The Voices of African-American Literature

Lerone Bennett, Jr. • Frank London Brown •
Arthur P. Davis • Frank Marshall Davis •
Owen Dodson • Mari Evans • Rudolph Fisher •
Dan Georgakas • Robert Hayden • Frank Horne •
Blyden Jackson • Lance Jeffers • Fenton Johnson •
George E. Kent • Alain Locke • Diane Oliver •
Stanley Sanders • Richard G. Stern • Sterling Stuckey •
Melvin B. Tolson

D0012065

About the Editor

Abraham Chapman was professor of English and Chairman of the American Literature survey courses at Wisconsin State University—Stevens Point. His writings include critical studies on American literature of the 19th and 20th centuries and book reviews for various leading periodicals. He was the author of *The Negro in American Literature*. In 1968 Professor Chapman received the Biennial College Language Association Creative Scholarship Award for his study *The Harlem Renaissance in Literary History*, published in *CLA Journal*.

BLACK VOICES

An Anthology of African-American Literature

Edited and with an Introduction
by Abraham Chapman

A SIGNET CLASSIC

SIGNET CLASSIC
Published by New American Library, a division of
Penguin Putnam Inc., 375 Hudson Street,
New York, New York 10014, U.S.A.
Penguin Books Ltd, 80 Strand,
London WC2R 0RL, England
Penguin Books Australia Ltd, Ringwood,
Victoria, Australia
Penguin Books Canada Ltd, 10 Alcorn Avenue,
Toronto, Ontario, Canada M4V 3B2
Penguin Books (N.Z.) Ltd, 182–190 Wairau Road,
Auckland 10, New Zealand

Penguin Books Ltd, Registered Offices:
Harmondsworth, Middlesex, England

Published by Signet Classic, an imprint of New American Library,
a division of Penguin Putnam Inc. Previously published in a Mentor edition.

First Signet Classic Printing, April 2001
10 9 8

Acknowledgments and Copyright Notices

JAMES BALDWIN, "Autobiographical Notes" copyright © 1955 by
James Baldwin, and "Many Thousands Gone" copyright © 1951, 1955
by James Baldwin, from *Notes of a Native Son* by James Baldwin.
Reprinted by permission of the Beacon Press.

LERONE BENNETT, JR., "Blues and Bitterness" from *New Negro
Poets U.S.A.* ed. by Langston Hughes, Indiana University Press. Re-
pinted by permission of the author.

(The following pages constitute an extension of this copyright page.)

REGISTERED TRADEMARK—MARCA REGISTRADA

The Library of Congress has cataloged the Mentor edition of this title as follows: 68-9045.

Printed in the United States of America

BOOKS ARE AVAILABLE AT QUANTITY DISCOUNTS WHEN USED TO PROMOTE PRODUCTS OR SERVICES. FOR INFORMATION PLEASE WRITE TO PREMIUM MARKETING DIVISION, PENGUIN PUTNAM INC., 375 HUDSON STREET, NEW YORK, NEW YORK 10014.

TO BELLE

who has always shared
the explorations, the
trials, and the harvest,
with love

CONTENTS

II. AUTOBIOGRAPHY

III. POETRY

IV. LITERARY CRITICISM

INTRODUCTION

A rich and varied body of literature has been created by black Americans which has become an organic part of the literature of the United States.

The Africans torn away from their native languages and cultures and transported to colonial America began to use English as a written language of literary expression more than 220 years ago. A slave girl, Lucy Terry, from Deerfield, Massachusetts, is recognized as the first American Negro poet. In 1746, she wrote *Bars Fight*, a verse account of an Indian raid. Jupiter Hammon, a Long Island slave, was the first Negro poet to be published, in 1760 (an eighty-eight-line religious poem printed as a broadside). In 1773, Phyllis Wheatley, a Boston slave, was the first Negro in America to publish a volume of verse (124 pages, printed in London).

Of earlier and far greater literary significance than these first published poems is the great Afro-American folk literature in English created by the slaves in the plantation South. The folk poetry, with its striking imagery and metaphors, is wedded to the music of the spirituals and secular songs which proved to be the cradle of the most distinctive American music. The lyrics of these songs were only one literary manifestation of the Afro-American imagination. The profusion of oral narratives and folktales was another. Professor Richard M. Dorson, a scholarly authority on American folklore, has written in his book, *American Negro Folktales:*

> One of the memorable bequests by the Negro to American civilization is his rich and diverse store of folktales. . . . Only the Negro, as a distinct element of the English-speaking population, maintained a full-blown storytelling tradition. A separate Negro subculture formed within the shell of American life, missing the bounties of general education and material progress, remaining a largely oral, self-contained society with its own unwritten history and literature.

It was only in the 1880's, with the publication of the *Uncle Remus* stories by Joel Chandler Harris, that the American reading public began to get its first inklings of a small portion

21

of this very rich literature—as told by a white Southern journalist. And it was not very much earlier, in the 1860's, that some of the old spirituals and slave songs were published for the first time.

The poetic and rhythmic qualities of the spirituals and the dramatic qualities of the folktales were blended with added qualities of emotional intensity and psychological suggestiveness in the creation of still another current of oral literary expression: the sermons of the Negro preachers.

The rich variety of Afro-American folk imagination and expression made its impact on the consciousness and sensibility of both black and white American writers and has entered the written literature of the United States in many different shapes and ways. This incomparable cultural harvest of the black man's experience, anguish, humor, and creativity in the United States remains a viable and potent source of folk and shared emotional experience which Negro writers in the twentieth century draw upon in accordance with their individual needs, talents, and literary visions. How it can feed diverse individual artists in different ways is evident if you turn to the work of three poets in this anthology, each different from the other: James Weldon Johnson, Sterling Brown, and Langston Hughes. And James Baldwin, who has become a master of the modern American essay as a literary form, has mined nuggets of the Negro preacher's sermon style which he has woven into his high literary mode of individual expression.

The earliest published prose writing by an Afro-American, as far as we know, also dates back more than two centuries. In 1760, the same year that witnessed the publication in Hartford of Jupiter Hammon's first broadside in verse, another slave with the same surname, Briton Hammon, published a narrative in Boston. It was an autobiographical pamphlet entitled *A Narrative of the Uncommon Sufferings and Surprising Deliverance of Briton Hammon, a Negro Man.* Of historical rather than literary interest, this pamphlet foreshadowed a fact of Afro-American literary history: Autobiographical narratives were to become the first genre of prose writing of literary importance.

From the 1780's to the end of the Civil War there was a steady flow of a literature destined in advance to be stillborn, a literature "in spite of," created in defiance of the laws making literacy for slaves a crime. It consisted of autobiographies and narratives written, and sometimes told, by slaves who had escaped slavery. One of the earliest important works of this type is *The Interesting Narrative of the Life of Olondah*

Equiano, or Gustavas Vassa, the African. Vernon Loggins, in his book *The Negro Author in America,* affirmed: "At the time it was published, in 1789, few books had been produced in America which afford such vivid, concrete, and picturesque narrative."

Nineteenth-century peaks of this literary form are the narratives by Frederick Douglass, William Wells Brown, and Samuel Ringgold Ward, leading Negroes in the antislavery movement. The Autobiography section of this anthology opens with selections from the 1845 *Narrative* of Frederick Douglass.

Another current of prose writing developed simultaneously with the slave narratives—protests against slavery and antislavery expository writing. The first noteworthy work in this field, an essay of unmistakable intellectual and stylistic importance, was "An Essay on Slavery" signed by "Othello," a Free Negro. This essay appeared in 1788 in two installments in the November and December issues of *American Museum,* one of the four major magazines founded in the United States after the American Revolution. From 1791 to 1796 Benjamin Banneker, the Negro of many talents who was appointed by Thomas Jefferson to the commission which laid out the plans for the city of Washington, published his widely circulated annual *Almanacks.* On August 19, 1791, Banneker sent a letter to Jefferson, who was then Secretary of State, condemning the degradation and barbarism of slavery and arguing for recognition of the human worth and equality of "the African race." This letter was published in Philadelphia in 1792 and, until the Civil War, was reprinted countless times as a classic of Negro-American protest against slavery. Some believe that Benjamin Banneker was the author of the anonymous "Othello" essay.

From the first decade of the nineteenth century the protest writings of Lemuel Haynes and Peter Williams are remembered. In 1829, David Walker's famous abolitionist pamphlet *Walker's Appeal* was published in Boston and became, in the words of Vernon Loggins, "the most widely circulated work that came from the pen of an American Negro before 1840."

In 1827, *Freedom's Journal,* the first Negro newspaper in the United States, began publication in New York City, four years before the birth of Garrison's famous Abolitionist organ *The Liberator.* The opening editorial in the first issue of the first Negro newspaper (March 16, 1827) declared: "We wish to plead our own cause. Too long have others spoken for us. Too long has the publick been deceived by misrepresentations, in things which concern us dearly. . . ."

A group of articulate writers, speakers, and fighters against slavery contributed to *Freedom's Journal*, including Samuel Ringgold Ward and William Wells Brown, who attracted public notice with their narratives. Poems by early Negro poets and versifiers were published in *Freedom's Journal* and in *The Liberator*.

We can detect a pattern in the development of Afro-American expression very similar to the general line of development of American writing. The real achievements in imaginative writing follow an initial period of expository, autobiographical, religious, and political writing. Significantly, the first fiction and first play by a Negro came from an active Abolitionist who contributed to *Freedom's Journal*. William Wells Brown, author of many important antislavery articles and books, also wrote the first novel by a Negro in the United States. The book, *Clotel*, was first published in London in 1853. A revised version was printed in the United States in 1864. William Wells Brown also wrote the first play by an American Negro, *The Escape; or, A Leap for Freedom*, published in 1858. Both his novel and play are of slight literary merit, but it is interesting that the Negro antislavery writings spill over into the first works of fiction and drama. Alain Locke, who is represented in the Literary Criticism section of this anthology with two essays, made an interesting point, in an article he wrote for *New World Writing* (1952):

If slavery molded the emotional and folk life of the Negro, it was the anti-slavery struggle that developed his intellect and spurred him to disciplined, articulate expression. Up to the Civil War, the growing anti-slavery movement was the midwife of Negro political and literary talent.

The modern period of literature by Negro authors, marked by the mastery of literary craftsmanship, achievements in form, and the critical definition of specific literary and cultural problems of Negro Americans within American culture, opens with the 1890's. Paul Laurence Dunbar, Charles Waddell Chesnutt, and W. E. B. Du Bois loom large in these literary beginnings. Poems by Dunbar and Du Bois, a story by Chesnutt, and selections from Du Bois's *The Souls of Black Folk*, respectively, open the Poetry, Fiction, and Literary Criticism sections of this anthology. With the exception of the autobiography of Frederick Douglass, all of the writing by the forty-four Negro American writers in this book is from this "modern" period—predominantly from the 1920's and later—and the selections in all of the four categories into which this anthology is divided extend to prose and poetry of the 1960's.

Very much of the literature created by black American writers in the twentieth century is unknown to the general reading public and little known even to students of American literature. Before any meaningful debate can take place on conflicting critical approaches and interpretations and on analyses of distinctive forms, structures, images, and themes, the literature itself will have to become better known. All too often, and for far too long, it has been a spurned or neglected part of our literary heritage.

The climate of indifference, neglect, or rejection in which this literature has developed is easy to document. Many important books in this field are inaccessible and out of print. One of the finest collections of Negro literature in the world, the Schomburg Collection—which is part of the New York Public Library in Harlem—does not have the budget to maintain itself and its rare books and manuscripts properly. Many public and college libraries have but the sparsest sprinkling of imaginative literature by black Americans. You can form your own idea of this state of affairs by checking in your local library to see how many of the books listed in the Bibliography at the end of this volume are available. In American literature courses in a number of high schools and colleges, books by Ralph Ellison, James Baldwin, and Richard Wright are today assigned and taught. But in most schools the voices of the black writers remain unheard and unknown, and this also holds true for a very large proportion of the nonintegrated or resegregated schools, with their overwhelming numbers of black students.

It is a fact of life that in our day a teacher in a ghetto school in the great cultural center of Boston can be fired for teaching his black students a poem by Langston Hughes. Officially, of course, for teaching an unauthorized poem (what a horrible educational practice, anyhow, that poems need the seals and licenses of some board of approval before they can be read and discussed by students in a free society). But far beyond Boston's school procedures, the question remains: How come the poem of a leading Negro American poet is *not authorized* for teaching in the city's schools, and not only in the ghetto schools?

If you have any questions about the banned poem, "Ballad of the Landlord," you can find it with other poems by Hughes in the Poetry section of this anthology. Boston, of course, is well known for its excessive sensitivity to obscenity.

But the banned poem by Hughes doesn't have any sexual undertones or overtones. Its obscenity in the eyes of the respectable, it would appear, is its harsh illumination of the injustices of slum-life realities.

While the Boston school authorities made news with the severity of their action, the problem is not peculiar to Boston alone. I have taught a special course on the Negro in American literature to urban high school teachers from all over the country. These teachers maintain that there are school authorities in the urban centers who insist the teachers be very wary of, or ignore, works by black writers, because these writings are too disturbing, or too realistic, or too angry, when there are already enough "problems" with the ghetto students. This constitutes a kind of literary or cultural segregation, a stifling of the black literary voices, in addition to being wrong in educational principle. The black students know the confining and frustrating realities of ghetto life as lived experience and need not turn to books for that. But literature by black writers can give the black students a meaningful ordering and illumination of the black experience in this country; it can show them the creative and imaginative power and achievements of the black man and can prove very important psychologically.

I am well aware that many schools in a number of cities have been doing excellent pioneer work in teaching significant works by black writers as an indispensable component of the English curriculum. But this is still too rare in our schools today. The fact that work by Negro American writers can still encounter hostility, suspicion, or no recognition at all, in schools in every part of the country, is part of the problem of the neglect of Negro American literature for reasons which are very frequently not literary.

As a result of the various walls standing between many black writers and the reading audience, large numbers of literate and cultured Americans, including a high proportion of English majors and students of literature in the colleges, are not aware that many meaningful literary works have been created by black Americans and are an organic part of the American literary heritage. Unfortunately we still have to contend, in our study of American literature, with the long and harsh tradition of the rejection of the Negro in our society and the historically built-in tendencies in American culture to ignore or play down the importance of the black Americans as creators of cultural values and aesthetic forms in the United States.

This is not unexplored territory. Many important studies,

anthologies, and specialized collections of writings have been published over the years—predominantly but not exclusively by Negro scholars, critics, writers, and poets. But symptomatic of the long resistance to the proper recognition of the literary works created by black Americans is the fact that, even today, you will search in vain in definitive up-to-date American literary histories, for some of the elementary facts about Negro American writers and writing. You will search in vain in almost all of the standard American literary reference works of today for the "Negro Renaissance" or "Harlem Renaissance," interchangeable terms widely used by students of the Negro in American literature to denote the extensive literary creativity of the New Negro movement that arose in the 1920's. This was the literary explosion that brought into American literature the early works of such writers as Langston Hughes, Alain Locke, Jean Toomer, Claude McKay, Countee Cullen, Sterling Brown, Arna Bontemps, and others, that you will find in this anthology. But our literary histories, with very rare exceptions, simply do not recognize the existence of any flowering of Negro expression, or any specific literary movement of black Americans, worthy of special notice.

This is clear evidence of how much remains to be done to become aware of the full diversity and scope of American literature, to open our ears and eyes to the voices and imaginative creations of black humanity in our midst. That is a prime purpose of this anthology. To bring to the general reading public and to the students of American literature in the high schools and colleges a large and diverse collection of writing by black Americans at a popular price—literature worth reading as literature and worthy, in my opinion, of inclusion in the American literature curriculum in the schools.

I have no special thesis about Negro American literature to advance or prove. If there is anything I would like to emphasize, it is the plural *Voices* in the title of this book, the individuality of each and every black writer, the diversity of styles and approaches to literature, the conflict of ideas, values, and varying attitudes to life, within black America. In my reading and experience I simply have not found any such thing as "the Negro."

Even the name "Negro" is today the subject of intense debate among Negroes. The question has been posed as to whether or not the word "Negro" should be abandoned and replaced by the words "black" or "Afro-American." Lerone Bennett, Jr., in a lengthy and interesting article on this problem in *Ebony* in November, 1967 wrote:

This question is at the root of a bitter national controversy over the proper designation for *identifiable* Americans of African descent. (More than 40 million "white" Americans, according to some scholars, have African ancestors.) A large and vocal group is pressing an aggressive campaign for the use of the word "Afro-American" as the only historically accurate and humanly significant designation of this large and pivotal portion of the American population. This group charges that the word "Negro" is an inaccurate epithet which perpetuates the master-slave mentality in the minds of both black and white Americans. An equally large, but not so vocal, group says the word "Negro" is as accurate and as euphonious as the words "black" and "Afro-American." This group is scornful of the premises of the advocates of change. A Negro by any other name, they say, would be as black and as beautiful—and as segregated. The times, they add, are too crucial for Negroes to dissipate their energy in fratricidal strife over names. But the pro-black contingent contends . . . that names are of the essence of the game of power and control. And they maintain that a change in name will short-circuit the stereotyped thinking patterns that undergird the system of racism in America. To make things even more complicated, a third group, composed primarily of Black Power advocates, has adopted a new vocabulary in which the word "black" is reserved for "black brothers and sisters who are emancipating themselves," and the word "Negro" is used contemptuously for Negroes "who are still in Whitey's bag and who still think of themselves and speak of themselves as Negroes."

In a deeper sense the new challenge to the name "Negro" is a reflection of the challenge to the racist conditions of life identified with the reality of being a Negro in America. It is a part of the fight for new identities and new realities of life for black Americans. *Ebony* and other Negro publications have initiated polls of their readers as to which name they prefer. At this writing, early in 1968, the first incomplete results of these polls are reported and the first choice is for "Afro-American," second choice for "black," and third choice for "Negro."

Because life in the black American community, as in every human community, is characterized by diversity, divisions, and conflicts, there can be no single approach to Negro life, the black experience, or the literature and culture created by Afro-Americans. We would consider America as a whole a very static, drab, and regimented country without the very deep and fundamental differences of opinion which mark our national and cultural life. We would reject any single thesis or sweeping generalization to define the literature or culture of the United States. I don't know why the vigorous debates and sharp political and cultural differences within the black communities should evoke surprise and wonder. Conflict of opinions and values is the way of life of every thinking and human community. The great debates in the black communities of America today only confirm again what needs no confirmation—that the black communities are as human, argumentative, and divided in opinions as any thinking community. For an idea of the different approaches to the literature of black writers by Negro scholars, academic critics, and writers, I have included, as a special feature of this anthology, a section devoted to literary criticism by Negro Americans, ranging chronologically from 1903 to 1967.

American literary criticism largely ignores most of the works by the Afro-American writers. In the last few decades, a few individual Negro writers, namely Ralph Ellison and James Baldwin, have won critical recognition and acclaim as major American authors. To a lesser degree the critical spotlight has also shone on Richard Wright, frequently in terms of his power, drive, and searing anger—but quite often as a negative example, as the archetypal author of the "protest novel," which is so commonly dismissed as a subliterary species.

Rarely are Wright, Ellison, and Baldwin seen and treated, in our general American literary criticism, as part of a bigger and older current of literary expression—a literary tradition created by Americans of African descent, a literary reality which is both organically American, created on American soil in the American language, with the same rights to recognition for its American authenticity as the literature created by the descendants of the immigrants from England and Europe. Rarely is this literature of the Afro-Americans seen by our general literary criticism in its full light and complete complexity. On the one hand it is part of a literature and culture shared with white America as a whole, inevitably shaped in significant part by the dictates of the American language itself and by the forms of literary expression developed in the United States. At the same time, it is also a distinct and special body of literature, in the sense that the historical memories and myths, experiences, and conditions of life of the black Americans have been deliberately kept separate and apart, for generations, from the priority of conditions and values established for white Americans.

There is little general critical recognition of the fact that central metaphors and concepts of Ellison and Baldwin, like "the invisible man" and "nobody knows my name"—the in-

visibility and denial of identity, the facelessness and name-
lessness, which are associated with the Ellison and Baldwin
dramatizations of the alienated Negro in America—are actually
deeply rooted in the group or folk consciousness of black
America and were given literary expression long before Ellison and Baldwin ever appeared on the literary scene.

In the dawn of this century, in *The Souls of Black Folk*
(1903), a classic literary expression of the sensibility, consciousness, and dilemmas of a black American intellectual,
W. E. B. Du Bois wrote:

> After the Egyptian and Indian, the Greek and Roman, the
> Teuton and Mongolian, the Negro is a sort of seventh son,
> born with a veil, and gifted with second-sight in this Ameri-
> can world,—a world which yields him no true self-conscious-
> ness, but only lets him see himself through the revelation of
> the other world. It is a peculiar sensation, this double-con-
> sciousness, this sense of always looking at one's self through
> the eyes of others, of measuring one's soul by the tape of a
> world that looks on in amused contempt and pity. One ever
> feels his twoness,—an American, a Negro; two souls, two
> thoughts, two unreconciled strivings; two warring ideals in
> one dark body, whose dogged strength alone keeps it from
> being torn asunder.

Many years later, in his book *Dusk of Dawn* (1940), Du
Bois described the psychological impact of caste segregation
in the following words:

> It is as though one, looking out from a dark cave in a side
> of an impending mountain, sees the world passing and speaks
> to it; speaks courteously and persuasively, showing them how
> these entombed souls are hindered in their natural movement,
> expression, and development; and how their loosening from
> prison would be a matter not simply of courtesy, sympathy,
> and help to them, but aid to all the world. . . . It gradually
> permeates the minds of the prisoners that the people passing
> do not hear; that some thick sheet of invisible but horribly
> tangible plate glass is between them and the world. They get
> excited; they talk louder; they gesticulate. Some of the pass-
> ing world stop in curiosity; these gesticulations seem so point-
> less; they laugh and pass on. They still either do not hear at
> all, or hear but dimly, and even what they hear, they do not
> understand. Then the people within may become hysterical.

The sense of duality, powerlessness, and rejection by a hostile society and environment, as expressed by Du Bois, comes
from the core of the consciousness of black America and is

reiterated time and again, in a multitude of ways, by Negro American writers.

James Weldon Johnson published an article entitled "The Dilemma of the Negro Author" in *The American Mercury* in December, 1928. The title of the article itself sounds the note of duality we heard earlier in Du Bois. Observing that the Negro author faces all of the difficulties common to all writers, Johnson went on to say that "the Aframerican author faces a special problem which the plain American author knows nothing about—the problem of the double audience. It is more than a double audience; it is a divided audience, an audience made up of two elements with differing and often opposite and antagonistic points of view. His audience is always both white America and black America." The theme is insistent: two worlds, two Americas, two antagonistic points of view.

Langston Hughes voiced this sense of division in an early poem, "As I Grew Older," the full text of which you will find in the Poetry section of this anthology:

It was a long time ago
I have almost forgotten my dream
But it was there then,
In front of me,
Bright like a sun—
My dream.

And then the wall rose,
Rose slowly,
Slowly,
Between me and my dream.
Rose slowly, slowly,
Dimming,
Hiding,
The light of my dream.
Rose until it touched the sky—
The wall.

We hear the motif again in a late essay by Richard Wright, "The Literature of the Negro in the United States," articulated this way:

Held in bondage, stripped of his culture, denied family life for centuries, made to labor for others, the Negro tried to learn to live the life of the New World in an atmosphere of rejection and hate. . . . For the development of Negro expression—as well as the whole of Negro life in America—

hovers always somewhere between the rise of man from his ancient, rural way of life to the complex, industrial life of our time. Let me sum up these differences by contrasts; entity vs. identity; pre-individualism vs. individualism; the determined vs. the free. . . . Entity, men integrated with their culture; and identity, men who are at odds with their culture, striving for personal identification.

Richard Wright expressed the duality and the sense of two-ness as a "versus" and identified the search for personal identity with being at odds with the prevailing culture in the United States.

In a symposium of prominent Negro writers broadcast by a New York City radio station in 1961, the moderator, Nat Hentoff, asked the late playwright Lorraine Hansberry the following question:

Miss Hansberry, in writing *A Raisin in the Sun*, to what extent did you feel a double role, both as a kind of social actionist "protester," and as a dramatist?

Lorraine Hansberry answered:

Well, given the Negro writer, we are necessarily aware of a special situation in the American setting. . . . We are doubly aware of conflict, because of the special pressures of being a Negro in America. . . . In my play I was dealing with a young man who would have, I feel, been a compelling object of conflict as a young American of his class of whatever racial background, with the exception of the incident at the end of the play, and with the exception, of course, of character depth, because a Negro character is a reality; there is no such thing as saying that a Negro could be a white person if you just changed the lines or something like this. This is a very arbitrary and superficial approach to Negro character. . . . I started to write about this family as I knew them in the context of those realities which I remembered as being true for this particular given set of people; and, at one point, it was just inevitable that a problem of some magnitude which was racial would intrude itself, because this is one of the realities of Negro life in America. But it was just as inevitable that for a large part of the play, they would be excluded. Because the duality of consciousness is so complete that it is perfectly true to say that Negroes do not sit around twenty-four hours a day, thinking, "I am a Negro."

And Chester Himes, in an essay entitled "Dilemma of the Negro Novelist in U.S." published in 1966 in the miscellaneous collection by various writers, *Beyond the Angry Black*, wrote:

From the start the American Negro writer is beset by conflicts. He is in conflict with himself, with his environment, with his public. The personal conflict will be the hardest. He must decide at the outset the extent of his honesty. He will find it no easy thing to reveal the truth of his experience or even to discover it. He will derive no pleasure from the recounting of his hurts. He will encounter more agony by his explorations into his own personality than most non-Negroes realize. For him to delineate the degrading effects of oppression will be like inflicting a wound upon himself. He will have begun an intellectual crusade that will take him through the horrors of the damned. And this must be his reward for his integrity: he will be reviled by the Negroes and whites alike. Most of all, he will find no valid interpretation of his experiences in terms of human values until the truth be known.

If he does not discover this truth, his life will be forever veiled in mystery, not only to whites, but to himself; and he will be heir to all the weird interpretations of his personality.

Because this is an anthology of literature by black Americans, appearing at a time when the tensions and harsh realities of race relations in the United States are critical and high on the social, economic, and political agendas of the nation, it may also help serve a public function which literature is preeminently qualified to perform: to illuminate the human realities of black America. Without minimizing the value of the factual knowledge offered by history, sociology, anthropology, and economics, literature offers a depth of insight into the hearts and minds of black Americans which cannot be approximated by the social sciences.

The literature in this anthology takes us into the inner worlds of black Americans, as seen and felt from the *inside*. Literature as a way of knowing and perceiving probes beyond the conscious, the fully known, and the fully thought out. With contrast and analogy, imaginative ways of ordering images and values, with metaphor and symbol which suggest and imply the shapes and intimations of things and conditions sensed and known in the psychic subsoil, literature searches and captures human hopes and fears, dreams and nightmares, aspirations and frustrations, desires and resentments, which do not register on the computer cards, statistical surveys, and government reports. If America had only done something about the truths and literary revelations in Richard Wright's *Native Son*, published in 1940, with its profound psychological illumination of how the prison box of the big city ghetto was generating violence and destruction as the only language and means of action that had any validity for the hemmed in Bigger Thomas, living in a world without viable alternatives, moving in an incomprehensible mausoleum of dead dreams and hopes—then our past summers of discontent might have been very different.

There is still another special insight into American life that we get from black writers: the look and the feel and the psychological texture of the behavior of white Americans as it is manifest to black Americans. Here, too, we have an area of great human complexities, of codes of behavior and hidden emotional recesses, of cruelty and guilt, of cold calculation and the irrational, crime and conscience, hate and love. Here we find further illumination of a major concern of modern literature, the walls that isolate and separate man from man and the barriers to human connection and communication, with particular attention to what the "curtain of color" does to people on both sides of such a curtain. If, in addition to aesthetic delight, we turn to literature for its power of human illumination, both as mirror and lamp, then certainly the mirrors and lamps created by the black writers have a special value for America—if we are ready to look at the truths they expose.

2

A long time ago in the literary history of the United States, when the great debate was unfolding on whether and when and *how* a distinctively American literature would develop on this continent, the question of the Negro in American literature was an organic part of the whole discussion. Some of the highly original and nonconformist writers of that day, seeking to probe the uniqueness of America, thought that the United States differed most from England and all other countries in its human composition and evolution, its absorption of people from all the continents, races, and regions of mankind. A truly American literature, these writers believed, would somehow express the new fusion of peoples and races in the new continent, the new human realities and conditions of life in the United States.

This conception was clearly voiced in the dawn of the "Golden Age" of American literature by Margaret Fuller, first editor of the transcendentalist journal *The Dial,* who later joined the staff of the New York *Tribune* as the first professional book reviewer in America. In her landmark essay "American Literature: Its Position in the Present Time, and Prospects for the Future" (1846), a composite of reviews she had first written for the *Tribune,* later published in her two-volume collection of writings *Papers on Literature and Art*, Margaret Fuller wrote:

> We have no sympathy with national vanity. We are not anxious to prove that there is as yet much American literature. Of those who think and write among us in the methods and of the thoughts of Europe, we are not impatient; if their minds are still best adapted to such food and such action. . . . Yet there is often between child and parent a reaction from excessive influence having been exerted, and such a one. we have experienced in behalf of our country against England. We use her language and receive in torrents the influence of her thought, yet it is in many respects uncongenial and injurious to our constitution. What suits Great Britain, with her insular position and consequent need to concentrate and intensify her life, her limited monarchy and spirit of trade, does not suit a mixed race continually enriched with new blood from other stocks the most unlike that of our first descent, with ample field and verge enough to range in and leave every impulse free, and abundant opportunity to develop a genius wide and full as our rivers. . . . That such a genius is to rise and work in this hemisphere we are confident; equally so that scarce the first faint streaks of that day's dawn are yet visible. . . . That day will not rise till the fusion of races among us is more complete. It will not rise till this nation shall attain sufficient moral and intellectual dignity to prize moral and intellectual no less highly than political freedom. . . .

A decade later, in the high tide of the "American Renaissance," Walt Whitman wrote in his Preface to the first (1855) edition of *Leaves of Grass*:

> Here is not merely a nation but a teeming nation of nations. . . . The American poets are to enclose old and new for America is the race of races. Of them a bard is to be commensurate with a people. To him the other continents arrive as contributions. . . . he gives them reception for their sake and his own sake.

Almost a century later, the American poet William Carlos Williams in his prose volume of poetic insights and interpretations of the American heritage, *In the American Grain*, wrote:

> The colored men and women whom I have known intimately have a racial character which has impressed me. I have not much bothered to know why, exactly, this has been so—
> The one thing that never seems to occur to anybody is that

the negroes have a quality which they have brought to America. . . . Poised against the *Mayflower* is the slave ship—manned by Yankees and Englishmen—bringing another race to try upon the New World. . . . There is a solidity, a racial irreducible minimum, which gives them poise in a world in which they have no authority.

The hopeful vision of Margaret Fuller, Walt Whitman, and many others—that the United States would realize the promise and potential of its genius by transcending racial exclusiveness and welcoming the contributions and qualities brought to this continent by all races and continents—clashed, and clashes to this day, with a tenacious, strong, and contrary current in American culture. It is in conflict with a cultural attitude and posture which Professor Horace M. Kallen, in his book *Cultural Pluralism and the American Idea* (1956), has designated as "a racism in culture":

It claimed that the American Idea and the American Way were hereditary to the Anglo-Saxon stock and to that stock only; that other stocks were incapable of producing them, learning them and living them. If, then, America is to survive as a culture of creed and code, it can do so only so long as the chosen Anglo-Saxon race retains its integrity of flesh and spirit and freely sustains and defends their American expression against alien contamination.

The famous Gunnar Myrdal study of the American Negro problem, published in 1944, dealt with this same reality in a strictly sociological context, and called it "the anti-amalgamation doctrine." This doctrine is the opposite of the "melting pot" theory, which envisaged the assimilation and amalgamation of the various streams of white immigrants to this country into an American synthesis. The "anti-amalgamation doctrine" works in-reverse and is described as follows in the Myrdal report:

The Negroes, on the other hand, are commonly assumed to be unassimilable, and this is the reason why the Negro problem is different from the ordinary minority problem in America. The Negroes are set apart, together with other colored peoples, principally the Chinese and Japanese. While all other groups are urged to become Americanized as quickly and completely as possible, the colored peoples are excluded from assimilation. (*Quoted from the Condensed Version of the Myrdal study* The Negro in America (1964) *by Arnold Rose.*)

We can detect signs and echoes of this "racism in culture,"

this "anti-amalgamation doctrine," which is rooted so deeply in the American consciousness and American social practices, in white America's critical approaches to the Negro in American literature. I hasten to make clear that I am not saying that all American critics, writers, and readers are racists. What I am saying is that it is very difficult to maintain, in theory and practice, that the Negro is unassimilable, so different and inherently incapable of fitting into America like other people that he must be kept separate and apart, and at the same time see that this despised Negro has been, and is, a real and significant creator of American cultural values and aesthetic forms. Racism and currents of conflict with racism, including the resistance to racism of black America, are organic elements in the dynamics of American culture. And, since the pressures of racism in American life and thinking remain more powerful and pervasive than the significant but weaker currents of antiracism, inescapably racist attitudes often spill over into the literary domain and blur America's literary and critical vision.

Evidence of how the pressures of racism penetrate literature can be found in the crowded gallery of stereotyped Negro characters in American fiction and drama—certainly not all Negro characters by white writers, but quite predominantly: the servile Negro, the comic Negro, the savage Negro. The opening lines of Sterling Brown's book *The Negro in American Fiction* (1937) declare bluntly: "The treatment of the Negro in American fiction, since it parallels his treatment in American life, has naturally been noted for injustice. Like other oppressed and exploited minorities, the Negro has been interpreted in a way to justify his exploitation."

Ralph Ellison, in an early essay now included in his book *Shadow and Act*, wrote: "Thus it is unfortunate for the Negro that the most powerful formulations of modern American fictional works have been so slanted against him that when he approaches for a glimpse of himself he discovers an image drained of humanity."

The racist attitudes and feelings which have spawned the well-exposed stereotypes of Negro character in American imaginative literature have also been responsible for distortions of critical criteria and for the double standards and special criteria we often encounter in American literary criticism when the works of Afro-American writers are discussed. Whether it stems from a fear of looking at the blackness of the black experience in America and the human consequences of American racism or whether it stems from some cultural variation of the doctrine of the "unassimilability" of the Negro, the fact is that we do encounter in American literary criticism various forms of rejection and negation of the meaning and value of the human experience of the Negro in America.

I shall later offer the evidence on which I base this assertion, but first I want to contrast the very common sympathetic approaches of modern literary criticism to the particularity and otherness of regional and ethnic individuality, as primary proof of why I think there is a reverse tendency in American criticism, a tendency to reject the unique value of the ethnic individuality of the Negro. What seems to be frequently reversed when the Negro enters the picture are the critical criteria—commonly accepted by more than one school of modern literary criticism—that literature is the art of the particular and individual, that the universal in literature is most fully achieved in the depth and completeness with which the uniqueness of the individual is portrayed, and that human freedom is a valid subject for artistic and literary exploration.

Let us see how some modern critics and writers approach and appreciate the particular ethnic and regional literary worlds of writers who are not Negro.

Albert Camus, the French writer of Algerian birth, declared in an interview included in his book *Resistance, Rebellion, and Death:* "No one is more closely attached to his Algerian province than I, and yet I have no trouble feeling a part of French tradition. . . . Silone [the Italian writer] speaks to all of Europe, and the reason I feel so close to him is that he is also so unbelievably rooted in his national and even provincial tradition."

William Faulkner declared in his well-known *Paris Review* interview: "Beginning with *Sartoris* I discovered that my own little postage stamp of native soil was worth writing about and that I would never live long enough to exhaust it. . . ."

Isaac Bashevis Singer, the Jewish writer who came to the United States from Poland in 1935, writes in Yiddish and has been widely hailed as a significant figure in the contemporary literary scene since his works began appearing in English in the 1950's, wrote in an article published in *Book World* early in 1968: "But the masters of literary prose have seldom left their territorial and cultural frontiers. There is no such thing as the international novel or international drama. Literature is by its very nature bound to a people, a region, a language, even a dialect."

James Joyce, writing outside his native Ireland, created his entire fictional world out of Dubliners, and this was no bar to his universal recognition as a giant of modern fiction.

W. B. Yeats, recognized as a major poet of the twentieth century, is not dismissed by any critic as "not universal" because he gave full expression to his Irish self, nor is he dubbed a "protest" propagandist by any serious critic because he stressed the thematic literary inspiration he derived from the Irish freedom movement. Yeats shed much light on the question I am now trying to examine in his essay "A General Introduction For My Work," written in 1937 for a complete edition of his works which did not appear, and later incorporated into his book *Essays and Introductions* (1961). Stating as his "first principle" that "a poet writes always of his personal life, in his finest work out of its tragedy, whatever it be, remorse, lost love, or loneliness," Yeats went on to say that he found his subject matter in the Irish resistance movement. He stated it in a very personal way: "It was through the old Fenian leader John O'Leary I found my theme." He speaks of O'Leary's long imprisonment, longer banishment, his pride, his integrity, and his dream—the dream of Irish freedom—that nourished and attracted young Irishmen to him and attracted the young Yeats too. He recalled that at the time he read only romantic literature and the Irish poets, some of which was not good poetry at all, and he added: "But they had one quality I admired and admire: they were not separated individual men; they spoke or tried to speak out of a people to a people; behind them stretched the generations."

This is a quality we also find, in a different way, in the works of the Negro writers in which we can also feel this sense of a people speaking out to a people, with a sense of the generations behind: mythic memories of the remote African past, memories of slavery and common experiences in America.

Yeats, of course, as an artist, voiced his strong hatred of didactic literature but at the same time took pains to disavow any idea that his Irish self separated him from world literature and humanity as a whole. Later in this same essay Yeats wrote:

> I hated and still hate with an ever growing hatred the literature of the point of view. I wanted, if my ignorance permitted, to get back to Homer, to those that fed at his table. I wanted to cry as all men cried, to laugh as all men laughed, and the young Ireland poets when not writing mere politics had the same want, but they did not know that the common and its befitting language is the research of a lifetime, and

when found may lack popular recognition. . . . If Irish literature goes on as my generation planned it, it may do something to keep the "Irishry" living. . . .

In his poetic approach, Yeats united three components which to others may seem irreconcilable or incompatible: to express the personal and private self, to express the common humanity the individual shares with all men, and to express the ethnic or racial self with its particular mythology and cultural past. If for "Irishry" we substitute black or Negro consciousness we can see that the best of the Afro-American writers have been struggling to express and blend the three components Yeats speaks of and a fourth as well, which has made the situation of the black writer in America even more complex: their personal selves, their universal humanity, the particular qualities and beauty of their blackness and ethnic specificity, and their American selves. These are not separate and boxed off compartments of the mind and soul, but the inseparable and intermingled elements of a total human being, of a whole person who blends diversities within himself. This is the rich blend we find in the best of the Negro American artists.

The significance of Yeats' experience and point of view for an understanding of certain aspects of American literature is stressed, in a different way and in another context, by Cleanth Brooks in his book *William Faulkner: The Yoknapatawpha Country*. Brooks writes:

> Any Southerner who reads Yeats' *Autobiographies* is bound to be startled, over and over again, by the analogies between Yeats' "literary situation" and that of the Southern author: the strength to be gained from the writer's sense of belonging to a living community and the special focus upon the world bestowed by one's having a precise location in time and history.

Certainly the Negro writer has this "sense of belonging to a living community" which should be appreciated as a source of strength. But the Negro writer and Negro community in the United States have historically been denied the advantages "bestowed by one's having a precise location in time and history." The Negro in America has been denied a proper location and place, has been in perpetual motion searching for a proper place he could call home. During slavery, the flight to freedom was the goal—the search for a home, a haven, the search for a possibility of secure belonging. After the Civil War, and to this day, this historical reality has expressed itself in the great migration from the South to the North and the patterns of flight and migration which are inherent in the spatial and plot movements in the novels of Richard Wright, Ralph Ellison, and James Baldwin. This opposite reality, of uprooting and dislocation, gave the Negro writer, to use the language of Brooks, a different "special focus upon the world," a focus of *denial* of a place, which we hear so clearly as far back as in the spirituals.

Here is how this theme is expressed time and again in lines chosen at random from different spirituals.

I'm rolling through an unfriendly worl'.

———

Sometimes I feel like a motherless child,
A long way from home. . . .

———

Swing low, sweet chariot,
Coming for to carry me home. . . .

———

I got a home in dat rock,
Don't you see? . . .
Poor man Laz'rus, poor as I,
When he died he found a home on high,
He had a home in dat rock,
Don't you see?

———

Deep river, my home is over Jordan.

———

I am a poor pilgrim of sorrow. . . .
I'm tryin' to make heaven my home.

Sometimes I am tossed and driven.
Sometimes I don't know where to roam.
I've heard of a city called heaven.
I've started to make it my home.

American literary criticism has still not come to terms with the "special focus upon the world" that the realities of being a black man in America have created for the Negro writers. And all too often the critical assumptions articulated by Camus, Faulkner, Singer, and Yeats are reversed into some kind of special critical doctrine for the black writer which seems to say or imply that to be meaningful for America, to be universal, the black writer has to be *other* than Negro, *other* than racial, *other* than what he actually and truly is.

What about the evidence for this statement? Let me begin with Louis Simpson, a fine contemporary American poet with a liberal and humane sensibility. When *Selected Poems* by Gwendolyn Brooks was published, he reviewed it among a group of new volumes of verse, in *Book Week* (October 27, 1963). Simpson wrote:

> Gwendolyn Brooks' *Selected Poems* contain some lively pictures of Negro life. I am not sure it is possible for a Negro to write well without making us aware he is a Negro; on the other hand, if being a Negro is the only subject, the writing is not important. . . . Miss Brooks must have had a devil of a time trying to write poetry in the United States, where there has been practically no Negro poetry worth talking about.

Why is writing about "being a Negro" a subject which "is not important"?—why, unless you somehow feel or believe that being a Negro is not important or that Negro life doesn't have values or meanings that are important? And why should there be anything wrong with our being aware of the Negro as author, anymore than it is wrong for us to be aware that Yeats is Irish and that Isaac Bashevis Singer is Jewish and that Ignazio Silone is Italian and that Dostoyevsky is unmistakably Russian and that Faulkner is very much a Mississippian? And why so cavalierly dismiss practically all Negro poetry in the United States with one fell swoop?

Or take another example, this one from academic criticism by Marcus Klein, a member of the Barnard College faculty. In his book *After Alienation: American Novels in Mid-Century* he devotes two chapters to Ralph Ellison and James Baldwin and considers them very seriously. He writes:

> But what seems characteristic of major Negro literature since mid-century is an urgency on the part of writers to be more than merely Negro. . . . The time has seemed to urge upon him [the Negro writer], rather, a necessity to discover his nonracial identity within the circumstances of race.

Why this emphasis on being more than "merely Negro" and "nonracial identity"? Perhaps the clearest answer is provided in a critical statement by William Faulkner. In the rich and complex fictional world of Faulkner we encounter many Negro characters, ranging from Negro stereotypes tainted by the racism of their Mississippi origin to Negro characters of great artistic stature, with depth and dignity and profound symbolic meaning, like Sam Fathers and Lucas Beuchamp in

Go Down, Moses. As man and critic, Faulkner, on numerous occasions, expressed the basic racist assumptions and attitudes of his society and his Mississippi environment, which Faulkner, the artist—at his best, but not always—succeeded in transcending. Let us look at one of his public nonliterary statements. In a speech delivered at the University of Virginia (February 20, 1958) and published in his book *Essays, Speeches and Public Letters,* Faulkner said:

> Perhaps the Negro is not yet capable of more than second class citizenship. His tragedy may be that so far he is competent for equality only in the ratio of his white blood. . . . For the sake of argument, let us agree that as yet the Negro is incapable of equality for the reason that he could not hold and keep it even if it were forced on him with bayonets; that once the bayonets were removed, the first smart and ruthless man black or white who came along would take it away from him, because he, the Negro, is not yet capable of, or refuses to accept, the responsibilities of equality.
>
> So we, the white man, must take him in hand and teach him that responsibility. . . . Let us teach him that, in order to be free and equal, he must first be worthy of it, and then forever afterward work to hold and keep and defend it. He must learn to cease forever more thinking like a Negro and acting like a Negro. This will not be easy for him.

Here we have the crux of the problem: the rejection by powerful forces in American life and thought of any positive qualities and values, in Negro life—the negation by cultivated people, by artists and poets, of the worth of "being a Negro" and "thinking like a Negro" and "acting like a Negro." In short, the repudiation of Negro identity and the vicious circle: on the one hand, the pressure to blot out the blackness of the black man, the pressure to make him like a white man —and, at the same time, the unrelenting pressure to slam the door of white society in his face and say: "Negro, keep out!"

These approaches to Negro life and literature contradict the critical premises voiced by T. S. Eliot in his famous review of James Joyce's *Ulysses,* which became axiomatic for much of modern criticism. Eliot declared that "in creation you are responsible for what you can do with material which you must simply accept. And in this material I include the emotions and feelings of the writer himself, which, for that writer, are simply material which he must accept—not virtues to be enlarged or vices to be diminished." Too much of American literary criticism is still not simply *accepting* the materials of the Negro writer—his subject matter and feelings and emotions, which are part of his material—and, in violation of well-established critical principles, is arguing with the material rather than addressing itself to how the writer has made artistic use of his particular material.

The underlying assumptions of Simpson, Klein, and Faulkner are the antitheses of the premises long held by Negro American writers.

Participating in a radio symposium in New York City in 1961, Langston Hughes said:

> My main material is the race problem—and I have found it most exciting and interesting and intriguing to deal with it in writing, and I haven't found the problem of being a Negro in any sense a hindrance to putting words on paper. It may be a hindrance sometimes to selling them. . . .
>
> Well now, I very often try to use social material in a humorous form and most of my writing from the very beginning has been aimed largely at a Negro reading public, because when I began to write I had no thought of achieving a wide public. My early work was always published in *The Crisis* of the N.A.A.C.P., and then in the *Opportunity* of the Urban League, and then the Negro papers like the Washington *Sentinel* and the Baltimore *Afro-American*, and so on. And I contend that since these things, which are Negro, largely for Negro readers, have in subsequent years achieved world-wide publication—my work has come out in South America, Japan, and all over Europe—that a regional Negro character like Simple, a character intended for the people who belong to his own race, if written about warmly enough, humanly enough, can achieve universality.
>
> And I don't see, as Jimmy Baldwin sometimes seems to imply, any limitations, in artistic terms, in being a Negro. I see none whatsoever. It seems to me that any Negro can write about anything he chooses, even the most narrow problems; if he can write about it forcefully and honestly and truly, it is very possible that that bit of writing will be read and understood, in Iceland or Uruguay.

Hughes was consistent in his position over a long period of years, a position which is really no more than not applying a reverse critical standard to the Negro writer. Some thirty-five years earlier, in his famous article "The Negro Artist and the Racial Mountain" published in *The Nation* (June 23, 1926), Hughes wrote:

> One of the most promising of the young Negro poets said to me once, "I want to be a poet—not a Negro poet," meaning, I believe, "I want to write like a white poet," meaning sub-consciously, "I would like to be a white poet," meaning behind that, "I would like to be white." And I was sorry the

young man said that, for no great poet has ever been afraid of being himself.

In one of his interesting essays, "The Literature of the Negro in the United States," which is included in his book *White Man, Listen!*, Richard Wright stated his views this way:

Around the turn of the century, two tendencies became evident in Negro expression. I'll call the first tendency: The Narcissistic Level, and the second tendency I'll call: The Forms of Things Unknown, which consists of folk utterances, spirituals, blues, work songs, and folklore.

These two main streams of Negro expression—The Narcissistic Level and The Forms of Things Unknown—remained almost distinctly apart until the depression struck our country in 1929. . . . Then there were those who hoped and felt that they would ultimately be accepted in their native land as free men, and they put forth their claims in a language that their nation had given them. These latter were more or less always middle class in their ideology. But it was among the migratory Negro workers that one found, rejected and ignorant though they were, strangely positive manifestations of expression, original contributions in terms of form and content.

Middle class Negroes borrowed the forms of the culture which they strove to make their own, but the migratory Negro worker improvised his cultural forms and filled those forms with a content wrung from a bleak and barren environment, an environment that stung, crushed, all but killed him. . . .

You remember the Greek legend of Narcissus who was condemned by Nemesis to fall in love with his own reflection which he saw in the water of a fountain? Well, the middle class Negro writers were condemned by America to stand before a Chinese Wall and wail that they were like other men, that they felt as others felt. It is this relatively static stance of emotion that I call The Narcissistic Level. These Negroes were in every respect the equal of whites; they were valid examples of personality types of Western culture; but they lived in a land where even insane white people were counted above them. They were men whom constant rejection had rendered impacted of feeling, choked of emotion. . . .

While this was happening in the upper levels of Negro life, a chronic and grinding poverty set in in the lower depths. Semi-literate black men and women drifted from city to city, ever seeking what was not to be found: jobs, homes, love—a chance to live as free men. . . .

Because I feel personally identified with the migrant Negro, his folk songs, his ditties, his wild tales of bad men; and because my own life was forged in the depths in which they live, I'll tell first of the Forms of Things Unknown. Numerically, this formless folk utterance accounts for the great majority of the Negro people in the United States, and it is my conviction that the subject matter of future novels resides in the lives of these nameless millions.

Wright affirmed not only the distinctive literary values and the rich forms and content forged in the depths and lower depths of urban Negro life, he also insisted on its value to America. Later in this same essay, Wright declared: "We write out of what life gives us in the form of experience. And there is a value in what we Negro writers say. Is it not clear to you that the American Negro is the only group in our nation that consistently and passionately raises the question of freedom?"

More recently, at the American Academy Conference on the Negro American which took place in 1965 and resulted in the two special issues of *Daedalus* devoted to "The Negro American," Ralph Ellison participated in the discussions and said:

One thing that is not clear to me is the implication that Negroes have come together and decided that we want to lose our identity as quickly as possible. Where does that idea come from? . . . If one assumes that a group, which has existed within this complicated society as long as ours, has failed to develop cultural patterns, views, structures, or whatever other sociological terms one may want to use, then it is quite logical to assume that they would want to get rid of that inhuman condition as quickly as possible. But I, as a novelist looking at Negro life, in terms of its ceremonies, its rituals, and its rather complicated assertions and denials of identity, feel that there are many, many things we would fight to preserve. . . .

There are great ideas of this society which are available to Negroes who have a little consciousness. . . . Contacts are being made. Judgments are being rendered. Choices are being made. I know that in the life styles of any number of groups in the nation, there are many things which Negroes would certainly reject, not because they held them in contempt, but because they do not satisfy our way of doing things and our feeling about things. Sociologists often assert that there is a Negro thing—a timbre of a voice, a style, a rhythm—in all of its positive and negative implications, the expression of a certain kind of American uniqueness. . . . If there is this uniqueness, why on earth would it not in some way be precious to the people who maintain it?

Later in the proceedings, which took the form of an elaborate exchange of views by a group of experts, Ellison added:

One concept that I wish we would get rid of is the concept of a main stream of American culture—which is an exact mirroring of segregation and second class citizenship. . . . The whole problem about whether there is a Negro culture might be cleared up if we said that there were many idioms of American culture, including, certainly, a Negro idiom of American culture in the South. We can trace it in many, many ways. We can trace it in terms of speech idioms, in terms of manners, in terms of dress, in terms of cuisine, and so on. But it is American, and it has existed a long time, it has refinements and crudities. It has all the aspects of a cultural reality. . . .

The feeling that I have about my own group is that it represents certain human values which are unique not in a Negritude sort of way, but in an American way. Because the group has survived, because it has maintained its sense of itself through all these years, it can be of benefit to the total society, the total culture.

John Oliver Killens, novelist and writer in residence at Fisk University, states another important view of a black writer in this way, in his volume of collected essays, *Black Man's Burden* (1965):

And now, in the middle of the twentieth century, I, the Negro, like my counterparts in Asia and Africa and South America and on the islands of the many seas, am refusing to be your "nigger" any longer. Even some of us "favored," "talented," "unusual," ones are refusing to be your educated, sophisticated, split-leveled "niggers" any more. We refuse to look at ourselves through the eyes of white America.

We are not fighting for the right to be like you. We respect ourselves too much for that. When we advocate freedom, we mean freedom for us to be black, or brown, and you to be white, and yet live together in a free and equal society. This is the only way that integration can bring dignity for both of us. . . . My fight is not for racial sameness but for racial equality and against racial prejudice and discrimination. I work for the day when black people will be free of the racist pressures to be white like you; a day when "good hair" and "high yaller" and bleaching cream and hair straighteners will be obsolete. What a tiresome place America would be if freedom meant we all had to think alike or be the same color or wear that same gray flannel suit! That road leads to the conformity of the graveyard!

The black cultural nationalists today not only take for granted the value and distinctness of their blackness but affirm a "black aesthetic" in literature and culture. Very revealing of the divergent and new currents of thinking among black writers today is the issue of the magazine *Negro Digest* for January, 1968. A large part of the magazine is devoted to a survey of the opinions of black writers, which is introduced in the following way by Hoyt W. Fuller, Managing Editor of the publication:

> There is a spirit of revolution abroad in the shadowy world of letters in black America. Not all black writers are attuned to it, of course, and some are even opposed to it which is to be expected also, one supposes. . . . There is, therefore, a wide divergence of opinion among black writers as to their role in society, as to their role in the Black Revolution, as to their role as artists—all these considerations tied into, and touching on, the others. *Negro Digest* polled some 38 black writers, both famous and unknown. . . . The questions elicited from the writers opinions relative to the books and writers which have influenced them, the writers who are "most important" to them in terms of achievement and promise, and what they think about the new movement toward "a black aesthetic" and the preoccupation with "the black experience," aspects of the larger Black Consciousness Movement.

Laurence P. Neal, a young black nationalist writer, expressed this view in the *Negro Digest* poll:

> There is no need to establish a "black aesthetic." Rather, it is important to understand that one already exists. The question is: where does it exist? . . . To explore the black experience means that we do not deny the reality and the power of the slave culture; the culture that produced the blues, spirituals, folk songs, work songs, and "jazz." It means that Afro-American life and its myriad of styles are expressed and examined in the fullest, most truthful manner possible. The models for what Black literature should be are found primarily in our folk culture, especially in the blues and jazz. . . .
>
> Strictly speaking it is not a matter of whether we write protest literature or not. I have written "love" poems that act to liberate the soul as much as any "war" poem I have written. No, it can't simply be about protest as such. Protest literature assumes that the people we are talking to do not understand the nature of their condition. In this narrow context, protest literature is finally a plea to white America for our human dignity. We cannot get it that way. We must address each other. We must touch each other's beauty, wonder, and pain.

Other Negro writers, like Saunders Redding and Robert Hayden, rejected the idea of a "black aesthetic." Redding asserted that "aesthetics has no racial, national or geographical boundaries," and Robert Hayden voiced sharp disagreement with the cultural black nationalism of LeRoi Jones. Poet and novelist Margaret Walker, on the other hand, wrote:

> The "black aesthetic" has a rich if undiscovered past. This goes back in time to the beginning of civilization in Egypt, Babylonia, India, China, Persia, and all the Islamic world that precedes the Renaissance of the Europeans. We have lived too long excluded by the Anglo-Saxon aesthetic. . . . Where else should the journey lead? The black writer IS the black experience. How can the human experience transcend humanity? It's the same thing.

The contemporary black writers polled by *Negro Digest* were asked who, in their opinions, was the most important black writer. Richard Wright headed the choices, with Langston Hughes and James Baldwin in second and third place and Ralph Ellison trailing Baldwin.

In reply to the question on "the most important living black poet" LeRoi Jones came out first, with Robert Hayden and Gwendolyn Brooks in second and third place and Margaret Walker in fourth.

This is a time of great liveliness, controversy, and creativity in the black literary world in the United States. The pages of *Negro Digest* month after month reflect the vitality of the black literary scene, and new literary publications are coming forward, like *The Journal of Black Poetry* and the Broadsides Press, which publishes black poetry. New literary voices are being heard, like those in *From the Ashes*, the collection of writing by the writers in Budd Schulberg's workshop in Watts, and in *ex umbra*, the magazine of the arts produced by the black students at North Carolina College at Durham.

I close this anthology reluctantly with the feeling that so much is happening and being born that it would be good to keep the book open and bring in still more of the new. But the end of this anthology is not conclusion, I hope, but further beginnings: greater appreciation of what black writers have contributed and are contributing to the diversity of American literature, and movement towards greater inclusion of works by Negro writers in our American literature courses in the high schools and colleges.

ABRAHAM CHAPMAN

Wisconsin State University—Stevens Point

1.

Fiction

CHARLES W. CHESNUTT (1858–1932)

American Negroes were writing and publishing fiction for nearly four decades before Charles Waddell Chesnutt's first short story appeared in The Atlantic Monthly *in 1887. But Chesnutt is commonly considered the first Negro writer in the United States to master the short story form and the craft of fiction. He succeeded during his lifetime in establishing national literary reputation as a novelist and short story writer. Born in Cleveland, Ohio, his biography first reverses, then reenacts, the dominant south-to-north migratory pattern of Negro life in the United States. He lived in North Carolina from the age of eight until he was twenty-five and dug deep into the Negro folklore and folkways of the South, which later found literary expression in his fiction. He left North Carolina in 1883 for New York, where he worked as a stenographer for Dow Jones, the commercial reporting agency. Chesnutt finally returned to Cleveland for the rest of his life, where he worked as a commercial and legal stenographer. During the early part of his writing career his identity as a Negro was concealed. Walter Hines Page, editor of* The Atlantic Monthly *when Chesnutt's stories were first being published there, believed that revealing the author's race would harm the reception of his work and so kept it a secret for close to a decade. In* The Atlantic Monthly *of May, 1900, William Dean Howells published an article entitled "Mr. Charles W. Chesnutt's Stories." The tone of the article reflects what a novelty fiction by an American Negro was to the American reading public of that day, though Howells emphasized that Chesnutt merited critical acclaim for his achievement as an artist and not for any reasons of race. As Howells put it:*

Now, however, it is known that the author of this story ["The Wife of His Youth"] is of Negro blood—diluted, indeed, in such measure that if he did not admit this descent few would imagine it, but still quite of that middle world, which lies next, though wholly outside, our own. Since his first story appeared he has contributed several others to these pages, and he now makes a showing palpable to criticism in a volume called The Wife of His Youth, and Other Stories of the Color Line; a volume of Southern sketches called The Conjure Woman; and a short life of Frederick Douglass in the Beacon Series of biographies. . . . But the volumes of fiction *are* remarkable above many, above most short stories by people entirely white. . . . It is not from their racial interest that we could first wish to speak of them, though that must have a very great and very just claim upon the critic. It is much more simply and directly, as works of art, that they make their appeal, and we must allow the force of this quite independently of the other interest.

Chesnutt studied law and passed the Ohio bar examination in 1887, with unusually high scores, but never practiced law because he found legal stenography a more lucrative profession. From 1905 until his death in 1932 Chesnutt wrote no further fiction. The Spingarn Gold Medal was awarded to Chesnutt in 1928 for his "pioneer work as a literary artist depicting the life and struggle of Americans of African descent." He is represented here by one of his last stories, "Baxter's Procrustes," taken from The Atlantic Monthly, *June, 1904.*

Baxter's Procrustes

Baxter's Procrustes is one of the publications of the Bodleian
Club. The Bodleian Club is composed of gentlemen of culture,
who are interested in books and book-collecting. It was
named, very obviously, after the famous library of the same
name, and not only became in our city a sort of shrine for
local worshipers of fine buildings and rare editions, but was
visited occasionally by pilgrims from afar. The Bodleian has
entertained Mark Twain, Joseph Jefferson, and other literary
and histrionic celebrities. It possesses quite a collection of
personal mementos of distinguished authors, among them a
paperweight which once belonged to Goethe, a lead pencil
used by Emerson, an autograph letter of Matthew Arnold,
and a chip from a tree felled by Mr. Gladstone. Its library
contains a number of rare books, including a fine collection
on chess, of which game several of the members are enthusiastic devotees.

The activities of the club are not, however, confined entirely to books. We have a very handsome clubhouse, and
much taste and discrimination have been exercised in its
adornment. There are many good paintings, including por-
traits of the various presidents of the club, which adorn the
entrance hall. After books, perhaps the most distinctive feature of the club is our collection of pipes. In a large rack in
the smoking-room—really a superfluity, since smoking is permitted all over the house—is as complete an assortment of
pipes as perhaps exists in the civilized world. Indeed, it is an
unwritten rule of the club that no one is eligible for membership who cannot produce a new variety of pipe, which is filed
with his application for membership, and, if he passes, deposited with the club collection, he, however, retaining the title
in himself. Once a year, upon the anniversary of the death of
Sir Walter Raleigh, who, it will be remembered, first introduced tobacco into England, the full membership of the club,
as a rule, turns out. A large supply of the very best smoking
mixture is laid in. At nine o'clock sharp each member takes
his pipe from the rack, fills it with tobacco, and then the
whole club, with the president at the head, all smoking furiously, march in solemn procession from room to room, upstairs and downstairs, making the tour of the clubhouse and
returning to the smoking-room. The president then delivers
an address, and each member is called upon to say some-

thing, either by way of a quotation or an original sentiment, in praise of the virtues of nicotine. This ceremony—facetiously known as "hitting the pipe"—being thus concluded, the membership pipes are carefully cleaned out and replaced in the club rack.

As I have said, however, the *raison d'être* of the club, and the feature upon which its fame chiefly rests, is its collection of rare books, and of these by far the most interesting are its own publications. Even its catalogues are works of art, published in numbered editions, and sought by libraries and book-collectors. Early in its history it began the occasional publication of books which should meet the club standard—books in which emphasis should be laid upon the qualities that make a book valuable in the eyes of collectors. Of these, age could not, of course, be imparted, but in the matter of fine and curious bindings, of hand-made linen papers, of uncut or deckle edges, of wide margins and limited editions, the club could control its own publications. The matter of contents was, it must be confessed, a less important consideration. At first it was felt by the publishing committee that nothing but the finest products of the human mind should be selected for enshrinement in the beautiful volumes which the club should issue. The length of the work was an important consideration,—long things were not compatible with wide margins and graceful slenderness. For instance, we brought out Coleridge's Ancient Mariner, an essay by Emerson, and another by Thoreau. Our Rubáiyát of Omar Khayyám was Heron-Allen's translation of the original MS. in the Bodleian Library at Oxford, which, though less poetical than FitzGerald's, was not so common. Several years ago we began to publish the works of our own members. Bascom's Essay on Pipes was a very creditable performance. It was published in a limited edition of one hundred copies, and since it had not previously appeared elsewhere and was copyrighted by the club, it was sufficiently rare to be valuable for that reason. The second publication of local origin was Baxter's Procrustes.

I have omitted to say that once or twice a year, at a meeting of which notice has been given, an auction is held at the Bodleian. The members of the club send in their duplicate copies, or books they for any reason wish to dispose of, which are auctioned off to the highest bidder. At these sales, which are well attended, the club's publications have of recent years formed the leading feature. Three years ago, number three of Bascom's Essay on Pipes sold for fifteen dollars;—the original cost of publication was one dollar and seventy-five cents.

Later in the evening an uncut copy of the same brought thirty dollars. At the next auction the price of the cut copy was run up to twenty-five dollars, while the uncut copy was knocked down at seventy-five dollars. The club had always appreciated the value of uncut copies, but this financial indorsement enhanced their desirability immensely. This rise in the Essay on Pipes was not without a sympathetic effect upon all the club publications. The Emerson essay rose from three dollars to seventeen, and the Thoreau, being an author less widely read, and by his own confession commercially unsuccessful, brought a somewhat higher figure. The prices, thus inflated, were not permitted to come down appreciably. Since every member of the club possessed one or more of these valuable editions, they were all manifestly interested in keeping up the price. The publication, however, which brought the highest prices, and, but for the sober second thought, might have wrecked the whole system, was Baxter's Procrustes.

Baxter was, perhaps, the most scholarly member of the club. A graduate of Harvard, he had traveled extensively, had read widely, and while not so enthusiastic a collector as some of us, possessed as fine a private library as any man of his age in the city. He was about thirty-five when he joined the club, and apparently some bitter experience—some disappointment in love or ambition—had left its mark upon his character. With light, curly hair, fair complexion, and gray eyes, one would have expected Baxter to be genial of temper, with a tendency toward wordiness of speech. But though he had occasional flashes of humor, his ordinary demeanor was characterized by a mild cynicism, which, with his gloomy pessimistic philosophy, so foreign to the temperament that should accompany his physical type, could only be accounted for upon the hypothesis of some secret sorrow such as I have suggested. What it might be no one knew. He had means and social position, and was an uncommonly handsome man. The fact that he remained unmarried at thirty-five furnished some support for the theory of a disappointment in love, though this the several intimates of Baxter who belonged to the club were not able to verify.

It had occurred to me, in a vague way, that perhaps Baxter might be an unsuccessful author. That he was a poet we knew very well, and typewritten copies of his verses had occasionally circulated among us. But Baxter had always expressed such a profound contempt for modern literature, had always spoken in terms of such unmeasured pity for the slaves of the pen, who were dependent upon the whim of an undiscriminating public for recognition and a livelihood, that

no one of us had ever suspected him of aspirations toward
publication, until, as I have said, it occurred to me one day
that Baxter's attitude with regard to publication might be
viewed in the light of effect as well as of cause,—that his
scorn of publicity might as easily arise from failure to
achieve it, as his never having published might be due to his
preconceived disdain of the vulgar popularity which one must
share with the pugilist or balloonist of the hour.

The notion of publishing Baxter's Procrustes did not emanate
from Baxter,—I must do him the justice to say this. But he had
spoken to several of the fellows about the theme of his poem,
until the notion that Baxter was at work upon something fine
had become pretty well disseminated throughout our membership. He would occasionally read brief passages to a small
coterie of friends in the sitting-room or library,—never more
than ten lines at once, or to more than five people at a time,—
and these excerpts gave at least a few of us a pretty fair idea of
the motive and scope of the poem. As I, for one, gathered, it
was quite along the line of Baxter's philosophy. Society was
the Procrustes which, like the Greek bandit of old, caught
every man born into the world, and endeavored to fit him to
some preconceived standard, generally to the one for which
he was least adapted. The world was full of men and women
who were merely square pegs in round holes, and *vice versa*.
Most marriages were unhappy because the contracting parties
were not properly mated. Religion was mostly superstition,
science for the most part sciolism, popular education merely
a means of forcing the stupid and repressing the bright, so
that all the youth of the rising generation might conform to
the same dull, dead level of democratic mediocrity. Life
would soon become so monotonously uniform and so uni-
formly monotonous as to be scarce worth the living.

It was Smith, I think, who first proposed that the club
publish Baxter's Procrustes. The poet himself did not seem
enthusiastic when the subject was broached; he demurred for
some little time, protesting that the poem was not worthy of
publication. But when it was proposed that the edition be
limited to fifty copies he agreed to consider the proposition.
When I suggested, having in mind my secret theory of Baxter's failure in authorship, that the edition would at least be
in the hands of friends, that it would be difficult for a hostile
critic to secure a copy, and that if it should not achieve success from a literary point of view, the extent of the failure
would be limited to the size of the edition, Baxter was visibly
impressed. When the literary committee at length decided to
request formally of Baxter the privilege of publishing his Pro-

crustes, he consented, with evident reluctance, upon condition
that he should supervise the printing, binding, and delivery of
the books, merely submitting to the committee, in advance,
the manuscript, and taking their views in regard to the bookmaking.

The manuscript was duly presented to the literary committee. Baxter having expressed the desire that the poem be
not read aloud at a meeting of the club, as was the custom,
since he wished it to be given to the world clad in suitable
garb, the committee went even farther. Having entire confidence in Baxter's taste and scholarship, they, with great deli-
cacy, refrained from even reading the manuscript, contenting
themselves with Baxter's statement of the general theme and
the topics grouped under it. The details of the bookmaking,
however, were gone into thoroughly. The paper was to be of
hand-made linen, from the Kelmscott Mills; the type black-
letter, with rubricated initials. The cover, which was Baxter's
own selection, was to be of dark green morocco, with a cap-
and-bells border in red inlays, and doublures of maroon morocco with a blind-tooled design. Baxter was authorized to
contract with the printer and superintend the publication.
The whole edition of fifty numbered copies was to be disposed of at auction, in advance, to the highest bidder, only
one copy to each, the proceeds to be devoted to paying for
the printing and binding, the remainder, if any, to go into the
club treasury, and Baxter himself to receive one copy by way
of remuneration. Baxter was inclined to protest at this, on the
ground that his copy would probably be worth more than the
royalties on the edition, at the usual ten per cent, would
amount to, but was finally prevailed upon to accept an author's copy.

While the Procrustes was under consideration, some one
read, at one of our meetings, a note from some magazine,
which stated that a sealed copy of a new translation of Cam-
panella's Sonnets, published by the Grolier Club, had been
sold for three hundred dollars. This impressed the members
greatly. It was a novel idea. A new work might thus be en-
shrined in a sort of holy of holies, which, if the collector so
desired, could be forever sacred from the profanation of any
vulgar or unappreciative eye. The possessor of such a treasure
could enjoy it by the eye of imagination, having at the same
time the exaltation of grasping what was for others the unat-
tainable. The literary committee were so impressed with this
idea that they presented it to Baxter in regard to the Procrustes. Baxter making no objection, the subscribers who
might wish their copies delivered sealed were directed to no-

tify the author. I sent in my name. A fine book, after all, was an investment, and if there was any way of enhancing its rarity, and therefore its value, I was quite willing to enjoy such an advantage.

When the Procrustes was ready for distribution, each subscriber received his copy by mail, in a neat pasteboard box. Each number was wrapped in a thin and transparent but very strong paper, through which the cover design and tooling were clearly visible. The number of the copy was indorsed upon the wrapper, the folds of which were securely fastened at each end with sealing-wax, upon which was impressed, as a guaranty of its inviolateness, the monogram of the club.

At the next meeting of the Bodleian a great deal was said about the Procrustes, and it was unanimously agreed that no finer specimen of bookmaking had ever been published by the club. By a curious coincidence, no one had brought his copy with him, and the two club copies had not yet been received from the binder, who, Baxter had reported, was retaining them for some extra fine work. Upon resolution, offered by a member who had not subscribed for the volume, a committee of three was appointed to review the Procrustes at the next literary meeting of the club. Of this committee it was my doubtful fortune to constitute one.

In pursuance of my duty in the premises, it of course became necessary for me to read the Procrustes. In all probability I should have cut my own copy for this purpose, had not one of the club auctions intervened between my appointment and the date set for the discussion of the Procrustes. At this meeting a copy of the book, still sealed, was offered for sale, and bought by a non-subscriber for the unprecedented price of one hundred and fifty dollars. After this a proper regard for my own interests would not permit me to spoil my copy by opening it, and I was therefore compelled to procure my information concerning the poem from some other source. As I had no desire to appear mercenary, I said nothing about my own copy, and made no attempt to borrow. I did, however, casually remark to Baxter that I should like to look at his copy of the proof sheets, since I wished to make some extended quotations for my review, and would rather not trust my copy to a typist for that purpose. Baxter assured me, with every evidence of regret, that he had considered them of so little importance that he had thrown them into the fire. The indifference of Baxter to literary values struck me as just a little overdone. The proof sheets of Hamlet, corrected in Shakespeare's own hand, would be well-nigh priceless.

At the next meeting of the club I observed that Thompson and Davis, who were with me on the reviewing committee, very soon brought up the question of the Procrustes in conversation in the smoking-room, and seemed anxious to get from the members their views concerning Baxter's production, I supposed upon the theory that the appreciation of any book review would depend more or less upon the degree to which it reflected the opinion of those to whom the review should be presented. I presumed, of course, that Thompson and Davis had each read the book,—they were among the subscribers,—and I was desirous of getting their point of view.

"What do you think," I inquired, "of the passage on Social Systems?" I have forgotten to say that the poem was in blank verse, and divided into parts, each with an appropriate title.

"Well," replied Davis, it seemed to me a little cautiously, "it is not exactly Spencerian, although it squints at the Spencerian view, with a slight deflection toward Hegelianism. I should consider it an harmonious fusion of the best views of all the modern philosophers, with a strong Baxterian flavor."

"Yes," said Thompson, "the charm of the chapter lies in this very quality. The style is an emanation from Baxter's own intellect,—he has written himself into the poem. By knowing Baxter we are able to appreciate the book, and after having read the book we feel that we are so much the more intimately acquainted with Baxter,—the real Baxter."

Baxter had come in during this colloquy, and was standing by the fireplace smoking a pipe. I was not exactly sure whether the faint smile which marked his face was a token of pleasure or cynicism; it was Baxterian, however, and I had already learned that Baxter's opinions upon any subject were not to be gathered always from his facial expression. For instance, when the club porter's crippled child died Baxter remarked, it seemed to me unfeelingly, that the poor little devil was doubtless better off, and that the porter himself had certainly been relieved of a burden; and only a week later the porter told me in confidence that Baxter had paid for an expensive operation, undertaken in the hope of prolonging the child's life. I therefore drew no conclusions from Baxter's somewhat enigmatical smile. He left the room at this point in the conversation, somewhat to my relief.

"By the way, Jones," said Davis, addressing me, "are you impressed by Baxter's view on Degeneration?"

Having often heard Baxter express himself upon the general downward tendency of modern civilization, I felt safe in discussing his views in a broad and general manner.

"I think," I replied, "that they are in harmony with those of Schopenhauer, without his bitterness; with those of Nordau, without his flippancy. His materialism is Haeckel's, presented with something of the charm of Omar Khayyám."

"Yes," chimed in Davis, "it answers the strenuous demand of our day—dissatisfaction with an unjustified optimism—and voices for us the courage of human philosophy facing the unknown."

I had a vague recollection of having read something like this somewhere, but so much has been written, that one can scarcely discuss any subject of importance without unconsciously borrowing, now and then, the thoughts or the language of others. Quotation, like imitation, is a superior grade of flattery.

"The Procrustes," said Thompson, to whom the metrical review had been apportioned, "is couched in sonorous lines, of haunting melody and charm; and yet so closely inter-related as to be scarcely quotable with justice to the author. To be appreciated the poem should be read as a whole,—I shall say as much in my review. What shall you say of the letterpress?" he concluded, addressing me. I was supposed to discuss the technical excellence of the volume from the connoisseur's viewpoint.

"The setting," I replied judicially, "is worthy of the gem. The dark green cover elaborately tooled, the old English lettering, the heavy linen paper, mark this as one of our very choicest publications. The letter-press is of course De Vinne's best,—there is nothing better on this side of the Atlantic. The text is a beautiful, slender stream, meandering gracefully through a wide meadow of margin."

For some reason I left the room for a minute. As I stepped into the hall, I almost ran into Baxter, who was standing near the door, facing a hunting print of a somewhat humorous character, hung upon the wall, and smiling with an immensely pleased expression.

"What a ridiculous scene!" he remarked. "Look at that fat old squire on that tall hunter! I'll wager dollars to doughnuts that he won't get over the first fence!"

It was a very good bluff, but did not deceive me. Under his mask of unconcern, Baxter was anxious to learn what we thought of his poem, and had stationed himself in the hall that he might overhear our discussion without embarrassing us by his presence. He had covered up his delight at our appreciation by this simulated interest in the hunting print.

When the night came for the review of the Procrustes there was a large attendance of members, and several visitors, among them a young English cousin of one of the members, on his first visit to the United States; some of us had met him at other clubs, and in society, and had found him a very jolly boy, with a youthful exuberance of spirits and a naïve ignorance of things American, that made his views refreshing and, at times, amusing.

The critical essays were well considered, if a trifle vague. Baxter received credit for poetic skill of a high order.

"Our brother Baxter," said Thompson, "should no longer bury his talent in a napkin. This gem, of course, belongs to the club, but the same brain from which issued this exquisite emanation can produce others to inspire and charm an appreciative world."

"The author's view of life," said Davis, "as expressed in these beautiful lines, will help us to fit our shoulders for the heavy burden of life, by bringing to our realization those profound truths of philosophy which find hope in despair and pleasure in pain. When he shall see fit to give to the wider world, in fuller form, the thoughts of which we have been vouchsafed this foretaste, let us hope that some little ray of his fame may rest upon the Bodleian, from which can never be taken away the proud privilege of saying that he was one of its members."

I then pointed out the beauties of the volume as a piece of bookmaking. I knew, from conversation with the publication committee, the style of type and rubrication, and could see the cover through the wrapper of my sealed copy. The dark green morocco, I said, in summing up, typified the author's serious view of life, as a thing to be endured as patiently as might be. The cap-and-bells border was significant of the shams by which the optimist sought to delude himself into the view that life was a desirable thing. The intricate blind-tooling of the doublure shadowed forth the blind fate which left us in ignorance of our future and our past, or of even what the day itself might bring forth. The black-letter type, with rubricated initials, signified a philosophic pessimism enlightened by the conviction that in duty one might find, after all, an excuse for life and a hope for humanity. Applying this test to the club, this work, which might be said to represent all that the Bodleian stood for, was in itself sufficient to justify the club's existence. If the Bodleian had done nothing else, if it should do nothing more, it had produced a masterpiece.

There was a sealed copy of the Procrustes, belonging, I believe, to one of the committee, lying on the table by which I stood, and I had picked it up and held it in my hand for a moment, to emphasize one of my periods, but had laid it down immediately. I noted, as I sat down, that young Hunkin, our English visitor, who sat at the other side of the table, had picked up the volume and was examining it with interest. When the last review was read, and the generous applause had subsided, there were cries for Baxter.

"Baxter! Baxter! Author! Author!"

Baxter had been sitting over in a corner during the reading of the reviews, and had succeeded remarkably well, it seemed to me, in concealing, under his mask of cynical indifference, the exulatation which I was sure he must feel. But this outburst of enthusiasm was too much even for Baxter, and it was clear that he was struggling with strong emotion when he rose to speak.

"Gentlemen, and fellow members of the Bodleian, it gives me unaffected pleasure—sincere pleasure—some day you may know how much pleasure—I cannot trust myself to say it now—to see the evident care with which your committee have read my poor verses, and the responsive sympathy with which my friends have entered into my views of life and conduct. I thank you again, and again, and when I say that I am too full for utterance,—I'm sure you will excuse me from saying any more."

Baxter took his seat, and the applause had begun again when it was broken by a sudden exclamation.

"By Jove!" exclaimed our English visitor, who still sat behind the table, "what an extraordinary book!"

Every one gathered around him.

"You see," he exclaimed, holding up the volume, "you fellows said so much about the bally book that I wanted to see what it was like; so I untied the ribbon, and cut the leaves with the paper knife lying there, and found—and found that there wasn't a single line in it, don't you know!"

Blank consternation followed this announcement, which proved only too true. Every one knew instinctively, without further investigation, that the club had been badly sold. In the resulting confusion Baxter escaped, but later was waited upon by a committee, to whom he made the rather lame excuse that he had always regarded uncut and sealed books as tommy-rot, and that he had merely been curious to see how far the thing could go; and that the result had justified his belief that a book with nothing in it was just as useful to a book-collector as one embodying a work of genius. He offered to pay all the bills for the sham Procrustes, or to replace the blank copies with the real thing, as we might choose. Of course, after such an insult, the club did not care for the poem. He was permitted to pay the expense, however, and it was more than hinted to him that his resignation from the club would be favorably acted upon. He never sent it in, and, as he went to Europe shortly afterwards, the affair had time to blow over.

In our first disgust at Baxter's duplicity, most of us cut our copies of the Procrustes, some of us mailed them to Baxter with cutting notes, and others threw them into the fire. A few wiser spirits held on to theirs, and this fact leaking out, it began to dawn upon the minds of the real collectors among us that the volume was something unique in the way of a publication.

"Baxter," said our president one evening to a select few of us who sat around the fireplace, "was wiser than we knew, or than he perhaps appreciated. His Procrustes, from the collector's point of view, is entirely logical, and might be considered as the acme of bookmaking. To the true collector, a book is a work of art, of which the contents are no more important than the words of an opera. Fine binding is a desideratum, and, for its cost, that of the Procrustes could not be improved upon. The paper is above criticism. The true collector loves wide margins, and Procrustes, being all margin, merely touches the vanishing point of the perspective. The smaller the edition, the greater the collector's eagerness to acquire a copy. There are but six uncut copies left, I am told, of the Procrustes, and three sealed copies, of one of which I am the fortunate possessor."

After this deliverance, it is not surprising that, at our next auction, a sealed copy of Baxter's Procrustes was knocked down, after spirited bidding, for two hundred and fifty dollars, the highest price ever brought by a single volume published by the club.

JEAN TOOMER (1894–1967)

With his single book Cane *(1923), a mosaic of poems, short stories, and intense sketches, Jean Toomer raised the innovation of the literary experimentation of the 20's and the modernist mode to new levels of artistic achievement in racial expression by an American Negro. Profoundly appreciated by other American writers, Toomer's new artistic ways did not win the audience and public recognition merited by his contribution to American writing at that time. The most promising of the talents and original voices of the Negro Renaissance, he died in the obscurity of a rest home near Philadelphia on March 30, 1967. Toomer was born in Washington, D. C., and attended the University of Wisconsin and the City College of New York. He began his literary career in 1918 with poems, sketches and reviews in a variety of national magazines. In 1922 he went to Georgia, where he worked for a while as principal of a school. It was from his contact with Negro life in the deep South that he created the most striking stories and poems in* Cane. *After* Cane, *as Professor Darwin T. Turner noted in a memorial tribute to Toomer: "He wrote; editors refused. Seeking an excuse for failure, he blamed his identification as a Negro. He denied that he came from Negro ancestry. Still the editors refused. . . . He continued to write and rewrite; two novels, two books of poems, a collection of stories, books of nonfiction, two books of aphorisms. But editors never again accepted a book for publication." He lived for a time in the artistic community of Carmel, California, later moving to Taos, New Mexico. Toomer finally settled in Bucks County, Pennsylvania, where he became a "literary ghost," a living writer remembered and revered for over forty years by a small group of critics and literary historians for his literary past. We present two stories from* Cane, *"Karintha," which opens the book as the first in a cycle of stories set in Georgia, and "Blood-Burning Moon," the story which concludes the Georgia cycle.*

Karintha

Her skin is like dusk on the eastern horizon,
O cant you see it, O cant you see it,
Her skin is like dusk on the eastern horizon
. . . When the sun goes down.

Men always wanted her, this Karintha, even as a child, Karintha carrying beauty, perfect as dusk when the sun goes
down. Old men rode her hobby-horse upon their knees.
Young men danced with her at frolics when they should have
been dancing with their grown-up girls. God grant us youth,
secretly prayed the old men. The young fellows counted the
time to pass before she would be old enough to mate with
them. This interest of the male, who wishes to ripen a growing thing too soon, could mean no good to her.
    Karintha, at twelve, was a wild flash that told the other
folks just what it was to live. At sunset, where there was no
wind, and the pine-smoke from over by the sawmill hugged
the earth, and you couldnt see more than a few feet in front,
her sudden darting past you was a bit of vivid color, like a
black bird that flashes in light. With the other children one
could hear, some distance off, their feet flopping in the two-
inch dust. Karintha's running was a whir. It had the sound of
the red dust that sometimes makes a spiral in the road. At
dusk, during the hush just after the sawmill had closed down,
and before any of the women had started their supper-getting-
ready songs, her voice, high-pitched, shrill, would put one's
ears to itching. But no one ever thought to make her stop because of it. She stoned the cows, and beat her dog, and
fought the other children. . . . Even the preacher, who
caught her at mischief, told himself that she was as innocently lovely as a November cotton flower. Already, rumors
were out about her. Homes in Georgia are most often built
on the two-room plan. In one, you cook and eat, in the other
you sleep, and there love goes on. Karintha had seen or
heard, perhaps she had felt her parents loving. One could but
imitate one's parents, for to follow them was the way of God.
She played "home" with a small boy who was not afraid to
do her bidding. That started the whole thing. Old men could
no longer ride her hobby-horse upon their knees. But young
men counted faster.

Her skin is like dusk,
O cant you see it,
Her skin is like dusk,
When the sun goes down.

Karintha is a woman. She who carries beauty, perfect as
dusk when the sun goes down. She has been married many
times. Old men remind her that a few years back they rode
her hobby-horse upon their knees. Karintha smiles, and in-
dulges them when she is in the mood for it. She has contempt
for them. Karintha is a woman. Young men run stills to
make her money. Young men go to the big cities and run on
the road. Young men go away to college. They all want to
bring her money. These are the young men who thought that
all they had to do was to count time. But Karintha is a
woman, and she has had a child. A child fell out of her
womb onto a bed of pine-needles in the forest. Pine-needles
are smooth and sweet. They are elastic to the feet of
rabbits . . . A sawmill was nearby. Its pyramidal sawdust
pile smouldered. It is a year before one completely burns.
Meanwhile, the smoke curls up and hangs in odd wraiths
about the trees, curls up, and spreads itself out over the valley . . . Weeks after Karintha returned home the smoke was
so heavy you tasted it in water. Some one made a song:

Smoke is on the hills. Rise up.
Smoke is on the hills, O rise
And take my soul to Jesus.

Karintha is a woman. Men do not know that the soul of
her was a growing thing ripened too soon. They will bring
their money; they will die not having found it out . . . Karintha at twenty, carrying beauty, perfect as dusk when the
sun goes down. Karintha. . .

Her skin is like dusk on the eastern horizon,
O cant you see it, O cant you see it,
Her skin is like dusk on the eastern horizon
. . . When the sun goes down.

Goes down . . .

Blood-Burning Moon

Up from the skeleton stone walls, up from the rotting floor
boards and the solid hand-hewn beams of oak of the pre-war
cotton factory, dusk came. Up from the dusk the full moon
came. Glowing like a fired pine-knot, it illumined the great
door and soft showered the Negro shanties aligned along the
single street of factory town. The full moon in the great door
was an omen. Negro women improvised songs against its
spell.

Louisa sang as she came over the crest of the hill from the
white folks' kitchen. Her skin was the color of oak leaves on
young trees in fall. Her breasts, firm and up-pointed like ripe
acorns. And her singing had the low murmur of winds in fig
trees. Bob Stone, younger son of the people she worked for,
loved her. By the way the world reckons things, he had won
her. By measure of that warm glow which came into her
mind at thought of him, he had won her. Tom Burwell,
whom the whole town called Big Boy, also loved her. But
working in the fields all day, and far away from her, gave
him no chance to show it. Though often enough of evenings
he had tried to. Somehow, he never got along. Strong as he
was with his hands upon the ax or plow, he found it difficult
to hold her. Or so he thought. But the fact was that he held
her to factory town more firmly than he thought, for his
black balanced, and pulled against, the white of Stone, when
she thought of them. And her mind was vaguely upon them
as she came over the crest of the hill, coming from the white
folks' kitchen. As she sang softly at the evil face of the full
moon.

A strange stir was in her. Indolently, she tried to fix upon
Bob or Tom as the cause of it. To meet Bob in the canebrake, as she was going to do an hour or so later, was nothing
new. And Tom's proposal which she felt on its way to her
could be indefinitely put off. Separately, there was no unusual
significance to either one. But for some reason, they jumbled
when her eyes gazed vacantly at the rising moon. And from
the jumble came the stir that was strangely within her. Her
lips trembled. The slow rhythm of her song grew agitant and
restless. Rusty black and tan spotted hounds, lying in the
dark corners of porches or prowling around back yards, put
their noses in the air and caught its tremor. They began
plaintively to yelp and howl. Chickens woke up and cackled.

Intermittently, all over the countryside dogs barked and roosters crowed as if heralding a weird dawn or some ungodly awakening. The women sang lustily. Their songs were cotton-wads to stop their ears. Louisa came down into factory town and sank wearily upon the step before her home. The moon was rising towards a thick cloud-bank which soon would hide it.

Red nigger moon. Sinner!
Blood-burning moon. Sinner!
Come out that fact'ry door.

2

Up from the deep dusk of a cleared spot on the edge of the forest a mellow glow arose and spread fan-wise into the low-hanging heavens. And all around the air was heavy with the scent of boiling cane. A large pile of cane-stalks lay like ribboned shadows upon the ground. A mule, harnessed to a pole, trudged lazily round and round the pivot of the grinder. Beneath a swaying oil lamp, a Negro alternately whipped out at the mule, and fed cane-stalks to the grinder. A fat boy waddled pails of fresh-ground juice between the grinder and the boiling stove. Steam came from the copper boiling pan. The scent of cane came from the copper pan and drenched the forest and the hill that sloped to factory town, beneath its fragrance. It drenched the men in the circle seated around the stove. Some of them chewed at the white pulp of stalks, but there was no need for them to, if all they wanted was to taste the cane. One tasted it in factory town. And from factory town one could see the soft haze thrown by the glowing stove upon the low-hanging heavens.

Old David Georgia stirred the thickening syrup with a long ladle, and ever so often drew it off. Old David Georgia tended his stove and told tales about the white folks, about moonshining and cotton picking, and about sweet nigger gals, to the men who sat there about his stove to listen to him. Tom Burwell chewed cane-stalk and laughed with the others till someone mentioned Louisa. Till someone said something about Louisa and Bob Stone, about the silk stockings she must have gotten from him. Blood ran up Tom's neck hotter than the glow that flooded from the stove. He sprang up. Glared at the men and said, "She's my gal." Will Manning laughed. Tom strode over to him. Yanked him up and knocked him to the ground. Several of Manning's friends got up to fight for him. Tom whipped out a long knife and would have cut them

to shreds if they hadnt ducked into the woods. Tom had had
enough. He nodded to Old David Georgia and swung down
the path to factory town. Just then, the dogs started barking
and the roosters began to crow. Tom felt funny. Away from
the fight, away from the stove, chill got to him. He shivered.
He shuddered when he saw the full moon rising towards the
cloud-bank. He who didnt give a godam for the fears of old
women. He forced his mind to fasten on Louisa. Bob Stone.
Better not be. He turned into the street and saw Louisa sitting before her home. He went towards her, ambling, touched
the brim of a marvelously shaped, spotted, felt hat, said he
wanted to say something to her, and then found that he didnt
know what he had to say, or if he did, that he couldnt say it.
He shoved his big fists in his overalls, grinned, and started to
move off.

"Youall want me, Tom?"

"Thats what us wants, sho, Louisa."

"Well, here I am—"

"An here I is, but that aint ahelpin none, all th same."

"You wanted to say somthing?"

"I did that, sho. But the words is like th spots on dice: no
matter how y fumbles em, there's times when they jes wont
come. I dunno why. Seems like th love I feels fo yo done
stole m tongue. I got it now. Whee! Louisa, honey, I oughtnt
tell y, I feel I oughtnt cause yo is young an goes t church
an I has had other gals, but Louisa I sho do love y. Lil gal,
Ise watched y from them first days when youall sat right there
befo yo door befo th well an sang sometimes in a way that
like t broke m heart. Ise carried y with me into th fields, day
after day, and after that, an I sho can plow when yo is there,
an I can pick cotton. Yassur! Come near beatin Barlo yesterday. I sho did. Yassur! An next year if ole Stone'll trust
me, I'll have a farm. My own. My bales will buy yo what y
gets from white folks now. Silk stockings an purple dresses
—course I dont believe what some folks been whisperin as t
how y gets them things now. White folks always did do for
niggers what they likes. An they jes cant help alikin yo,
Louisa. Bob Stone likes y. Course he does. But not th way
folks is awhisperin. Does he, hon?"

"I dont know what you mean, Tom."

"Course y dont. Ise already cut two niggers. Had t hon, t
tell em so. Niggers always tryin t make somethin outa nothin.
An then besides, white folks aint up t them tricks so much
nowadays. Godam better not be. Leastawise not with you.
Cause I wouldnt stand f it. Nassur."

"What would you do, Tom?"

"Cut him jes like I cut a nigger."

"No, Tom—"

"I said I would an there ain't no mo to it. But that aint th talk f now. Sing, honey Louisa, an while I'm listenin t y I'll be makin love."

Tom took her hand in his. Against the tough thickness of his own, hers felt soft and small. His huge body slipped down to the step beside her. The full moon sank upward into the deep purple of the cloud-bank. An old woman brought a lighted lamp and hung it on the common well whose bulky shadow squatted in the middle of the road, opposite Tom and Louisa. The old woman lifted the well-lid, took hold the chain, and began drawing up the heavy bucket. As she did so, she sang. Figures shifted, restless-like, between lamp and window in the front rooms of the shanties. Shadows of the figures fought each other on the gray dust of the road. Figures raised the windows and joined the old woman in song. Louisa and Tom, the whole street, singing:

> Red nigger moon. Sinner!
> Blood-burning moon. Sinner!
> Come out that fact'ry door.

3

Bob Stone sauntered from his veranda out into the gloom of fir trees and magnolias. The clear white of his skin paled, and the flush of his cheeks turned purple. As if to balance this outer change, his mind became consciously a white man's. He passed the house with its huge open hearth which, in the days of slavery, was the plantation cookery. He saw Louisa bent over that hearth. He went in as a master should and took her. Direct, honest, bold. None of this sneaking that he had to go through now. The contrast was repulsive to him. His family had lost ground. Hell no, his family still owned the niggers, practically. Damned if they did, or he wouldnt have to duck around so. What would they think if they knew? His mother? His sister? He shouldnt mention them, shouldnt think of them in this connection. There in the dark he blushed at doing so. Fellows about town were all right, but how about his friends up North? He could see them, incredible, repulsed. They didnt know. The thought first made him laugh. Then, with their eyes still upon him, he began to feel embarrassed. He felt the need of explaining things to them. Explain hell. They wouldnt understand, and moreover, who ever heard of a Southerner getting on his knees to any Yankee, or anyone. No sir. He was going to see Louisa to-night, and love

her. She was lovely—in her way. Nigger way. What way was
that? Damned if he knew. Must know. He'd known her long
enough to know. Was there something about niggers that you
couldnt know? Listening to them at church didnt tell you
anything. Looking at them didnt tell you anything. Talking to
them didnt tell you anything—unless it was gossip, unless
they wanted to talk. Of course, about farming, and licker,
and craps—but those werent nigger. Nigger was something
more. How much more? Something to be afraid of, more?
Hell no. Who ever heard of being afraid of a nigger? Tom
Burwell. Cartwell had told him that Tom went with Louisa
after she reached home. No sir. No nigger had ever been
with his girl. He'd like to see one try. Some position for him
to be in. Him, Bob Stone, of the Stone family, in a scrap with
a nigger over a nigger girl. In the good old days . . . Ha!
Those were the days. His family had lost ground. Not so
much, though. Enough for him to have to cut through old
Lemon's canefield by way of the woods, that he might meet
her. She was worth it. Beautiful nigger gal. Why nigger? Why
not, just gal? No, it was because she was nigger that he went
to her. Sweet . . . The scent of boiling cane came to him.
Then he saw the rich glow of the stove. He heard the voices
of the men circled around it. He was about to skirt the clearing when he heard his own name mentioned. He stopped.
Quivering. Leaning against a tree, he listened.

"Bad nigger. Yassur, he sho is one bad nigger when he gets
started."

"Tom Burwell's been on th gang three times fo cuttin
men."

"What y think he's a gwine t do t Bob Stone?"

"Dunno yet. He aint found out. When he does— Baby!"

"Young Stone aint no quitter an I ken tell y that. Blood of
th old uns in his veins."

"Thats right. He'll scrap, sho."

"Be gettin too hot f niggers round this away."

"Shut up, nigger. Y dont know what y talkin bout."

Bob Stone's ears burned as though he had been holding
them over the stove. Sizzling heat welled up within him. His
feet felt as if they rested on red-hot coals. They stung him to
quick movement. He circled the fringe of the glowing. Not a
twig cracked beneath his feet. He reached the path that led to
factory town. Plunged furiously down it. Halfway along, a
blindness within him veered him aside. He crashed into the
bordering canebrake. Cane leaves cut his face and lips. He
tasted blood. He threw himself down and dug his fingers in
the ground. The earth was cool. Cane-roots took the fever

from his hands. After a long while, or so it seemed to him, the thought came to him that it must be time to see Louisa. He got to his feet and walked calmly to their meeting place. No Louisa. Tom Burwell had her. Veins in his forehead bulged and distended. Saliva moistened the dried blood on his lips. He bit down on his lips. He tasted blood. Not his own blood; Tom Burwell's blood. Bob drove through the cane and out again upon the road. A hound swung down the path before him towards factory town. Bob couldn't see it. The dog loped aside to let him pass. Bob's blind rushing made him stumble over it. He fell with a thud that dazed him. The hound yelped. Answering yelps came from all over the countryside. Chickens cackled. Roosters crowed, heralding the bloodshot eyes of southern awakening. Singers in the town were silenced. They shut their windows down. Palpitant between the rooster crows, a chill hush settled upon the huddled forms of Tom and Louisa. A figure rushed from the shadow and stood before them. Tom popped to his feet.

"Whats y want?"

"I'm Bob Stone."

"Yassur—and I'm Tom Burwell. Whats y want?"

Bob lunged at him. Tom side-stepped, caught him by the shoulder, and flung him to the ground. Straddled him.

"Let me up."

"Yassur—but watch yo doins, Bob Stone."

A few dark figures, drawn by the sound of scuffle, stood about them. Bob sprang to his feet.

"Fight like a man, Tom Burwell, an I'll lick y."

Again he lunged. Tom side-stepped and flung him to the ground. Straddled him.

"Get off me, you godam nigger you."

"Yo sho has started somethin now. Get up."

Tom yanked him up and began hammering at him. Each blow sounded as if it smashed into a precious, irreplaceable soft something. Beneath them, Bob staggered back. He reached in his pocket and whipped out a knife. "That's my game, sho."

Blue flash, a steel blade slashed across Bob Stone's throat. He had a sweetish sick feeling. Blood began to flow. Then he felt a sharp twitch of pain. He let his knife drop. He slapped one hand against his neck. He pressed the other on top of his head as if to hold it down. He groaned. He turned, and staggered towards the crest of the hill in the direction of white town. Negroes who had seen the fight slunk into their homes and blew the lamps out. Louisa, dazed, hysterical, refused to go indoors. She slipped, crumpled, her body loosely propped against the woodwork of the well. Tom Burwell leaned against it. He seemed rooted there.

Bob reached Broad Street. White men rushed up to him. He collapsed in their arms.

"Tom Burwell. . . ."

White men like ants upon a forage rushed about. Except for the taut hum of their moving, all was silent. Shotguns, revolvers, rope, kerosene, torches. Two high-powered cars with glaring search-lights. They came together. The taut hum rose to a low roar. Then nothing could be heard but the flop of their feet in the thick dust of the road. The moving body of their silence preceded them over the crest of the hill into factory town. It flattened the Negroes beneath it. It rolled to the wall of the factory, where it stopped. Tom knew that they were coming. He couldnt move. And then he saw the search-lights of the two cars glaring down on him. A quick shock went through him. He stiffened. He started to run. A yell went up from the mob. Tom wheeled about and faced them. They poured down on him. They swarmed. A large man with dead-white face and flabby cheeks came to him and almost jabbed a gun-barrel through his guts.

"Hands behind y, nigger."

Tom's wrists were bound. The big man shoved him to the well. Burn him over it, and when the woodwork caved in, his body would drop to the bottom. Two deaths for a godam nigger.

Louisa was driven back. The mob pushed in. Its pressure, its momentum was too great. Drag him to the factory. Wood and stakes already there. Tom moved in the direction indicated. But they had to drag him. They reached the great door. Too many to get in there. The mob divided and flowed around the walls to either side. The big man shoved him through the door. The mob pressed in from the sides. Taut humming. No words. A stake was sunk into the ground. Rotting floor boards piled around it. Kerosene poured on the rotting floor boards. Tom bound to the stake. His breast was bare. Nails scratches let little lines of blood trickle down and mat into the hair. His face, his eyes were set and stony. Except for irregular breathing, one would have thought him already dead. Torches were flung onto the pile. A great flare muffled in black smoke shot upward. The mob yelled. The mob was silent. Now Tom could be seen within the flames. Only his head, erect, lean, like a blackened stone. Stench of burning flesh soaked the air. Tom's eyes popped. His head settled downward. The mob yelled. Its yell echoed against the skeleton stone walls and sounded like a hundred yells. Like a hundred mobs yelling. Its yell thudded against the thick front wall and fell back. Ghost of a yell slipped through the flames and out the great door of the factory. It fluttered like a dying thing down the single street of factory town. Louisa, upon the step before her home, did not hear it, but her eyes opened slowly. They saw the full moon glowing in the great door. The full moon, an evil thing, an omen, soft showering the homes of folks she knew. Where were they, these people? She'd sing, and perhaps they'd come out and join her. Perhaps Tom Burwell would come. At any rate, the full moon in the great door was an omen which she must sing to:

Red nigger moon. Sinner!
Blood-burning moon. Sinner!
Come out that fact'ry door.

RUDOLPH FISHER (1897–1934)

Prominently associated with the "Negro Renaissance," the literary movement and fictional portrayal of Harlem in the 1920's, Rudolph Fisher was born in Washington, D. C., and received degrees from Brown University and Howard University Medical School. Fisher completed his medical studies at Columbia University, and became a physician-author practicing roentgenology and writing in New York City. His first short story was published in The Atlantic Monthly. *Fisher published two novels and many short stories and sketches of Harlem during his lifetime. Several of his short stories were included in annual anthologies of* Best Short Stories. *He is represented in this anthology by a story he first published in the Baltimore* Afro-American, *the famous Negro newspaper. The story subsequently appeared in* Best Short Stories by Afro-American Writers (1925–1950), *selected and edited by Nick Aaron Ford and H. L. Faggett (Boston, 1950).*

Common Meter

The Arcadia, on Harlem's Lenox Avenue, is "The World's Largest and Finest Ballroom—Admission Eighty-Five Cents." Jazz is its holy spirit, which moves it continuously from nine till two every night. Observe above the brilliant entrance this legend in white fire:

TWO — ORCHESTRAS — TWO

Below this in red:

FESS BAXTER'S FIREMEN

Alongside in blue:

BUS WILLIAMS' BLUE DEVILS

Still lower in gold:

HEAR THEM OUTPLAY EACH OTHER

So much outside. Inside, a blazing lobby, flanked by marble stairways. Upstairs, an enormous dance hall the length of a city block. Low ceilings blushing pink with rows of inverted dome-lights. A broad dancing area, bounded on three sides by a wide soft-carpeted promenade, on the fourth by an ample platform accommodating the two orchestras.

People. Flesh. A fly-thick jam of dancers on the floor, grimly jostling each other; a milling herd of thirsty-eyed boys, moving slowly, searchingly over the carpeted promenade; a congregation of languid girls, lounging in rows of easy chairs here and there, bodies and faces unconcerned, dark eyes furtively alert. A restless multitude of empty, romance-hungry lives.

Bus Williams' jolly round brown face beamed down on the crowd as he directed his popular hit—*She's Still My Baby*:

You take her out to walk
And give her baby-talk,
But talk or walk, walk or talk —
    She's still my baby!

But the cheese-colored countenance of Fessenden Baxter, his professional rival, who with his orchestra occupied the adjacent half of the platform, was totally oblivious to *She's Still My Baby*.

Baxter had just caught sight of a girl, and catching sight of girls was one of his special accomplishments. Unbelief, wonder, amazement registered in turn on his blunt, bright features. He passed a hand over his straightened brown hair and bent to Perry Parker, his trumpetist.

"P.P., do you see what I see, or is it only the gin?"

"Both of us had the gin," said P.P., "so both of us sees the same thing."

"Judas Priest! Look at that figure, boy!"

"Never was no good at figures," said P.P.

"I've got to get me an armful of that baby."

"Lay off, papa," advised P.P.

"What do you mean, lay off?"

"Lay off. You and your boy got enough to fight over already, ain't you?"

"My boy?"

"Your boy, Bus."

"You mean that's Bus Williams' folks?"

"No lie. Miss Jean Ambrose, lord. The newest hostess. Bus got her the job."

Fess Baxter's eyes followed the girl. "Oh, he got her the job, did he?—Well, I'm going to fix it so she won't need any job. Woman like that's got no business working anywhere."

"Gin," murmured P.P.

"Gin hell," said Baxter. "Gunpowder wouldn't make a mama look as good as that."

"Gunpowder wouldn't make you look so damn good, either."

"You hold the cat's tail," suggested Baxter.

"I'm tryin' to save yours," said P.P.

"Save your breath for that horn."

"Maybe," P.P. insisted, "she ain't so possible as she looks."

"Huh. They can all be taught."

"I've seen some that couldn't."

"Oh you have?—Well, P.P., my boy, remember, that's you."

Beyond the brass rail that limited the rectangular dance area at one lateral extreme there were many small round tables and clusters of chairs. Bus Williams and the youngest hostess occupied one of these tables while Fess Baxter's Firemen strutted their stuff.

Bus ignored the tall glass before him, apparently endeavoring to drain the girl's beauty with his eyes; a useless effort, since it lessened neither her loveliness nor his thirst. Indeed the more he looked the less able was he to stop looking. Oblivious, the girl was engrossed in the crowd. Her amber skin grew clearer and the roses imprisoned in it brighter as her merry black eyes danced over the jostling company.

"Think you'll like it?" he asked.

"Like it?" She was a child of Harlem and she spoke its language. "Boy, I'm having the time of my life. Imagine getting paid for this!"

"You ought to get a bonus for beauty."

"Nice time to think of that—after I'm hired."

"You look like a full course dinner—and I'm starved."

"Hold the personalities, papa."

"No stuff. Wish I could raise a loan on you. Baby—what a roll I'd tote."

"Thanks. Try that big farmer over there hootin' it with Sister Full-bosom. Boy, what a side-show they'd make!"

"Yea. But what I'm lookin' for is a leadin' lady."

"Yea? I got a picture of any lady leadin' you anywhere."

"You could, Jean."

"Be yourself, brother."

"I ain't bein' nobody else."

"Well, be somebody else, then."

"Remember the orphanage?"

"Time, papa. Stay out of my past."

"Sure—if you let me into your future."

"Speaking of the orphanage—?"

"You wouldn't know it now. They got new buildings all over the place."

"Somehow that fails to thrill me."

"You always were a knock-out, even in those days. You had the prettiest hair of any of the girls out there—and the sassiest hip-switch."

"Look at Fred and Adele Astaire over there. How long they been doing blackface?"

"I used to watch you even then. Know what I used to say?"

"Yea. 'Toot-a-toot-toot' on a bugle."

"That ain't all. I used to say to myself, 'Boy, when that sister grows up, I'm going to—'."

Her eyes grew suddenly onyx and stopped him like an abruptly reversed traffic signal.

"What's the matter?" he said.

She smiled and began nibbling the straw in her glass.

"What's the matter, Jean?"

"Nothing, Innocence. Nothing. Your boy plays a devilish one-step, doesn't he?"

"Say. You think I'm jivin', don't you?"

"No, darling. I think you're selling insurance."

"Think I'm gettin' previous, just because I got you the job."

"Funny, I never have much luck with jobs."

"Well, I don't care what you think, I'm going to say it."

"Let's dance."

"I used to say to myself, 'When that kid grows up, I'm going to ask her to marry me.' "

She called his bluff. "Well, I'm grown up."

"Marry me, will you, Jean?"

Her eyes relented a little in admiration of his audacity. Rarely did a sober aspirant have the courage to mention marriage.

"You're good, Bus. I mean, you're good."

"Every guy ain't a wolf, you know, Jean."

"No. Some are just ordinary meat-hounds."

From the change in his face she saw the depth of the thrust, saw pain where she had anticipated chagrin.

"Let's dance," she suggested again, a little more gently.

They had hardly begun when the number ended, and Fess Baxter stood before them, an ingratiating grin on his Swiss-cheese-colored face.

"Your turn, young fellow," he said to Bus.

"Thoughtful of you, reminding me," said Bus. "This is Mr. Baxter, Miss Ambrose."

"It's always been one of my ambitions," said Baxter, "to dance with a sure-enough angel."

"Just what I'd like to see you doin'," grinned Bus.

"Start up your stuff and watch us," said Baxter. "Step on it, brother. You're holding up traffic."

"Hope you get pinched for speedin'," said Bus, departing.

The Blue Devils were in good form tonight, were really "bearin' down" on their blues. Bus, their leader, however, was only going through the motions, waving his baton idly. His eyes followed Jean and Baxter, and it was nothing to his credit that the jazz maintained its spirit. Occasionally he lost the pair: a brace of young wild birds double-timed through the forest, miraculously avoiding the trees: an extremely ardent couple, welded together, did a decidedly localized mess-around; that gigantic black farmer whom Jean had pointed out sashayed into the line of vision, swung about, backed off, being fancy. . . .

Abruptly, as if someone had caught and held his right arm, Bus' baton halted above his head. His men kept on playing under the impulse of their own momentum, but Bus was a creature apart. Slowly his baton drooped, like the crest of a proud bird, beaten. His eyes died on their object and all his features sagged. On the floor forty feet away, amid the surrounding clot of dancers, Jean and Baxter had stopped moving and were standing perfectly still. The girl had clasped her partner close about the shoulders with both arms. Her face was buried in his chest.

Baxter, who was facing the platform, looked up and saw Bus staring. He drew the girl closer, grinned, and shut one eye.

They stood so a moment or an hour till Bus dragged his eyes away. Automatically he resumed beating time. Every moment or so his baton wavered, slowed, and hurried to catch up. The blues were very low-down, the nakedest of jazz, a series of periodic wails against a background of steady, slow rhythm, each pounding pulse descending inevitably, like leaden strokes of fate. Bus found himself singing the words of this grief-stricken lamentation:

Trouble—trouble has followed me all my days,
Trouble—trouble has followed my all my days—
Seems like trouble's gonna follow me always.

The mob demanded an encore, a mob that knew its blues and liked them blue. Bus complied. Each refrain became bluer as it was caught up by a different voice: the wailing clarinet, the weeping C sax, the moaning B-flat sax, the trombone, and Bus' own plaintive tenor:

Baby—baby—my baby's gone away.
Baby—baby—my baby's gone away—
Seems like baby—my baby's gone to stay.

Presently the thing beat itself out, and Bus turned to acknowledge applause. He broke a bow off in half. Directly before the platform stood Jean alone, looking up at him.

He jumped down. "Dance?"

"No. Listen. You know what I said at the table?"

"At the table?"

"About—wolves?"

"Oh—that—?"

"Yea. I didn't mean anything personal. Honest, I didn't." Her eyes besought his. "You didn't think I meant anything personal, did you?"

"Course not," he laughed. "I know now you didn't mean anything." He laughed again. "Neither one of us meant anything."

With a wry little smile, he watched her slip off through the crowd.

From his side of the platform Bus overheard Fess Baxter talking to Perry Parker. Baxter had a custom of talking while he conducted, the jazz serving to blanket his words. The blanket was not quite heavy enough tonight.

"P. P., old pooter, she fell."

Parker was resting while the C sax took the lead. "She did?"

"No lie. She says, 'You don't leave me any time for cash customers.' "

"Yea?"

"Yea. And I says, 'I'm a cash customer, baby. Just name your price.' "

Instantly Bus was across the platform and at him, clutched him by the collar, bent him back over the edge of the platform; and it was clear from the look in Bus's eyes that he wasn't just being playful.

"Name her!"

"Hey—what the hell you doin'!"

"Name her or I'll drop you and jump in your face. I swear to—"

"Nellie!" gurgled Fessenden Baxter.

"Nellie who—damn it?"

"Nellie—Gray!"

"All right then!"

Baxter found himself again erect with dizzy suddenness.

The music had stopped, for the players had momentarily lost their breath. Baxter swore and impelled his men into action, surreptitiously adjusting his ruffled plumage.

The crowd had an idea what it was all about and many good-naturedly derided the victim as they passed:

" 'Smatter, Fess? Goin' in for toe-dancin'?"

"Nice back-dive, papa, but this ain't no swimmin'-pool."

Curry, the large, bald, yellow manager, also had an idea what it was all about and lost no time accosting Bus.

"Tryin' to start somethin'?"

"No. Tryin' to stop somethin'."

"Well, if you gonna stop it with your hands, stop it outside. I ain't got no permit for prize fights in here— 'Course, if you guys can't get on together I can maybe struggle along without one of y' till I find somebody."

Bus said nothing.

"Listen. You birds fight it out with them jazz sticks, y' hear? Them's your weapons. Nex' Monday night's the jazz contest. You'll find out who's the best man next Monday night. Might win more'n a lovin' cup. And y' might lose more. Get me?"

He stood looking sleekly sarcastic a moment, then went to give Baxter like counsel.

Rumor spread through the Arcadia's regulars as night succeeded night.

A pair of buddies retired to the men's room to share a half-pint of gin. One said to the other between gulps:

"Lord today! Ain't them two roosters bearin' down on the jazz!"

"No lie. They mussa had some this same licker."

"Licker hell. Ain't you heard 'bout it?"

" 'Bout what?"

"They fightin', Oscar, fightin'."

"Gimme that bottle 'fo' you swaller it. Fightin'? What you mean, fightin'?"

"Fightin' over that new mama."

"The honey-dew?"

"Right. They can't use knives and they can't use knucks. And so they got to fight it out with jazz."

"Yea? Hell of a way to fight."

"That's the only way they'd be any fight. Bus Williams'd knock that yaller boy's can off in a scrap."

"I know it. Y'ought-a-seen him grab him las' night."

"I did. They tell me she promised it to the one 'at wins this cup nex' monday night."

"Yea? Wisht I knowed some music."

"Sho-nuff sheba all right. I got a long shout with her last night, Papa, an' she's got ever'thing!"

"Too damn easy on the eyes. Women like that ain't no good 'cep'n to start trouble."

"She sho' could start it for me. I'd 'a' been dancin' with her yet, but my two-bitses give out. Spent two hardearned bucks dancin' with her, too."

"Shuh! Might as well th'ow yo' money in the street. What you git dancin' with them hostesses?"

"You right there, brother. All I got out o' that one was two dollars worth o' disappointment."

Two girl friends, lounging in adjacent easy chairs, discussed the situation.

"I can't see what she's got so much more'n anybody else."

"Me neither. I could look a lot better'n that if I didn't have to work all day."

"No lie. Scrubbin' floors never made no bathin' beauties."

"I heard Fess Baxter jivin' her while they was dancin'. He's got a line, no stuff."

"He'd never catch me with it."

"No, dearie. He's got two good eyes too, y'know."

"Maybe that's why he couldn't see you flaggin' 'im."

"Be yourself, sister. He says to her, 'Baby, when the boss hands me that cup—'."

"Hates hisself, don't he?"

" 'When the boss hands me that cup,' he says, 'I'm gonna put it right in your arms.' "

"Yea. And I suppose he goes with the cup."

"So she laughs and says, 'Think you can beat him?' So he says, 'Beat him? Huh, that bozo couldn't play a hand organ.' "

"He don't mean her no good though, this Baxter."

"How do you know?"

"A kack like that never means a woman no good. The other one ast her to step off with him."

"What!"

"Etta Pipp heard him. They was drinkin' and she was at the next table."

"Well, ain't that somethin'! Ast her to step off with him! What'd she say?"

"Etta couldn't hear no more."

"Jus' goes to show ya. What chance has a honest workin' girl got?"

Bus confided in Tappen, his drummer.

"Tap," he said, "ain't it funny how a woman always seems to fall for a wolf?"

"No lie," Tap agreed. "When a guy gets too deep, he's long-gone."

"How do you account for it, Tap?"

"I don't. I jes' play 'em light. When I feel it gettin' heavy —boy, I run like hell."

"Tap, what would you do if you fell for a girl and saw her neckin' another guy?"

"I wouldn't fall," said Tappen, "so I wouldn't have to do nothin'."

"Well, but s'posin' you did?"

"Well, if she was my girl, I'd knock the can off both of 'em."

"S'posin' she wasn't your girl?"

"Well, if she wasn't my girl, it wouldn't be none of my business."

"Yea, but a guy kind o' hates to see an old friend gettin' jived."

"Stay out, papa. Only way to protect yourself."

"S'posin' you didn't want to protect yourself? S'posin' you wanted to protect the woman?"

"Hmph! Who ever heard of a woman needin' protection?"

"Ladies and gentlemen!" sang Curry to the tense crowd that
gorged the Arcadia. "Tonight is the night of the only contest
of its kind in recorded history! On my left, Mr. Bus Williams,
chief of the Blue Devils. On my right, Mr. Fessenden Baxter,
leader of the Firemen. On this stand, the solid gold loving-
cup. The winner will claim the jazz championship of the
world!"

"And the sweet mama too, how 'bout it?" called a wag.

"Each outfit will play three numbers: a one-step, a fox-
trot, and a blues number. With this stop watch which you see
in my hand, I will time your applause after each number.
The leader receiving the longest total applause wins the loving-cup!"

"Yea—and some lovin'-up wid it!"

"I will now toss a coin to see who plays the first number!"

"Toss it out here!"

"Bus Williams's Blue Devils, ladies and gentlemen, will
play the first number!"

Bus's philosophy of jazz held tone to be merely the vehicle
of rhythm. He spent much time devising new rhythmic patterns with which to vary his presentations. Accordingly he
depended largely on Tappen, his master percussionist, who
knew every rhythmic monkey-shine with which to delight a
gaping throng.

Bus had conceived the present piece as a chase, in which
an agile clarinet eluded impetuous and turbulent traps. The
other instruments were to be observers, chorusing their excitement while they urged the principals on.

From the moment the piece started something was obviously wrong. The clarinet was elusive enough, but its agility
was without purpose. Nothing pursued it. People stopped
dancing in the middle of the number and turned puzzled
faces toward the platform. The trap-drummer was going
through the motions faithfully but to no avail. His traps were
voiceless, emitted mere shadows of sound. He was a deaf
mute making a speech.

Brief, perfunctory, disappointed applause rose and fell at
the number's end. Curry announced its duration:

"Fifteen seconds flat!"

Fess Baxter, with great gusto, leaped to his post.

"The Firemen will play their first number!"

Bus was consulting Tappen.

"For the love o' Pete, Tap—?"

"Love o' hell. Look a' here."

Bus looked—first at the trapdrum, then at the bass; snapped them with a finger, thumped them with his knuckles. There was almost no sound; each drum-sheet was dead, lax instead of taut, and the cause was immediately clear: each bore a short curved knife-cut following its edge a brief distance, a wound unnoticeable at a glance, but fatal to the instrument.

Bus looked at Tappen, Tappen looked at Bus.

"The cream-colored son of a buzzard!"

Fess Baxter, gleeful and oblivious, was directing a whirlwind number, sweeping the crowd about the floor at an exciting, exhausting pace, distorting, expanding, etherealizing their emotions with swift-changing dissonances. Contrary to Bus Williams's philosophy, Baxter considered rhythm a mere rack upon which to hang his tonal tricks. The present piece was dizzy with sudden disharmonies, unexpected twists of phrase, successive false resolutions. Incidentally, however, there was nothing wrong with Baxter's drums.

Boiling over, Bus would have started for him, but Tappen grabbed his coat.

"Hold it, papa. That's a sure way to lose. Maybe we can choke him yet."

"Yea—?"

"I'll play the wood. And I still got cymbals and sandpaper."

"Yea—and a triangle. Hell of a lot o' good they are."

"Can't quit," said Tappen.

"Well," said Bus.

Baxter's number ended in a furor.

"Three minutes and twenty seconds!" bellowed Curry as the applause eventually died out.

Bus began his second number, a fox-trot. In the midst of it he saw Jean dancing, beseeching him with bewildered dismay in her eyes, a look that at once crushed and crazed him. Tappen rapped on the rim of his trap drum, tapped his triangle, stamped the pedal that clapped the cymbals, but the result was a toneless and hollow clatter, a weightless noise that bounced back from the multitude instead of penetrating into it. The players also, distracted by the loss, were operating far below par, and not all their leader's frantic false enthusiasm could compensate for the gaping absence of bass. The very spine had been ripped out of their music, and Tappen's desperate efforts were but the hopeless flutterings of a stricken, limp, pulseless heart.

"Forty-five seconds!" Curry announced. "Making a total so

far of one minute flat for the Blue Devils! The Firemen will now play their second number!"

The Firemen's fox-trot was Baxter's re-arrangement of Burleigh's "Jean, My Jean," and Baxter, riding his present advantage hard, stressed all that he had put into it of tonal ingenuity. The thing was delirious with strange harmonies, iridescent with odd color-changes, and its very flamboyance, its musical fine-writing and conceits delighted the dancers.

But it failed to delight Jean Ambrose, whom by its title it was intended to flatter. She rushed to Bus.

"What is it?" She was a-quiver.

"Drums gone. Somebody cut the pigskin the last minute."

"What? Somebody? Who?"

"Cut 'em with a knife close to the rim."

"Cut? He cut—? Oh, Bus!"

She flashed Baxter a look that would have crumpled his assurance had he seen it. "Can't you— Listen." She was at once wild and calm. "It's the bass. You got to have—I know! Make 'em stamp their feet! Your boys, I mean. That'll do it. All of 'em. Turn the blues into a shout."

"Yea? Gee. Maybe—"

"Try it! You've got to win this thing."

An uproar that seemed endless greeted Baxter's version of "Jean." The girl, back out on the floor, managed to smile as Baxter acknowledged the acclaim by gesturing toward her.

"The present score, ladies and gentlemen, is—for the Blue Devils, one minute even; for the Firemen, six minutes and thirty seconds! The Devils will now play their last number!" Curry's intonation of "last" moved the mob to laughter.

Into that laughter Bus grimly led his men like a captain leading his command into fire. He had chosen the parent of blue songs, the old St. Louis Blues, and he adduced every device that had ever adorned that classic. Clarinets wailed, saxophones moaned, trumpets wept wretchedly, trombones laughed bitterly, even the great bass horn sobbed dismally from the depths. And so perfectly did the misery in the music express the actual despair of the situation that the crowd was caught from the start. Soon dancers closed their eyes, forgot their jostling neighbors, lost themselves bodily in the easy sway of that slow, fateful measure, vaguely aware that some quality hitherto lost had at last been found. They were too wholly absorbed to note just how that quality had been found: that every player softly dropped his heel where each bass-drum beat would have come, giving each major impulse a body and breadth that no drum could have achieved. Zoom-zoom-zoom-zoom. It was not a mere sound; it was a vibrant throb that took hold of the crowd and rocked it.

They had been rocked thus before, this multitude. Two hundred years ago they had swayed to that same slow fateful measure, lifting their lamentation to heaven, pounding the earth with their feet, seeking the mercy of a new God through the medium of an old rhythm, zoom-zoom. They had rocked so a thousand years ago in a city whose walls were jungle, forfending the wrath of a terrible black God who spoke in storm and pestilence, had swayed and wailed to that same slow period, beaten on a wild boar's skin stretched over the end of a hollow tree-trunk. Zoom-zoom-zoom-zoom. Not a sound but an emotion that laid hold on their bodies and swung them into the past. Blues—low-down blues indeed —blues that reached their souls' depths.

But slowly the color changed. Each player allowed his heel to drop less and less softly. Solo parts faded out, and the orchestra began to gather power as a whole. The rhythm persisted, the unfaltering common meter of blues, but the blueness itself, the sorrow, the despair, began to give way to hope. Ere long hope came to the verge of realization— mounted it—rose above it. The deep and regular impulses now vibrated like nearing thunder, a mighty, inescapable, all-embracing dominance, stressed by the contrast of windtone; an all-pervading atmosphere through which soared wild-winged birds. Rapturously, rhapsodically, the number rose to madness and at the height of its madness, burst into sudden silence.

Illusion broke. Dancers awoke, dropped to reality with a jolt. Suddenly the crowd appreciated that Bus Williams had returned to form, had put on a comeback, had struck off a masterpiece. And the crowd showed its appreciation. It applauded its palms sore.

Curry's suspense-ridden announcement ended:

"Total—for the Blue Devils, seven minutes and forty seconds! For the Firemen, six minutes and thirty seconds! Maybe that wasn't the Devils' last number after all! The Firemen will play their last number!"

It was needless for Baxter to attempt the depths and heights just attained by Bus Williams's Blue Devils. His speed, his subordination of rhythm to tone, his exotic coloring, all were useless in a low-down blues song. The crowd moreover, had nestled upon the broad, sustaining bosom of a shout. Nothing else warmed them. The end of Baxter's last piece left them chilled and unsatisfied.

But if Baxter realized that he was beaten, his attitude failed to reveal it. Even when the major volume of applause died out in a few seconds, he maintained his self-assured grin. The reason was soon apparent: although the audience as a whole had stopped applauding, two small groups of assiduous handclappers, one at either extreme of the dancing-area, kept up a diminutive, violent clatter.

Again Bus and Tappen exchanged sardonic stares.

"Damn' if he ain't paid somebody to clap!"

Only the threatening hisses and boos of the majority terminated this clatter, whereupon Curry summed up:

"For Bus Williams's Blue Devils—seven minutes and forty seconds! For Fess Baxter's Firemen—eight minutes flat!"

He presented Baxter the loving-cup amid a hubbub of murmurs, handclaps, shouts, and hisses that drowned whatever he said. Then the hubbub hushed. Baxter was assisting Jean Ambrose to the platform. With a bow and a flourish he handed the girl the cup.

She held it for a moment in both arms, uncertain, hesitant. But there was nothing uncertain or hesitant in the mob's reaction. Feeble applause was overwhelmed in a deluge of disapprobation. Cries of "Crooked!" "Don't take it!" "Crown the cheat!" "He stole it!" stood out. Tappen put his finger in the slit in his trap-drum, ripped it to a gash, held up the mutilated instrument, and cried, "Look what he done to my traps!" A few hardboiled ruffians close to the platform moved menacingly toward the victor. "Grab 'im! Knock his can off!"

Jean's uncertainty abruptly vanished. She wheeled with the trophy in close embrace and sailed across the platform toward the defeated Bus Williams. She smiled into his astonished face and thrust the cup into his arms.

"Hot damn, mama! That's the time!" cried a jubilant voice from the floor, and instantly the gathering storm of menace broke into a cloudburst of delight. That romance-hungry multitude saw Bus Williams throw his baton into the air and gather the girl and the loving-cup into his arms. And they went utterly wild—laughed, shouted, yelled and whistled till the walls of the Arcadia bulged.

Jazz emerged as the mad noise subsided: Bus Williams's Blue Devils playing *"She's Still My Baby."*

ARNA BONTEMPS (1902–1973)

*As poet, novelist, author of short stories and juvenile literature,
critic, anthologist, playwright, librarian, and educator, Arna Bontemps was a central figure in the creation, dissemination, and teaching of Negro American literature. He was born in Alexandria,
Louisiana, raised and educated in California, and graduated from
Pacific Union College in 1923. He came to Harlem at the beginning
of the Harlem Renaissance and became one of its best known writers. His poetry first appeared in* The Crisis, *in the summer of 1924.
In 1926 and 1927 his poems* "Golgotha Is a Mountain" *and* "The
Return" *won the Alexander Pushkin Awards for Poetry offered by*
Opportunity: Journal of Negro Life. *In 1927 he also won first prize
in the poetry contest sponsored by* The Crisis. *He pursued graduate
studies in English at the University of Chicago during the Depression years and later earned an M.A. in librarianship. Bontemps
became University Librarian at Fisk University in 1943, a position
he held for twenty-two years before joining the faculty of the University of Illinois, Chicago Circle, in the fall of 1966. In 1969, he
became a lecturer and curator of the James Weldon Johnson Collection at Yale University, a position he held until 1971. His anthologies
ies (some edited in collaboration with Langston Hughes), his books
for young people, and his nonfiction, have become even more widely
known than his three novels. His* Story of the Negro *received the
Jane Addams Children's Book Award in 1956. His* Anyplace but
Here *(written in collaboration with Jack Conroy) won the James L.
Dow Award of the Society of Midland Authors in 1967. He has also
received citations and special recognition for* Lonesome Boy *(1955),*
Frederick Douglass *(1958),* 100 Years of Negro Freedom *(1961),
and* American Negro Poetry *(1963). The following short story,* "A
Summer Tragedy," *was written in 1933. Bontemps is also repre-
sented in other sections of this anthology with poems and an autobiographical essay.*

A Summer Tragedy

Old Jeff Patton, the black share farmer, fumbled with his bow tie. His fingers trembled and the high stiff collar pinched his throat. A fellow loses his hand for such vanities after thirty or forty years of simple life. Once a year, or maybe twice if there's a wedding among his kinfolks, he may spruce up; but generally fancy clothes do nothing but adorn the wall of the big room and feed the moths. That had been Jeff Patton's experience. He had not worn his stiff-bosomed shirt more than a dozen times in all his married life. His swallow-tailed coat lay on the bed beside him, freshly brushed and pressed, but it was as full of holes as the overalls in which he worked on weekdays. The moths had used it badly. Jeff twisted his mouth into a hideous toothless grimace as he contended with the obstinate bow. He stamped his good foot and decided to give up the struggle.

"Jennie," he called.

"What's that, Jeff?" His wife's shrunken voice came out of the adjoining room like an echo. It was hardly bigger than a whisper.

"I reckon you'll have to he'p me wid this heah bow tie, baby," he said meekly. "Dog if I can hitch it up."

Her answer was not strong enough to reach him, but presently the old woman came to the door, feeling her way with a stick. She had a wasted, dead-leaf appearance. Her body, as scrawny and gnarled as a string bean, seemed less than nothing in the ocean of frayed and faded petticoats that surrounded her. These hung an inch or two above the tops of her heavy unlaced shoes and showed little grotesque piles where the stockings had fallen down from her negligible legs.

"You oughta could do a heap mo' wid a thing like that'n me—beingst as you got yo' good sight."

"Looks like I oughta could," he admitted. "But ma fingers is gone democrat on me. I get all mixed up in the looking glass an' can't tell wicha way to twist the devilish thing."

Jennie sat on the side of the bed and old Jeff Patton got down on one knee while she tied the bow knot. It was a slow and painful ordeal for each of them in this position. Jeff's bones cracked, his knee ached, and it was only after a half dozen attempts that Jennie worked a semblance of a bow into the tie.

"I got to dress maself now," the old woman whispered.

"These is ma old shoes an' stockings, and I ain't so much as unwrapped ma dress."

"Well, don't worry 'bout me no mo', baby," Jeff said. "That 'bout finishes me. All I gotta do now is slip on that old coat 'n ves' an' I'll be fixed to leave."

Jennie disappeared again through the dim passage into the shed room. Being blind was no handicap to her in that black hole. Jeff heard the cane placed against the wall beside the door and knew that his wife was on easy ground. He put on his coat, took a battered top hat from the bedpost and hobbled to the front door. He was ready to travel. As soon as Jennie could get on her Sunday shoes and her old black silk dress, they would start.

Outside the tiny log house, the day was warm and mellow with sunshine. A host of wasps were humming with busy excitement in the trunk of a dead sycamore. Gray squirrels were searching through the grass for hickory nuts and blue jays were in the trees, hopping from branch to branch. Pine woods stretched away to the left like a black sea. Among them were scattered scores of log houses like Jeff's, houses of black share farmers. Cows and pigs wandered freely among the trees. There was no danger of loss. Each farmer knew his own stock and knew his neighbor's as well as he knew his neighbor's children.

Down the slope to the right were the cultivated acres on which the colored folks worked. They extended to the river, more than two miles away, and they were today green with the unmade cotton crop. A tiny thread of a road, which passed directly in front of Jeff's place, ran through these green fields like a pencil mark.

Jeff, standing outside the door, with his absurd hat in his left hand, surveyed the wide scene tenderly. He had been forty-five years on these acres. He loved them with the unexplained affection that others have for the countries to which they belong.

The sun was hot on his head, his collar still pinched his throat, and the Sunday clothes were intolerably hot. Jeff transferred the hat to his right hand and began fanning with it. Suddenly the whisper that was Jennie's voice came out of the shed room.

"You can bring the car round front whilst you's waitin'," it said feebly. There was a tired pause; then it added, "I'll soon be fixed to go."

"A'right, baby," Jeff answered. "I'll get it in a minute."

But he didn't move. A thought struck him that made his mouth fall open. The mention of the car brought to his mind, with new intensity, the trip he and Jennie were about to take. Fear came into his eyes; excitement took his breath. Lord, Jesus!

"Jeff . . . O Jeff," the old woman's whisper called.

He awakened with a jolt. "Hunh, baby?"

"What you doin'?"

"Nuthin. Jes studyin'. I jes been turnin' things round'n round in ma mind."

"You could be gettin' the car," she said.

"Oh yes, right away, baby."

He started round to the shed, limping heavily on his bad leg. There were three frizzly chickens in the yard. All his other chickens had been killed or stolen recently. But the frizzly chickens had been saved somehow. That was fortunate indeed, for these curious creatures had a way of devouring "Poison" from the yard and in that way protecting against conjure and black luck and spells. But even the frizzly chickens seemed now to be in a stupor. Jeff thought they had some ailment; he expected all three of them to die shortly.

The shed in which the old T-model Ford stood was only a grass roof held up by four corner poles. It had been built by tremulous hands at a time when the little rattletrap car had been regarded as a peculiar treasure. And, miraculously, despite wind and downpour it still stood.

Jeff adjusted the crank and put his weight upon it. The engine came to life with a sputter and bang that rattled the old car from radiator to taillight. Jeff hopped into the seat and put his foot on the accelerator. The sputtering and banging increased. The rattling became more violent. That was good. It was good banging, good sputtering and rattling, and it meant that the aged car was still in running condition. She could be depended on for this trip.

Again Jeff's thought halted as if paralyzed. The suggestion of the trip fell into the machinery of his mind like a wrench. He felt dazed and weak. He swung the car out into the yard, made a half turn and drove around to the front door. When he took his hands off the wheel, he noticed that he was trembling violently. He cut off the motor and climbed to the ground to wait for Jennie.

A few minutes later she was at the window, her voice rattling against the pane like a broken shutter.

"I'm ready, Jeff."

He did not answer, but limped into the house and took her by the arm. He led her slowly through the big room, down the step and across the yard.

"You reckon I'd oughta lock the do'?" he asked softly.

They stopped and Jennie weighed the question. Finally she shook her head.

"Ne' mind the do'," she said. "I don't see no cause to lock up things."

"You right," Jeff agreed. "No cause to lock up."

Jeff opened the door and helped his wife into the car. A quick shudder passed over him. Jesus! Again he trembled.

"How come you shaking so?" Jennie whispered.

"I don't know," he said.

"You mus' be scairt, Jeff."

"No, baby, I ain't scairt."

He slammed the door after her and went around to crank up again. The motor started easily. Jeff wished that it had not been so responsive. He would have liked a few more minutes in which to turn things around in his head. As it was, with Jennie chiding him about being afraid, he had to keep going. He swung the car into the little pencil-mark road and started off toward the river, driving very slowly, very cautiously.

Chugging across the green countryside, the small battered Ford seemed tiny indeed. Jeff felt a familiar excitement, a thrill, as they came down the first slope to the immense levels on which the cotton was growing. He could not help reflecting that the crops were good. He knew what that meant, too; he had made forty-five of them with his own hands. It was true that he had worn out nearly a dozen mules, but that was the fault of old man Stevenson, the owner of the land. Major Stevenson had the odd notion that one mule was all a share farmer needed to work a thirty-acre plot. It was an expensive notion, the way it killed mules from overwork, but the old man held to it. Jeff thought it killed a good many share farmers as well as mules, but he had no sympathy for them. He had always been strong, and he had been taught to have no patience with weakness in men. Women or children might be tolerated if they were puny, but a weak man was a curse. Of course, his own children—

Jeff's thought halted there. He and Jennie never mentioned their dead children any more. And naturally he did not wish to dwell upon them in his mind. Before he knew it, some remark would slip out of his mouth and that would make Jennie feel blue. Perhaps she would cry. A woman like Jennie could not easily throw off the grief that comes from losing five grown children within two years. Even Jeff was still staggered by the blow. His memory had not been much good recently. He frequently talked to himself. And, although he had kept it a secret, he knew that his courage had left him. He was terrified by the least unfamiliar sound at night. He was reluctant to venture far from home in the daytime. And that habit of trembling when he felt fearful was now far beyond his control. Sometimes he became afraid and trembled without knowing what had frightened him. The feeling would just come over him like a chill.

The car rattled slowly over the dusty road. Jennie sat erect and silent, with a little absurd hat pinned to her hair. Her useless eyes seemed very large, very white in their deep sockets. Suddenly Jeff heard her voice, and he inclined his head to catch the words.

"Is we passed Delia Moore's house yet?" she asked.

"Not yet," he said.

"You must be drivin' mighty slow, Jeff."

"We might just as well take our time, baby."

There was a pause. A little puff of steam was coming out of the radiator of the car. Heat wavered above the hood. Delia Moore's house was nearly half a mile away. After a moment Jennie spoke again.

"You ain't really scairt, is you, Jeff?"

"Nah, baby, I ain't scairt."

"You know how we agreed—we gotta keep on goin'."

Jewels of perspiration appeared on Jeff's forehead. His eyes rounded, blinked, became fixed on the road.

"I don't know," he said with a shiver. "I reckon it's the only thing to do."

"Hm."

A flock of guinea fowls, pecking in the road, were scattered by the passing car. Some of them took to their wings; others hid under bushes. A blue jay, swaying on a leafy twig, was annoying a roadside squirrel. Jeff held an even speed till he came near Delia's place. Then he slowed down noticeably.

Delia's house was really no house at all, but an abandoned store building converted into a dwelling. It sat near a crossroads, beneath a single black cedar tree. There Delia, a cattish old creature of Jennie's age, lived alone. She had been there more years than anybody could remember, and long ago had won the disfavor of such women as Jennie. For in her young days Delia had been gayer, yellower and saucier than seemed proper in those parts. Her ways with menfolks had been dark and suspicious. And the fact that she had had as many husbands as children did not help her reputation.

"Yonder's old Delia," Jeff said as they passed.

"What she doin'?"

"Jes sittin' in the do'," he said.

"She see us?"

"Hm," Jeff said. "Musta did."

That relieved Jennie. It strengthened her to know that her old enemy had seen her pass in her best clothes. That would give the old she-devil something to chew her gums and fret about, Jennie thought. Wouldn't she have a fit if she didn't find out? Old evil Delia! This would be just the thing for her. It would .pay her back for being so evil. It would also pay her, Jennie thought, for the way she used to grin at Jeff— long ago when her teeth were good.

The road became smooth and red, and Jeff could tell by the smell of the air that they were nearing the river. He could see the rise where the road turned and ran along parallel to the stream. The car chugged on monotonously. After a long silent spell, Jennie leaned against Jeff and spoke.

"How many bale o' cotton you think we got standin'?" she said.

Jeff wrinkled his forehead as he calculated.

" 'Bout twenty-five, I reckon."

"How many you make las' year?"

"Twenty-eight," he said. "How come you ask that?"

"I's jes thinkin'," Jennie said quietly.

"It don't make a speck o' difference though," Jeff reflected. "If we get much or if we get little, we still gonna be in debt to old man Stevenson when he gets through counting up agin us. It's took us a long time to learn that."

Jennie was not listening to these words. She had fallen into a trance-like meditation. Her lips twitched. She chewed her gums and rubbed her gnarled hands nervously. Suddenly she leaned forward, buried her face in the nervous hands and burst into tears. She cried aloud in a dry cracked voice that suggested the rattle of fodder on dead stalks. She cried aloud like a child, for she had never learned to suppress a genuine sob. Her slight old frame shook heavily and seemed hardly able to sustain such violent grief.

"What's the matter, baby?" Jeff asked awkwardly. "Why you cryin' like all that?"

"I's jes thinkin'," she said.

"So you the one what's scairt now, hunh?"

"I ain't scairt, Jeff. I's jes thinkin' 'bout leavin' eve'thing like this—eve'thing we been used to. It's right sad-like."

Jeff did not answer, and presently Jennie buried her face again and cried.

The sun was almost overhead. It beat down furiously on the dusty wagon-path road, on the parched roadside grass and the tiny battered car. Jeff's hands, gripping the wheel, be- came wet with perspiration; his forehead sparkled. Jeff's lips parted. His. mouth shaped a hideous grimace. His face suggested the face of a man being burned. But the torture passed and his expression softened again.

"You mustn't cry, baby," he said to his wife. "We gotta be strong. We can't break down."

Jennie waited a few seconds, then said, "You reckon we oughta do it, Jeff? You reckon we oughta go 'head an' do it, really?"

Jeff's voice choked; his eyes blurred. He was terrified to hear Jennie say the thing that had been in his mind all morning. She had egged him on when he had wanted more than anything in the world to wait, to reconsider, to think things over a little longer. Now she was getting cold feet. Actually there was no need of thinking the question through again. It would only end in making the same painful decision once more. Jeff knew that. There was no need of fooling around longer.

"We jes as well to do like we planned," he said. "They ain't nothin' else for us now—it's the bes' thing."

Jeff thought of the handicaps, the near impossibility, of making another crop with his leg bothering him more and more each week. Then there was always the chance that he would have another stroke, like the one that had made him lame. Another one might kill him. The least it could do would be to leave him helpless. Jeff gasped—Lord, Jesus! He could not bear to think of being helpless, like a baby, on Jennie's hands. Frail, blind Jennie.

The little pounding motor of the car worked harder and harder. The puff of steam from the cracked radiator became larger. Jeff realized that they were climbing a little rise. A moment later the road turned abruptly and he looked down upon the face of the river.

"Jeff."

"Hunh?"

"Is that the water I hear?"

"Hm. Tha's it."

"Well, which way you goin' now?"

"Down this-a way," he said. "The road runs 'long 'side o' the water a lil piece."

She waited a while calmly. Then she said, "Drive faster."

"A'right, baby," Jeff said.

The water roared in the bed of the river. It was fifty or sixty feet below the level of the road. Between the road and the water there was a long smooth slope, sharply inclined. The slope was dry, the clay hardened by prolonged summer heat. The water below, roaring in a narrow channel, was noisy and wild.

"Jeff."

"Hunh?"

"How far you goin'?"

"Jes a lil piece down the road."

"You ain't scairt, is you, Jeff?"

"Nah, baby," he said trembling. "I ain't scairt."

"Remember how we planned it, Jeff. We gotta do it like we said. Brave-like."

"Hm."

Jeff's brain darkened. Things suddenly seemed unreal, like figures in a dream. Thoughts swam in his mind foolishly, hysterically, like little blind fish in a pool within a dense cave. They rushed, crossed one another, jostled, collided, retreated and rushed again. Jeff soon became dizzy. He shuddered violently and turned to his wife.

"Jennie, I can't do it. I can't." His voice broke pitifully.

She did not appear to be listening. All the grief had gone from her face. She sat erect, her unseeing eyes wide open, strained and frightful. Her glossy black skin had become dull. She seemed as thin, as sharp and bony, as a starved bird. Now, having suffered and endured the sadness of tearing herself away from beloved things, she showed no anguish. She was absorbed with her own thoughts, and she didn't even hear Jeff's voice shouting in her ear.

Jeff said nothing more. For an instant there was light in his cavernous brain. The great chamber was, for less than a second, peopled by characters he knew and loved. They were simple, healthy creatures, and they behaved in a manner that he could understand. They had quality. But since he had already taken leave of them long ago, the remembrance did not break his heart again. Young Jeff Patton was among them, the Jeff Patton of fifty years ago who went down to New Orleans with a crowd of country boys to the Mardi Gras doings. The gay young crowd, boys with candy-striped shirts and rouged-brown girls in noisy silks, was like a picture in his head. Yet it did not make him sad. On that very trip Slim Burns had killed Joe Beasley—the crowd had been broken up. Since then Jeff Patton's world had been the Greenbriar Plantation. If there had been other Mardi Gras carnivals, he had not heard of them. Since then there had been no time; the years had fallen on him like waves. Now he was old, worn out. Another paralytic stroke (like the one he had already suffered) would put him on his back for keeps. In that condition, with a frail blind woman to look after him, he would be worse off than if he were dead.

Suddenly Jeff's hands became steady. He actually felt

brave. He slowed down the motor of the car and carefully pulled off the road. Below, the water of the stream boomed, a soft thunder in the deep channel. Jeff ran the car onto the clay slope, pointed it directly toward the stream and put his foot heavily on the accelerator. The little car leaped furiously down the steep incline toward the water. The movement was nearly as swift and direct as a fall. The two old black folks, sitting quietly side by side, showed no excitement. In another instant the car hit the water and dropped immediately out of sight.

A little later it lodged in the mud of a shallow place. One wheel of the crushed and upturned little Ford became visible above the rushing water.

LANGSTON HUGHES (1902–1967)

The most prolific and perhaps best-known of modern Negro American writers, Langston Hughes was the only Negro poet who lived entirely on the professional earnings of his literary activities in a long and diverse literary career. He was born in Joplin, Missouri, but for most of his childhood Hughes lived with his grandmother in Lawrence, Kansas. Hughes recalled that his Kansas grandmother was the last surviving widow of John Brown's Raid—in his words, "her first husband having been one of the five colored men to die so gloriously at Harper's Ferry." She died when he was thirteen and he then went to live with his mother in Lincoln, Illinois. A year later they moved to Cleveland, where he attended Central High School and began writing poetry. After graduation he spent fifteen months in Mexico with his father, who had been living there for some years. Here Hughes learned Spanish and wrote "The Negro Speaks of Rivers," which was published in The Crisis *(1921). He attended Columbia University for a year in 1921, leaving to work as a seaman for almost two years. His travels brought him to the West Coast of Africa and North-ern Europe. In 1924 he went to Paris, where he worked in nightclubs, and then on to Italy. By the end of the year*

Hughes worked his way back to New York on a tramp steamer, painting and scrubbing decks. He spent the next year in Washington, employed in the office of the Association for the Study of Negro Life and History, and later as a bus-boy at the Wardman Park Hotel. It was there that Vachel Lindsay read some of his poems and Hughes (as he recalled) "was discovered by the newspapers." He received his first prize for poetry in 1925 from Opportunity *magazine and went on to become a major figure of the "Harlem Renaissance." He resumed his college education at Lincoln University, in Pennsylvania, where he wrote his first novel,* Not Without Laughter *(1930). More than twelve volumes of his poems were published during his lifetime and a final collection,* The Panther and the Lash *(1967), was issued posthumously. He was frequently introduced to audiences as "the Poet Laureate of Harlem." He won the Witter Bynner undergraduate prize for excellence in poetry in 1926 and was awarded Rosenwald and Guggenheim fellowships and a grant from the American Academy of Arts and Letters. He received the Anisfield Wolfe award in 1959 and the Spingarn Medal in 1960. His prodigious literary activities and versatility are evident in the large number of books listed in the Bibliography at the end of this volume. A favorite fictional character created by Hughes is Jesse B. Semple of Harlem. As the Simple tales grew in number and were assembled periodically in book form, they ultimately filled four volumes. Seven tales of Simple are presented here, preceded by the author's Foreword explaining who Simple is. More of Hughes' work will be found in the Poetry and Literary Criticism sections of this anthology.*

Tales of Simple

Foreword: Who Is Simple?

I cannot truthfully state, as some novelists do at the beginnings of their books, that these stories are about "nobody living or dead." The facts are that these tales are about a great many people—although they are stories about no specific persons as such. But it is impossible to live in Harlem and not know at least a hundred Simples, fifty Joyces, twenty-five Zaritas, a number of Boyds, and several Cousin Minnies—or reasonable facsimiles thereof.

"Simple Speaks His Mind" had hardly been published when I walked into a Harlem cafe one night and the proprietor said, "Listen, I don't know where you got that character, Jesse B. Semple, but I want you to meet one of my customers who is *just* like him." He called to a fellow at the end of the bar. "Watch how he walks," he said, "exactly like Simple. And I'll bet he won't be talking to you two minutes before he'll tell you how long he's been standing on his feet, and how much his bunions hurt—just like your book begins."

The barman was right. Even as the customer approached, he cried, "Man, my feet hurt! If you want to see me, why don't you come over here where I am? I stands on my feet all day."

"And I stand on mine all night," said the barman. Without me saying a word, a conversation began so much like the opening chapter in my book that even I was a bit amazed to see how nearly life can be like fiction—or vice versa.

Simple, as a character, originated during the war. His first words came directly out of the mouth of a young man who lived just down the block from me. One night I ran into him in a neighborhood bar and he said, "Come on back to the booth and meet my girl friend." I did and he treated me to a beer. Not knowing much about the young man, I asked where he worked. He said, "In a war plant."

I said, "What do you make?"

He said, "Cranks."

I said, "What kind of cranks?"

He said, "Oh, man, I don't know what kind of cranks."

I said, "Well, do they crank cars, tanks, buses, planes or what?"

He said, "I don't know what them cranks crank."

Whereupon, his girl friend, a little put out at this ignorance of his job, said, "You've been working there long enough. Looks like by now you ought to know what them cranks crank."

"Aw, woman," he said, "you know white folks don't tell colored folks what cranks crank."

That was the beginning of Simple. I have long since lost track of the fellow who uttered those words. But out of the mystery as to what the cranks of this world crank, to whom they belong and why, there evolved the character in this book, wondering and laughing at the numerous problems of white folks, colored folks, and just folks—including himself. He talks about the wife he used to have, the woman he loves today, and his one-time play-girl, Zarita. Usually over a glass of beer, he tells me his tales, mostly in high humor, but sometimes with a pain in his soul as sharp as the occasional hurt of that bunion on his right foot. Sometimes, as the old blues says, Simple might be "laughing to keep from crying." But even then, he keeps you laughing, too. If there were not a lot of genial souls in Harlem as talkative as Simple, I would never have these tales to write down that are "just like him." He is my ace-boy, Simple. I hope you like him, too.

LANGSTON HUGHES

New York City
August, 1961

Feet Live Their Own Life

"If you want to know about my life," said Simple as he blew the foam from the top of the newly filled glass the bartender put before him, "don't look at my face, don't look at my hands. Look at my feet and see if you can tell how long I been standing on them."

"I cannot see your feet through your shoes," I said.

"You do not need to see through my shoes," said Simple. "Can't you tell by the shoes I wear—not pointed, not rocking-chair, not French-toed, not nothing but big, long, broad, and flat—that I been standing on these feet a long time and carrying some heavy burdens? They ain't flat from standing at no bar, neither, because I always sets at a bar. Can't you tell that? You know I do not hang out in a bar unless it has stools, don't you?"

"That I have observed," I said, "but I did not connect it with your past life."

"Everything I do is connected up with my past life," said Simple. "From Virginia to Joyce, from my wife to Zarita, from my mother's milk to this glass of beer, everything is connected up."

"I trust you will connect up with that dollar I just loaned you when you get paid," I said. "And who is Virginia? You never told me about her."

"Virginia is where I was borned," said Simple. "I *would* be borned in a state named after a woman. From that day on, women never give me no peace."

"You, I fear, are boasting. If the women were running after you as much as you run after them, you would not be able to sit here on this bar stool in peace. I don't see any women coming to call you out to go home, as some of these fellows' wives do around here."

"Joyce better not come in no bar looking for me," said Simple. "That is why me and my wife busted up—one reason. I do not like to be called out of no bar by a female. It's a man's perogative to just set and drink sometimes."

"How do you connect that prerogative with your past?" I asked.

"When I was a wee small child," said Simple, "I had no place to set and think in, being as how I was raised up with three brothers, two sisters, seven cousins, one married aunt, a common-law uncle, and the minister's grandchild—and the house only had four rooms. I never had no place just to set and think. Neither to set and drink—not even much my milk before some hongry child snatched it out of my hand. I were not the youngest, neither a girl, nor the cutest. I don't know why, but I don't think nobody liked me much. Which is why I was afraid to like anybody for a long time myself. When I did like somebody, I was full-grown and then I picked out the wrong woman because I had no practice in liking anybody before that. We did not get along."

"Is that when you took to drink?"

"Drink took to me," said Simple. "Whiskey just naturally likes me but beer likes me better. By the time I got married I had got to the point where a cold bottle was almost as good as a warm bed, especially when the bottle could not talk and the bed-warmer could. I do not like a woman to talk to me too much—I mean about me. Which is why I like Joyce. Joyce most in generally talks about herself."

"I am still looking at your feet," I said, "and I swear they do not reveal your life to me. Your feet are no open book."

"You have eyes but you see not," said Simple. "These feet have stood on every rock from the Rock of Ages to 135th and Lenox. These feet have supported everything from a cotton bale to a hongry woman. These feet have walked ten thousand miles working for white folks and another ten thousand keeping up with colored. These feet have stood at altars, crap tables, free lunches, bars, graves, kitchen doors, betting windows, hospital clinics, WPA desks, social security railings, and in all kinds of lines from soup lines to the draft. If I just had four feet, I could have stood in more places longer. As it is, I done wore out seven hundred pairs of shoes, eighty-nine tennis shoes, twelve summer sandals, also six loafers. The socks that these feet have bought could build a knitting mill. The corns I've cut away would dull a German razor. The bunions I forgot would make you ache from now till Judgment Day. If anybody was to write the history of my life, they should start with my feet."

"Your feet are not all that extraordinary," I said. "Besides, everything you are saying is general. Tell me specifically some one thing your feet have done that makes them different from any other feet in the world, just one."

"Do you see that window in that white man's store across the street?" asked Simple. "Well, this right foot of mine broke out that window in the Harlem riots right smack in the middle. Didn't no other foot in the world break that window but mine. And this left foot carried me off running as soon as my right foot came down. Nobody else's feet saved me from the cops that night but these *two* feet right here. Don't tell me these feet ain't had a life of their own."

"For shame," I said, "going around kicking out windows. Why?"

"Why?" said Simple. "You have to ask my great-great-grandpa why. He must of been simple—else why did he let them capture him in Africa and sell him for a slave to breed my great-grandpa in slavery to breed my grandpa in slavery to breed my pa to breed me to look at that window and say, 'It ain't mine! Bam-mmm-mm-m!' and kick it out?"

"This bar glass is not yours either," I said. "Why don't you smash it?"

"It's got my beer in it," said Simple.

Just then Zarita came in wearing her Thursday-night rab-bit-skin coat. She didn't stop at the bar, being dressed up, but went straight back to a booth. Simple's hand went up, his beer went down, and the glass back to its wet spot on the bar.

"Excuse me a minute," he said, sliding off the stool.

Just to give him pause, the dozens, that old verbal game of maligning a friend's female relatives, came to mind. "Wait," I said. "You have told me about what to ask your great-great-grandpa. But I want to know what to ask your great-great-*grandma.*"

"I don't play the dozens that far back," said Simple, fol-lowing Zarita into the smoky juke-box blue of the back room.

Temptation

"When the Lord said, 'Let there be light,' and there was light, what I want to know is where was us colored people?"

"What do you mean, 'Where were we colored people?'" I said.

"We must *not* of been there," said Simple, "because we are still dark. Either He did not include me or else I were not there."

"The Lord was not referring to people when He said, 'Let there be light.' He was referring to the elements, the atmo-sphere, the air."

"He must have included some people," said Simple, "because white people are light, in fact, *white*, whilst I am dark. How come? I say, we were not there."

"Then where do you think we were?"

"Late as usual," said Simple, "old C. P. Time. We must have been down the road a piece and did not get back on time."

"There was no C. P. Time in those days," I said. "In fact, no people were created—so there couldn't be any Colored People's Time. The Lord God had not yet breathed the breath of life into anyone."

"No?" said Simple.

"No," said I, "because it wasn't until Genesis 2 and 7 that God 'formed man of the dust of the earth and breathed into his nostrils the breath of life and man became a living soul.' His name was Adam. Then He took one of Adam's ribs and made a woman."

"Then trouble began," said Simple. "Thank God, they was both white."

"How do you know Adam and Eve were white?" I asked.

"When I was a kid I seen them on the Sunday school cards," said Simple. "Ever since I been seeing a Sunday School card, they was white. That is why I want to know where was us Negroes when the Lord said, 'Let there be light'?"

"Oh, man, you have a color complex so bad you want to trace it back to the Bible."

"No, I don't. I just want to know how come Adam and Eve was white. If they had started out black, this world might not be in the fix it is today. Eve might not of paid that serpent no attention. I never did know a Negro yet that liked a snake."

"That snake is a symbol," I said, "a symbol of temptation and sin. And that symbol would be the same, no matter what the race."

"I am not talking about no symbol," said Simple. "I am talking about the day when Eve took that apple and Adam et. From then on the human race has been in trouble. There ain't a colored woman living what would take no apple from a snake—and she better not give no snake-apples to her husband!"

"Adam and Eve are symbols, too," I said.

"You are simple yourself," said Simple. "But I just wish we colored folks had been somewhere around at the start. I do not know where we was when Eden was a garden, but we sure didn't get in on none of the crops. If we had, we would not be so poor today. White folks started out ahead and they are still ahead. Look at me!"

"I am looking," I said.

"Made in the image of God," said Simple, "but I never did see anybody like me on a Sunday school card."

"Probably nobody looked like you in Biblical days," I said. "The American Negro did not exist in B.C. You're a product of Caucasia and Africa, Harlem and Dixie. You've been conditioned entirely by our environment, our modern times."

"Times have been hard," said Simple, "but still I am a child of God."

"In the cosmic sense, we are all children of God."

"I have been baptized," said Simple, "also anointed with oil. When I were a child I come through at the mourners' bench. I was converted. I have listened to Daddy Grace and et with Father Divine, moaned with Elder Lawson and prayed with Adam Powell. Also I have been to the Episcopalians with Joyce. But if a snake were to come up to me and offer *me* an apple, I would say, 'Varmint, be on your way! No fruit today! Bud, you got the wrong stud now, so get along somehow, be off down the road because you're lower than a toad!' Then that serpent would respect me as a wise man—and this world would not be where it is—all on account of an apple. That apple has turned into an atom now."

"To hear you talk, if you had been in the Garden of Eden, the world would still be a Paradise," I said. "Man would not have fallen into sin."

"Not *this* man," said Simple. "I would have stayed in that garden making grape wine, singing like Crosby, and feeling fine! I would not be scuffling out in this rough world, neither would I be in Harlem. If I was Adam I would just stay in Eden in that garden with no rent to pay, no landladies to dodge, no time clock to punch—and *my* picture on a Sunday school card. I'd be a *real gone guy* even if I didn't have but one name—Adam—and no initials."

"You would be *real gone* all right. But you were not there. So, my dear fellow, I trust you will not let your rather late arrival on our contemporary stage distort your perspective."

"No," said Simple.

Bop

Somebody upstairs in Simple's house had the combination turned up loud with an old Dizzy Gillespie record spinning like mad filling the Sabbath with Bop as I passed.

"Set down here on the stoop with me and listen to the music," said Simple.

"I've heard your landlady doesn't like tenants sitting on her stoop," I said.

"Pay it no mind," said Simple. "Ool-ya-koo," he sang. "Hey Ba-Ba-Re-Bop! Be-Bop! Mop!"

"All that nonsense singing reminds me of Cab Calloway back in the old *scat* days," I said, "around 1930 when he was chanting, 'Hi-de-*hie*-de-ho! Hee-de-*hee*-de-hee!'"

"Not at all," said Simple, "absolutely not at all."

"Re-Bop certainly sounds like scat to me," I insisted.

"No," said Simple, "Daddy-o, you are wrong. Besides, it was not *Re*-Bop. It is *Be*-bop."

"What's the difference," I asked, "between *Re* and *Be*?"

"A lot," said Simple. "Re-Bop was an imitation like most of the white boys play. Be-Bop is the real thing like the colored boys play."

"You bring race into everything," I said, "even music."

"It is in everything," said Simple.

"Anyway, Be-Bop is passé, gone, finished."

"It may be gone, but its riffs remain behind," said Simple. "Be-Bop music was certainly colored folks' music—which is why white folks found it so hard to imitate. But there are some few white boys that latched onto it right well. And no wonder, because they sat and listened to Dizzy, Thelonius, Tad Dameron, Charlie Parker, also Mary Lou, all night long every time they got a chance, and bought their records by the dozen to copy their riffs. The ones that sing tried to make up new Be-Bop words, but them white folks don't know what they are singing about, even yet."

"It all sounds like pure nonsense syllables to me."

"Nonsense, nothing!" cried Simple. "Bop makes plenty of sense."

"What kind of sense?"

"You must not know where Bop comes from," said Simple, astonished at my ignorance.

"I do not know," I said. "Where?"

"From the police," said Simple.

"What do you mean, from the police?"

"From the police beating Negroes' heads," said Simple. "Every time a cop hits a Negro with his billy club, that old club say, 'BOP! BOP! . . . BE-BOP! . . . MOP! . . . BOP!'

"That Negro hollers, 'Ooool-ya-koo! Ou-o-o!'

"Old Cop just keeps on, 'MOP! MOP! . . . BE-BOP! . . . MOP!' That's where Be-Bop came from, beaten right out of some Negro's head into them horns and saxophones and piano keys that plays it. Do you call that nonsense?"

"If it's true, I do not," I said.

"That's why so many white folks don't dig Bop," said Simple. "White folks do not get their heads beat *just for being white*. But me——a cop is liable to grab me almost any time and beat my head——*just* for being colored.

"In some parts of this American country as soon as the polices see me, they say, 'Boy, what are you doing in this neighborhood?'

"I say, 'Coming from work, sir.'

"They say, 'Where do you work?'

"Then I have to go into my whole pedigree because I am a black man in a white neighborhood. And if my answers do not satisfy them, BOP! MOP! . . . BE-BOP! . . . MOP! If they do not hit me, they have already hurt my soul. *A dark man shall see dark days.* Bop comes out of them dark days. That's why real Bop is mad, wild, frantic, crazy——and not to be dug unless you've seen dark days, too. Folks who ain't suffered much cannot play Bop, neither appreciate it. They think Bop is nonsense——like you. They think it's just *crazy* crazy. They do not know Bop is also MAD crazy, SAD crazy, FRANTIC WILD CRAZY——beat out of somebody's head! That's what Bop is. Them young colored kids who started it, they know what Bop is."

"Your explanation depresses me," I said.

"Your nonsense depresses me," said Simple.

Census

"I have had so many hardships in this life," said Simple, "that it is a wonder I'll live until I die. I was born young, black, voteless, poor, and hungry, in a state where white folks did not even put Negroes on the census. My daddy said he were never counted in his life by the United States government. And nobody could find a birth certificate for me nowhere. It were not until I come to Harlem that one day a census taker dropped around to my house and asked me where were I born and why, also my age and if I was still living. I said, 'Yes, I am here, in spite of all.'

" 'All of what?' asked the census taker. 'Give me the data.'

" 'All my corns and bunions, for one,' I said. 'I were borned with corns. Most colored peoples get corns so young, they must be inherited. As for bunions, they seem to come natural, we stands on our feet so much. These feet of mine have stood in everything from soup lines to the draft board. They have supported everything from a packing trunk to a hongry woman. My feet have walked ten thousand miles running errands for white folks and another ten thousand trying to keep up with colored. My feet have stood before altars, at crap tables, bars, graves, kitchen doors, welfare windows, and social security railings. Be sure and include my feet on that census you are taking,' I told that man.

"Then I went on to tell him how my feet have helped to keep the American shoe industry going, due to the money I have spent on my feet. 'I have wore out seven hundred pairs of shoes, eight-nine tennis shoes, forty-four summer sandals, and two hundred and two loafers. The socks my feet have bought could build a knitting mill. The razor blades I have used cutting away my corns could pay for a razor plant. Oh, my feet have helped to make America rich, and I am still standing on them.

" 'I stepped on a rusty nail once, and mighty near had lockjaw. And from my feet up, so many other things have happened to me, since, it is a wonder I made it through this world. In my time, I have been cut, stabbed, run over, hit by a car, tromped by a horse, robbed, fooled, deceived, double-crossed, dealt seconds, and mighty near blackmailed—but I am still here! I have been laid off, fired and not rehired, Jim Crowed, segregated, insulted, eliminated, locked in, locked out, locked up, left holding the bag, and denied relief. I have been caught in the rain, caught in jails, caught short with my rent, and caught with the wrong woman—but I am still here!

" 'My mama should have named me Job instead of Jesse B. Semple. I have been underfed, underpaid, undernourished, and everything but undertaken—yet I am still here. The only thing I am afraid of now—is that I will die before my time. So man, put me on your census now this year, because I may not be here when the next census comes around.'

"The census man said, 'What do you expect to die of—complaining?'

" 'No,' I said, 'I expect to ugly away.' At which I thought the man would laugh. Instead you know he nodded his head, and wrote it down. He were white and did not know I was making a joke. Do you reckon that man really thought I am homely?"

Coffee Break

"My boss is white," said Simple.

"Most bosses are," I said.

"And being white and curious, my boss keeps asking me just what does THE Negro want. Yesterday he tackled me during the coffee break, talking about THE Negro. He always says 'THE Negro,' as if there was not 50-11 different kinds of Negroes in the U.S.A.," complained Simple. "My boss says, 'Now that you-all have got the Civil Rights Bill and the Supreme Court, Adam Powell in Congress, Ralph Bunche in the United Nations, and Leontyne Price singing in the Metropolitan Opera, plus Dr. Martin Luther King getting the Nobel Prize, what more do you want? I am asking you, just what does THE Negro want?'"

"'I am not THE Negro,' I says. 'I am *me*.'

"'Well,' says my boss, 'you represent THE Negro.'

"'I do not,' I says. 'I represent my own self.'

"'Ralph Bunche represents you, then,' says my boss, 'and Thurgood Marshall and Martin Luther King. Do they not?'

"'I am proud to be represented by such men, if you say they represent me,' I said. 'But all them men you name are *way* up there, and they do not drink beer in my bar. I have never seen a single one of them mens on Lenox Avenue in my natural life. So far as I know, they do not even live in Harlem. I cannot find them in the telephone book. They all got private numbers. But since you say they represent THE Negro, why do you not ask them what THE Negro wants?'

"'I cannot get to them,' says my boss.

"'Neither can I,' I says, 'so we both is in the same boat.'

"'Well then, to come nearer home,' says my boss, 'Roy Wilkins fights your battles, also James Farmer.'

"'They do not drink in my bar, neither,' I said.

"'Don't Wilkins and Farmer live in Harlem?' he asked.

"'Not to my knowledge,' I said. 'And I bet they have not been to the Apollo since Jackie Mabley cracked the first joke.'

"'I do not know him,' said my boss, 'but I see Nipsey Russell and Bill Cosby on TV.'

"'Jackie Mabley is no *him*,' I said. 'She is a *she*—better known as Moms.'

"'Oh,' said my boss.

"'And Moms Mabley has a story on one of her records about Little Cindy Ella and the magic slippers going to the Junior Prom at Ole Miss which tells all about what THE Negro wants.'

"'What's its conclusion?' asked my boss.

"'When the clock strikes midnight, Little Cindy Ella is dancing with the President of the Ku Klux Klan, says Moms, but at the stroke of twelve, Cindy Ella turns back to her natural self, black, and her blonde wig turns to a stocking cap —and her trial comes up next week.'

" 'A symbolic tale,' says my boss, 'meaning, I take it, that THE Negro is in jail. But you are not in jail.'

" 'That's what you think,' I said.

" 'Anyhow, you claim you are not THE Negro,' said my boss.

" 'I am not,' I said. 'I am *this* Negro.'

" 'Then what do *you* want?' asked my boss.

" 'To get out of jail,' I said.

" 'What jail?'

" 'The jail you got me in.'

" 'Me?' yells my boss. 'I have not got you in jail. Why, boy, I like you. I am a liberal. I voted for Kennedy. And this time for Johnson. I believe in integration. Now that you got it, though, what more do you want?'

" 'Reintegration,' I said.

" 'Meaning by that, what?'

" 'That you be integrated with *me*, not me with you.'

" 'Do you mean that I come and live in Harlem?' asked my boss. 'Never!'

" 'I live in Harlem,' I said.

" 'You are adjusted to it,' said my boss. 'But there is so much crime in Harlem.'

" 'There are no two-hundred-thousand-dollar bank robberies, though,' I said, 'of which there was three lately *elsewhere* —all done by white folks, and nary one in Harlem. The biggest and best crime is outside of Harlem. We never has no half-million-dollar jewelry robberies, no missing star sapphires. You better come uptown with me and reintegrate.'

" 'Negroes are the ones who want to be integrated,' said my boss.

" 'And white folks are the ones who do *not* want to be,' I said.

" 'Up to a point, we do,' said my boss.

" 'That is what THE Negro wants,' I said, 'to remove that *point*.'

" 'The coffee break is over,' said my boss."

Cracker Prayer

"Well," said Simple, "this other old cracker down in Virginia who acted like Mr. Wincliff what kicked my shins, one night he were down on his knees praying. Since he were getting right ageable, he wanted to be straight with God before he departed his life and headed for the Kingdom. So he lifted his voice and said, 'Oh, Lord, help me to get right, do right, be right, and die right before I ascends to Thy sight. Help me

to make my peace with Nigras, Lord, because I have hated
them all my life. If I do not go to heaven, Lord, I certainly
do not want to go to hell with all them Nigras down there
waiting to meet me. I hear the Devil is in league with Nigras,
and if the Devil associates with Nigras, he must be a Yankee
who would not give me protection. Lord, take me to Thy
Kingdom where I will not have to associate with a hell full of
Nigras. Do You hear me, Lord?'

"The Lord answered and said, 'I hearest thee, Colonel
Cushenberry. What else wilst thou have of me?'

"The old cracker prayed on, 'Lord, Lord, dear Lord, since
I did not have a nice old colored mammy in my childhood,
give me one in heaven, Lord. My family were too poor to
afford a black mammy for any of my father's eight children.
I were mammyless as a child. Give me a mammy in heaven,
Lord. Also a nice old Nigress to polish my golden slippers
and keep the dust off of my wings. But, Lord, if there be educated Nigras in heaven, keep them out of my sight. The
only thing I hate worse than an educated Nigra is an integrated one. Do not let me meet no New York Nigras in
heaven, Lord, nor none what ever flirted with the NAACP or
Eleanor Roosevelt. As You is my Father, Lord, lead me not
into black pastures, but deliver me from integration, for
Thine is the power to make all men as white as snow. But I
would still know a Nigra even though he were white, by the
way he sings, also by certain other characteristics which I will
not go into now because a prayer is no place to explain everything. But You understand as well as I do, Lord, why a
Nigra is something special.

" 'Lord, could I ask You one question? Did You make Nigras just to bedevil white folks? Was they put here on earth
to be a trial and tribulation to the South? Did You create the
NAACP to add fire to brimstone? You know, Lord, as soon
as a Nigra gets an inch he wants an el. Give him an el, and
he wants it ALL. Pretty soon a white man will not be able to
sing "Come to Jesus" without a Nigra wanting to sing along
with him. And you know Nigras can outsing us, Lord.

" 'Lord, You know I think it would be a good idea if You
would send Christ down to earth again. It is about time for
the Second Coming, because I don't believe Christ knows
what Nigras is up to in this modern day and age. They is up
to devilment, Lord—riding in the same train coaches with us,
setting beside us on busses, sending their little Nigra children
to school with our little white children. Even talking about
they do not like to be segregated in jail no more—that a jail
is a public place for which they also pay taxes.

" 'Lord, separate the black taxes from the white taxes, black sheep from white sheep, and Nigra soldiers from white soldiers before the next war comes around. I do not want my grandson atomized with no Nigra. Lord, dispatch Christ down here before it is too late. Great Lord God, Jehovah, Father, send Your Only Begotten Son in a Cloud of Fire to straighten out this world again and put Nigras back in their places before that last trumpet sounds. When I get ready to go to Glory, Lord, and put on my white robe and prepare to step into Thy chariot, I do not want no Nigras lined up telling me the Supreme Court has decreed integrated seats in the Celestial Chariot, too. If I hear tell of such, Lord, I elect to stay right here on earth where at least Faubus is on my side.' "

Promulgations

"If I was setting in the High Court in Washington," said Simple, "where they do not give out no sentences for crimes, but where they gives out promulgations, I would promulgate. Up them long white steps behind them tall white pillars in that great big marble hall with the eagle of the U.S.A., where at I would bang my gavel and promulgate."

"Promulgate what?" I asked.

"Laws," said Simple. "After that I would promulgate the promulgations that would take place if people did not obey my laws. I see no sense in passing laws if nobody pays them any mind."

"What would happen if people did not obey your promulgations?" I asked.

"Woe be unto them," said Simple. "I would not be setting in that High Court paid a big salary just to read something off a paper. I would be there with a robe on to see that what I read was carried out. I would gird on my sword, like in the Bible, and prepare to do battle. For instant, 'Love thy neighbor as thyself.' The first man I caught who did not love his neighbor as hisself, I would make him change places with his neighbor—the rich with the poor, the white with the black, and Governor Faubus with me."

"I know you have lost your mind," I said. "How could you accomplish such an objective?"

"With education," said Simple, "which white folks favors. I would make Governor Faubus go to school again in Little Rock and study with them integrated students there and learn all over again the facts of life."

"You are telling me *what* you would do," I said, "not *how* you would do it. How could you make Faubus do anything?"

"I would say, 'Faubus! Faubus! Come out of that clothes closet or wherever you are hiding and face me. *Me*, Jesse B., who has promulgated your attendance in my presence! I decrees now and from here on out that you straighten up and fly right. Cast off your mask of ignorance and hate and go study your history. You have not yet learned that "taxation without representation is tyranny," which I learned in grade school. You have also not learned that "all men are created equal," which I learned before I quit school. Educate yourself, Faubus, so that you can better rule your state.' "

"Suppose he paid you no attention?" I said.

"Then I would whisper something in his ear," said Simple. "I would tell him that the secret records in the hands of my committee show that he has got colored blood. Whilst he was trying to recover from that shock, I would continue with some facts I made up.

" 'Governor Faubus, did you know your great-great-grandfather were black?'

"He would say, 'What?'

"I would say, 'Look at me, Governor, I am your third cousin.' Whereupon Faubus would faint. Whilst he was fainted, I would pick him up and take him to a mixed school. When he come to, he would be integrated. That is the way I would work my promulgations," said Simple.

"I should think you would rapidly become a national figure," I said, "with your picture in *Time, Life, Newsweek, Ebony*, and *Jet*."

"Yes," said Simple. "Then in my spare time I would take up the international situation. I would call a Summit Meeting and get together with all the big heads of state in the world."

"I gather you would drop your judgeship for the nonce and become a diplomat."

"A hip-to-mat," said Simple, "minding everybody's business but my own. I would call my valet to tell my confidential secretary to inform my aide to bring me my attaché case. I would put on my swallowtail coat, striped trousers, and high hat, get into my limousine, and ride to the Summit looking like an Englishman. But what would be different about me is I would be black. I would take my black face, black hands, and black demands right up to the top and set down and say, 'Gimme a microphone, turn on the TVs, and hook up the national hookups. I want the world to hear my message.' Then I would promulgate at large as I proceeded to chair the agenda."

"Proceed," I said.

"Which I would do," said Simple, "no sooner than the audience got settled, the diplomats got their earphones strapped on, and the translators got their dictionaries out, also the stenographers got their machines ready to take my message from Harlem down for the record. The press galleries would be full of reporters waiting to wire my words around the world, and I would be prepared to send them, Jack. I would be ready."

"Give forth," I said.

"Bread and meat come first," said Simple. " 'Gentlemens of the Summit, I want you-all to think how you can provide everybody in the world with bread and meat. Civil rights comes next. Let everybody have civil rights, white, black, yellow, brown, gray, grizzle, or green. No Jim-Crow-take-low can't go for anybody! Let Arabs go to Israel and Israels go to Egypt, Chinese come to America and Negroes live in Australia, if any be so foolish as to want to. Let Willie Mays live in Levittown and Casey Stengel live in Ghana if he so desires. And let me drink at the Stork Club if I get tired of Small's Paradise. Open house before open skies. After which comes peace, which you can't have nohow as long as peoples and nations is snatching and grabbing over pork chops and payola so as not to starve to death. No peace could be had nowhow with white nations against dark.

" 'You big countries of the world has got to wake up to the sense your leaders wasn't born with, and the peoples has got to reach out their hands to each others' over the leaders' heads, just like I am talking over your leaders' heads now, because so many leaders is in the game for payola and sayola, not do-ola. But me, self-appointed, I am beholden to nobody. Right now I cannot do much, but I can say all.

" 'I therefore say to you, gentlemens of the Summit, you may not pay attention to me now, but some sweet day you will. I will get tired of your stuff and your bluff. I will take your own golf stick and wham the world so far up into orbit until you will be shaken off the surface of the earth and everybody will wonder where have all the white folks gone. Gentlemens of the Summit, you-all had better get together and straighten up and fly right—else in due time you will have to contend with what Harlem thinks. Do I hear some of you-all say, "It do not matter what Harlem thinks"?

" 'I regret to inform you, gentlemens of the Summit, that IT DO!' "

RICHARD WRIGHT (1908–1960)

Going far beyond the "protest novel" label which has been tagged to his fiction by some critics, Richard Wright brought into American literature in a radically new way, the feeling and the texture of the complex psychological tensions simmering in the black ghetto of urban America. Bigger Thomas in Native Son *is a literary archetype of the hemmed-in, frustrated, and rejected black American in the ghetto who is propelled into violence by overwhelming conditions and forces. Wright was born on a plantation near Natchez, Mississippi, spent his youth in Memphis, Tennessee, and reached Chicago in his teens where he worked at odd jobs while experiencing his genesis as a writer. He participated in the traumatic mass migration of Negroes from the South to the North which produced the great centers of urban Negro life in the North. In his fiction he gave literary expression to the human and psychological meanings of this complex process of uprooting and rerooting. When he was born, about ninety per cent of the Negroes in the United States lived in the South. He was one of the many who made the northward trek which resulted in a quadrupling of the proportion of Negroes in the North during his lifetime. As he wrote in the last years of his life: "I feel personally identified with the migrant Negro, his folk songs, his ditties, his wild tales of bad men . . . because my own life was forged in the depths in which they live." He found his voice in the literary and political ferment of the Left in the 30's. His first writing was published in the Communist press, and for a while he was Harlem correspondent of* The Daily Worker; *later he voiced sharp conflict with Communist policies. His first book, a collection of short stories entitled* Uncle Tom's Children (1938), *won the annual award of* Story *magazine. His novel* Native Son, *published in 1940, became the first novel by an American Negro to enter the full mainstream of American literature, both in terms of its mass audience and its subsequent influence. It was a best seller, the first novel by a Negro to become a Book-of-the-Month Club selection, and became the first novel by a Negro to appear in the Modern Library editions. In 1945 he published* Black Boy, *an autobiographical account of his childhood and youth in the South. LeRoi Jones has written: "The most completely valid social novels and social criticisms of South and North, nonurban and urban Negro life, are Wright's* Black Boy *and* Native Son." *After the publication of* Black Boy, *Wright went to Paris. He lived there as an expatriate for about fifteen years until his death in 1960. He traveled in Europe and Africa and continued to write fiction and nonfiction during his long exile, but critical opinion recognizes his earlier pre-Paris fiction as his most significant work. The short story that follows, with its obvious allusion in the title to the Dostoyevskyan Underground—redefined and applied here to the nightmarish hell of an urban Negro—was written at the peak of Wright's literary activity in America. An earlier draft was first published in* Accent *magazine in 1942. The present revised and enlarged version was published in* Cross-Section *1944 and later included in his posthumously published collection of short stories,* Eight Men. *Other works by Richard Wright appear in the Autobiography, Poetry, and Literary Criticism sections.*

The Man Who Lived Underground

I've got to hide, he told himself. His chest heaved as he waited, crouching in a dark corner of the vestibule. He was tired of running and dodging. Either he had to find a place to hide, or he had to surrender. A police car swished by through the rain, its siren rising sharply. They're looking for me all over . . . He crept to the door and squinted through the fogged plate glass. He stiffened as the siren rose and died in the distance. Yes, he had to hide, but where? He gritted his teeth. Then a sudden movement in the street caught his attention. A throng of tiny columns of water snaked into the air from the perforations of a manhole cover. The columns stopped abruptly, as though the perforations had become clogged; a gray spout of sewer water jutted up from underground and lifted the circular metal cover, juggled it for a moment, then let it fall with a clang.

He hatched a tentative plan: he would wait until the siren sounded far off, then he would go out. He smoked and waited, tense. At last the siren gave him his signal; it wailed, dying, going away from him. He stepped to the sidewalk, then paused and looked curiously at the open manhole, half expecting the cover to leap up again. He went to the center of the street and stooped and peered into the hole, but could see nothing. Water rustled in the black depths.

He started with terror; the siren sounded so near that he had the idea that he had been dreaming and had awakened to find the car upon him. He dropped instinctively to his knees and his hands grasped the rim of the manhole. The siren seemed to hoot directly above him and with a wild gasp of exertion he snatched the cover far enough off to admit his body. He swung his legs over the opening and lowered himself into watery darkness. He hung for an eternal moment to the rim by his finger tips, then he felt rough metal prongs and at once he knew that sewer workmen used these ridges to lower themselves into manholes. Fist over fist, he let his body sink until he could feel no more prongs. He swayed in dank space; the siren seemed to howl at the very rim of the manhole. He dropped and was washed violently into an ocean of warm, leaping water. His head was battered against a wall and he wondered if this were death. Frenziedly his fingers clawed and sank into a crevice. He steadied himself and measured the strength of the current with his own muscular tension. He stood slowly in water that dashed past his knees with fearful velocity.

He heard a prolonged scream of brakes and the siren broke off. Oh, God! They had found him! Looming above his head in the rain a white face hovered over the hole. "How did this damn thing get off?" he heard a policeman ask. He saw the steel cover move slowly until the hole looked like a quarter moon turned black. "Give me a hand here," someone called. The cover clanged into place, muffling the sights and sounds of the upper world. Knee-deep in the pulsing current, he breathed with aching chest, filling his lungs with the hot stench of yeasty rot.

From the perforations of the manhole cover, delicate lances of hazy violet sifted down and wove a mottled pattern upon the surface of the streaking current. His lips parted as a car swept past along the wet pavement overhead, its heavy rumble soon dying out, like the hum of a plane speeding through a dense cloud. He had never thought that cars could sound like that; everyting seemed strange and unreal under here. He stood in darkness for a long time, knee-deep in rustling water, musing.

The odor of rot had become so general that he no longer smelled it. He got his cigarettes, but discovered that his matches were wet. He searched and found a dry folder in the pocket of his shirt and managed to strike one; it flared weirdly in the wet gloom, glowing greenishly, turning red, orange, then yellow. He lit a crumpled cigarette; then, by the flickering light of the match, he looked for support so that he would not have to keep his muscles flexed against the pouring water. His pupils narrowed and he saw to either side of him two steaming walls that rose and curved inward some six feet above his head to form a dripping, mouse-colored dome. The bottom of the sewer was a sloping V-trough. To the left, the sewer vanished in ashen fog. To the right was a steep down-curve into which water plunged.

He saw now that had he not regained his feet in time, he would have been swept to death, or had he entered any other manhole he would have probably drowned. Above the rush of the current he heard sharper juttings of water; tiny streams were spewing into the sewer from smaller conduits. The match died; he struck another and saw a mass of debris sweep past him and clog the throat of the down-curve. At once the water began rising rapidly. Could he climb out before he drowned? A long hiss sounded and the debris was sucked from sight; the current lowered. He understood now what had made the water toss the manhole cover; the down-curve had become temporarily obstructed and the perforations had become clogged.

He was in danger; he might slide into a down-curve; he might wander with a lighted match into a pocket of gas and blow himself up; or he might contract some horrible disease . . . Though he wanted to leave, an irrational impulse held him rooted. To the left, the convex ceiling swooped to a height of less than five feet. With cigarette slanting from pursed lips, he waded with taut muscles, his feet sloshing over the slimy bottom, his shoes sinking into spongy slop, the slate-colored water cracking in creamy foam against his knees. Pressing his flat left palm against the lowered ceiling, he struck another match and saw a metal pole nestling in a niche of the wall. Yes, some sewer workman had left it. He reached for it, then jerked his head away as a whisper of scurrying life whisked past and was still. He held the match close and saw a huge rat, wet with slime, blinking beady eyes and baring tiny fangs. The light blinded the rat and the frizzled head moved aimlessly. He grabbed the pole and let it fly against the rat's soft body; there was shrill piping and the grizzly body splashed into the dun-colored water and was snatched out of sight, spinning in the scuttling stream.

He swallowed and pushed on, following the curve of the

misty cavern, sounding the water with the pole. By the faint
light of another manhole cover he saw, amid loose wet brick,
a hole with walls of damp earth leading into blackness. Gingerly he poked the pole into it; it was hollow and went beyond the length of the pole. He shoved the pole before him,
hoisted himself upward, got to his hands and knees, and
crawled. After a few yards he paused, struck to wonderment
by the silence; it seemed that he had traveled a million miles
away from the world. As he inched forward again he could
sense the bottom of the dirt tunnel becoming dry and lower-
ing slightly. Slowly he rose and to his astonishment he stood
erect. He could not hear the rustling of the water now and he
felt confoundingly alone, yet lured by the darkness and silence.

He crept a long way, then stopped, curious, afraid. He put
his right foot forward and it dangled in space; he drew back
in fear. He thrust the pole outward and it swung in emptiness. He trembled, imagining the earth crumbling and burying him alive. He scratched a match and saw that the dirt
floor sheered away steeply and widened into a sort of cave
some five feet below him. An old sewer, he muttered. He
cocked his head, hearing a feathery cadence which he could
not identify. The match ceased to burn.

Using the pole as a kind of ladder, he slid down and stood
in darkness. The air was a little fresher and he could still
hear vague noises. Where was he? He felt suddenly that
someone was standing near him and he turned sharply, but
there was only darkness. He poked cautiously and felt a brick
wall; he followed it and the strange sounds grew louder. He
ought to get out of here. This was crazy. He could not remain here for any length of time; there was no food and no
place to sleep. But the faint sounds tantalized him; they were
strange but familiar. Was it a motor? A baby crying? Music?
A siren? He groped on, and the sounds came so clearly that
he could feel the pitch and timbre of human voices. Yes,
singing! That was it! He listened with open mouth. It was a
church service. Enchanted, he groped toward the waves of
melody.

Jesus, take me to your home above
And fold me in the bosom of Thy love......

The singing was on the other side of a brick wall. Excited,
he wanted to watch the service without being seen. Whose
church was it? He knew most of the churches in this area
above ground, but the singing sounded too strange and de-

tached for him to guess. He looked to the left, to the right, down to the black dirt, then upward and was startled to see a bright sliver of light slicing the darkness like the blade of a razor. He struck one of his two remaining matches and saw rusty pipes running along an old concrete ceiling. Photographically he located the exact position of the pipes in his mind. The match flame sank and he sprang upward; his hands clutched a pipe. He swung his legs and tossed his body onto the bed of pipes and they creaked, swaying up and down; he thought that the tier was about to crash, but nothing happened. He edged to the crevice and saw a segment of black men and women, dressed in white robes, singing, holding tattered songbooks in their black palms. His first impulse was to laugh, but he checked himself.

What was he doing? He was crushed with a sense of guilt. Would God strike him dead for that? The singing swept on and he shook his head, disagreeing in spite of himself. They oughtn't to do that, he thought. But he could think of no reason *why* they should not do it. Just singing with the air of the sewer blowing in on them . . . He felt that he was gazing upon something abysmally obscene, yet he could not bring himself to leave.

After a long time he grew numb and dropped to the dirt. Pain throbbed in his legs and a deeper pain, induced by the sight of those black people groveling and begging for something they could never get, churned in him. A vague conviction made him feel that those people should stand unrepentant and yield no quarter in singing and praying, yet *he* had run away from the police, had pleaded with them to believe in *his* innocence. He shook his head, bewildered.

How long had he been down here? He did not know. This was a new kind of living for him; the intensity of feelings he had experienced when looking at the church people sing made him certain that he had been down here a long time, but his mind told him that the time must have been short. In this darkness the only notion he had of time was when a match flared and measured time by its fleeting light. He groped back through the hole toward the sewer and the waves of song subsided and finally he could not hear them at all. He came to where the earth hole ended and he heard the noise of the current and time lived again for him, measuring the moments by the wash of water.

The rain must have slackened, for the flow of water had lessened and came only to his ankles. Ought he to go up into the streets and take his chances on hiding somewhere else? But they would surely catch him. The mere thought of dodging and running again from the police made him tense. No, he would stay and plot how to elude them. But what could he do down here? He walked forward into the sewer and came to another manhole cover; he stood beneath it, debating. Fine pencils of gold spilled suddenly from the little circles in the manhole cover and trembled on the surface of the current. Yes, street lamps . . . It must be night . . .

He went forward for about a quarter of an hour, wading aimlessly, poking the pole carefully before him. Then he stopped, his eyes fixed and intent. What's that? A strangely familiar image attracted and repelled him. Lit by the yellow stems from another manhole cover was a tiny nude body of a baby snagged by debris and half-submerged in water. Thinking that the baby was alive, he moved impulsively to save it, but his roused feelings told him that it was dead, cold, nothing, the same nothingness he had felt while watching the men and women singing in the church. Water blossomed about the tiny legs, the tiny arms, the tiny head, and rushed onward. The eyes were closed, as though in sleep; the fists were clenched, as though in protest; and the mouth gaped black in a soundless cry.

He straightened and drew in his breath, feeling that he had been staring for all eternity at the ripples of veined water skimming impersonally over the shriveled limbs. He felt as condemned as when the policemen had accused him. Involuntarily he lifted his hand to brush the vision away, but his arm fell listlessly to his side. Then he acted; he closed his eyes and reached forward slowly with the soggy shoe of his right foot and shoved the dead baby from where it had been lodged. He kept his eyes closed, seeing the little body twisting in the current as it floated from sight. He opened his eyes, shivered, placed his knuckles in the sockets, hearing the water speed in the somber shadows.

He tramped on, sensing at times a sudden quickening in the current as he passed some conduit whose waters were swelling the stream that slid by his feet. A few minutes later he was standing under another manhole cover, listening to the faint rumble of noises above ground. Streetcars and trucks, he mused. He looked down and saw a stagnant pool of gray-green sludge; at intervals a balloon pocket rose from the scum, glistening a bluish-purple, and burst. Then another. He turned, shook his head, and tramped back to the dirt cave by the church, his lips quivering.

Back in the cave, he sat and leaned his back against a dirt wall. His body was trembling slightly. Finally his senses quieted and he slept. When he awakened he felt stiff and cold. He had to leave this foul place, but leaving meant facing those policemen who had wrongly accused him. No, he could not go back aboveground. He remembered the beating they had given him and how he had signed his name to a confession, a confession which he had not even read. He had been too tired when they had shouted at him, demanding that he sign his name; he had signed it to end his pain.

He stood and groped about in the darkness. The church singing had stopped. How long had he slept? He did not know. But he felt refreshed and hungry. He doubled his fist nervously, realizing that he could not make a decision. As he walked about he stumbled over an old rusty iron pipe. He picked it up and felt a jagged edge. Yes, there was a brick wall and he could dig into it. What would he find? Smiling, he groped to the brick wall, sat, and began digging idly into damp cement. I can't make any noise, he cautioned himself. As time passed he grew thirsty, but there was no water. He had to kill time or go aboveground. The cement came out of the wall easily; he extracted four bricks and felt a soft draft blowing into his face. He stopped, afraid. What was beyond? He waited a long time and nothing happened; then he began digging again, soundlessly, slowly; he enlarged the hole and crawled through into a dark room and collided with another wall. He felt his way to the right; the wall ended and his fingers toyed in space, like the antennae of an insect.

He fumbled on and his feet struck something hollow, like wood. What's this? He felt with his fingers. Steps . . . He stooped and pulled off his shoes and mounted the stairs and saw a yellow chink of light shining and heard a low voice speaking. He placed his eye to a keyhole and saw the nude waxen figure of a man stretched out upon a white table. The voice, low-pitched and vibrant, mumbled indistinguishable words, neither rising nor falling. He craned his neck and squinted to see the man who was talking, but he could not locate him. Above the naked figure was suspended a huge glass container filled with a blood-red liquid from which a white rubber tube dangled. He crouched closer to the door and saw the tip end of a black object lined with pink satin. A coffin, he breathed. This is an undertaker's establishment . . . A fine-spun lace of ice covered his body and he shuddered. A throaty chuckle sounded in the depths of the yellow room.

He turned to leave. Three steps down it occurred to him that a light switch should be nearby; he felt along the wall, found an electric button, pressed it, and a blinding glare smote his pupils so hard that he was sightless, defenseless. His pupils contracted and he wrinkled his nostrils at a peculiar odor. At once he knew that he had been dimly aware of this odor in the darkness, but the light had brought it sharply to his attention. Some kind of stuff they use to embalm, he thought. He went down the steps and saw piles of lumber, coffins, and a long workbench. In one corner was a tool chest. Yes, he could use tools, could tunnel through walls with them. He lifted the lid of the chest and saw nails, a hammer, a crowbar, a screwdriver, a light bulb, a long length of electric wire. Good! He would lug these back to his cave.

He was about to hoist the chest to his shoulders when he discovered a door behind the furnace. Where did it lead? He tried to open it and found it securely bolted. Using the crowbar so as to make no sound, he pried the door open; it swung on creaking hinges, outward. Fresh air came to his face and he caught the faint roar of faraway sound. Easy now, he told himself. He widened the door and a lump of coal rattled toward him. A coalbin . . . Evidently the door led into another basement. The roaring noise was louder now, but he could not identify it. Where was he? He groped slowly over the coal pile, then ranged in darkness over a gritty floor. The roaring noise seemed to come from above him, then below, His fingers followed a wall until he touched a wooden ridge. A door, he breathed.

The noise died to a low pitch; he felt his skin prickle. It seemed that he was playing a game with an unseen person whose intelligence outstripped his. He put his ear to the flat surface of the door. Yes, voices . . . Was this a prize fight stadium? The sound of the voices came near and sharp, but he could not tell if they were joyous or despairing. He twisted the knob until he heard a soft click and felt the springy weight of the door swinging toward him. He was afraid to open it, yet captured by curiosity and wonder. He jerked the door wide and saw on the far side of the basement a furnace glowing red. Ten feet away was still another door, half ajar. He crossed and peered through the door into an empty, high-ceilinged corridor that terminated in a dark complex of shadow. The belling voices rolled about him and his eagerness mounted. He stepped into the corridor and the voices swelled louder. He crept on and came to a narrow stairway leading circularly upward; there was no question but what he was going to ascend those stairs.

Mounting the spiraled staircase, he heard the voices roll in a steady wave, then leap to crescendo, only to die away, but always remaining audible. Ahead of him glowed red letters: E—X—I—T. At the top of the steps he paused in front of a black curtain that fluttered uncertainly. He parted the folds and looked into a convex depth that gleamed with clusters of shimmering lights. Sprawling below him was a stretch of human faces, tilted upward, chanting, whistling, screaming, laughing. Dangling before the faces, high upon a screen of silver, were jerking shadows. A movie, he said with slow laughter breaking from his lips.

He stood in a box in the reserved section of a movie house and the impulse he had had to tell the people in the church to stop their singing seized him. These people were laughing at their lives, he thought with amazement. They were shouting and yelling at the animated shadows of themselves. His compassion fired his imagination and he stepped out of the box, walked out upon thin air, walked on down to the audience; and, hovering in the air just above them, he stretched out his hand to touch them . . . His tension snapped and he found himself back in the box, looking down into the sea of faces. No; it could not be done; he could not awaken them. He sighed. Yes, these people were children, sleeping in their living, awake in their dying.

He turned away, parted the black curtain, and looked out. He saw no one. He started down the white stone steps and when he reached the bottom he saw a man in trim blue uniform coming toward him. So used had he become to being underground that he thought that he could walk past the man, as though he were a ghost. But the man stopped. And he stopped.

"Looking for the men's room, sir?" the man asked, and, without waiting for an answer, he turned and pointed. "This way, sir. The first door to your right."

He watched the man turn and walk up the steps and go out of sight. Then he laughed. What a funny fellow! He went back to the basement and stood in the red darkness, watching the glowing embers in the furnace. He went to the sink and turned the faucet and the water flowed in a smooth silent stream that looked like a spout of blood. He brushed the mad image from his mind and began to wash his hands leisurely, looking about for the usual bar of soap. He found one and rubbed it in his palms until a rich lather bloomed in his cupped fingers, like a scarlet sponge. He scrubbed and rinsed his hands meticulously, then hunted for a towel; there was none. He shut off the water, pulled off his shirt, dried his hands on it; when he put it on again he was grateful for the cool dampness that came to his skin.

Yes, he was thirsty; he turned on the faucet again, bowled his fingers and when the water bubbled over the brim of his cupped palms, he drank in long, slow swallows. His bladder grew tight; he shut off the water, faced the wall, bent his head, and watched a red stream strike the floor. His nostrils wrinkled against acrid wisps of vapor; though he had tramped in the waters of the sewer, he stepped back from the wall so that his shoes, wet with sewer slime, would not touch his urine.

He heard footsteps and crawled quickly into the coalbin. Lumps rattled noisily. The footsteps came into the basement and stopped. Who was it? Had someone heard him and come down to investigate? He waited, crouching, sweating. For a long time there was silence, then he heard the clang of metal and a brighter glow lit the room. Somebody's tending the furnace, he thought. Footsteps came closer and he stiffened. Looming before him was a white face lined with coal dust, the face of an old man with watery blue eyes. Highlights spotted his gaunt cheekbones, and he held a huge shovel. There was a screechy scrape of metal against stone, and the old man lifted a shovelful of coal and went from sight.

The room dimmed momentarily, then a yellow glare came as coal flared at the furnace door. Six times the old man came to the bin and went to the furnace with shovels of coal, but not once did he lift his eyes. Finally he dropped the shovel, mopped his face with a dirty handkerchief, and sighed: "Wheeew!" He turned slowly and trudged out of the basement, his footsteps dying away.

He stood, and lumps of coal clattered down the pile. He stepped from the bin and was startled to see the shadowy outline of an electric bulb hanging above his head. Why had not the old man turned it on? Oh, yes . . . He understood. The old man had worked here for so long that he had no need for light; he had learned a way of seeing in his dark world, like those sightless worms that inch along underground by a sense of touch.

His eyes fell upon a lunch pail and he was afraid to hope that it was full. He picked it up; it was heavy. He opened it. *Sandwiches!* He looked guiltily around; he was alone. He searched farther and found a folder of matches and a half-empty tin of tobacco; he put them eagerly into his pocket and clicked off the light. With the lunch pail under his arm, he went through the door, groped over the pile of coal, and stood again in the lighted basement of the undertaking establishment. I've got to get those tools, he told himself. And turn off that light. He tiptoed back up the steps and switched off the light; the invisible voice still droned on behind the door. He crept down and, seeing with his fingers, opened the lunch pail and tore off a piece of paper bag and brought out the tin and spilled grains of tobacco into the makeshift concave. He rolled it and wet it with spittle, then inserted one end into his mouth and lit it: he sucked smoke that bit his lungs. The nicotine reached his brain, went out along his arms to his finger tips, down to his stomach, and over all the tired nerves of his body.

He carted the tools to the hole he had made in the wall. Would the noise of the falling chest betray him? But he would have to take a chance; he had to have those tools. He lifted the chest and shoved it; it hit the dirt on the other side of the wall with a loud clatter. He waited, listening; nothing happened. Head first, he slithered through and stood in the cave. He grinned, filled with a cunning idea. Yes, he would now go back into the basement of the undertaking establishment and crouch behind the coal pile and dig another hole. Sure! Fumbling, he opened the tool chest and extracted a crowbar, a screwdriver, and a hammer; he fastened them securely about his person.

With another lumpish cigarette in his flexed lips, he crawled back through the hole and over the coal pile and sat, facing the brick wall. He jabbed with the crowbar and the cement sheered away; quicker than he thought, a brick came loose. He worked an hour; the other bricks did not come easily. He sighed, weak from effort. I ought to rest a little, he thought. I'm hungry. He felt his way back to the cave and stumbled along the wall till he came to the tool chest. He sat upon it, opened the lunch pail, and took out two thick sandwiches. He smelled them. Pork chops . . . His mouth watered. He closed his eyes and devoured a sandwich, savoring the smooth rye bread and juicy meat. He ate rapidly, gulping down lumpy mouthfuls that made him long for water. He ate the other sandwich and found an apple and gobbled that up too, sucking the core till the last trace of flavor was drained from it. Then, like a dog, he ground the meat bones with his teeth, enjoying the salty, tangy marrow. He finished and stretched out full length on the ground and went to sleep. . . .

. . . His body was washed by cold water that gradually turned warm and he was buoyed upon a stream and swept out to sea where waves rolled gently and suddenly he found himself walking upon the water how strange and delightful to walk upon the water and he came upon a nude woman holding a nude baby in her arms and the woman was sinking into the water holding the baby above her head and screaming *help* and he ran over the water to the woman and he reached her just before she went down and he took the baby from her

hands and stood watching the breaking bubbles where the
woman sank and he called *lady* and still no answer yes dive
down there and rescue that woman but he could not take this
baby with him and he stooped and laid the baby tenderly
upon the surface of the water expecting it to sink but it
floated and he leaped into the water and held his breath and
strained his eyes to see through the gloomy volume of water
but there was no woman and he opened his mouth and called
lady and the water bubbled and his chest ached and his arms
were tired but he could not see the woman and he called
again *lady lady* and his feet touched sand at the bottom of
the sea and his chest felt as though it would burst and he
bent his knees and propelled himself upward and water
rushed past him and his head bobbed out and he breathed
deeply and looked around where was the baby the baby was
gone and he rushed over the water looking for the baby calling *where is it* and the empty sky and sea threw back his
voice *where is it* and he began to doubt that he could stand
upon the water and then he was sinking and as he struggled
the water rushed him downward spinning dizzily and he
opened his mouth to call for help and water surged into his
lungs and he choked . . .

He groaned and leaped erect in the dark, his eyes wide.
The images of terror that thronged his brain would not let
him sleep. He rose, made sure that the tools were hitched to
his belt, and groped his way to the coal pile and found the
rectangular gap from which he had taken the bricks. He took
out the crowbar and hacked. Then dread paralyzed him. How
long had he slept? Was it day or night now? He had to be
careful. Someone might hear him if it were day. He hewed
softly for hours at the cement, working silently. Faintly quivering in the air above him was the dim sound of yelling
voices. Crazy people, he muttered. They're still there in that
movie . . .

Having rested, he found the digging much easier. He soon
had a dozen bricks out. His spirits rose. He took out another
brick and his fingers fluttered in space. Good! What lay
ahead of him? Another basement? He made the hole larger,
climbed through, walked over an uneven floor and felt a
metal surface. He lighted a match and saw that he was standing behind a furance in a basement; before him, on the far
side of the room, was a door. He crossed and opened it; it
was full of odds and ends. Daylight spilled from a window
above his head.

Then he was aware of a soft, continuous tapping. What
was it? A clock? No, it was louder than a clock and more

irregular. He placed an old empty box beneath the window, stood upon it, and looked into an areaway. He eased the window up and crawled through; the sound of the tapping came clearly now. He glanced about; he was alone. Then he looked upward at a series of window ledges. The tapping identified itself. That's a typewriter, he said to himself. It seemed to be coming from just above. He grasped the ridges of a rain pipe and lifted himself upward; through a half-inch opening of window he saw a doorknob about three feet away. No, it was not a doorknob; it was a small circular disk made of stainless steel with many fine markings upon it. He held his breath: an eerie white hand, seemingly detached from its arm, touched the metal knob and whirled it, first to the left, then to the right. It's a safe! . . . Suddenly he could see the dial no more; a huge metal door swung slowly toward him and he was looking into a safe filled with green wads of paper money, rows of coins wrapped in brown paper, and glass jars and boxes of various sizes. His heart quickened. Good Lord! The white hand went in and out of the safe, taking wads of bills and cylinders of coins. The hand vanished and he heard the muffled click of the big door as it closed. Only the steel dial was visible now. The typewriter still tapped in his ears, but he could not see it. He blinked, wondering if what he had seen was real. There was more money in that safe than he had seen in all his life.

As he clung to the rain pipe, a daring idea came to him and he pulled the screwdriver from his belt. If the white hand twirled that dial again, he would be able to see how far to the left and right it spun and he would have the combination! His blood tingled. I can scratch the numbers right here, he thought. Holding the pipe with one hand, he made the sharp edge of the screwdriver bite into the brick wall. Yes, he could do it. Now, he was set. Now, he had a reason for staying here in the underground. He waited for a long time, but the white hand did not return. Goddamn! Had he been more alert, he would have counted the twirls and he would have had the combination. He got down and stood in the areaway, sunk in reflection.

How could he get into that room? He climbed back into the basement and saw wooden steps leading upward. Was that the room where the safe stood? Fearing that the dial was now being twirled, he clambered through the window, hoisted himself up the rain pipe, and peered; he saw only the naked gleam of the steel dial. He got down and doubled his fists. Well, he would explore the basement. He returned to the basement room and mounted the steps to the door and squinted through the keyhole; all was dark, but the tapping was still somewhere near, still faint and directionless. He pushed the door in; along one wall of a room was a table piled with radios and electrical equipment. A radio shop, he muttered.

Well, he could rig up a radio in his cave. He found a sack, slid the radio into it, and slung it across his back. Closing the door, he went down the steps and stood again in the basement, disappointed. He had not solved the problem of the steel dial and he was irked. He set the radio on the floor and again hoisted himself through the window and up the rain pipe and squinted; the metal door was swinging shut. Goddamn! He's worked the combination again. If I had been patient, I'd have had it! How could he get into that room? He *had* to get into it. He could jimmy the window, but it would be much better if he could get in without any traces. To the right of him, he calculated, should be the basement of the building that held the safe; therefore, if he dug a hole right *here*, he ought to reach his goal.

He began a quiet scraping; it was hard work, for the bricks were not damp. He eventually got one out and lowered it softly to the floor. He had to be careful; perhaps people were beyond this wall. He extracted a second layer of brick and found still another. He gritted his teeth, ready to quit. I'll dig one more, he resolved. When the next brick came out he felt air blowing into his face. He waited to be challenged, but nothing happened.

He enlarged the hole and pulled himself through and stood in quiet darkness. He scratched a match to flame and saw steps; he mounted and peered through a keyhole: Darkness . . . He strained to hear the typewriter, but there was only silence. Maybe the office had closed? He twisted the knob and swung the door in; a frigid blast made him shiver. In the shadows before him were halves and quarters of hogs and lambs and steers hanging from metal hooks on the low ceiling, red meat encased in folds of cold white fat. Fronting him was frost-coated glass from behind which came indistinguishable sounds. The odor of fresh raw meat sickened him and he backed away. A meat market, he whispered.

He ducked his head, suddenly blinded by light. He narrowed his eyes; the red-white rows of meat were drenched in yellow glare. A man wearing a crimson-spotted jacket came in and took down a bloody meat clever. He eased the door to, holding it ajar just enough to watch the man, hoping that the darkness in which he stood would keep him from being seen. The man took down a hunk of steer and placed it upon a bloody wooden block and bent forward and whacked with the cleaver. The man's face was hard, square, grim; a jet of mustache smudged his upper lip and a glistening cowlick of hair fell over his left eye. Each time he lifted the cleaver and brought it down upon the meat, he let out a short, deep-chested grunt. After he had cut the meat, he wiped blood off the wooden block with a sticky wad of gunny sack and hung the cleaver upon a hook. His face was proud as he placed the chunk of meat in the crook of his elbow and left.

The door slammed and the light went off; once more he stood in shadow. His tension ebbed. From behind the frosted glass he heard the man's voice: "Forty-eight cents a pound, ma'am." He shuddered, feeling that there was something he had to do. But what? He stared fixedly at the cleaver, then he sneezed and was terrified for fear that the man had heard him. But the door did not open. He took down the cleaver and examined the sharp edge smeared with cold blood. Behind the ice-coated glass a cash register rang with a vibrating, musical tinkle.

Absent-mindedly holding the meat cleaver, he rubbed the glass with his thumb and cleared a spot that enabled him to see into the front of the store. The shop was empty, save for the man who was now putting on his hat and coat. Beyond the front window a wan sun shone in the streets; people passed and now and then a fragment of laughter or the whir of a speeding auto came to him. He peered closer and saw on the right counter of the shop a mosquito netting covering pears, grapes, lemons, oranges, bananas, peaches, and plums. His stomach contracted.

The man clicked out the light and he gritted his teeth, muttering, Don't lock the icebox door . . . The man went through the door of the shop and locked it from the outside. Thank God! Now, he would eat some more! He waited, trembling. The sun died and its rays lingered on in the sky, turning the streets to dusk. He opened the door and stepped inside the shop. In reverse letters across the front window was: NICK'S FRUITS AND MEATS. He laughed, picked up a soft ripe yellow pear and bit into it; juice squirted; his mouth ached as his saliva glands reacted to the acid of the fruit. He ate three pears, gobbled six bananas, and made away with several oranges, taking a bite out of their tops and holding them to his lips and squeezing them as he hungrily sucked the juice.

He found a faucet, turned it on, laid the cleaver aside, pursed his lips under the stream until his stomach felt about to burst. He straightened and belched, feeling satisfied for the first time since he had been underground. He sat upon the floor, rolled and lit a cigarette, his bloodshot eyes squinting against the film of drifting smoke. He watched a patch of sky turn red, then purple; night fell and he lit another cigarette, brooding. Some part of him was trying to remember the world he had left, and another part of him did not want to remember it. Sprawling before him in his mind was his wife, Mrs. Wooten for whom he worked, the three policemen who had picked him up . . . He possessed them now more completely than he had ever possessed them when he had lived aboveground. How this had come about he could not say, but he had no desire to go back to them. He laughed, crushed the cigarette, and stood up.

He went to the front door and gazed out. Emotionally he hovered between the world aboveground and the world underground. He longed to go out, but sober judgment urged him to remain here. Then impulsively he pried the lock loose with one swift twist of the crowbar; the door swung outward. Through the twilight he saw a white man and a white woman coming toward him. He held himself tense, waiting for them to pass; but they came directly to the door and confronted him.

"I want to buy a pound of grapes," the woman said.

Terrified, he stepped back into the store. The white man stood to one side and the woman entered.

"Give me a pound of dark ones," the woman said.

The white man came slowly forward, blinking his eyes.

"Where's Nick?" the man asked.

"Were you just closing?" the woman asked.

"Yes, ma'am," he mumbled. For a second he did not breathe, then he mumbled again: "Yes, ma'am."

"I'm sorry," the woman said.

The street lamps came on, lighting the store somewhat. Ought he run? But that would raise an alarm. He moved slowly, dreamily, to a counter and lifted up a bunch of grapes and showed them to the woman.

"Fine," the woman said. "But isn't that more than a pound?"

He did not answer. The man was staring at him intently.

"Put them in a bag for me," the woman said, fumbling with her purse.

"Yes, ma'am."

He saw a pile of paper bags under a narrow ledge; he opened one and put the grapes in.

"Thanks," the woman said, taking the bag and placing a dime in his dark palm.

"Where's Nick?" the man asked again. "At supper?"

"Sir? Yes, sir," he breathed.

They left the store and he stood trembling in the doorway. When they were out of sight, he burst out laughing and crying. A trolley car rolled noisily past and he controlled himself quickly. He flung the dime to the pavement with a gesture of contempt and stepped into the warm night air. A few shy stars trembled above him. The look of things was beautiful, yet he felt a lurking threat. He went to an unattended newsstand and looked at a stack of papers. He saw a headline: HUNT NEGRO FOR MURDER.

He felt that someone had slipped up on him from behind and was stripping off his clothes; he looked about wildly, went quickly back into the store, picked up the meat cleaver where he had left it near the sink, then made his way through the icebox to the basement. He stood for a long time, breathing heavily. They know I didn't do anything, he muttered. But how could he prove it? He had signed a confession. Though innocent, he felt guilty, condemned. He struck a match and held it near the steel blade, fascinated and repelled by the dried blotches of blood. Then his fingers gripped the handle of the cleaver with all the strength of his body, he wanted to fling the cleaver from him, but he could not. The match flame wavered and fled; he struggled through the hole and put the cleaver in the sack with the radio. He was determined to keep it, for what purpose he did not know.

He was about to leave when he remembered the safe. Where was it? He wanted to give up, but felt that he ought to make one more try. Opposite the last hole he had dug, he tunneled again, plying the crowbar. Once he was so exhausted that he lay on the concrete floor and panted. Finally he made another hole. He wriggled through and his nostrils filled with the fresh smell of coal. He struck a match; yes, the usual steps led upward. He tiptoed to a door and eased it open. A fair-haired white girl stood in front of a steel cabinet, her blue eyes wide upon him. She turned chalky and gave a high-pitched scream. He bounded down the steps and raced to his hole and clambered through, replacing the bricks with nervous haste. He paused, hearing loud voices.

"What's the matter, Alice?"

"A man . . ."

"What man? Where?"

"A man was at that door . . ."

"Oh nonsense!"

"He was looking at me through the door!"

"Aw, you're dreaming."

"I *did* see a man!"

The girl was crying now.

"There's nobody here."

Another man's voice sounded.

"What is it, Bob?"

"Alice says she saw a man in here, in that door!"

"Let's take a look."

He waited, poised for flight. Footsteps descended the stairs.

"There's nobody down here."

"The window's locked."

"And there's no door."

"You ought to fire that dame."

"Oh, I don't know. Women are that way."

"She's too hysterical."

The men laughed. Footsteps sounded again on the stairs. A door slammed. He sighed, relieved that he had escaped. But he had not done what he had set out to do; his glimpse of the room had been too brief to determine if the safe was there. He had to know. Boldly he groped through the hole once more; he reached the steps and pulled off his shoes and tiptoed up and peered through the keyhole. His head accidentally touched the door and it swung silently in a fraction of an inch; he saw the girl bent over the cabinet, her back to him. Beyond her was the safe. He crept back down the steps, thinking exultingly: I found it!

Now he had to get the combination. Even if the window in the areaway was locked and bolted, he could gain entrance when the office closed. He scoured through the hole he had dug and stood again in the basement where he had left the radio and the clever. Again he crawled out of the window and lifted himself up the rain pipe and peered. The steel dial showed lonely and bright, reflecting the yellow glow of an unseen light. Resigned to a long wait, he sat and leaned against a wall. From far off came the faint sounds of life aboveground; once he looked with a baffled expression at the dark sky. Frequently he rose and climbed the pipe to see the white hand spin the dial, but nothing happened. He bit his lip with impatience. It was not the money that was luring him, but the mere fact that he could get it with impunity. Was the hand now twirling the dial? He rose and looked, but the white hand was not in sight.

Perhaps it would be better to watch continuously? Yes; he clung to the pipe and watched the dial until his eyes thickened with tears. Exhausted, he stood again in the areaway. He heard a door being shut and he clawed up the pipe and looked. He jerked tense as a vague figure passed in front of him. He stared unblinkingly, hugging the pipe with one hand and holding the screwdriver with the other, ready to etch the combination upon the wall. His ears caught: *Dong . . . Dong . . . Dong . . . Dong . . . Dong . . . Dong . . . Dong . . .* Seven o'clock, he whispered Maybe they were closing now? What kind of a store would be open as late as this? he wondered. Did anyone live in the rear? Was there a night watchman? Perhaps the safe was *already* locked for the night! Goddamn! While he had been eating in that shop, they had locked up everything . . . Then, just as he was about to give up, the white hand touched the dial and turned it once to the right and stopped at six. With quivering fingers, he etched 1—R—6 upon the brick wall with the tip of the screwdriver. The hand twirled the dial twice to the left and stopped at two, and he engraved 2—L—2 upon the wall. The dial was spun four times to the right and stopped at six again; he wrote 4—R—6. The dial rotated three times to the left and was centered straight up and down; he wrote 3—L—0. The door swung open and again he saw the piles of green money and the rows of wrapped coins. I got it, he said grimly.

Then he was stone still, astonished. There were two hands now. A right hand lifted a wad of green bills and deftly slipped it up the sleeve of a left arm. The hands trembled; again the right hand slipped a packet of bills up the left sleeve. He's stealing, he said to himself. He grew indignant, as if the money belonged to him. Though *he* had planned to steal the money, he despised and pitied the man. He felt that his stealing the money and the man's stealing were two entirely different things. He wanted to steal the money merely for the sensation involved in getting it, and he had no intention whatever of spending a penny of it; but he knew that the man who was now stealing it was going to spend it, perhaps for pleasure. The huge steel door closed with a soft click.

Though angry, he was somewhat satisfied. The office would close soon. I'll clean the place out, he mused. He imagined the entire office staff cringing with fear; the police would question everyone for a crime they had not committed, just as they had questioned him. And they would have no idea of how the money had been stolen until they discovered the holes, he had tunneled in the walls of the basements. He lowered himself and laughed mischievously, with the abandoned glee of an adolescent.

He flattened himself against the wall as the window above him closed with rasping sound. He looked; somebody was bolting the window securely with a metal screen. That won't help you, he snickered to himself. He clung to the rain pipe until the yellow light in the office went out. He went back into the basement, picked up the sack containing the radio and cleaver, and crawled through the two holes he had dug and groped his way into the basement of the building that held the safe. He moved in slow motion, breathing softly. Be careful now, he told himself. There might be a night watch-man . . . In his memory was the combination written in bold white characters as upon a blackboard. Eel-like he squeezed through the last hole and crept up the steps and put his hand on the knob and pushed the door in about three inches. Then his courage ebbed; his imagination wove dangers for him.

Perhaps the night watchman was waiting in there, ready to shoot. He dangled his cap on a forefinger and poked it past the jamb of the door. If anyone fired, they would hit his cap; but nothing happened. He widened the door, holding the crowbar high above his head, ready to beat off an assailant. He stood like that for five minutes; the rumble of a streetcar brought him to himself. He entered the room. Moonlight floated in from a wide window. He confronted the safe, then checked himself. Better take a look around first . . . He stepped about and found a closed door. Was the night watch-man in there? He opened it and saw a washbowl, a faucet, and a commode. To the left was still another door that opened into a huge dark room that seemed empty; on the far side of that room he made out the shadow of still another door. Nobody's here, he told himself.

He turned back to the safe and fingered the dial; it spun with ease. He laughed and twirled it just for fun. Get to work, he told himself. He turned the dial to the figures he saw on the blackboard of his memory; it was so easy that he felt that the safe had not been locked at all. The heavy door eased loose and he caught hold of the handle and pulled hard, but the door swung open with a slow momentum of its own. Breathless, he gaped at wads of green bills, rows of wrapped coins, curious glass jars full of white pellets, and many oblong green metal boxes. He glanced guiltily over his shoulder; it seemed impossible that someone should not call to him to stop.

They'll be surprised in the morning, he thought. He opened the top of the sack and lifted a wad of compactly tied bills; the money was crisp and new. He admired the smooth, clean-cut edges. The fellows in Washington sure know how to make this stuff, he mused. He rubbed the money with his fin-gers, as though expecting it to reveal hidden qualities. He lifted the wad to his nose and smelled the fresh odor of ink.

Just like any other paper, he mumbled. He dropped the wad into the sack and picked up another. Holding the bag, he thought and laughed.

There was in him no sense of possessiveness; he was in-'trigued with the form and color of the money, with the manifold reactions which he knew that men aboveground held toward it. The sack was one-third full when it occurred to him to examine the denominations of the bills; without realizing it, he had put many wads of one-dollar bills into the sack, Aw, nuts, he said in disgust. Take the big ones . . . He dumped the one-dollar bills onto the floor and swept all the hundred-dollar bills he could find into the sack, then he raked in rolls of coins with crooked fingers.

He walked to a desk upon which sat a typewriter, the same machine which the blond girl had used. He was fascinated by it; never in his life had he used one of them. It was a queer instrument of business, something beyond the rim of his life. Whenever he had been in an office where a girl was typing, he had almost always spoken in whispers. Remembering vaguely what he had seen others do, he inserted a sheet of paper into the machine; it went in lopsided and he did not know how to straighten it. Spelling in a soft diffident voice, he pecked out his name on the keys: *freddaniels.* He looked at it and laughed. He would learn to type correctly one of these days.

Yes, he would take the typewriter too. He lifted the machine and placed it atop the bulk of money in the sack. He did not feel that he was stealing, for the cleaver, the radio, the money, and the typewriter were all on the same level of value, all meant the same thing to him. They were the serious toys of the men who lived in the dead world of sunshine and rain he had left, the world that had condemned him, branded him guilty.

But what kind of a place is this? He wondered. What was in that dark room to his rear? He felt for his matches and found that he had only one left. He leaned the sack against the safe and groped forward into the room, encountering smooth, metallic objects that felt like machines. Baffled, he touched a wall and tried vainly to locate an electric switch. Well, he *had* to strike his last match. He knelt and struck it, cupping the flame near the floor with his palms. The place seemed to be a factory, with benches and tables. There were bulbs with green shades spaced about the tables; he turned on a light and twisted it low so that the glare was limited. There were stools at the benches and he concluded that men worked here at some trade. He wandered and found a few half-used folders of matches. If only he could find more cigarettes! But there were none.

But what kind of a place was this? On a bench he saw a pad of paper captioned: PEER'S—MANUFACTURING JEWELERS. His lips formed an "O," then he snapped off the light and ran back to the safe and lifted one of the glass jars and stared at the tiny white pellets. Gingerly he picked up one and found that it was wrapped in tissue paper. He peeled the paper and saw a glittering stone that looked like glass, glinting white and blue sparks. Diamonds, he breathed.

Roughly he tore the paper from the pellets and soon his palm quivered with precious fire. Trembling, he took all four glass jars from the safe and put them into the sack. He grabbed one of the metal boxes, shook it, and heard a tinny rattle. He pried off the lid with the screwdriver. Rings! Hundreds of them . . . Were they worth anything? He scooped up a handful and jets of fire shot fitfully from the stones. These are diamonds too, he said. He pried open another box. Watches! A chorus of soft, metallic ticking filled his ears. For a moment he could not move, then he dumped all the boxes into the sack.

He shut the safe door, then stood looking around, anxious not to overlook anything. Oh! He had seen a door in the room where the machines were. What was in there? More valuables? He re-entered the room, crossed the floor, and stood undecided before the door. He finally caught hold of the knob and pushed the door in; the room beyond was dark. He advanced cautiously inside and ran his fingers along the wall for the usual switch, then he was stark still. *Something had moved in the room!* What was it? Ought he to creep out, taking the rings and diamonds and money? Why risk what he already had? He waited and the ensuing silence gave him confidence to explore further. Dare he strike a match? Would not a match flame make him a good target? He tensed again as he heard a faint sigh; he was now convinced that there was something alive near him, something that lived and breathed. On tiptoe he felt slowly along the wall, hoping that he would not collide with anything. Luck was with him; he found the light switch.

No; don't turn the light on . . . Then suddenly he realized that he did not know in what direction the door was. Goddamn! He had to turn the light on or strike a match. He fingered the switch for a long time, then thought of an idea. He knelt upon the floor, reached his arm up to the switch and flicked the button, hoping that if anyone shot, the bullet would go above his head. The moment the light came on he narrowed his eyes to see quickly. He sucked in his breath and his body gave a violent twitch and was still. In front of him, so close that it made him want to bound up and scream, was a human face.

He was afraid to move lest he touch the man. If the man had opened his eyes at that moment, there was no telling what he might have done. The man—long and rawboned—was stretched out on his back upon a little cot, sleeping in his clothes, his head cushioned by a dirty pillow; his face, clouded by a dark stubble of beard, looked straight up to the ceiling. The man sighed, and he grew tense to defend himself; the man mumbled and turned his face away from the light. I've got to turn off that light, he thought. Just as he was about to rise, he saw a gun and cartridge belt on the floor at the man's side. Yes, he would take the gun and cartridge belt, not to use them, but just to keep them, as one takes a memento from a country fair. He picked them up and was about to click off the light when his eyes fell upon a photograph perched upon a chair near the man's head; it was the picture of a woman, smiling, shown against a background of open fields; at the woman's side were two young children, a boy and a girl. He smiled indulgently; he could send a bullet into that man's brain and time would be over for him . . .

He clicked off the light and crept silently back into the room where the safe stood; he fastened the cartridge belt about him and adjusted the holster at his right hip. He strutted about the room on tiptoe, lolling his head nonchalantly, then paused abruptly, pulled the gun, and pointed it with grim face toward an imaginary foe. "Boom!" he whispered fiercely. Then he bent forward with silent laughter. That's just like they do it in the movies, he said.

He contemplated his loot for a long time, then got a towel from the washroom and tied the sack securely. When he looked up he was momentarily frightened by his shadow looming on the wall before him. He lifted the sack, dragged it down the basement steps, lugged it across the basement, gasping for breath. After he had struggled through the hole, he clumsily replaced the bricks, then tussled with the sack until he got it to the cave. He stood in the dark, wet with sweat, brooding about the diamonds, the rings, the watches, the money; he remembered the singing in the church, the people yelling in the movie, the dead baby, the nude man stretched out upon the white table . . . He saw these items hovering before his eyes and felt that some dim meaning linked them together, that some magical relationship made them kin. He stared with vacant eyes, convinced that all of these images, with their tongueless reality, were striving to tell him something . . .

Later, seeing with his fingers, he untied the sack and set each item neatly upon the dirt floor. Exploring, he took the bulb, the socket, and the wire out of the tool chest; he was elated to find a double socket at one end of the wire. He crammed the stuff into his pockets and hoisted himself upon the rusty pipes and squinted into the church; it was dim and empty. Somewhere in this wall were live electric wires; but where? He lowered himself, groped and tapped the wall with the butt of the screwdriver, listening vainly for hollow sounds. I'll just take a chance and dig, he said.

For an hour he tried to dislodge a brick, and when he struck a match, he found that he had dug a depth of only an inch! No use in digging here, he sighed. By the flickering light of a match, he looked upward, then lowered his eyes, only to glance up again, startled. Directly above his head, beyond the pipes, was a wealth of electric wiring. I'll be damned, he snickered.

He got an old dull knife from the chest and, seeing again with his fingers, separated the two strands of wire and cut away the insulation. Twice he received a slight shock. He scraped the wiring clean and managed to join the two twin ends, then screwed in the bulb. The sudden illumination blinded him and he shut his lids to kill the pain in his eyeballs. I've got that much done, he thought jubilantly.

He placed the bulb on the dirt floor and the light cast a blatant glare on the bleak clay walls. Next he plugged one end of the wire that dangled from the radio into the light socket and bent down and switched on the button; almost at once there was the harsh sound of static, but no words or music. Why won't it work? he wondered. Had he damaged the mechanism in any way? Maybe it needed grounding? Yes . . . He rummaged in the tool chest and found another length of wire, fastened it to the ground of the radio, and then tied the opposite end to a pipe. Rising and growing distinct, a slow strain of music entranced him with its measured sound. He sat upon the chest, deliriously happy.

Later he searched again in the chest and found a half-gallon can of glue; he opened it and smelled a sharp odor. Then he recalled that he had not even looked at the money. He took a wad of green bills and weighed it in his palm, then broke the seal and held one of the bills up to the light and studied it closely. *The United States of America will pay to the bearer on demand one hundred dollars,* he read in slow speech; then: *This note is legal tender for all debts, public*

and private. . . . He broke into a musing laugh, feeling that
he was reading of the doings of people who lived on some
far-off planet. He turned the bill over and saw on the other
side of it a delicately beautiful building gleaming with paint
and set amidst green grass. He had no desire whatever to
count the money; it was what it stood for—the various currents of life swirling aboveground—that captivated him. Next
he opened the rolls of coins and let them slide from their
paper wrappings to the ground; the bright, new gleaming
pennies and nickels and dimes piled high at his feet, a glowing mound of shimmering copper and silver. He sifted them
through his fingers, listening to their tinkle as they struck the
conical heap.

Oh, yes! He had forgotten. He would now write his name
on the typewriter. He inserted a piece of paper and poised his
fingers to write. But what was his name? He stared, trying to
remember. He stood and glared about the dirt cave, his name
on the tip of his lips. But it would not come to him. Why was
he here? Yes, he had been running away from the police. But
why? His mind was blank. He bit his lips and sat again, feeling a vague terror. But why worry? He laughed, then pecked
slowly: *itwasalonghotday*. He was determined to type the sentence without making any mistakes. How did one make capital letters? He experimented and luckily discovered how to
lock the machine for capital letters and then shift it back to
lower case. Next he discovered how to make spaces, then he
wrote neatly and correctly: *It was a long hot day*. Just why
he selected that sentence he did not know; it was merely the
ritual of performing the thing that appealed to him. He took
the sheet out of the machine and looked around with stiff
neck and hard eyes and spoke to an imaginary person:

"Yes, I'll have the contracts ready tomorrow."

He laughed. That's just the way they talk, he said. He grew
weary of the game and pushed the machine aside. His eyes
fell upon the can of glue, and a mischievous idea bloomed in
him, filling him with nervous eagerness. He leaped up and
opened the can of glue, then broke the seals on all the wads
of money. I'm going to have some wallpaper, he said with a
luxurious, physical laugh that made him bend at the knees.
He took the towel with which he had tied the sack and balled
it into a swab and dipped it into the can of glue and dabbed
glue onto the wall; then he pasted one green bill by the side
of another. He stepped back and cocked his head. Jesus!
That's funny . . . He slapped his thighs and guffawed. He
had triumphed over the world aboveground! He was free! If

only people could see this! He wanted to run from this cave and yell his discovery to the world.

He swabbed all the dirt walls of the cave and pasted them with green bills; when he had finished the walls blazed with a yellow-green fire. Yes, this room would be his hide-out; between him and the world that had branded him guilty would stand this mocking symbol. He had not stolen the money; he had simply picked it up, just as a man would pick up firewood in a forest. And that was how the world aboveground now seemed to him, a wild forest filled with death.

The walls of money finally palled on him and he looked about for new interests to feed his emotions. The cleaver! He drove a nail into the wall and hung the bloody cleaver upon it. Still another idea welled up. He pried open the metal boxes and lined them side by side on the dirt floor. He grinned at the gold and fire. From one box he lifted up a fistful of ticking gold watches and dangled them by their gleaming chains. He stared with an idle smile, then began to wind them up; he did not attempt to set them at any given hour, for there was no time for him now. He took a fistful of nails and drove them into the papered walls and hung the watches upon them, letting them swing down by their glittering chains, trembling and ticking busily against the backdrop of green with the lemon sheen of the electric light shining upon the metal watch casings, converting the golden disks into blobs of liquid yellow. Hardly had he hung up the last watch than the idea extended itself; he took more nails from the chest and drove them into the green paper and took the boxes of rings and went from nail to nail and hung up the golden bands. The blue and white sparks from the stones filled the cave with brittle laughter, as though enjoying his hilarious secret. People certainly can do some funny things, he said to himself.

He sat upon the tool chest, alternately laughing and shaking his head soberly. Hours later he became conscious of the gun sagging at his hip and he pulled it from the holster. He had seen men fire guns in movies, but somehow his life had never led him into contact with firearms. A desire to feel the sensation others felt in firing came over him. But someone might hear . . . Well, what if they did? They would not know where the shot had come from. Not in their wildest notions would they think that it had come from under the streets! He tightened his finger on the trigger; there was a deafening report and it seemed that the entire underground had caved in upon his eardrums; and in the same instant there flashed an orange-blue spurt of flame that died quickly but lingered on as a vivid after-image. He smelled the acrid stench of burnt powder filling his lungs and he dropped the gun abruptly.

The intensity of his feelings died and he hung the gun and cartridge belt upon the wall. Next he lifted the jars of diamonds and turned them bottom upward, dumping the white pellets upon the ground. One by one he picked them up and peeled the tissue paper from them and piled them in a neat heap. He wiped his sweaty hands on his trousers, lit a cigarette, and commenced playing another game. He imagined that he was a rich man who lived aboveground in the obscene sunshine and he was strolling through a park of a summer morning, smiling, nodding to his neighbors, sucking an after-breakfast cigar. Many times he crossed the floor of the cave, avoiding the diamonds with his feet, yet subtly gauging his footsteps so that his shoes, wet with sewer slime, would strike the diamonds at some undetermined moment. After twenty minutes of sauntering, his right foot smashed into the heap and diamonds lay scattered in all directions, glinting with a million tiny chuckles of icy laughter. Oh, shucks, he mumbled in mock regret, intrigued by the damage he had wrought. He continued walking, ignoring the brittle fire. He felt that he had a glorious victory locked in his heart.

He stooped and flung the diamonds more evenly over the floor and they showered rich sparks, collaborating with him. He went over the floor and trampled the stones just deep enough for them to be faintly visible, as though they were set delicately in the prongs of a thousand rings. A ghostly light bathed the cave. He sat on the chest and frowned. Maybe *any*thing's right, he mumbled. Yes, if the world as men had made it was right, then anything else was right, any act a man took to satisfy himself, murder, theft, torture.

He straightened with a start. What was happening to him? He was drawn to these crazy thoughts, yet they made him feel vaguely guilty. He would stretch out upon the ground, then get up; he would want to crawl again through the holes he had dug, but would restrain himself; he would think of going again up into the streets, but fear would hold him still. He stood in the middle of the cave, surrounded by green walls and a laughing floor, trembling. He was going to do something, but what? Yes, he was afraid of himself, afraid of doing some nameless thing.

To control himself, he turned on the radio. A melancholy piece of music rose. Brooding over the diamonds on the floor was like looking up into a sky full of restless stars; then the illusion turned into its opposite: he was high up in the air looking down at the twinkling lights of a sprawling city. The music ended and a man recited news events. In the same attitude in which he had contemplated the city, so now, as he heard the cultivated tone, he looked down upon land and sea as men fought, as cities were razed, as planes scattered death upon open towns, as long lines of trenches wavered and broke. He heard the names of generals and the names of mountains and the names of countries and the names and numbers of divisions that were in action on different battle fronts. He saw black smoke billowing from the stacks of warships as they neared each other over wastes of water and he heard their huge guns thunder as red-hot shells screamed across the surface of night seas. He saw hundreds of planes wheeling and droning in the sky and heard the clatter of machine guns as they fought each other and he saw planes falling in plumes of smoke and blaze of fire. He saw steel tanks rumbling across fields of ripe wheat to meet other tanks and there was a loud clang of steel as numberless tanks collided. He saw troops with fixed bayonets charging in waves against other troops who held fixed bayonets and men groaned as steel ripped into their bodies and they went down to die . . . The voice of the radio faded and he was staring at the diamonds on the floor at his feet.

He shut off the radio, fighting an irrational compulsion to act. He walked aimlessly about the cave, touching the walls with his finger tips. Suddenly he stood still. *What was the matter with him?* Yes, he knew . . . It was these walls; these crazy walls were filling him with a wild urge to climb out into the dark sunshine aboveground. Quickly he doused the light to banish the shouting walls, then sat again upon the tool chest. Yes, he was trapped. His muscles were flexed taut and sweat ran down his face. He knew now that he could not stay here and he could not go out. He lit a cigarette with shaking fingers; the match flame revealed the green-papered walls with militant distinctness; the purple on the gun barrel glinted like a threat; the meat cleaver brooded with its eloquent splotches of blood; the mound of silver and copper smoldered angrily; the diamonds winked at him from the floor; and the gold watches ticked and trembled, crowning time the king of consciousness, defining the limits of living . . . The match blaze died and he bolted from where he stood and collided brutally with the nails upon the walls. The spell was broken. He shuddered, feeling that, in spite of his fear, sooner or later he would go up into that dead sunshine and somehow say something to somebody about all this.

He sat again upon the tool chest. Fatigue weighed upon his

forehead and eyes. Minutes passed and he relaxed. He dozed, but his imagination was alert. He saw himself rising, wading again in the sweeping water of the sewer; he came to a manhole and climbed out and was amazed to discover that he had hoisted himself into a room filled with armed policemen who were watching him intently. He jumped awake in the dark; he had not moved. He sighed, closed his eyes, and slept again; this time his imagination designed a scheme of protection for him. His dreaming made him feel that he was standing in a room watching over his own nude body lying stiff and cold upon a white table. At the far end of the room he saw a crowd of people huddled in a corner, afraid of his body. Though lying dead upon the table, he was standing in some mysterious way at his side, warding off the people, guarding his body, and laughing to himself as he observed the situation. They're scared of me, he thought.

He awakened with a start, leaped to his feet, and stood in the center of the black cave. It was a full minute before he moved again. He hovered between sleeping and waking, unprotected, a prey of wild fears. He could neither see nor hear. One part of him was asleep; his blood coursed slowly and his flesh was numb. On the other hand he was roused to a strange, high pitch of tension. He lifted his fingers to his face, as though about to weep. Gradually his hands lowered and he struck a match, looking about, expecting to see a door through which he could walk to safety: but there was no door, only the green walls and the moving floor. The match flame died and it was dark again.

Five minutes later he was still standing when the thought came to him that he had been asleep. Yes . . . But he was not yet fully awake; he was still queerly blind and deaf. How long had he slept? Where was he? Then suddenly he recalled the green-papered walls of the cave and in the same instant he heard loud singing coming from the church beyond the wall. Yes, they woke me up, he muttered. He hoisted himself and lay atop the bed of pipes and brought his face to the narrow slit. Men and women stood here and there between pews. A song ended and a young black girl tossed back her head and closed her eyes and broke plaintively into another hymn:

Glad, glad, glad, oh, so glad
I got Jesus in my soul . . .

Those few words were all she sang, but what her words did not say, her emotions said as she repeated the lines, varying the mood and tempo, making her tone express meanings

which her conscious mind did not know. Another woman
melted her voice with the girl's, and then an old man's voice
merged with that of the two women. Soon the entire congregation was singing:

Glad, glad, glad, oh, so glad
I got Jesus in my soul ...

They're wrong, he whispered in the lyric darkness. He felt
that their search for a happiness they could never find made
them feel that they had committed some dreadful offense
which they could not remember or understand. He was now
in possession of the feeling that had gripped him when he
had first come into the underground. It came to him in a series of questions: Why was this sense of guilt so seemingly
innate, so easy to come by, to think, to feel, so verily physical? It seemed that when one felt this guilt one was retracing
in one's feelings a faint pattern designed long before; it
seemed that one was always trying to remember a gigantic
shock that had left a haunting impression upon one's body
which one could not forget or shake off, but which had been
forgotten by the conscious mind, creating in one's life a state
of eternal anxiety.

He had to tear himself away from this; he got down from
the pipes. His nerves were so taut that he seemed to feel his
brain pushing through his skull. He felt that he had to do
something, but he could not figure out what it was. Yet he
knew that if he stood here until he made up his mind, he
would never move. He crawled through the hole he had
made in the brick wall and the exertion afforded him respite
from tension. When he entered the basement of the radio
store, he stopped in fear, hearing loud voices.

"Come on, boy! Tell us what you did with the radio!"

"Mister, I didn't steal the radio! I swear!"

He heard a dull thumping sound and he imagined a boy
being struck violently.

"Please, mister!"

"Did you take it to a pawn shop?"

"No, sir! I didn't steal the radio! I got a radio at home,"
the boy's voice pleaded hysterically. "Go to my home and
look!"

There came to his ears the sound of another blow. It was
so funny that he had to clap his hand over his mouth to keep
from laughing out loud. They're beating some poor boy, he
whispered to himself, shaking his head. He felt a sort of distant pity for the boy and wondered if he ought to bring back

the radio and leave it in the basement. No. Perhaps it was a good thing that they were beating the boy; perhaps the beating would bring to the boy's attention, for the first time in his life, the secret of his existence, the guilt that he could never get rid of.

Smiling, he scampered over a coal pile and stood again in the basement of the building where he had stolen the money and jewelry. He lifted himself into the areaway, climbed the rain pipe, and squinted through a two-inch opening of window. The guilty familiarity of what he saw made his muscles tighten. Framed before him in a bright tableau of daylight was the night watchman sitting upon the edge of a chair, stripped to the waist, his head sagging forward, his eyes red and puffy. The watchman's face and shoulders were stippled with red and black welts. Back of the watchman stood the safe, the steel door wide open showing the empty vault. Yes, they think he did it, he mused.

Footsteps sounded in the room and a man in a blue suit passed in front of him, then another, then still another. Policemen, he breathed. Yes, they were trying to make the watchman confess, just as they had once made him confess to a crime he had not done. He stared into the room, trying to recall something. Oh . . . Those were the same policemen who had beaten him, had made him sign that paper when he had been too tired and sick to care. Now, they were doing the same thing to the watchman. His heart pounded as he saw one of the policemen shake a finger into the watchman's face.

"Why don't you admit it's an inside job, Thompson?" the policeman said.

"I've told you all I know," the watchman mumbled through swollen lips.

"But nobody was here but you!" the policeman shouted.

"I was sleeping," the watchman said. "It was wrong, but I was sleeping all that night!"

"Stop telling us that lie!"

"It's the truth!"

"When did you get the combination?"

"I don't know how to open the safe," the watchman said.

He clung to the rain pipe, tense; he wanted to laugh, but he controlled himself. He felt a great sense of power; yes, he could go back to the cave, rip the money off the walls, pick up the diamonds and rings, and bring them here and write a note, telling them where to look for their foolish toys. No . . . What good would that do? It was not worth the effort. The watchman was guilty; although he was not guilty of the crime of which he had been accused, he was guilty, had always been guilty. The only thing that worried him was that the man who had been really stealing was not being accused. But he consoled himself: they'll catch him sometime during his life.

He saw one of the policemen slap the watchman across the mouth.

"Come clean, you bastard!"

"I've told you all I know," the watchman mumbled like a child.

One of the police went to the rear of the watchman's chair and jerked it from under him; the watchman pitched forward upon his face.

"Get up!" a policeman said.

Trembling, the watchman pulled himself up and sat limply again in the chair.

"Now, are you going to talk?"

"I've told you all I know," the watchman gasped.

"Where did you hide the stuff?"

"I didn't take it!"

"Thompson, your brains are in your feet," one of the policemen said. "We're going to string you up and get them back into your skull."

He watched the policemen clamp handcuffs on the watchman's wrists and ankles; then they lifted the watchman and swung him upside-down and hoisted his feet to the edge of a door. The watchman hung, head down, his eyes bulging. They're crazy, he whispered to himself as he clung to the ridges of the pipe.

"You going to talk?" a policeman shouted into the watchman's ear.

He heard the watchman groan.

"We'll let you hang there till you talk, see?"

He saw the watchman close his eyes.

"Let's take 'im down. He passed out," a policeman said.

He grinned as he watched them take the body down and dump it carelessly upon the floor. The policeman took off the handcuffs.

"Let 'im come to. Let's get a smoke," a policeman said.

The three policemen left the scope of his vision. A door slammed. He had an impulse to yell to the watchman that he could escape through the hole in the basement and live with him in the cave. But he wouldn't understand, he told himself. After a moment he saw the watchman rise and stand swaying from weakness. He stumbled across the room to a desk, opened a drawer, and took out a gun. He's going to kill himself, he thought, intent, eager, detached, yearning to see the end of the man's actions. As the watchman stared vaguely about he lifted the gun to his temple; he stood like that for some minutes, biting his lips until a line of blood etched its way down a corner of his chin. No, he oughtn't do that, he said to himself in a mood of pity.

"Don't!" he half whispered and half yelled.

The watchman looked wildly about; he had heard him. But it did not help; there was a loud report and the watchman's head jerked violently and he fell like a log and lay prone, the gun clattering over the floor.

The three policemen came running into the room with drawn guns. One of the policemen knelt and rolled the watchman's body over and stared at a ragged, scarlet hole in the temple.

"Our hunch was right," the kneeling policeman said. "He was guilty, all right."

"Well, this ends the case," another policeman said

"He knew he was licked," the third one said with grim satisfaction.

He eased down the rain pipe, crawled back through the holes he had made, and went back into his cave. A fever burned in his bones. He had to act, yet he was afraid. His eyes stared in the darkness as though propped open by invisible hands, as though they had become lidless. His muscles were rigid and he stood for what seemed to him a thousand years.

When he moved again his actions were informed with precision, his muscular system reinforced from a reservoir of energy. He crawled through the hole of earth, dropped into the gray sewer current, and sloshed ahead. When his right foot went forward at a street intersection, he fell backward and shot down into water. In a spasm of terror his right hand grabbed the concrete ledge of a down-curve and he felt the streaking water tugging violently at his body. The current reached his neck and for a moment he was still. He knew that if he moved clumsily he would be sucked under. He held onto the ledge with both hands and slowly pulled himself up. He sighed, standing once more in the sweeping water, thankful that he had missed death.

He waded on through sludge, moving with care, until he came to a web of light sifting down from a manhole cover. He saw steel hooks running up the side of the sewer wall; he caught hold and lifted himself and put his shoulder to the cover and moved it an inch. A crash of sound came to him as he looked into a hot glare of sunshine through which blurred shapes moved. Fear scalded him and he dropped back into the pallid current and stood paralyzed in the shadows. A heavy car rumbled past overhead, jarring the pavement, warning him to stay in his world of dark light, knocking the cover back into place with an imperious clang.

He did not know how much fear he felt, for fear claimed him completely; yet it was not a fear of the police or of people, but a cold dread at the thought of the actions he knew he would perform if he went out into that cruel sunshine. His mind said no; his body said yes; and his mind could not understand his feelings. A low whine broke from him and he was in the act of uncoiling. He climbed upward and heard the faint honking of auto horns. Like a frantic cat clutching a rag, he clung to the steel prongs and heaved his shoulder against the cover and pushed it off halfway. For a split second his eyes were drowned in the terror of yellow light and he was in a deeper darkness than he had ever known in the underground.

Partly out of the hole, he blinked, regaining enough sight to make out meaningful forms. An odd thing was happening: No one was rushing forward to challenge him. He had imagined the moment of his emergence as a desperate tussle with men who wanted to cart him off to be killed; instead, life froze about him as the traffic stopped. He pushed the cover aside, stood, swaying in a world so fragile that he expected it to collapse and drop him into some deep void. But nobody seemed to pay him heed. The cars were now swerving to shun him and the gaping hole.

"Why in hell don't you put up a red light, dummy?" a raucous voice yelled.

He understood; they thought that he was a sewer workman. He walked toward the sidewalk, weaving unsteadily through the moving traffic.

"Look where you're going, nigger!"

"That's right! Stay there and get killed!"

"You blind, you bastard?"

"Go home and sleep your drunk off!"

A policeman stood at the curb, looking in the opposite direction. When he passed the policeman, he feared that he would be grabbed, but nothing happened. Where was he? Was this real? He wanted to look about to get his bearings, but felt that something awful would happen to him if he did. He wandered into a spacious doorway of a store that sold men's clothing and saw his reflection in a long mirror: his cheekbones protruded from a hairy black face; his greasy cap

was perched askew upon his head and his eyes were red and
glassy. His shirt and trousers were caked with mud and hung
loosely. His hands were gummed with a black stickness. He
threw back his head and laughed so loudly·that passers-by
stopped and stared.

He ambled on down the sidewalk, not having the merest
notion of where he was going. Yet, sleeping within him, was
the drive to go somewhere and say something to somebody.
Half an hour later his ears caught the sound of spirited singing.

The Lamb, the Lamb, the Lamb
  I hear thy voice a-calling
The Lamb, the Lamb, the Lamb
  I feel thy grace a-falling

A church! he exclaimed. He broke into a run and came to
brick steps leading downward to a subbasement. This is it!
The church into which he had peered. Yes, he was going in
and tell them. What? He did not know; but, once face to face
with them, he would think of what to say. Must be Sunday,
he mused. He ran down the steps and jerked the door open;
the church was crowded and a deluge of song swept over
him.

The Lamb, the Lamb, the Lamb
  Tell me again your story
The Lamb, the Lamb, the Lamb
  Flood my soul with your glory

He stared at the singing faces with a trembling smile.
"Say!" he shouted.
Many turned to look at him, but the song rolled on. His
arm was jerked violently.
"I'm sorry, Brother, but you can't do that in here," a man
said.
"But, mister!"
"You can't act rowdy in God's house," the man said.
"He's filthy," another man said.
"But I want to tell 'em," he said loudly.
"He stinks," someone muttered.
The song had stopped, but at once another one began.

Oh, wondrous sight upon the cross
  Vision sweet and divine
Oh, wondrous sight upon the cross
  Full of such love sublime

He attempted to twist away, but other hands grabbed him and rushed him into the doorway.

"Let me alone!" he screamed, struggling.

"Get out!"

"He's drunk," somebody said. "He ought to be ashamed!"

"He acts crazy!"

He felt that he was failing and he grew frantic.

"But, mister, let me tell—"

"Get away from this door, or I'll call the police!"

He stared, his trembling smile fading in a sense of wonderment.

"The police," he repeated vacantly.

"Now, get!"

He was pushed toward the brick steps and the door banged shut. The waves of song came.

Oh, wondrous sight, wondrous sight
  Lift my heavy heart above
Oh, wondrous sight, wondrous sight
  Fill my weary soul with love

He was smiling again now. Yes, the police . . . That was it! Why had he not thought of it before? The idea had been deep down in him, and only now did it assume supreme importance. He looked up and saw a street sign: COURT STREET—HARTSDALE AVENUE. He turned and walked northward, his mind filled with the image of the police station. Yes, that was where they had beaten him, accused him, and had made him sign a confession of his guilt. He would go there and clear up everything, make a statement. What statement? He did not know. He was the statement, and since it was all so clear to him, surely he would be able to make it clear to others.

He came to the corner of Hartsdale Avenue and turned westward. Yeah, there's the station. . . . A policeman came down the steps and walked past him without a glance. He mounted the stone steps and went through the door, paused; he was in a hallway where several policemen were standing, talking, smoking. One turned to him.

"What do you want, boy?"

He looked at the policeman and laughed.

"What in hell are you laughing about?" the policeman asked.

He stopped laughing and stared. His whole being was full of what he wanted to say to them, but he could not say it.

"Are you looking for the Desk Sergeant?"

"Yes, sir," he said quickly; then: "Oh, no, sir."

"Well, make up your mind, now."

Four policemen grouped themselves around him.

"I'm looking for the men," he said.

"What men?"

Peculiarly, at that moment he could not remember the names of the policemen; he recalled their beating him, the confession he had signed, and how he had run away from them. He saw the cave next to the church, the money on the walls, the guns, the rings, the cleaver, the watches, and the diamonds on the floor.

"They brought me here," he began.

"When?"

His mind flew back over the blur of the time lived in the underground blackness. He had no idea of how much time had elapsed, but the intensity of what had happened to him told him that it could not have transpired in a short space of time, yet his mind told him that time must have been brief.

"It was a long time ago." He spoke like a child relating a dimly remembered dream. "It was a long time," he repeated, following the promptings of his emotions. "They beat me . . . I was scared . . . I ran away."

A policeman raised a finger to his temple and made a derisive circle.

"Nuts," the policeman said.

"Do you know what place this is, boy?"

"Yes, sir. The police station," he answered sturdily, almost proudly.

"Well, who do you want to see?"

"The men," he said again, feeling that surely they knew the men. "You know the men," he said in a hurt tone.

"What's your name?"

He opened his lips to answer and no words came. He had forgotten. But what did it matter if he had? It was not important.

"Where do you live?"

Where did he live? It had been so long ago since he had lived up here in this strange world that he felt it was foolish even to try to remember. Then for a moment the old mood that had dominated him in the underground surged back. He leaned forward and spoke eagerly.

"They said I killed the woman."

"What woman?" a policeman asked.

"And I signed a paper that said I was guilty," he went on, ignoring their questions. "Then I ran off . . ."

"Did you run off from an institution?"

"No, sir," he said, blinking and shaking his head. "I came

from under the ground. I pushed off the manhole cover and climbed out . . ."

"All right, now," a policeman said, placing an arm about his shoulder. "We'll send you to the psycho and you'll be taken care of."

"Maybe he's a Fifth Columnist!" a policeman shouted.

There was laughter and, despite his anxiety, he joined in. But the laughter lasted so long that it irked him.

"I got to find those men," he protested mildly.

"Say, boy, what have you been drinking?"

"Water," he said. "I got some water in a basement."

"Were the men you ran away from dressed in white, boy?"

"No, sir," he said brightly. "They were men like you."

An elderly policeman caught hold of his arm.

"Try and think hard. Where did they pick you up?"

He knitted his brows in an effort to remember, but he was blank inside. The policeman stood before him demanding logical answers and he could no longer think with his mind; he thought with his feelings and no words came.

"I was guilty," he said. "Oh, no, sir. I wasn't then, I mean, mister!"

"Aw, talk sense. Now, where did they pick you up?"

He felt challenged and his mind began reconstructing events in reverse; his feelings ranged back over the long hours and he saw the cave, the sewer, the bloody room where it was said that a woman had been killed.

"Oh, yes, sir," he said, smiling. "I was coming from Mrs. Wooten's."

"Who is she?"

"I work for her."

"Where does she live?"

"Next door to Mrs. Peabody, the woman who was killed."

The policemen were very quiet now, looking at him intently.

"What do you know about Mrs. Peabody's death, boy?"

"Nothing, sir. But they said I killed her. But it doesn't make any difference. I'm guilty!"

"What are you talking about, boy?"

His smile faded and he was possessed with memories of the underground; he saw the cave next to the church and his lips moved to speak. But how could he say it? The distance between what he felt and what these men meant was vast. Something told him, as he stood there looking into their faces, that he would never be able to tell them, that they would never believe him even if he told them.

"All the people I saw was guilty," he began slowly.

"Aw, nuts," a policemen muttered.

"Say," another policeman said, "that Peabody woman was killed over on Winewood. That's Number Ten's beat."

"Where's Number Ten?" a policeman asked.

"Upstairs in the swing room," someone answered.

"Take this boy up, Sam," a policeman ordered.

"O.K. Come along, boy."

An elderly policeman caught hold of his arm and led him up a flight of wooden stairs, down a long hall, and to a door.

"Squad Ten!" the policeman called through the door.

"What?" a gruff voice answered.

"Someone to see you!"

"About what?"

The old policeman pushed the door in and then shoved him into the room.

He stared, his lips open, his heart barely beating. Before him were the three policemen who had picked him up and had beaten him to extract the confession. They were seated about a small table, playing cards. The air was blue with smoke and sunshine poured through a high window, lighting up fantastic smoke shapes. He saw one of the policemen look up; the policeman's face was tired and a cigarette dropped limply from one corner of his mouth and both of his fat, puffy eyes were squinting and his hands gripped his cards.

"Lawson!" the man exclaimed.

The moment the man's name sounded he remembered the names of all of them: Lawson, Murphy, and Johnson. How simple it was. He waited, smiling, wondering how they would react when they knew that he had come back.

"Looking for me?" the man who had been called Lawson mumbled, sorting his cards. "For what?"

So far only Murphy, the red-headed one, had recognized him.

"Don't you-all remember me?" he blurted, running to the table.

All three of the policemen were looking at him now. Lawson, who seemed the leader, jumped to his feet.

"Where in hell have you been?"

"Do you know 'im, Lawson?" the old policeman asked.

"Huh?" Lawson frowned. "Oh, yes. I'll handle 'im." The old policeman left the room and Lawson crossed to the door and turned the key in the lock. "Come here, boy," he ordered in a cold tone.

He did not move: he looked from face to face. Yes, he would tell them about his cave.

"He looks batty to me," Johnson said, the one who had not spoken before.

"Why in hell did you come back here?" Lawson said.

"I—I just didn't want to run away no more," he said. "I'm all right, now." He paused; the men's attitude puzzled him.

"You've been hiding, huh?" Lawson asked in a tone that denoted that he had not heard his previous words. "You told us you were sick, and when we left you in the room, you jumped out of the window and ran away."

Panic filled him. Yes, they were indifferent to what he would say! They were waiting for him to speak and they would laugh at him. He had to rescue himself from this bog; he had to force the reality of himself upon them.

"Mister, I took a sackful of money and pasted it on the walls . . ." he began.

"I'll be damned," Lawson said.

"Listen," said Murphy, "let me tell you something for your own good. We don't want you, see? You're free, free as air. Now go home and forget it. It was all a mistake. We caught the guy who did the Peabody job. He wasn't colored at all. He was an Eyetalian."

"Shut up!" Lawson yelled. "Have you no sense!"

"But I want to tell 'im," Murphy said.

"We can't let this crazy fool go," Lawson exploded. "He acts nuts, but this may be a stunt . . ."

"I was down in the basement," he began in a childlike tone as though repeating a lesson learned by heart; "and I went into a movie . . ." His voice failed. He was getting ahead of his story. First, he ought to tell them about the singing in the church, but what words could he use? He looked at them appealingly. "I went into a shop and took a sackful of money and diamonds and watches and rings . . . I didn't steal 'em; I'll give 'em all back. I just took 'em to play with . . ." He paused, stunned by their disbelieving eyes.

Lawson lit a cigarette and looked at him coldly.

"What did you do with the money?" he asked in a quiet, waiting voice.

"I pasted the hundred-dollar bills on the walls."

"What walls?" Lawson asked.

"The walls of the dirt room," he said, smiling, "the room next to the church. I hung up the rings and the watches and I stamped the diamonds into the dirt . . ." He saw that they were not understanding what he was saying. He grew frantic to make them believe, his voice tumbled on eagerly. "I saw a dead baby and a dead man . . ."

"Aw, you're nuts," Lawson snarled, shoving him into a chair.

"But, mister . . ."

"Johnson, where's the paper he signed?" Lawson asked.

"What paper?"

"The confession, fool!"

Johnson pulled out his billfold and extracted a crumpled piece of paper.

"Yes, sir, mister," he said, stretching forth his hand. "That's the paper I signed . . ."

Lawson slapped him and he would have toppled had his chair not struck a wall behind him. Lawson scratched a match and held the paper over the flame; the confession burned down to Lawson's fingertips.

He stared, thunderstruck; the sun of the underground was fleeing and the terrible darkness of the day stood before him. They did not believe him, but he *had* to make them believe him!

"But, mister . . ."

"It's going to be all right, boy," Lawson said with a quiet, soothing laugh. "I've burned your confession, see? You didn't sign anything." Lawson came close to him with the black ashes cupped in his palm. "You don't remember a thing about this, do you?"

"Don't you-all be scared of me," he pleaded, sensing their uneasiness. "I'll sign another paper, if you want me to. I'll show you the cave."

"What's your game, boy?" Lawson asked suddenly.

"What are you trying to find out?" Johnson asked.

"Who sent you here?" Murphy demanded.

"Nobody sent me, mister," he said. "I just want to show you the room . . ."

"Aw, he's plumb bats," Murphy said. "Let's ship 'im to the psycho."

"No," Lawson said. "He's playing a game and I wish to God I knew what it was."

There flashed through his mind a definite way to make them believe him; he rose from the chair with nervous excitement.

"Wister, I saw the night watchman blow his brains out because you accused him of stealing," he told them. "But he didn't steal the money and diamonds. I took 'em."

Tigerishly Lawson grabbed his collar and lifted him bodily. *"Who told you about that?"*

"Don't get excited, Lawson," Johnson said. "He read about it in the papers."

Lawson flung him away.

"He couldn't have," Lawson said, pulling papers from his pocket. "I haven't turned in the reports yet."

"Then how *did* he find out?" Murphy asked.

"Let's get out of here," Lawson said with quick resolution. "Listen, boy, we're going to take you to a nice, quiet place, see?"

"Yes, sir," he said. "And I'll show you the underground."

"Goddamn," Lawson muttered, fastening the gun at his hip. He narrowed his eyes at Johnson and Murphy. "Listen," he spoke just above a whisper, "say nothing about this, you hear?"

"O.K.," Johnson said.

"Sure," Murphy said.

Lawson unlocked the door and Johnson and Murphy led him down the stairs. The hallway was crowded with policemen.

"What have you got there, Lawson?"

"What did he do, Lawson?"

"He's psycho, ain't he, Lawson?"

Lawson did not answer; Johnson and Murphy led him to the car parked at the curb, pushed him into the back seat. Lawson got behind the steering wheel and the car rolled forward.

"What's up, Lawson?" Murphy asked.

"Listen," Lawson began slowly, "we tell the papers that he spilled about the Peabody job, then he escapes. The Wop is caught and we tell the papers that we steered them wrong to trap the real guy, see? Now this dope shows up and acts nuts. If we let him go, he'll squeal that we framed him, see?"

"I'm all right, mister," he said, feeling Murphy's and Johnson's arms locked rigidly into his. "I'm guilty . . . I'll show you everything in the underground. I laughed and laughed . . ."

"Shut that fool up!" Lawson ordered.

Johnson tapped him across the head with a blackjack and he fell back against the seat cushion, dazed.

"Yes, sir," he mumbled. "I'm all right."

The car sped along Hartsdale Avenue, then swung onto Pine Street and rolled to State Street, then turned south. It slowed to a stop, turned in the middle of a block, and headed north again.

"You're going around in circles, Lawson," Murphy said.

Lawson did not answer; he was hunched over the steering wheel. Finally he pulled the car to a stop at the curb.

"Say, boy, tell us the truth," Lawson asked quietly. "Where did you hide?"

"I didn't hide, mister."

The three policemen were staring at him now; he felt that for the first time they were willing to understand him.

"Then what happened?"

"Mister, when I looked through all of those holes and saw how people were living, I loved 'em. . . ."

"Cut out that crazy talk!" Lawson snapped. "Who sent you back here?"

"Nobody, mister."

"Maybe he's talking straight," Johnson ventured.

"All right," Lawson said. "Nobody hid you. Now, tell us *where* you hid."

"I went underground . . ."

"What goddamn underground do you keep talking about?"

"I just went . . ." He paused and looked into the street, then pointed to a manhole cover. "I went down in there and stayed."

"In the *sewer?*"

"Yes, sir."

The policemen burst into a sudden laugh and ended quickly. Lawson swung the car around and drove to Woodside Avenue; he brought the car to a stop in front of a tall apartment building.

"What're we going to do, Lawson?" Murphy asked.

"I'm taking him up to my place," Lawson said. "We've got to wait until night. There's nothing we can do now."

They took him out of the car and led him into a vestibule.

"Take the steps," Lawson muttered.

They led him up four flights of stairs and into the living room of a small apartment. Johnson and Murphy let go of his arms and he stood uncertainly in the middle of the room.

"Now, listen, boy," Lawson began, "forget those wild lies you've been telling us. Where did you hide?"

"I just went underground, like I told you."

The room rocked with laughter. Lawson went to a cabinet and got a bottle of whisky; he placed glasses for Johnson and Murphy. The three of them drank.

He felt that he could not explain himself to them. He tried to muster all the sprawling images that floated in him; the images stood out sharply in his mind, but he could not make them have the meaning for others that they had for him. He felt so helpless that he began to cry.

"He's nuts, all right," Johnson said. "All nuts cry like that."

Murphy crossed the room and slapped him.

"Stop that raving!"

A sense of excitement flooded him; he ran to Murphy and grabbed his arm.

"Let me show you the cave," he said. "Come on, and you'll see!"

Before he knew it a sharp blow had clipped him on the chin; darkness covered his eyes. He dimly felt himself being lifted and laid out on the sofa. He heard low voices and struggled to rise, but hard hands held him down. His brain was clearing now. He pulled to a sitting posture and stared with glazed eyes. It had grown dark. How long had he been out?

"Say, boy," Lawson said soothingly, "will you show us the underground?"

His eyes shone and his heart swelled with gratitude. Lawson believed him! He rose, glad; he grabbed Lawson's arm, making the policeman spill whisky from the glass to his shirt.

"Take it easy, goddammit," Lawson said.

"Yes, sir."

"O.K. We'll take you down. But you'd better be telling us the truth, you hear?"

He clapped his hands in wild joy.

"I'll show you everything!"

He had triumphed at last! He would now do what he had felt was compelling him all along. At last he would be free of his burden.

"Take 'im down," Lawson ordered.

They led him down to the vestibule; when he reached the sidewalk he saw that it was night and a fine rain was falling.

"It's just like when I went down," he told them.

"What?" Lawson asked.

"The rain," he said, sweeping his arm in a wide arc. "It was raining when I went down. The rain made the water rise and lift the cover off."

"Cut it out," Lawson snapped.

They did not believe him now, but they would. A mood of high selflessness throbbed in him. He could barely contain his rising spirits. They would see what he had seen; they would feel what he had felt. He would lead them through all the holes he had dug and . . . He wanted to make a hymn, prance about in physical ecstasy, throw his arms about the policemen in fellowship.

"Get into the car," Lawson ordered.

He climbed in and Johnson and Murphy sat at either side

of him; Lawson slid behind the steering wheel and started the
motor.

"Now, tell us where to go," Lawson said.

"It's right around the corner from where the lady was
killed," he said.

The car rolled slowly and he closed his eyes, remembering
the song he had heard in the church, the song that had
wrought him to such a high pitch of terror and pity. He sang
softly, lolling his head:

Glad, glad, glad, oh, so glad
I got Jesus in my soul . . .

"Mister," he said, stopping his song, "you ought to see how
funny the rings look on the wall." He giggled. "I fired a pistol, too. Just once, to see how it felt."

"What do you suppose he's suffering from?" Johnson
asked.

"Delusions of grandeur, maybe," Murphy said.

"Maybe it's because he lives in a white man's world," Lawson said.

"Say, boy, what did you eat down there?" Murphy asked,
prodding Johnson anticipatorily with his elbow.

"Pears, oranges, bananas, and pork chops," he said.

The car filled with laughter.

"You didn't eat any watermelon?" Lawson asked, smiling.

"No, sir," he answered calmly. "I didn't see any."

The three policemen roared harder and louder.

"Boy, you're sure some case," Murphy said, shaking his
head in wonder.

The car pulled to a curb.

"All right, boy," Lawson said. "Tell us where to go."

He peered through the rain and saw where he had gone
down. The streets, save for a few dim lamps glowing softly
through the rain, were dark and empty.

"Right there, mister," he said, pointing.

"Come on; let's take a look," Lawson said.

"Well, suppose he did hide down there," Johnson said,
"what is that supposed to prove?"

"I don't believe he hid down there," Murphy said.

"It won't hurt to look," Lawson said. "Leave things to
me."

Lawson got out of the car and looked up and down the
street.

He was eager to show them the cave now. If he could
show them what he had seen, then they would feel what he

had felt and they in turn would show it to others and those others would feel as they had felt, and soon everybody would be governed by the same impulse of pity.

"Take 'im out," Lawson ordered.

Johnson and Murphy opened the door and pushed him out; he stood trembling in the rain, smiling. Again Lawson looked up and down the street; no one was in sight. The rain came down hard, slanting like black wires across the wind-swept air.

"All right," Lawson said. "Show us."

He walked to the center of the street, stopped and inserted a finger in one of the tiny holes of the cover and tugged, but he was too weak to budge it.

"Did you really go down in there, boy?" Lawson asked; there was a doubt in his voice.

"Yes, sir. Just a minute. I'll show you."

"Help 'im get that damn thing off," Lawson said.

Johnson stepped forward and lifted the cover; it clanged against the wet pavement. The hole gaped round and black.

"I went down in there," he announced with pride.

Lawson gazed at him for a long time without speaking, then he reached his right hand to his holster and drew his gun.

"Mister, I got a gun just like that down there," he said, laughing and looking into Lawson's face. "I fired it once then hung it on the wall. I'll show you."

"Show us how you went down," Lawson said quietly.

"I'll go down first, mister, and then you-all can come after me, hear?" He spoke like a little boy playing a game.

"Sure, sure," Lawson said soothingly. "Go ahead. We'll come."

He looked brightly at the policemen; he was bursting with happiness. He bent down and placed his hands on the rim of the hole and sat on the edge, his feet dangling into watery darkness. He heard the familiar drone of the gray current. He lowered his body and hung for a moment by his fingers, then he went downward on the steel prongs, hand over hand, until he reached the last rung. He dropped and his feet hit the water and he felt the stiff current trying to suck him away. He balanced himself quickly and looked back upward at the policemen.

"Come on, you-all!" he yelled, casting his voice above the rustling at his feet.

The vague forms that towered above him in the rain did not move. He laughed, feeling that they doubted him. But, once they saw the things he had done, they would never doubt again.

"Come on! The cave isn't far!" he yelled. "But be careful when your feet hit the water, because the current's pretty rough down here!"

Lawson still held the gun. Murphy and Johnson looked at Lawson quizzically.

"What are we going to do, Lawson?" Murphy asked.

"We are not going to follow that crazy nigger down into that sewer, are we?" Johnson asked.

"Come on, you-all!" he begged in a shout.

He saw Lawson raise the gun and point it directly at him. Lawson's face twitched, as though he were hesitating.

Then there was a thunderous report and a streak of fire ripped through his chest. He was hurled into the water, flat on his back. He looked in amazement at the blurred white faces looming above him. They shot me, he said to himself. The water flowed past him, blossoming in foam about his arms, his legs, and his head. His jaw sagged and his mouth gaped soundless. A vast pain gripped his head and gradually squeezed out consciousness. As from a great distance he heard hollow voices.

"What did you shoot him for, Lawson?"

"I had to."

"Why?"

"You've got to shoot his kind. They'd wreck things."

As though in a deep dream, he heard a metallic clank; they had replaced the manhole cover, shutting out forever the sound of wind and rain. From overhead came the muffled roar of a powerful motor and the swish of a speeding car. He felt the strong tide pushing him slowly into the middle of the sewer, turning him about. For a split second there hovered before his eyes the glittering cave, the shouting walls, and the laughing floor . . . Then his mouth was full of thick, bitter water. The current spun him around. He sighed and closed his eyes, a whirling object rushing alone in the darkness, veering, tossing, lost in the heart of the earth.

ANN PETRY (1911–1997)

Ann Petry, born and raised in Old Saybrook, Connecticut, made a striking literary debut with her first novel, The Street *(1946), set in Harlem and completed on a Houghton Mifflin Literary Fellowship. That same year Martha Foley dedicated her annual volume* The Best American Short Stories 1946 *to Ann Petry and included a short story Petry had first published in* The Crisis. *It was only after her marriage in 1938 that Ann Petry left New England to live in Harlem, where she began a newspaper career, first with the* Amsterdam News *and later with* The People's Voice. *After some years of journalism, she went into experimental education in a Harlem grade school. Her first novel drew upon her life and experiences in Harlem. In 1985, she was awarded a special citation by the city of Philadelphia. She wrote two additional novels, short stories, books for children, and a biography of Harriet Tubman. "In Darkness and Confusion," which follows, is a novella which grew imaginatively out of the Harlem riot of 1943. It is reprinted from* Cross-Section 1947, *a collection of American writing edited by Edwin Seaver.*

In Darkness and Confusion

William Jones took a sip of coffee and then put his cup down on the kitchen table. It didn't taste right and he was annoyed because he always looked forward to eating breakfast. He usually got out of bed as soon as he woke up and hurried into the kitchen. Then he would take a long time heating the corn bread left over from dinner the night before, letting the coffee brew until it was strong and clear, frying bacon and scrambling eggs. He would eat very slowly—savoring the early-morning quiet and the just-rightness of the food he'd fixed.

There was no question about early morning being the best

part of the day, he thought. But this Saturday morning in
July it was too hot in the apartment. There were too many
nagging worries that kept drifting through his mind. In the
heat he couldn't think clearly—so that all of them pressed in
against him, weighed him down.

He pushed his plate away from him. The eggs had cooked
too long; much as he liked corn bread it tasted like sand this
morning—grainy and coarse inside his throat. He couldn't
help wondering if it scratched the inside of his stomach in the
same way.

Pink was moving around in the bedroom. He cocked his
head on one side, listening to her. He could tell exactly what
she was doing, as though he were in there with her. The soft
heavy sound of her stockinged feet as she walked over to the
dresser. The dresser drawer being pulled out. That meant she
was getting a clean slip. Then the thud of her two hundred
pounds landing in the rocker by the window. She was sitting
down to comb her hair. Untwisting the small braids she'd
made the night before. She would unwind them one by one,
putting the hairpins in her mouth as she went along. Now she
was brushing it, for he could hear the creak of the rocker;
she was rocking back and forth, humming under her breath
as she brushed.

He decided that as soon as she came into the kitchen he
would go back to the bedroom, get dressed, and go to work.
For his mind was already on the mailbox. He didn't feel like
talking to Pink. There simply had to be a letter from Sam
today. There had to be.

He was thinking about it so hard that he didn't hear Pink
walk toward the kitchen.

When he looked up she was standing in the doorway. She
was a short, enormously fat woman. The only garment she
had on was a bright pink slip that magnified the size of her
body. The skin on her arms and shoulders and chest was star-
tlingly black against the pink material. In spite of the brisk
brushing she had given her hair, it stood up stiffly all over
her head in short wiry lengths, as though she wore a turban
of some rough dark-gray material.

He got up from the table quickly when he saw her. "Hot,
ain't it?" he said, and patted her arm as he went past her toward the bedroom.

She looked at the food on his plate. "You didn't want no
breakfast?" she asked.

"Too hot," he said over his shoulder.

He closed the bedroom door behind him gently. If she saw
the door was shut, she'd know that he was kind of low in his

mind this morning and that he didn't feel like talking. At first he moved about with energy—getting a clean work shirt, giving his shoes a hasty brushing, hunting for a pair of clean socks. Then he stood still in the middle of the room, holding his dark work pants in his hand while he listened to the rush and roar of water running in the bathtub.

Annie May was up and taking a bath. And he wondered if that meant she was going to work. Days when she went to work she used a hot comb on her hair before she ate her breakfast, so that before he left the house in the morning it was filled with the smell of hot irons sizzling against hair grease.

He frowned. Something had to be done about Annie May. Here she was only eighteen years old and staying out practically all night long. He hadn't said anything to Pink about it, but Annie May crept into the house at three and four and five in the morning. He would hear her key go in the latch and then the telltale click as the lock drew back. She would shut the door very softly and turn the bolt. She'd stand there awhile, waiting to see if they woke up. Then she'd take her shoes off and pad down the hall in her stockinged feet.

When she turned the light on in the bathroom, he could see the clock on the dresser. This morning it was four-thirty when she came in. Pink, lying beside him, went on peacefully snoring. He was glad that she didn't wake up easy. It would only worry her to know that Annie May was carrying on like that.

Annie May put her hands on her hips and threw her head back and laughed whenever he tried to tell her she had to come home earlier. The smoky smell of the hot irons started seeping into the bedroom and he finished dressing quickly.

He stopped in the kitchen on his way out. "Got to get to the store early today," he explained. He was sure Pink knew he was hurrying downstairs to look in the mailbox. But she nodded and held her face up for his kiss. When he brushed his lips against her forehead he saw that her face was wet with perspiration. He thought with all that weight she must feel the heat something awful.

Annie May nodded at him without speaking. She was hastily swallowing a cup of coffee. Her dark thin hands made a pattern against the thick white cup she was holding. She had pulled her hair out so straight with the hot combs that, he thought, it was like a shiny skullcap fitted tight to her head. He was surprised to see that her lips were heavily coated with lipstick. When she was going to work she didn't use any, and he wondered why she was up so early if she wasn't working.

He could see the red outline of her mouth on the cup.

He hadn't intended to say anything. It was the sight of the lipstick on the cup that forced the words out. "You ain't workin' today?"

"No," she said lazily. "Think I'll go shopping." She winked at Pink, and it infuriated him.

"How you expect to keep a job when you don't show up half the time?" he asked.

"I can always get another one." She lifted the coffee cup to her mouth with both hands and her eyes laughed at him over the rim of the cup.

"What time did you come home last night?" he asked abruptly.

She stared out of the window at the blank brick wall that faced the kitchen. "I dunno," she said finally. "It wasn't late."

He didn't know what to say. Probably she was out dancing somewhere. Or maybe she wasn't. He was fairly certain that she wasn't. Yet he couldn't let Pink know what he was thinking. He shifted his feet uneasily and watched Annie May swallow the coffee. She was drinking it fast.

"You know you ain't too big to get your butt whipped," he said finally.

She looked at him out of the corner of her eyes. And he saw a deep smoldering sullenness in her face that startled him. He was conscious that Pink was watching both of them with a growing apprehension.

Then Annie May giggled. "You and who else?" she said lightly. Pink roared with laughter. And Annie May laughed with her.

He banged the kitchen door hard as he went out. Striding down the outside hall, he could still hear them laughing. And even though he knew Pink's laughter was due to relief because nothing unpleasant had happened, he was angry. Lately every time Annie May looked at him there was open, jeering laughter in her eyes, as though she dared him to say anything to her. Almost as though she thought he was a fool for working so hard.

She had been a nice little girl when she first came to live with them six years ago. He groped in his mind for words to describe what he thought Annie May had become. A Jezebel, he decided grimly. That was it.

And he didn't want Pink to know what Annie May was really like. Because Annie May's mother, Lottie, had been Pink's sister. And when Lottie died, Pink took Annie May. Right away she started finding excuses for anything she did that was wrong. If he scolded Annie May he had to listen to a sharp lecture from Pink. It always started off the same way: "Don't care what she done, William. You ain't goin' to lay a finger on her. She ain't got no father and mother except us. . . ."

The quick spurt of anger and irritation at Annie May had sent him hurrying down the first flight of stairs. But he slowed his pace on the next flight because the hallways were so dark that he knew if he wasn't careful he'd walk over a step. As he trudged down the long flights of stairs he began to think about Pink. And the hot irritation in him disappeared as it usually did when he thought about her. She was so fat she couldn't keep on climbing all these steep stairs. They would have to find another place to live—on a first floor where it would be easier for her. They'd lived on this top floor for years, and all the time Pink kept getting heavier and heavier. Every time she went to the clinic the doctor said the stairs were bad for her. So they'd start looking for another apartment and then because the top floors cost less, why, they stayed where they were. And——

Then he stopped thinking about Pink because he had reached the first floor. He walked over to the mailboxes and took a deep breath. Today there'd be a letter. He knew it. There had to be. It had been too long a time since they had had a letter from Sam. The last ones that came he'd said the same thing. Over and over. Like a refrain. "Ma, I can't stand this much longer." And then the letters just stopped.

As he stood there, looking at the mailbox, half afraid to open it for fear there would be no letter, he thought back to the night Sam graduated from high school. It was a warm June night. He and Pink got all dressed up in their best clothes. And he kept thinking me and Pink have got as far as we can go. But Sam—he made up his mind Sam wasn't going to earn his living with a mop and a broom. He was going to earn it wearing a starched white collar, and a shine on his shoes and a crease in his pants.

After he finished high school Sam got a job redcapping at Grand Central. He started saving his money because he was going to go to Lincoln—a college in Pennsylvania. It looked like it was no time at all before he was twenty-one. And in the army. Pink cried when he left. Her huge body shook with her sobbing. He remembered that he had only felt queer and lost. There was this war and all the young men were being drafted. But why Sam—why did he have to go?

It was always in the back of his mind. Next thing Sam was in a camp in Georgia. He and Pink never talked about his being in Georgia. The closest they ever came to it was one night when she said, "I hope he gets used to it quick down there. Bein' born right here in New York there's lots he won't understand."

Then Sam's letters stopped coming. He'd come home from work and say to Pink casually, "Sam write today?" She'd shake her head without saying anything.

The days crawled past. And finally she burst out. "What you keep askin' for? You think I wouldn't tell you?" And she started crying.

He put his arm around her and patted her shoulder. She leaned hard against him. "Oh, Lord," she said. "He's my baby. What they done to him?"

Her crying like that tore him in little pieces. His mind kept going around in circles. Around and around. He couldn't think what to do. Finally one night after work he sat down at the kitchen table and wrote Sam a letter. He had written very few letters in his life because Pink had always done it for him. And now standing in front of the mailbox he could even remember the feel of the pencil in his hand; how the paper looked—blank and challenging—lying there in front of him; that the kitchen clock was ticking and it kept getting louder and louder. It was hot that night, too, and he held the pencil so tight that the inside of his hand was covered with sweat.

He had sat and thought a long time. Then he wrote: "Is you all right? Your Pa." It was the best he could do. He licked the envelope and addressed it with the feeling that Sam would understand.

He fumbled for his key ring, found the mailbox key, and opened the box quickly. It was empty. Even though he could see it was empty he felt around inside it. Then he closed the box and walked toward the street door.

The brilliant sunlight outside made him blink after the darkness of the hall. Even now, so early in the morning, it was hot in the street. And he thought it was going to be a hard day to get through, what with the heat and its being Saturday and all. Lately he couldn't seem to think about anything but Sam. Even at the drugstore where he worked as a porter, he would catch himself leaning on the broom or pausing in his mopping to wonder what had happened to him.

The man who owned the store would say to him sharply, "Boy, what the hell's the matter with you? Can't you keep your mind on what you're doing?" And he would go on washing windows, or mopping the floor, or sweeping the sidewalk. But his thoughts, somehow, no matter what he was doing, drifted back to Sam.

As he walked toward the drugstore he looked at the houses

on both sides of the street. He knew this street as he knew the creases in the old felt hat he wore the year round. No matter how you looked at it, it wasn't a good street to live on. It was a long cross-town street. Almost half of it on one side consisted of the backs of the three theaters on One Hundred Twenty-fifth Street—a long blank wall of gray brick. There were few trees on the street. Even these were a source of danger, for at night shadowy, vague shapes emerged from the street's darkness, lurking near the trees, dodging behind them. He had never been accosted by any of those disembodied figures, but the very stealth of their movements revealed a dishonest intent that frightened him. So when he came home at night he walked an extra block or more in order to go through One Hundred Twenty-fifth Street and enter the street from Eighth Avenue.

Early in the morning like this, the street slept. Window shades were drawn down tight against the morning sun. The few people he passed were walking briskly on their way to work. But in those houses where the people still slept, the window shades would go up about noon, and radios would blast music all up and down the street. The bold-eyed women who lived in these houses would lounge in the open windows and call to each other back and forth across the street.

Sometimes when he was on his way home to lunch they would call out to him as he went past, "Come on in, Poppa!" And he would stare straight ahead and start walking faster.

When Sam turned sixteen it seemed to him the street was unbearable. After lunch he and Sam went through this block together—Sam to school and he on his way back to the drugstore. He'd seen Sam stare at the lounging women in the windows. His face was expressionless, but his eyes were curious.

"I catch you goin' near one of them women and I'll beat you up and down the block," he'd said grimly.

Sam didn't answer him. Instead he looked down at him with a strangely adult look, for even at sixteen Sam had been a good five inches taller than he. After that when they passed through the block, Sam looked straight ahead. And William got the uncomfortable feeling that he had already explored the possibilities that the block offered. Yet he couldn't be sure. And he couldn't bring himself to ask him. Instead he walked along beside him, thinking desperately, We gotta move. I'll talk to Pink. We gotta move this time for sure.

That Sunday after Pink came home from church they looked for a new place. They went in and out of apartment houses along Seventh Avenue and Eighth Avenue, One Hundred Thirty-fifth Street, One Hundred Forty-fifth Street. Most of the apartments they didn't even look at. They just asked the super how much the rents were.

It was late when they headed for home. He had irritably agreed with Pink that they'd better stay where they were. Twenty-two dollars a month was all they could afford.

"It ain't a fit place to live, though," he said. They were walking down Seventh Avenue. The street looked wide to him, and he thought with distaste of their apartment. The rooms weren't big enough for a man to move around in without bumping into something. Sometimes he thought that was why Annie May spent so much time away from home. Even at thirteen she couldn't stand being cooped up like that in such a small amount of space.

And Pink said, "You want to live on Park Avenue? With a doorman bowin' you in and out. 'Good mornin', Mr. William Jones. Does the weather suit you this mornin'?'" Her voice was sharp, like the crack of a whip.

That was five years ago. And now again they ought to move on account of Pink not being able to stand the stairs any more. He decided that Monday night after work he'd start looking for a place.

It was even hotter in the drugstore than it was in the street. He forced himself to go inside and put on a limp work coat. Then broom in hand he went to stand in the doorway. He waved to the superintendent of the building on the corner. And watched him as he lugged garbage cans out of the areaway and rolled them to the curb. Now, that's the kind of work he didn't want Sam to have to do. He tried to decide why that was. It wasn't just because Sam was his boy and it was hard work. He searched his mind for the reason. It didn't pay enough for a man to live on decently. That was it. He wanted Sam to have a job where he could make enough to have good clothes and a nice home.

Sam's being in the army wasn't so bad, he thought. It was his being in Georgia that was bad. They didn't treat colored people right down there. Everybody knew that. If he could figure out some way to get him farther north Pink wouldn't have to worry about him so much.

The very sound of the word "Georgia" did something to him inside. His mother had been born there. She had talked about it a lot and painted such vivid pictures of it that he felt he knew the place—the heat, the smell of the earth, how cotton looked. And something more. The way her mouth had folded together whenever she had said, "They hate niggers down there. Don't you never none of you children go down there."

That was years ago, yet even now, standing here on Fifth Avenue, remembering the way she said it turned his skin clammy cold in spite of the heat. And of all the places in the world, Sam had to go to Georgia. Sam, who was born right here in New York, who had finished high school here—they had to put him in the army and send him to Georgia.

He tightened his grip on the broom and started sweeping the sidewalk in long, even strokes. Gradually the rhythm of the motion stilled the agitation in him. The regular back-and-forth motion was so pleasant that he kept on sweeping long after the sidewalk was clean. When Mr. Yudkin, who owned the store, arrived at eight-thirty he was still outside with the broom. Even now he didn't feel much like talking, so he only nodded in response to the druggist's brisk, "Good morning! Hot today!"

William followed him into the store and began polishing the big mirror in back of the soda fountain. He watched the man out of the corner of his eye as he washed his hands in the back room and exchanged his suit coat for a crisp white laboratory coat. And he thought maybe when the war is over Sam ought to study to be a druggist instead of a doctor or a lawyer.

As the morning wore along, customers came in in a steady stream. They got Bromo-Seltzers, cigarettes, aspirin, cough medicine, baby bottles. He delivered two prescriptions that cost five dollars. And the cash register rang so often it almost played a tune. Listening to it he said to himself, yes, Sam ought to be a druggist. It's clean work and it pays good.

A little after eleven o'clock three young girls came in. "Cokes," they said, and climbed up on the stools in front of the fountain. William was placing new stock on the shelves and he studied them from the top of the stepladder. As far as he could see, they looked exactly alike. All three of them. And like Annie May. Too thin. Too much lipstick. Their dresses were too short and too tight. Their hair was piled on top of their heads in slicked set curls.

"Aw, I quit that job," one of them said. "I wouldn't get up that early in the morning for nothing in the world."

That was like Annie May, too. She was always changing jobs. Because she could never get to work on time. If she was due at a place at nine she got there at ten. If at ten, then she arrived about eleven. He knew, too, that she didn't earn enough money to pay for all the cheap, bright-colored dresses she was forever buying.

Her girl friends looked just like her and just like these girls. He'd seen her coming out of the movie houses on One

Hundred Twenty-fifth Street with two or three of them. They were all chewing gum and they nudged each other and talked too loud and laughed too loud. They stared hard at every man who went past them.

Mr. Yudkin looked up at him sharply, and he shifted his glance away from the girls and began putting big bottles of Father John's medicine neatly on the shelf in front of him. As he stacked the bottles up he wondered if Annie May would have been different if she'd stayed in high school. She had stopped going when she was sixteen. He had spoken to Pink about it. "She oughtn't to stop school. She's too young," he'd said.

And because Annie May was Pink's sister's child all Pink had done had been to shake her head comfortably. "She's tired of going to school. Poor little thing. Leave her alone."

So he hadn't said anything more. Pink always took up for her. And he and Pink didn't fuss at each other like some folks do. He didn't say anything to Pink about it, but he took the afternoon off from work to go to see the principal of the school. He had to wait two hours to see her. And he studied the pictures on the walls in the outer office, and looked down at his shoes while he tried to put into words what he'd say—and how he wanted to say it.

The principal was a large-bosomed white woman. She listened to him long enough to learn that he was Annie May's uncle. "Ah, yes, Mr. Jones," she said. "Now in my opinion——"

And he was buried under a flow of words, a mountain of words, that went on and on. Her voice was high-pitched and loud, and she kept talking until he lost all sense of what she was saying. There was one phrase she kept using that sort of jumped at him out of the mass of words—"a slow learner."

He left her office feeling confused and embarrassed. If he could only have found the words he could have explained that Annie May was bright as a dollar. She wasn't any "slow learner." Before he knew it he was out in the street, conscious only that he'd lost a whole afternoon's pay and he never had got to say what he'd come for. And he was boiling mad with himself. All he'd wanted was to ask the principal to help him persuade Annie May to finish school. But he'd never got the words together.

When he hung up his soiled work coat in the broom closet at eight o'clock that night he felt as though he'd been sweeping floors, dusting fixtures, cleaning fountains, and running errands since the beginning of time itself. He looked at himself in the cracked mirror that hung on the door of the closet.

There was no question about it; he'd grown older-looking since Sam went in the army. His hair was turning a frizzled gray at the temples. His jawbones showed up sharper. There was a stoop in his shoulders.

"Guess I'll get a haircut," he said softly. He didn't really need one. But on a Saturday night the barbershop would be crowded. He'd have to wait a long time before Al got around to him. It would be good to listen to the talk that went on— the arguments that would get started and never really end. For a little while all the nagging worry about Sam would be pushed so far back in his mind, he wouldn't be aware of it.

The instant he entered the barbershop he could feel himself begin to relax inside. All the chairs were full. There were a lot of customers waiting. He waved a greeting to the barbers. "Hot, ain't it?" he said and mopped his forehead.

He stood there a minute, listening to the hum of conversation, before he picked out a place to sit. Some of the talk, he knew, would be violent, and he always avoided those discussions because he didn't like violence—even when it was only talk. Scraps of talk drifted past him.

"White folks got us by the balls——"

"Well, I dunno. It ain't just white folks. There's poor white folks gettin' their guts squeezed out, too——"

"Sure. But they're white. They can stand it better."

"Sadie had two dollars on 546 yesterday and it came out and——"

"You're wrong, man. Ain't no two ways about it. This country's set up so that——"

"Only thing to do, if you ask me, is shoot all them crackers and start out new——"

He finally settled himself in one of the chairs in the corner —not too far from the window and right in the middle of a group of regular customers who were arguing hotly about the war. It was a good seat. By looking in the long mirror in front of the barbers he could see the length of the shop.

Almost immediately he joined in the conversation. "Them Japs ain't got a chance——" he started. And he was feeling good. He'd come in at just the right time. He took a deep breath before he went on. Most every time he started talking about the Japs the others listened with deep respect. Because he knew more about them than the other customers. Pink worked for some Navy people and she told him what they said.

He looked along the line of waiting customers, watching their reaction to his words. Pretty soon they'd all be listening to him. And then he stopped talking abruptly. A soldier was sitting in the far corner of the shop, staring down at his shoes. Why, that's Scummy, he thought. He's at the same camp where Sam is. He forgot what he was about to say. He got up and walked over to Scummy. He swallowed all the questions about Sam that trembled on his lips.

"Hiya, son," he said. "Sure is good to see you."

As he shook hands with the boy he looked him over carefully. He's changed, he thought. He was older. There was something about his eyes that was different than before. He didn't-seem to want to talk. After that first quick look at William he kept his eyes down, staring at his shoes.

Finally William couldn't hold the question back any longer. It came out fast. "How's Sam?"

Scummy picked up a newspaper from the chair beside him. "He's all right," he mumbled. There was a long silence. Then he raised his head and looked directly at William. "Was the las' time I seen him." He put a curious emphasis on the word "las'".

William was conscious of a trembling that started in his stomach. It went all through his body. He was aware that conversation in the barbership had stopped. There was a cone of silence in which he could hear the scraping noise of the razors—a harsh sound, loud in the silence. Al was putting thick oil on a customer's hair and he turned and looked with the hair-oil bottle still in his hand, tilted up over the customer's head. The men sitting in the tilted-back barber's chairs twisted their necks around—awkwardly, slowly—so they could look at Scummy.

"What you mean—the las' time?" William asked sharply. The words beat against his ears. He wished the men in the barbershop would start talking again, for he kept hearing his own words. "What you mean—the las' time?" Just as though he were saying them over and over again. Something had gone wrong with his breathing, too. He couldn't seem to get enough air in through his nose.

Scummy got up. There was something about him that William couldn't give a name to. It made the trembling in his stomach worse.

"The las' time I seen him he was O.K." Scummy's voice made a snarling noise in the barbershop.

One part of William's mind said, yes, that's it. It's hate that makes him look different. It's hate in his eyes. You can see it. It's in his voice, and you can hear it. He's filled with it.

"Since I seen him las'," he went on slowly, "he got shot by a white MP. Because he wouldn't go to the nigger end of a bus. He had a bullet put through his guts. He took the MP's gun away from him and shot the bastard in the shoulder." He put the newspaper down and started toward the door; when he reached it he turned around. "They court-martialed him," he said softly. "He got twenty years at hard labor. The notice was posted in the camp the day I left." Then he walked out of the shop. He didn't look back.

There was no sound in the barbershop as William watched him go down the street. Even the razors had stopped. Al was still holding the hair-oil bottle over the head of his customer. The heavy oil was falling on the face of the man sitting in the chair. It was coming down slowly—one drop at a time.

The men in the shop looked at William and then looked away. He thought, I mustn't tell Pink. She mustn't ever get to know. I can go down to the mailbox early in the morning and I can get somebody else to look in it in the afternoon, so if a notice comes I can tear it up.

The barbers started cutting hair again. There was the murmur of conversation in the shop. Customers got up out of the tilted-back chairs. Someone said to him, "You can take my place."

He nodded and walked over to the empty chair. His legs were weak and shaky. He couldn't seem to think at all. His mind kept dodging away from the thought of Sam in prison. Instead the familiar details of Sam's growing up kept creeping into his thoughts. All the time the boy was in grammar school he made good marks. Time went so fast it seemed like it was just overnight and he was in long pants. And then in high school.

He made the basketball team in high school. The whole school was proud of him, for his picture had been in one of the white papers. They got two papers that day. Pink cut the pictures out and stuck one in the mirror of the dresser in their bedroom. She gave him one to carry in his wallet.

While Al cut his hair he stared at himself in the mirror until he felt as though his eyes were crossed. First he thought, maybe it isn't true. Maybe Scummy was joking. But a man who was joking didn't look like Scummy looked. He wondered if Scummy was AWOL. That would be bad. He told himself sternly that he mustn't think about Sam here in the barbershop—wait until he got home.

He was suddenly angry with Annie May. She was just plain no good. Why couldn't something have happened to her? Why did it have to be Sam? Then he was ashamed. He tried to find an excuse for having wanted harm to come to her. It looked like all his life he'd wanted a little something for himself and Pink and then when Sam came along he forgot about those things. He wanted Sam to have all the things that he and Pink couldn't get. It got to be too late for them to have them. But Sam—again he told himself not to think about him. To wait until he got home and in bed.

Al took the cloth from around his neck, and he got up out of the chair. Then he was out on the street, heading toward home. The heat that came from the pavement seeped through the soles of his shoes. He had forgotten how hot it was. He forced himself to wonder what it would be like to live in the country. Sometimes on hot nights like this, after he got home from work, he went to sit in the park. It was always cooler there. It would probably be cool in the country. But then it might be cold in winter—even colder than the city.

The instant he got in the house he took off his shoes and his shirt. The heat in the apartment was like a blanket—it made his skin itch and crawl in a thousand places. He went into the living room, where he leaned out of the window, trying to cool off. Not yet, he told himself. He mustn't think about it yet.

He leaned farther out of the window, to get away from the innumerable odors that came from the boxlike rooms in back of him. They cut off his breath, and he focused his mind on them. There was the greasy smell of cabbage and collard greens, smell of old wood and soapsuds and disinfectant, a lingering smell of gas from the kitchen stove, and over it all Annie May's perfume.

Then he turned his attention to the street. Up and down as far as he could see, folks were sitting on the stoops. Not talking. Just sitting. Somewhere up the street a baby wailed. A woman's voice rose sharply as she told it to shut up.

Pink wouldn't be home until late. The white folks she worked for were having a dinner party tonight. And no matter how late she got home on Saturday night she always stopped on Eighth Avenue to shop for her Sunday dinner. She never trusted him to do it. It's a good thing, he thought. If she ever took a look at me tonight she'd know there was something wrong.

A key clicked in the lock, and he drew back from the window. He was sitting on the couch when Annie May came in the room.

"You're home early, ain't you?" he asked.

"Oh, I'm going out again," she said.

"You shouldn't stay out so late like you did last night," he said mildly. He hadn't really meant to say it. But what with Sam—

"What you think I'm going to do? Sit here every night and make small talk with you?" Her voice was defiant. Loud.

"No," he said, and then added, "but nice girls ain't runnin' around the streets at four o'clock in the mornin'." Now that he'd started he couldn't seem to stop. "Oh, I know what time you come home. And it ain't right. If you don't stop it you can get some other place to stay."

"It's O.K. with me," she said lightly. She chewed the gum in her mouth so it made a cracking noise. "I don't know what Auntie Pink married a little runt like you for, anyhow. It wouldn't bother me a bit if I never saw you again." She walked toward the hall. "I'm going away for the week end," she added over her shoulder. "And I'll move out on Monday."

"What you mean for the week end?" he asked sharply. "Where you goin'?"

"None of your damn business," she said, and slammed the bathroom door hard.

The sharp sound of the door closing hurt his ears so that he winced, wondering why he had grown so sensitive to sounds in the last few hours. What'd she have to say that for, anyway, he asked himself. Five feet five wasn't so short for a man. He was taller than Pink, anyhow. Yet compared to Sam, he supposed he was a runt, for Sam had just kept on growing until he was six feet tall. At the thought he got up from the chair quickly, undressed, and got in bed. He lay there trying to still the trembling in his stomach; trying even now not to think about Sam, because it would be best to wait until Pink was in bed and sound asleep so that no expression on his face, no least little motion, would betray his agitation.

When he heard Pink come up the stairs just before midnight he closed his eyes. All of him was listening to her. He could hear her panting outside on the landing. There was a long pause before she put her key in the door. It took her all that time to get her breath back. She's getting old, he thought. I mustn't let her know about Sam.

She came into the bedroom, and he pretended to be asleep. He made himself breathe slowly. Evenly. Thinking, I can get through tomorrow all right. I won't get up much before she goes to church. She'll be so busy getting dressed she won't notice me.

She went out of the room and he heard the soft murmur of her voice talking to Annie May. "Don't you pay no attention, honey. He don't mean a word of it. I know menfolks. They's always tired and out of sorts by the time Saturdays come around."

"But I'm not going to stay here any more."

"Yes, you is. You think I'm goin' to let my sister's child be turned out? You goin' to be right here."

They lowered their voices. There was laughter. Pink's deep and rich and slow. Annie May's high-pitched and nervous. Pink said, "You looks lovely, honey. Now, have a good time."

The front door closed. This time Annie May didn't slam it. He turned over on his back, making the springs creak. Instantly Pink came into the bedroom to look at him. He lay still, with his eyes closed, holding his breath for fear she would want to talk to him about what he'd said to Annie May and would wake him up. After she moved away from the door he opened his eyes.

There must be some meaning in back of what had happened to Sam. Maybe it was some kind of judgment from the Lord, he thought. Perhaps he shouldn't have stopped going to church. His only concession to Sunday was to put on his best suit. He wore it just that one day, and Pink pressed the pants late on Saturday night. But in the last few years it got so that every time he went to church he wanted to stand up and yell, "You Goddamn fools! How much more you goin' to take?"

He'd get to thinking about the street they lived on, and the sight of the minister with his clean white collar turned hind side to and the sound of his buttery voice were too much. One Sunday he'd actually gotten on his feet, for the minister was talking about the streets of gold up in heaven; the words were right on the tip of his tongue when Pink reached out and pinched his behind sharply. He yelped and sat down. Someone in back of him giggled. In spite of himself a slow smile had spread over his face. He stayed quiet through the rest of the service, but after that he didn't go to church at all.

This street where he and Pink lived was like the one where his mother had lived. It looked like he and Pink ought to have gotten further than his mother had. She had scrubbed floors, washed, and ironed in the white folks' kitchens. They were doing practically the same thing. That was another reason he stopped going to church. He couldn't figure out why these things had to stay the same, and if the Lord didn't intend it like that, why didn't He change it?

He began thinking about Sam again, so he shifted his attention to the sounds Pink was making in the kitchen. She was getting the rolls ready for tomorrow. Scrubbing the sweet potatoes. Washing the greens. Cutting up the chicken. Then the thump of the iron. Hot as it was, she was pressing his pants. He resisted the impulse to get up and tell her not to do it.

A little later, when she turned the light on in the bathroom, he knew she was getting ready for bed. And he held his eyes tightly shut, made his body rigidly still. As long as he could make her think he was sound asleep she wouldn't take a real good look at him. One real good look and she'd know there was something wrong. The bed sagged under her weight as she knelt down to say her prayers. Then she was lying down beside him. She sighed under her breath as her head hit the pillow.

He must have slept part of the time, but in the morning it seemed to him that he had looked up at the ceiling most of the night. He couldn't remember actually going to sleep.

When he finally got up, Pink was dressed and ready for church. He sat down in a chair in the living room away from the window, so the light wouldn't shine on his face. As he looked at her he wished that he could find relief from the confusion of his thoughts by taking part in the singing and the shouting that would go on in church. But he couldn't. And Pink never said anything about his not going to church. Only sometimes like today, when she was ready to go, she looked at him a little wistfully.

She had on her Sunday dress. It was made of a printed material—big red and black poppies splashed on a cream-colored background. He wouldn't let himself look right into her eyes, and in order that she wouldn't notice the evasiveness of his glance he stared at the dress. It fit snugly over her best corset, and the corset in turn constricted her thighs and tightly encased the rolls of flesh around her waist. She didn't move away, and he couldn't keep on inspecting the dress, so he shifted his gaze up to the wide cream-colored straw hat she was wearing far back on her head. Next he noticed that she was easing her feet by standing on the outer edges of the high-heeled patent-leather pumps she wore.

He reached out and patted her arm. "You look nice," he said, picking up the comic section of the paper.

She stood there looking at him while she pulled a pair of white cotton gloves over her roughened hands. "Is you all right, honey?" she asked.

"Course," he said, holding the paper up in front of his face.

"You shouldn't talk so mean to Annie May," she said gently.

"Yeah, I know," he said, and hoped she understood that he was apologizing. He didn't dare lower the paper while she was standing there looking at him so intently. Why doesn't she go, he thought.

"There's grits and eggs for breakfast."

"O.K." He tried to make his voice sound as though he were so absorbed in what he was reading that he couldn't give her all of his attention. She walked toward the door, and he lowered the paper to watch her, thinking that her legs looked too small for her body under the vastness of the printed dress, that womenfolks sure were funny—she's got that great big pocketbook swinging on her arm and hardly anything in it. Sam used to love to tease her about the size of the handbags she carried.

When she closed the outside door and started down the stairs, the heat in the little room struck him in the face. He almost called her back so that he wouldn't be there by himself—left alone to brood over Sam. He decided that when she came home from church he would make love to her. Even in the heat the softness of her body, the smoothness of her skin, would comfort him.

He pulled his chair up close to the open window. Now he could let himself go. He could begin to figure out something to do about Sam. There's gotta be something, he thought. But his mind wouldn't stay put. It kept going back to the time Sam graduated from high school. Nineteen seventy-five his dark-blue suit had cost. He and Pink had figured and figured and finally they'd managed it. Sam had looked good in the suit; he was so tall and his shoulders were so broad it looked like a tailor-made suit on him. When he got his diploma everybody went wild—he'd played center on the basketball team, and a lot of folks recognized him.

The trembling in his stomach got worse as he thought about Sam. He was aware that it had never stopped since Scummy had said those words "the las' time." It had gone on all last night until now there was a tautness and a tension in him that left him feeling as though his eardrums were strained wide open, listening for sounds. They must be a foot wide open, he thought. Open and pulsing with the strain of being open. Even his nostrils were stretched open like that. He could feel them. And a weight behind his eyes.

He went to sleep sitting there in the chair. When he woke up his whole body was wet with sweat. It musta got hotter while I slept, he thought. He was conscious of an ache in his jawbones. It's from holding 'em shut so tight. Even his tongue —he'd been holding it so still in his mouth it felt like it was glued there.

Attracted by the sound of voices, he looked out of the window. Across the way a man and a woman were arguing. Their voices rose and fell on the hot, still air. He could look directly into the room where they were standing, and he saw that they were half undressed.

The woman slapped the man across the face. The sound was like a pistol shot, and for an instant William felt his jaw relax. It seemed to him that the whole block grew quiet and waited. He waited with it. The man grabbed his belt and lashed out at the woman. He watched the belt rise and fall against her brown skin. The woman screamed with the regularity of clockwork. The street came alive again. There was the sound of voices, the rattle of dishes. A baby whined. The woman's voice became a murmur of pain in the background.

"I gotta get me some beer," he said aloud. It would cool him off. It would help him to think. He dressed quickly, telling himself that Pink wouldn't be home for hours yet and by that time the beer smell would be gone from his breath.

The street outside was full of kids playing tag. They were all dressed up in their Sunday clothes. Red socks, blue socks, danced in front of him all the way to the corner. The sight of them piled up the quivering in his stomach. Sam used to play in this block on Sunday afternoons. As he walked along, women thrust their heads out of the opened windows, calling to the children. It seemed to him that all the voices were Pink's voice saying, "You, Sammie, stop that runnin' in your good cloes!"

He was so glad to get away from the sight of the children that he ignored the heat inside the barroom of the hotel on the corner and determinedly edged his way past girls in sheer summer dresses and men in loud plaid jackets and tight-legged cream-colored pants until he finally reached the long bar.

There was such a sense of hot excitement in the place that he turned to look around him. Men with slicked, straightened hair were staring through half-closed eyes at the girls lined up at the bar. One man sitting at a table close by kept running his hand up and down the bare arm of the girl leaning against him. Up and down. Down and up. William winced and looked away. The jukebox was going full blast, filling the room with high, raw music that beat about his ears in a queer mixture of violence and love and hate and terror. He stared at the brilliantly colored moving lights on the front of the jukebox as he listened to it, wishing that he had stayed at home, for the music made the room hotter.

"Make it a beer," he said to the bartender.

The beer glass was cold. He held it in his hand, savoring the chill of it, before he raised it to his lips. He drank it down fast. Immediately he felt the air grow cooler. The smell of beer and whisky that hung in the room lifted.

"Fill it up again," he said. He still had that awful trembling in his stomach, but he felt as though he were really beginning to think. Really think. He found he was arguing with himself.

"Sam mighta been like this. Spendin' Sunday afternoons whorin'."

"But he was part of·me and part of Pink. He had a chance——"

"Yeah. A chance to live in one of them hell-hole flats. A chance to get himself a woman to beat."

"He woulda finished college and got a good job. Mebbe been a druggist or a doctor or a lawyer——"

"Yeah. Or mebbe got himself a stable of women to rent out on the block——"

He licked the suds from his lips. The man at the table nearby had stopped stroking the girl's arm. He was kissing her—forcing her closer and closer to him.

"Yeah," William jeered at himself. "That coulda been Sam on a hot Sunday afternoon——"

As he stood there arguing with himself he thought it was getting warmer in the bar. The lights were dimmer. I better go home, he thought. I gotta live with this thing some time. Drinking beer in this place ain't going to help any. He looked out toward the lobby of the hotel, attracted by the sound of voices. A white cop was arguing with a frowzy-looking girl who had obviously had too much to drink.

"I got a right in here. I'm mindin' my own business," she said with one eye on the bar.

"Aw, go chase yourself." The cop gave her a push toward the door. She stumbled against a chair.

William watched her in amusement. "Better than a movie," he told himself.

She straightened up and tugged at her girdle. "You white son of a bitch," she said.

The cop's face turned a furious red. He walked toward the woman, waving his nightstick. It was then that William saw the soldier. Tall. Straight. Creases in his khaki pants. An overseas cap cocked over one eye. Looks like Sam looked that one time he was home on furlough, he thought.

The soldier grabbed the cop's arm and twisted the nightstick out of his hand. He threw it half the length of the small lobby. It rattled along the floor and came to a dead stop under a chair.

"Now what'd he want to do that for?" William said softly.

He knew that night after night the cop had to come back to this hotel. He's the law, he thought, and he can't let— Then he stopped thinking about him, for the cop raised his arm. The soldier aimed a blow at the cop's chin. The cop ducked and reached for his gun. The soldier turned to run.

It's happening too fast, William thought. It's like one of those horse-race reels they run over fast at the movies. Then he froze inside. The quivering in his stomach got worse. The soldier was heading toward the door. Running. His foot was on the threshold when the cop fired. The soldier dropped. He folded up as neatly as the brown-paper bags Pink brought home from the store, emptied, and then carefully put in the kitchen cupboard.

The noise of the shot stayed in his eardrums. He couldn't get it out. "Jesus Christ!" he said. Then again, "Jesus Christ!" The beer glass was warm. He put it down on the bar with such violence some of the beer slopped over on his shirt. He stared at the wet place, thinking Pink would be mad as hell. Him out drinking in a bar on Sunday. There was a stillness in which he was conscious of the stink of the beer, the heat in the room, and he could still hear the sound of the shot. Somebody dropped a glass, and the tinkle of it hurt his ears.

Then everybody was moving toward the lobby. The doors between the bar and the lobby slammed shut. High, excited talk broke out.

The tall, thin black man standing next to him said, "That ties it. It ain't even safe here where we live. Not no more. I'm goin' to get me a white bastard of a cop and nail his hide to a street sign."

"Is the soldier dead?" someone asked.

"He wasn't movin' none," came the answer.

They pushed hard against the doors leading to the lobby. The doors stayed shut.

He stood still, watching them. The anger that went through him was so great that he had to hold on to the bar to keep from falling. He felt as though he were going to burst wide open. It was like having seen Sam killed before his eyes. Then he heard the whine of an ambulance siren. His eardrums seemed to be waiting to pick it up.

"Come on, what you waitin' for?" he snarled the words at the people milling around the lobby doors. "Come on!" he repeated, running toward the street.

The crowd followed him to the One Hundred Twenty-sixth Street entrance of the hotel. He got there in time to see a stretcher bearing a limp khaki-clad figure disappear inside the ambulance in front of the door. The ambulance pulled away fast, and he stared after it stupidly.

He hadn't known what he was going to do, but he felt cheated. Let down. He noticed that it was beginning to get dark. More and more people were coming into the street. He wondered where they'd come from and how they'd heard about the shooting so quickly. Every time he looked around there were more of them. Curious, eager voices kept asking, "What happened? What happened?" The answer was always the same. Hard. Angry. "A white cop shot a soldier."

Someone said, "Come on to the hospital. Find out what happened to him."

In front of the hotel he had been in the front of the crowd. Now there were so many people in back of him and in front of him that when they started toward the hospital, he moved along with them. He hadn't decided to go—the forward movement picked him up and moved him along without any intention on his part. He got the feeling that he had lost his identity as a person with a free will of his own. It frightened him at first. Then he began to feel powerful. He was surrounded by hundreds of people like himself. They were all together. They could do anything.

As the crowd moved slowly down Eighth Avenue, he saw that there were cops lined up on both sides of the street. Mounted cops kept coming out of the side streets, shouting, "Break it up! Keep moving. Keep moving."

The cops were scared of them. He could tell. Their faces were dead white in the semidarkness. He started saying the words over separately to himself. Dead. White. He laughed. White cops. White MP's. They got us coming and going, he thought. He laughed again. Dead. White. The words were funny said separately like that. He stopped laughing suddenly because a part of his mind repeated: twenty years, twenty years.

He licked his lips. It was hot as all hell tonight. He imagined what it would be like to be drinking swallow after swallow of ice-cold beer. His throat worked and he swallowed audibly.

The big black man walking beside him turned and looked down at him. "You all right, brother?" he asked curiously.

"Yeah," he nodded. "It's them sons of bitches of cops. They're scared of us." He shuddered. The heat was terrible. The tide of hate quivering in his stomach made him hotter. "Wish I had some beer," he said.

The man seemed to understand not only what he had said but all the things he had left unsaid. For he nodded and smiled. And William thought this was an extraordinary night. It was as though, standing so close together, so many of them like this——as though they knew each other's thoughts. It was a wonderful thing.

The crowd carried him along. Smoothly. Easily. He wasn't really walking. Just gliding. He was aware that the shuffling feet of the crowd made a muffled rhythm on the concrete sidewalk. It was slow, inevitable. An ominous sound, like a funeral march. With the regularity of a drumbeat. No. It's more like a pulse beat, he thought. It isn't a loud noise. It just keeps repeating over and over. But not that regular, because it builds up to something. It keeps building up.

The mounted cops rode their horses into the crowd. Trying to break it up into smaller groups. Then the rhythm was broken. Seconds later it started again. Each time the tempo was a little faster. He found he was breathing the same way. Faster and faster. As though he were running. There were more and more cops. All of them white. They had moved the colored cops out.

"They done that before," he muttered.

"What?" said the man next to him.

"They moved the colored cops out," he said.

He heard the man repeat it to someone standing beside him. It became part of the slow shuffling rhythm on the sidewalk. "They moved the colored cops." He heard it go back and back through the crowd until it was only a whisper of hate on the still, hot air. "They moved the colored cops."

As the crowd shuffled back and forth in front of the hospital, he caught snatches of conversation. "The soldier was dead when they put him in the ambulance." "Always tryin' to fool us." "Christ! Just let me get my hands on one of them cops."

He was thinking about the hospital and he didn't take part in any of the conversations. Even now across the long span of years he could remember the helpless, awful rage that had sent him hurrying home from this same hospital. Not saying anything. Getting home by some kind of instinct.

Pink had come to this hospital when she had had her last child. He could hear again the cold contempt in the voice of the nurse as she listened to Pink's loud grieving. "You people have too many children anyway," she said.

It left him speechless. He had his hat in his hand and he remembered how he wished afterward that he'd put it on in front of her to show her what he thought of her. As it was, all the bitter answer that finally surged into his throat seemed to choke him. No words would come out. So he stared at her lean, spare body. He let his eyes stay a long time on her flat breasts. White uniform. White shoes. White stockings. White skin.

Then he mumbled, "It's too bad your eyes ain't white, too." And turned on his heel and walked out.

It wasn't any kind of answer. She probably didn't even know what he was talking about. The baby dead, and all he could think of was to tell her her eyes ought to be white. White shoes, white stockings, white uniform, white skin, and blue eyes.

Staring at the hospital, he saw with satisfaction that frightened faces were appearing at the windows. Some of the lights went out. He began to feel that this night was the first time he'd ever really been alive. Tonight everything was going to be changed. There was a growing, swelling sense of power in him. He felt the same thing in the people around him.

The cops were aware of it, too, he thought. They were out in full force. Mounties, patrolmen, emergency squads. Radio cars that looked like oversize bugs crawled through the side streets. Waited near the curbs. Their white tops stood out in the darkness. "White folks riding in white cars." He wasn't aware that he had said it aloud until he heard the words go through the crowd. "White folks in white cars." The laughter that followed the words had a rough, raw rhythm. It repeated the pattern of the shuffling feet.

Someone said, "They got him at the station house. He ain't here." And the crowd started moving toward One Hundred Twenty-third Street.

Great God in the morning, William thought, everybody's out here. There were girls in thin summer dresses, boys in long coats and tight-legged pants, old women dragging kids along by the hand. A man on crutches jerked himself past to the rhythm of the shuffling feet. A blind man tapped his way through the center of the crowd, and it divided into two separate streams as it swept by him. At every street corner William noticed someone stopped to help the blind man up over the curb.

The street in front of the police station was so packed with people that he couldn't get near it. As far as he could see they weren't doing anything. They were simply standing there. Waiting for something to happen. He recognized a few of them: the woman with the loose, rolling eyes who sold shopping bags on One Hundred Twenty-fifth Street; the lucky-number peddler—the man with the white parrot on his shoulder; three sisters of the Heavenly Rest for All movement—barefooted women in loose white robes.

Then, for no reason that he could discover, everybody moved toward One Hundred Twenty-fifth Street. The motion of the crowd was slower now because it kept increasing in size as people coming from late church services were drawn into it. It was easy to identify them, he thought. The women wore white gloves. The kids were all slicked up. Despite the more gradual movement he was still being carried along effortlessly, easily. When someone in front of him barred his way, he pushed against the person irritably, frowning in annoyance because the smooth forward flow of his progress had been stopped.

It was Pink who stood in front of him. He stopped frowning when he recognized her. She had a brown-paper bag tucked under her arm, and he knew she had stopped at the corner store to get the big bottle of cream soda she always brought home on Sundays. The sight of it made him envious, for it meant that this Sunday had been going along in an orderly, normal fashion for her while he— She was staring at him so hard he was suddenly horribly conscious of the smell of the beer that had spilled on his shirt. He knew she had smelled it, too, by the tighter grip she took on her pocketbook.

"What you doing out here in this mob? A Sunday evening and you drinking beer," she said grimly.

For a moment he couldn't answer her. All he could think of was Sam. He almost said, "I saw Sam shot this afternoon," and he swallowed hard.

"This afternoon I saw a white cop kill a colored soldier," he said. "In the bar where I was drinking beer. I saw it. That's why I'm here. The glass of beer I was drinking went on my clothes. The cop shot him in the back. That's why I'm here."

He paused for a moment, took a deep breath. This was how it ought to be, he decided. She had to know sometime and this was the right place to tell her. In this semidarkness, in this confusion of noises, with the low, harsh rhythm of the footsteps sounding against the noise of the horses' hoofs.

His voice thickened. "I saw Scummy yesterday," he went on. "He told me Sam's doing time at hard labor. That's why we ain't heard from him. A white MP shot him when he wouldn't go to the nigger end of a bus. Sam shot the MP. They gave him twenty years at hard labor."

He knew he hadn't made it clear how to him the soldier in the bar was Sam; that it was like seeing his own son shot before his very eyes. I don't even know whether the soldier was dead, he thought. What made me tell her about Sam out here in the street like this, anyway? He realized with a sense of shock that he really didn't care that he had told her. He felt strong, powerful, aloof. All the time he'd been talking he wouldn't look right at her. Now, suddenly, he was looking at her as though she were a total stranger. He was coldly wondering what she'd do. He was prepared for anything.

But he wasn't prepared for the wail that came from her throat. The sound hung in the hot air. It made the awful quivering in his stomach worse. It echoed and re-echoed the length of the street. Somewhere in the distance a horse whinnied. A woman standing way back in the crowd groaned as though the sorrow and the anguish in that cry were more than she could bear.

Pink stood there for a moment. Silent. Brooding. Then she lifted the big bottle of soda high in the air. She threw it with all her might. It made a wide arc and landed in the exact center of the plate-glass window of a furniture store. The glass crashed in with a sound like a gunshot.

A sigh went up from the crowd. They surged toward the broken window. Pink followed close behind. When she reached the window, all the glass had been broken in. Reaching far inside, she grabbed a small footstool and then turned to hurl it through the window of the dress shop next door. He kept close behind her, watching her as she seized a new missile from each store window that she broke.

Plate-glass windows were being smashed all up and down One Hundred Twenty-fifth Street—on both sides of the street. The violent, explosive sound fed the sense of power in him. Pink had started this. He was proud of her, for she had shown herself to be a fit mate for a man of his type. He stayed as close to her as he could. So in spite of the crashing, splintering sounds and the swarming, violent activity around him, he knew the exact moment when she lost her big straw hat; when she took off the high-heeled patent-leather shoes and flung them away, striding swiftly along in her stockinged feet. That her dress was hanging crooked on her.

He was right in back of her when she stopped in front of a hat store. She carefully appraised all the hats inside the broken window. Finally she reached out, selected a small hat covered with purple violets, and fastened it securely on her head.

"Woman's got good sense," a man said.

"Man, oh, man! Let me get in there," said a rawboned woman who thrust her way forward through the jam of people to seize two hats from the window.

A roar of approval went up from the crowd. From then on

when a window was smashed it was bare of merchandise when the people streamed past it. White folks owned these stores. They'd lose and lose and lose, he thought with satisfaction. The words "twenty years" re-echoed in his mind. I'll be an old man, he thought. Then: I may be dead before Sam gets out of prison.

The feeling of great power and strength left him. He was so confused by its loss that he decided this thing happening in the street wasn't real. It was so dark, there were so many people shouting and running about, that he almost convinced himself he was having a nightmare. He was aware that his hearing had now grown so acute he could pick up the tiniest sounds: the quickened breathing and the soft, gloating laughter of the crowd; even the sound of his own heart beating. He could hear these things under the noise of the breaking glass, under the shouts that were coming from both sides of the street. They forced him to face the fact that this was no dream but a reality from which he couldn't escape. The quivering in his stomach kept increasing as he walked along.

Pink was striding through the crowd just ahead of him. He studied her to see if she, too, was feeling as he did. But the outrage that ran through her had made her younger. She was tireless. Most of the time she was leading the crowd. It was all he could do to keep up with her, and finally he gave up the attempt—it made him too tired.

He stopped to watch a girl who was standing in a store window, clutching a clothes model tightly around the waist. "What's she want that for?" he said aloud. For the model had been stripped of clothing by the passing crowd, and he thought its pinkish torso was faintly obscene in its resemblance to a female figure.

The girl was young and thin. Her back was turned toward him, and there was something so ferocious about the way her dark hands gripped the naked model that he resisted the onward movement of the crowd to stare in fascination. The girl turned around. Her nervous hands were tight around the dummy's waist. It was Annie May.

"Ah, no!" he said, and let his breath come out with a sigh.

Her hands crept around the throat of the model and she sent it hurtling through the air above the heads of the crowd. It landed short of a window across the street. The legs shattered. The head rolled toward the curb. The waist snapped neatly in two. Only the torso remained whole and in one piece.

Annie May stood in the empty window and laughed with the crowd when someone kicked the torso into the street. He stood there, staring at her. He felt that now for the first time he understood her. She had never had anything but badly paying jobs—working for young white women who probably despised her. She was like Sam on that bus in Georgia. She didn't want just the nigger end of things, and here in Harlem there wasn't anything else for her. All along she'd been trying the only way she knew how to squeeze out of life a little something for herself.

He tried to get closer to the window where she was standing. He had to tell her that he understood. And the crowd, tired of the obstruction that he had made by standing still, swept him up and carried him past. He stopped thinking and let himself be carried along on a vast wave of feeling. There was so much plate glass on the sidewalk that it made a grinding noise under the feet of the hurrying crowd. It was a dull, harsh sound that set his teeth on edge and quickened the trembling of his stomach.

Now all the store windows that he passed were broken. The people hurrying by him carried tables, lamps, shoeboxes, clothing. A woman next to him held a wedding cake in her hands—it went up in tiers of white frosting with a small bride and groom mounted at the top. Her hands were bleeding, and he began to look closely at the people nearest him. Most of them, too, had cuts on their hands and legs. Then he saw there was blood on the sidewalk in front of the windows; blood dripping down the jagged edges of the broken windows. And he wanted desperately to go home.

He was conscious that the rhythm of the crowd had changed. It was faster, and it had taken on an ugly note. The cops were using their nightsticks. Police wagons drew up to the curbs. When they pulled away, they were full of men and women who carried loot from the stores in their hands.

The police cars slipping through the streets were joined by other cars with loudspeakers on top. The voices coming through the loudspeakers were harsh. They added to the noise and the confusion. He tried to listen to what the voices were saying. But the words had no meaning for him. He caught one phrase over and over: "Good people of Harlem." It made him feel sick.

He repeated the words "of Harlem." We don't belong anywhere, he thought. There ain't no room for us anywhere. There wasn't no room for Sam in a bus in Georgia. There ain't no room for us here in New York. There ain't no place but top floors. The top-floor black people. And he laughed, and the sound stuck in his throat.

After that he snatched a suit from the window of a men's

clothing store. It was a summer suit. The material felt crisp and cool. He walked away with it under his arm. He'd never owned a suit like that. He simply sweated out the summer in the same dark pants he wore in winter. Even while he stroked the material, a part of his mind sneered—you got summer pants; Sam's got twenty years.

He was surprised to find that he was almost at Lenox Avenue, for he hadn't remembered crossing Seventh. At the corner the cops were shoving a group of young boys and girls into a police wagon. He paused to watch. Annie May was in the middle of the group. She had a yellow-fox jacket dangling from one hand.

"Annie May!" he shouted. "Annie May!" The crowd pushed him along faster and faster. She hadn't seen him. He let himself be carried forward by the movement of the crowd. He had to find Pink and tell her that the cops had taken Annie May.

He peered into the dimness of the street ahead of him, looking for her; then he elbowed his way toward the curb so that he could see the other side of the street. He forgot about finding Pink, for directly opposite him was the music store that he passed every night coming home from work. Young boys and girls were always lounging on the sidewalk in front of it. They danced a few steps while they listened to the records being played inside the shop. All the records sounded the same—a terribly magnified woman's voice bleating out a blues song in a voice that sounded to him like that of an animal in heat—an old animal, tired and beaten, but with an insinuating know-how left in her. The white men who went past the store smiled as their eyes lingered on the young girls swaying to the music.

"White folks got us comin' and goin'. Backwards and forwards," he muttered. He fought his way out of the crowd and walked toward a no-parking sign that stood in front of the store. He rolled it up over the curb. It was heavy, and the effort made him pant. It took all his strength to send it crashing through the glass on the door.

Almost immediately an old woman and a young man slipped inside the narrow shop. He followed them. He watched them smash the records that lined the shelves. He hadn't thought of actually breaking the records, but once he started he found the crisp, snapping noise pleasant. The feeling of power began to return. He didn't like these records, so they had to be destroyed.

When they left the music store there wasn't a whole record left. The old woman came out of the store last. As he hurried off up the street he could have sworn he smelled the sharp, acrid smell of smoke. He turned and looked back. He was right. A thin wisp of smoke was coming through the store door. The old woman had long since disappeared in the crowd.

Farther up the street he looked back again. The fire in the record shop was burning merrily. It was making a glow that lit up that part of the street. There was a new rhythm now. It was faster and faster. Even the voices coming from the loudspeakers had taken on the urgency of speed.

Fire trucks roared up the street. He threw his head back and laughed when he saw them. That's right, he thought. Burn the whole damn place down. It was wonderful. Then he frowned. "Twenty years at hard labor." The words came back to him. He was a fool. Fire wouldn't wipe that out. There wasn't anything that would wipe it out.

He remembered then that he had to find Pink. To tell her about Annie May. He overtook her in the next block. She's got more stuff, he thought. She had a table lamp in one hand, a large enamel kettle in the other. The lightweight summer coat drapped across her shoulders was so small it barely covered her enormous arms. She was watching a group of boys assault the steel gates in front of a liquor store. She frowned at them so ferociously he wondered what she was going to do. Hating liquor the way she did, he half expected her to cuff the boys and send them on their way up the street.

She turned and looked at the crowd in back of her. When she saw him she beckoned to him. "Hold these," she said. He took the lamp, the kettle, and the coat she held out to him, and he saw that her face was wet with perspiration. The print dress was darkly stained with it.

She fastened the hat with the purple flowers securely on her head. Then she walked over to the gate. "Git out the way," she said to the boys. Bracing herself in front of the gate, she started tugging at it. The gate resisted. She pulled at it with a sudden access of such furious strength that he was frightened. Watching her, he got the feeling that the resistance of the gate had transformed it in her mind. It was no longer a gate—it had become the world that had taken her son, and she was wreaking vengeance on it.

The gate began to bend and sway under her assault. Then it was down. She stood there for a moment, staring at her hands—big drops of blood oozed slowly over the palms. Then she turned to the crowd that had stopped to watch.

"Come on, you niggers," she said. Her eyes were little and evil and triumphant. "Come on and drink up the white man's liquor." As she strode off up the street, the beflowered hat dangled precariously from the back of her head.

When he caught up with her she was moaning, talking to herself in husky whispers. She stopped when she saw him and put her hand on his arm.

"It's hot, ain't it?" she said, panting.

In the midst of all this violence, the sheer commonplaceness of her question startled him. He looked at her closely. The rage that had been in her was gone, leaving her completely exhausted. She was breathing too fast in uneven gasps that shook her body. Rivulets of sweat streamed down her face. It was as though her triumph over the metal gate had finished her. The gate won anyway, he thought.

"Let's go home, Pink," he said. He had to shout to make his voice carry over the roar of the crowd, the sound of breaking glass.

He realized she didn't have the strength to speak, for she only nodded in reply to his suggestion. Once we get home she'll be all right, he thought. It was suddenly urgent that they get home, where it was quiet, where he could think, where he could take something to still the tremors in his stomach. He tried to get her to walk a little faster, but she kept slowing down until, when they entered their own street, it seemed to him they were barely moving.

In the middle of the block she stood still. "I can't make it," she said. "I'm too tired."

Even as he put his arm around her she started going down. He tried to hold her up, but her great weight was too much for him. She went down slowly, inevitably, like a great ship capsizing. Until all of her huge body was crumpled on the sidewalk.

"Pink," he said. "Pink. You gotta get up," he said it over and over again.

She didn't answer. He leaned over and touched her gently. Almost immediately afterward he straightened up. All his life, moments of despair and frustration had left him speechless—strangled by the words that rose in his throat. This time the words poured out.

He sent his voice raging into the darkness and the awful confusion of noises. "The sons of bitches," he shouted. "The sons of bitches."

RALPH ELLISON (1914–1994)

With a single novel, Invisible Man—*honored with the National Book Award in 1952 and judged, in 1965, "the most distinguished single work" published in the past twenty years by a* Book Week *poll of some two hundred critics, authors, and editors—Ralph Ellison reached the summit of the American literary establishment. Never before had a Negro writer been so accepted by the dominant critical circles, discussed as a major figure of contemporary American literature rather than as a "race" writer. Ellison was born in Oklahoma City and originally intended to be a musician. He majored in music at Tuskegee Institute, and when he came to New York City in 1936, he planned to study music and sculpture. Ellison had a lifelong interest in jazz, and among his numerous jobs before he established himself as a writer, he was a jazz trumpeter. Ellison was Writer in Residence at Rutgers University, Visiting Fellow at Yale, and lectured and read from his works at colleges, universities, and academic gatherings throughout the United States. He published a volume of critical essays,* Shadow and Act, *and excerpts from a second novel appeared in literary journals for many years before being posthumously published in 1999 under the title* Juneteenth. *He is represented here with the Prologue to* Invisible Man, *the best possible introduction to his literary world. His views on literature are expressed in an interview with him in the Literary Criticism section.*

Invisible Man: Prologue

I am an invisible man. No, I am not a spook like those who haunted Edgar Allan Poe; nor am I one of your Hollywood-movie ectoplasms. I am a man of substance, of flesh and bone, fiber and liquids—and I might even be said to possess a

mind. I am invisible, understand, simply because people refuse to see me. Like the bodiless heads you see sometimes in
circus sideshows, it is as though I have been surrounded by
mirrors of hard, distorting glass. When they approach me
they see only my surroundings, themselves, or figments of
their imagination—indeed, everything and anything except
me.

Nor is my invisibility exactly a matter of a bio-chemical
accident to my epidermis. That invisibility to which I refer
occurs because of a peculiar disposition of the eyes of those
with whom I come in contact. A matter of the construction
of their *inner* eyes, those eyes with which they look through
their physical eyes upon reality. I am not complaining, nor
am I protesting either. It is sometimes advantageous to be unseen, although it is most often rather wearing on the nerves.
Then too, you're constantly being bumped against by those of
poor vision. Or again, you often doubt if you really exist.
You wonder whether you aren't simply a phantom in other
people's minds. Say, a figure in a nightmare which the sleeper
tries with all his strength to destroy. It's when you feel like
this that, out of resentment, you begin to bump people back.
And, let me confess, you feel that way most of the time. You
ache with the need to convince yourself that you do exist in
the real world, that you're a part of all the sound and anguish, and you strike out with your fists, you curse and you
swear to make them recognize you. And, alas, it's seldom
successful.

One night I accidentally bumped into a man, and perhaps
because of the near darkness he saw me and called me an
insulting name. I sprang at him, seized his coat lapels and demanded that he apologize. He was a tall blond man, and as
my face came close to his he looked insolently out of his blue
eyes and cursed me, his breath hot in my face as he struggled. I pulled his chin down sharp upon the crown of my
head, butting him as I had seen the West Indians do, and I
felt his flesh tear and the blood gush out, and I yelled, "Apologize! Apologize!" But he continued to curse and struggle,
and I butted him again and again until he went down heavily,
on his knees, profusely bleeding. I kicked him repeatedly, in
a frenzy because he still uttered insults though his lips were
frothy with blood. Oh yes, I kicked him! And in my outrage
I got out my knife and prepared to slit his throat, right there
beneath the lamplight in the deserted street, holding him by
the collar with one hand, and opening the knife with my
teeth—when it occurred to me that the man had not *seen* me,
actually; that he, as far as he knew, was in the midst of a

walking nightmare! And I stopped the blade, slicing the air as I pushed him away, letting him fall back to the street. I stared at him hard as the lights of a car stabbed through the darkness. He lay there, moaning on the asphalt; a man almost killed by a phantom. It unnerved me. I was both disgusted and ashamed. I was like a drunken man myself, wavering about on weakened legs. Then I was amused. Something in this man's thick head had sprung out and beaten him within an inch of his life. I began to laugh at this crazy discovery. Would he have awakened at the point of death? Would Death himself have freed him for wakeful living? But I didn't linger. I ran away into the dark, laughing so hard I feared I might rupture myself. The next day I saw his picture in the *Daily News,* beneath a caption stating that he had been "mugged." Poor fool, poor blind fool, I thought with sincere compassion, mugged by an invisible man!

Most of the time (although I do not choose as I once did to deny the violence of my days by ignoring it) I am not so overtly violent. I remember that I am invisible and walk softly so as not to awaken the sleeping ones. Sometimes it is best not to awaken them; there are few things in the world as dangerous as sleepwalkers. I learned in time though that it is possible to carry on a fight against them without their realizing it. For instance, I have been carrying on a fight with Monopolated Light & Power for some time now. I use their service and pay them nothing at all, and they don't know it. Oh, they suspect that power is being drained off, but they don't know where. All they know is that according to the master meter back there in their power station a hell of a lot of free current is disappearing somewhere into the jungle of Harlem. The joke, of course, is that I don't live in Harlem but in a border area. Several years ago (before I discovered the advantage of being invisible) I went through the routine process of buying service and paying their outrageous rates. But no more. I gave up all that, along with my apartment, and my old way of life: That way based upon the fallacious assumption that I, like other men, was visible. Now, aware of my invisibility, I live rent-free in a building rented strictly to whites, in a section of the basement that was shut off and forgotten during the nineteenth century, which I discovered when I was trying to escape in the night from Ras the Destroyer. But that's getting too far ahead of the story, almost to the end, although the end is in the beginning and lies far ahead.

The point now is that I found a home—or a hole in the ground, as you will. Now don't jump to the conclusion that because I call my home a "hole" it is damp and cold like a grave; there are cold holes and warm holes. Mine is a warm hole. And remember, a bear retires to his hole for the winter and lives until spring; then he comes strolling out like the Easter chick breaking from its shell. I say all this to assure you that it is incorrect to assume that, because I'm invisible and live in a hole, I am dead. I am neither dead nor in a state of suspended animation. Call me Jack-the-Bear, for I am in a state of hibernation.

My hole is warm and full of light. Yes, *full* of light. I doubt if there is a brighter spot in all New York than this hole of mine, and I do not exclude Broadway. Or the Empire State Building on a photographer's dream night. But that is taking advantage of you. Those two spots are among the darkest of our whole civilization—pardon me, our whole *culture* (an important distinction, I've heard)—which might sound like a hoax, or a contradiction, but that (by contradiction, I mean) is how the world moves: Not like an arrow, but a boomerang. (Beware of those who speak of the *spiral* of history; they are preparing a boomerang. Keep a steel helmet handy.) I know; I have been boomeranged across my head so much that I now can see the darkness of lightness. And I love light. Perhaps you'll think it strange that an invisible man should need light, desire light, love light. But maybe it is exactly because I *am* invisible. Light confirms my reality, gives birth to my form. A beautiful girl once told me of a recurring nightmare in which she lay in the center of a large dark room and felt her face expand until it filled the whole room, becoming a formless mass while her eyes ran in bilious jelly up the chimney. And so it is with me. Without light I am not only invisible, but formless as well; and to be unaware of one's form is to live a death. I myself, after existing some twenty years, did not become alive until I discovered my invisibility.

That is why I fight my battle with Monopolated Light & Power. The deeper reason, I mean: It allows me to feel my vital aliveness. I also fight them for taking so much of my money before I learned to protect myself. In my hole in the basement there are exactly 1,369 lights. I've wired the entire ceiling, every inch of it. And not with fluorescent bulbs, but with the older, more-expensive-to-operate kind, the filament type. An act of sabotage, you know. I've already begun to wire the wall. A junk man I know, a man of vision, has supplied me with wire and sockets. Nothing, storm or flood, must get in the way of our need for light and ever more and brighter light. The truth is the light and light is the truth.

When I finish all four walls, then I'll start on the floor. Just how that will go, I don't know. Yet when you have lived invisible as long as I have you develop a certain ingenuity. I'll solve the problem. And maybe I'll invent a gadget to place my coffeepot on the fire while I lie in bed, and even invent a gadget to warm my bed—like the fellow I saw in one of the picture magazines who made himself a gadget to warm his shoes! Though invisible, I am in the great American tradition of tinkers. That makes me kin to Ford, Edison and Franklin. Call me, since I have a theory and a concept, a "thinker-tinker." Yes, I'll warm my shoes; they need it, they're usually full of holes. I'll do that and more.

Now I have one radio-phonograph; I plan to have five. There is a certain acoustical deadness in my hole, and when I have music I want to *feel* its vibration, not only with my ear but with my whole body. I'd like to hear five recordings of Louis Armstrong playing and singing "What Did I Do to Be so Black and Blue"—all at the same time. Sometimes now I listen to Louis while I have my favorite dessert of vanilla ice cream and sloe gin. I pour the red liquid over the white mound, watching it glisten and the vapor rising as Louis bends that military instrument into a beam of lyrical sound. Perhaps I like Louis Armstrong because he's made poetry out of being invisible. I think it must be because he's unaware that he *is* invisible. And my own grasp of invisibility aids me to understand his music. Once when I asked for a cigarette, some jokers gave me a reefer, which I lighted when I got home and sat listening to my phonograph. It was a strange evening. Invisibility, let me explain, gives one a slightly different sense of time, you're never quite on the beat. Sometimes you're ahead and sometimes behind. Instead of the swift and imperceptible flowing of time, you are aware of its nodes, those points where time stands still or from which it leaps ahead. And you slip into the breaks and look around. That's what you hear vaguely in Louis' music.

Once I saw a prizefighter boxing a yokel. The fighter was swift and amazingly scientific. His body was one violent flow of rapid rhythmic action. He hit the yokel a hundred times while the yokel held up his arms in stunned surprise. But suddenly the yokel, rolling about in the gale of boxing gloves, struck one blow and knocked science, speed and footwork as cold as a well-digger's posterior. The smart money hit the canvas. The long shot got the nod. The yokel had simply stepped inside of his opponent's sense of time. So under the spell of the reefer I discovered a new analytical way of listening to music. The unheard sounds came through, and each melodic line existed of itself, stood out clearly from all the rest, said its piece, and waited patiently for the other voices to speak. That night I found myself hearing not only in time, but in space as well. I not only entered the music but descended, like Dante, into its depths. And *beneath the swiftness of the hot tempo there was a slower tempo and a cave and I entered it and looked around and heard an old woman singing a spiritual as full of Weltschmerz as flamenco, and beneath that lay a still lower level on which I saw a beautiful girl the color of ivory pleading in a voice like my mother's as she stood before a group of slave owners who bid for her naked body, and below that I found a lower level and a more rapid tempo and I heard someone shout:*

"Brothers and sisters, my text this morning is the 'Blackness of Blackness.'"

And a congregation of voices answered: "That blackness is most black, brother, most black . . ."

"In the beginning . . ."

"At the very start," they cried.

". . . there was blackness . . ."

"Preach it . . ."

". . . and the sun . . ."

"The sun, Lawd . . ."

". . . was bloody red . . ."

"Red . . ."

"Now black is . . ." the preacher shouted.

"Bloody . . ."

"I said black is . . ."

"Preach it, brother . . ."

". . . an' black ain't . . ."

"Red, Lawd, red: He said it's red!"

"Amen, brother . . ."

"Black will git you . . ."

"Yes, it will . . ."

". . . an' black won't . . ."

"Naw, it won't!"

"It do . . ."

"It do, Lawd . . ."

". . . an' it don't."

"Halleluiah . . ."

". . . It'll put you, glory, glory, Oh my Lawd, in the WHALE'S BELLY."

"Preach it, dear brother . . ."

". . . an' make you tempt . . ."

"Good God a-mighty!"

"Old Aunt Nelly!"

"Black will make you . . ."

"Black . . ."

". . . or black will un-make you."

"Ain't it the truth, Lawd?"

And at that point a voice of trombone timbre screamed at me, *"Git out of here, you fool! Is you ready to commit treason?"*

And I tore myself away, hearing the old singer of spirituals moaning, *"Go curse your God, boy, and die."*

I stopped and questioned her, asked her what was wrong.

"I dearly loved my master, son," she said.

"You should have hated him," I said.

"He gave me several sons," she said, *"and because I loved my sons I learned to love their father though I hated him too."*

"I too have become acquainted with ambivalence," I said. *"That's why I'm here."*

"What's that?"

"Nothing, a word that doesn't explain it. Why do you moan?"

"I moan this way 'cause he's dead," she said.

"Then tell me, who is that laughing upstairs?"

"Them's my sons. They glad."

"Yes, I can understand that too," I said.

"I laughs too, but I moans too. He promised to set us free but he never could bring hisself to do it. Still I loved him . . ."

"Loved him? You mean . . ."

"Oh yes, but I loved something else even more."

"What more?"

"Freedom."

"Freedom," I said. *"Maybe freedom lies in hating."*

"Naw, son, it's in loving. I loved him and give him the poison and he withered away like a frost-bit apple. Them boys woulda tore him to pieces with they homemake knives."

"A mistake was made somewhere," I said, *"I'm confused."* And I wished to say other things, but the laughter upstairs became too loud and moan-like for me and I tried to break out of it, but I couldn't. Just as I was leaving I felt an urgent desire to ask her what freedom was and went back. She sat with her head in her hands, moaning softly; her leather-brown face was filled with sadness.

"Old woman, what is this freedom you love so well?" I asked around a corner of my mind.

She looked surprised, then thoughtful, then baffled. *"I done forgot, son. It's all mixed up. First I think it's one thing, then*

I think it's another. It gits my head to spinning. I guess now it ain't nothing but knowing how to say what I got up in my head. But it's a hard job, son. Too much is done happen to me in too short a time. Hit's like I have a fever. Ever' time I starts to walk my head gits swirling and I falls down. Or if it ain't that, it's the boys; they gits to laughing and wants to kill up the white folks. They's bitter, that's what they is . . ."

"But what about freedom?"

"Leave me 'lone, boy; my head, aches!"

I left her, feeling dizzy myself. I didn't get far.

Suddenly one of the sons, a big fellow six feet tall, appeared out of nowhere and struck me with his fist.

"What's the matter, man?" I cried.

"You made Ma cry!"

"But how?" I said, dodging a blow.

"Askin' her them questions, that's how. Git outa here and stay, and next time you got questions like that, ask yourself!"

He held me in a grip like cold stone, his fingers fastening upon my windpipe until I thought I would suffocate before he finally allowed me to go. I stumbled about dazed, the music beating hysterically in my ears. It was dark. My head cleared and I wandered down a dark narrow passage, thinking I heard his footsteps hurrying behind me. I was sore, and into my being had come a profound craving for tranquillity, for peace and quiet, a state I felt I could never achieve. For one thing, the trumpet was blaring and the rhythm was too hectic. A tom-tom beating like heart-thuds began drowning out the trumpet, filling my ears. I longed for water and I heard it rushing through the cold mains my fingers touched as I felt my way, but I couldn't stop to search because of the footsteps behind me.

"Hey, Ras," I called. "Is it you, Destroyer? Rinehart?"

No answer, only the rhythmic footsteps behind me. Once I tried crossing the road, but a speeding machine struck me, scraping the skin from my leg as it roared past.

Then somehow I came out of it, ascending hastily from this underworld of sound to hear Louis Armstrong innocently asking,

What did I do
To be so black
And blue?

At first I was afraid; this familiar music had demanded action, the kind of which I was incapable, and yet had I lingered there beneath the surface I might have attempted to act. Nevertheless, I know now that few really listen to this music. I sat on the chair's edge in a soaking sweat, as though each of my 1,369 bulbs had everyone become a klieg light in an individual setting for a third degree with Ras and Rinehart in charge. It was exhausting—as though I had held my breath continuously for an hour under the terrifying serenity that comes from days of intense hunger. And yet, it was a strangely satisfying experience for an invisible man to hear the silence of sound. I had discovered unrecognized compulsions of my being—even though I could not answer "yes" to their promptings. I haven't smoked a reefer since, however; not because they're illegal, but because to *see* around corners is enough (that is not unusual when you are invisible). But to hear around them is too much; it inhibits action. And despite Brother Jack and all that sad, lost period of the Brotherhood, I believe in nothing if not in action.

Please, a definition: A hibernation is a covert preparation for a more overt action.

Besides, the drug destroys one's sense of time completely. If that happened, I might forget to dodge some bright morning and some cluck would run me down with an orange and yellow street car, or a bilious bus! Or I might forget to leave my hole when the moment for action presents itself.

Meanwhile I enjoy my life with the compliments of Monopolated Light & Power. Since you never recognize me even when in closest contact with me, and since, no doubt, you'll hardly believe that I exist, it won't matter if you know that I tapped a power line leading into the building and ran it into my hole in the ground. Before that I lived in the darkness into which I was chased, but now I see. I've illuminated the blackness of my invisibility—and vice versa. And so I play the invisible music of my isolation. The last statement doesn't seem just right, does it? But it is; you hear this music simply because music is heard and seldom seen, except by musicians. Could this compulsion to put invisibility down in black and white be thus an urge to make music of invisibility? But I am an orator, a rabble rouser—Am? I *was*, and perhaps shall be again. Who knows? All sickness is not unto death, neither is invisibility.

I can hear you say, "What a horrible, irresponsible bastard!" And you're right. I leap to agree with you. I am one of the most irresponsible beings that ever lived. Irresponsibility is part of my invisibility; any way you face it, it is a denial. But to whom can I be responsible, and why should I be, when you refuse to see me? And wait until I reveal how truly irresponsible I am. Responsibility rests upon recognition, and recognition is a form of agreement. Take the man whom I almost killed: Who was responsible for that near murder—I? I don't think so, and I refuse it. I won't buy it. You can't give it to me. *He* bumped *me, he* insulted *me.* Shouldn't he, for his own personal safety, have recognized my hysteria, my "danger potential"? He, let us say, was lost in a dream world. But didn't *he* control that dream world—which, alas, is only too real!—and didn't *he* rule me out of it? And if he had yelled for a policeman, wouldn't *I* have been taken for the offending one? Yes, yes, yes! Let me agree with you, I was the irresponsible one; for I should have used my knife to protect the higher interests of society. Some day that kind of foolishness will cause us tragic trouble. All dreamers and sleepwalkers must pay the price, and even the invisible victim is responsible for the fate of all. But I shirked that responsibility; I became too snarled in the incompatible notions that buzzed within my brain. I was a coward.

But what did *I* do to be so blue? Bear with me.

FRANK LONDON BROWN (1927–1962)

An urban literary voice of the 50's and 60's, Frank London Brown was born in Kansas City, Missouri, attended Wilberforce University and the Chicago Kent College of Law and received his B.A. at Roosevelt University in Chicago. He worked as a machinist, union organizer, government employee, jazz singer, journalist, and editor. He reached the higher echelons of modern jazz and appeared with Thelonius Monk at the Gate of Horn in Chicago and the Five Spot in New York. Trumbull Park, his first novel, was published in 1959. Brown published many articles and short stories in Downbeat, *the* Chicago Review, Ebony, *The* Negro Digest, *the* Chicago Tribune, *the* Chicago Sun-Times, *and the* Southwest Review. *He was Associate Editor of* Ebony *magazine. Brown was the first to read short stories, rather than poetry, to jazz accompaniment. He received the John Hay Whitney Foundation Award for creative writing and a University of*

Chicago Fellowship. At the time of his death, at the age of thirty-four, he was working on a revised draft of his second novel and was director of the Union Leadership Program of the University of Chicago, while completing his doctorate in political science at the University of Chicago. His short story "McDougal," rooted in his experience in the world of jazz, is reprinted from the Chicago literary review Phoenix Magazine *(Fall, 1961). A critical evaluation of Frank London Brown's literary work, by Sterling Stuckey, appears in the Literary Criticism section of this anthology.*

McDougal

The bass was walking. Nothing but the bass. And the rhythm section waited, counting time with the tap of a foot or the tip of a finger against the piano top. Pro had just finished his solo and the blood in his neck was pumping so hard it made his head hurt. Sweat shone upon the brown backs of his fingers and the moisture stained the bright brass of his tenor where he held it. Jake, young eyeglass-wearing boy from Dallas, had stopped playing the drums, and he too was sweating, and slight stains were beginning to appear upon his thin cotton coat, and his dark skin caught the purple haze from the overhead spotlight and the sweat that gathered on his flat cheekbones seemed purple. Percy R. Brookins bent over the piano tapping the black keys but not hard enough to make a sound.

Everybody seemed to be waiting.

And the bass was walking. Doom-de-doom-doom-doom-doom-doom!

A tall thin white man whose black hair shone with sweat stood beside the tenorman, lanky, ginger-brown Pro.

Pro had wailed—had blown choruses that dripped with the smell of cornbread and cabbage and had roared like a late "L" and had cried like a blues singer on the last night of a good gig.

Now it was the white man's turn, right after the bass solo was over . . . and he waited and Pro waited and so did Jake the drummer, and Percy R. Brookins. Little Jug was going into his eighth chorus and showed no sign of letting up.

DOOM-DE-DOOM-DOOM-DOOM-DOOM-DOOM!

Jake looked out into the audience. And the shadowy faces were hard to see behind the bright colored lights that ringed the bandstand. Yet he felt that they too waited . . . Pro had laid down some righteous sound—he had told so much truth —told it so plainly, so passionately that it had scared everybody in the place, even Pro, and now he waited for the affirming bass to finish so that he could hear what the white man had to say.

McDougal was his name. And his young face had many wrinkles and his young body slouched and his shoulders hung round and loose. He was listening to Little Jug's bass yet he also seemed to be listening to something else, almost as if he were still listening to the truth Pro had told.

And the bass walked.

Jake leaned over his drums and whispered to Percy R. Brookins.

"That cat sure looks beat don't he?"

Percy R. Brookins nodded, and then put his hand to the side of his mouth, and whispered back.

"His old lady's pregnant again."

"Again?! What's that? Number three?"

"Number four," Percy R. Brookins answered.

"Hell I'd look sad too . . . Is he still living on Forty Seventh Street?"

The drums slid in underneath the bass and the bass dropped out amid strong applause and a few "Yeahs!" And Jake, not having realized it, cut in where McDougal was to begin his solo. He smiled sheepishly at Percy R. Brookins and the piano player hunched his shoulders and smiled.

McDougal didn't look around, he didn't move from his slouched one-sided stance, he didn't stop staring beyond the audience and beyond the room itself. Yet his left foot kept time with the light bombs the drummer dropped and the husky soft scrape of the brushes.

Little Jug pulled a handkerchief from his back pocket and wiped his cheeks and around the back of his neck, then he stared at the black, glistening back of McDougal's head and then leaned down and whispered to Percy R. Brookins.

"Your boy sure could stand a haircut. He looks as bad as Ol' Theo." And they both knew how bad Ol' Theo looked and they both frowned and laughed.

Percy R. Brookins touched a chord lightly to give some color to Jake's solo and then he said.

"Man, that cat has suffered for that brownskin woman."

Little Jug added.

"And those . . . three little brownskin crumb-crushers."

Percy R. Brookins, hit another chord and then

"Do you know none of the white folks'll rent to him now?"

Little Jug laughed.

"Why hell yes . . . will they rent to me?"

"Sure they will, down on Forty Seventh Street."

Little Jug nodded at Jake and Jake made a couple of breaks that meant that he was about to give in to McDougal.

Percy R. Brookins turned to face his piano and then he got an idea and he turned to Little Jug and spoke with a serious look behind the curious smile on his face.

"You know that cat's after us? I mean he's out to blow the real thing. You know what I mean? Like he's no Harry James? Do you know that?"

Little Jug ran into some triplets and skipped a couple of beats and brought McDougal in right on time.

At the same time McDougal rode in on a long, hollow, gut bucket note that made Percy R. Brookins laugh, and caused Pro to cock his head and rub his cheek. The tall worried looking white man bent his trumpet to the floor and hunched his shoulders and closed his eyes and blew.

Little Jug answered Percy R. Brookins question about McDougal.

"I been knowing that . . . he knows the happenings . . . I mean about where we get it, you dig? I mean like with Leola and those kids and Forty Seventh Street and those jive landlords, you dig? The man's been burnt, Percy. Listen to that somitch—listen to him!"

McDougal's eyes were closed and he did not see the dark woman with the dark cotton suit that ballooned away from the great bulge of her stomach. He didn't see her ease into a chair at the back of the dark smoky room. He didn't see the smile on her face or the sweat upon her flat nose.

PAULE MARSHALL (1929–   )

Winning critical recognition as a significant and accomplished writer of her generation, Paule Marshall was born in Brooklyn, of West Indian parents who emigrated from

*Barbados to the United States shortly after World War I. She
began writing sketches and poems before she was ten years
old. After graduating Phi Beta Kappa from Brooklyn College,
Marshall worked in libraries and was a feature writer for the
magazine* Our World, *for which she traveled on assignments
to the West Indies and Brazil. In her writing she has captured
the idiom and patterns of Barbadian speech and has drawn
on her experiences in the Caribbean as well as in the United
States. She was a Guggenheim Fellow and a MacArthur Foundation fellow, and she has received grants from the American
Academy of Arts and Letters, the Ford Foundation and the
National Endowment for the Arts. Her autobiographical story
"To Da-duh, In Memoriam," which appeared initially in the
West Indian magazine* New World *in 1967, was published here
for the first time in the United States.*

To Da-duh, In Memoriam

". . . Oh Nana! all of you is not involved in this evil business
Death,
Nor all of us in Life."
—From "At My Grandmother's Grave," by Lebert Bethune

I did not see her at first I remember. For not only was it dark
inside the crowded disembarkation shed in spite of the daylight flooding in from outside, but standing there waiting for
her with my mother and sister I was still somewhat blinded
from the sheen of tropical sunlight on the water of the bay
which we had just crossed in the landing boat, leaving behind
us the ship that had brought us from New York lying in the
offing. Besides, being only nine years of age at the time and
knowing nothing of islands I was busy attending to the alien
sights and sounds of Barbados, the unfamiliar smells.

I did not see her, but I was alerted to her approach by my
mother's hand which suddenly tightened around mine, and
looking up I traced her gaze through the gloom in the shed
until I finally made out the small, purposeful, painfully erect
figure of the old woman headed our way.

Her face was drowned in the shadow of an ugly rolled-
brim brown felt hat, but the details of her slight body and of

the struggle taking place within it were clear enough—an intense, unrelenting struggle between her back which was beginning to bend ever so slightly under the weight of her eighty odd years and the rest of her which sought to deny those years and hold that back straight, keep it in line. Moving swiftly toward us (so swiftly it seemed she did not intend stopping when she reached us but would sweep past us out the doorway which opened onto the sea and like Christ walk upon the water!), she was caught between the sunlight at her end of the building and the darkness inside—and for a moment she appeared to contain them both: the light in the long severe old-fashioned white dress she wore which brought the sense of a past that was still alive into our bustling present and in the snatch of white at her eye; the darkness in her black high-top shoes and in her face which was visible now that she was closer.

It was as stark and fleshless as a death mask, that face. The maggots might have already done their work, leaving only the framework of bone beneath the ruined skin and deep wells at the temple and jaw. But her eyes were alive, unnervingly so for one so old, with a sharp light that flicked out of the dim clouded depths like a lizard's tongue to snap up all in her view. Those eyes betrayed a child's curiosity about the world, and I wondered vaguely seeing them, and seeing the way the bodice of her ancient dress had collapsed in on her flat chest (what had happened to her breasts?), whether she might not be some kind of child at the same time that she was a woman, with fourteen children, my mother included, to prove it. Perhaps she was both, both child and woman, darkness and light, past and present, life and death—all the opposites contained and reconciled in her.

"My Da-duh," my mother said formally and stepped forward. The name sounded like thunder fading softly in the distance.

"Child," Da-duh said, and her tone, her quick scrutiny of my mother, the brief embrace in which they appeared to shy from each other rather than touch, wiped out the fifteen years my mother had been away and restored the old relationship. My mother, who was such a formidable figure in my eyes, had suddenly with a word been reduced to my status.

"Yes, God is good," Da-duh said with a nod that was like a tic. "He has spared me to see my child again."

We were led forward then, apologetically because not only did Da-duh prefer boys but she also liked her grandchildren to be "white," that is, fair-skinned; and we had, I was to dis-

cover, a number of cousins, the outside children of white es-
tate managers and the like, who qualified. We, though, were
as black as she.

My sister being the oldest was presented first. "This one
takes after the father," my mother said and waited to be re-
proved.

Frowning, Da-duh tilted my sister's face toward the light.
But her frown soon gave way to a grudging smile, for my
sister with her large mild eyes and little broad winged nose,
with our father's high-cheeked Barbadian cast to her face,
was pretty.

"She's goin' be lucky," Da-duh said and patted her once on
the cheek. "Any girl-child that takes after the father does be
lucky."

She turned then to me. But oddly enough she did not
touch me. Instead leaning close, she peered hard at me, and
then quickly drew back. I thought I saw her hand start up as
though to shield her eyes. It was almost as if she saw not
only me, a thin truculent child who it was said took after no
one but myself, but something in me which for some reason
she found disturbing, even threatening. We looked silently at
each other for a long time there in the noisy shed, our gaze
locked. She was the first to look away.

"But Adry," she said to my mother and her laugh was
cracked, thin, apprehensive. "Where did you get this one
here with this fierce look?"

"We don't know where she came out of, my Da-duh," my
mother said, laughing also. Even I smiled to myself. After all
I had won the encounter. Da-duh had recognized my small
strength—and this was all I ever asked of the adults in my
life then.

"Come, soul," Da-duh said and took my hand. "You must
be one of those New York terrors you hear so much about."

She led us, me at her side and my sister and mother behind, out of the shed into the sunlight that was like a bright
driving summer rain and over to a group of people clustered
beside a decrepit lorry. They were our relatives, most of them
from St. Andrews although Da-duh herself lived in St.
Thomas, the women wearing bright print dresses, the colors
vivid against their darkness, the men rusty black suits that encased them like straitjackets. Da-duh, holding fast to my
hand, became my anchor as they circled round us like a nervous sea, exclaiming, touching us with their calloused hands,
embracing us shyly. They laughed in awed bursts: "But look
Adry got big-big children!"/ "And see the nice things they

wearing, wrist watch and all!/ "I tell you, Adry has done all right for sheself in New York. . . ."

Da-duh, ashamed at their wonder, embarrassed for them, admonished them the while. "But oh Christ," she said, "why you all got to get on like you never saw people from 'Away' before? You would think New York is the only place in the world to hear wunna. That's why I don't like to go anyplace with you St. Andrews people, you know. You all ain't been colonized."

We were in the back of the lorry finally, packed in among the barrels of ham, flour, cornmeal and rice and the trunks of clothes that my mother had brought as gifts. We made our way slowly through Bridgetown's clogged streets, part of a funereal procession of cars and open-sided buses, bicycles and donkey carts. The dim little limestone shops and offices along the way marched with us, at the same mournful pace, toward the same grave ceremony—as did the people, the women balancing huge baskets on top their heads as if they were no more than hats they wore to shade them from the sun. Looking over the edge of the lorry I watched as their feet slurred the dust. I listened, and their voices, raw and loud and dissonant in the heat, seemed to be grappling with each other high overhead.

Da-duh sat on a trunk in our midst, a monarch amid her court. She still held my hand, but it was different now. I had suddenly become her anchor, for I felt her fear of the lorry with its asthmatic motor (a fear and distrust, I later learned, she held of all machines) beating like a pulse in her rough palm.

As soon as we left Bridgetown behind though, she relaxed, and while the others around us talked she gazed at the canes standing tall on either side of the winding marl road. "C'dear," she said softly to herself after a time. "The canes this side are pretty enough."

They were too much for me. I thought of them as giant weeds that had overrun the island, leaving scarcely any room for the small tottering houses of sunbleached pine we passed or the people, dark streaks as our lorry hurtled by. I suddenly feared that we were journeying, unaware that we were, toward some dangerous place where the canes, grown as high and thick as a forest, would close in on us and run us through with their stiletto blades. I longed then for the familiar: for the street in Brooklyn where I lived, for my father who had refused to accompany us ("Blowing out good money on foolishness," he had said of the trip), for a game of tag with my friends under the chestnut tree outside our aging brownstone house.

"Yes, but wait till you see St. Thomas canes," Da-duh was saying to me. "They's canes father, bo," she gave a proud arrogant nod. "Tomorrow, God willing, I goin' take you out in the ground and show them to you."

True to her word Da-duh took me with her the following day out into the ground. It was a fairly large plot adjoining her weathered board and shingle house and consisting of a small orchard, a good-sized canepiece and behind the canes, where the land sloped abruptly down, a gully. She had purchased it with Panama money sent her by her eldest son, my uncle Joseph, who had died working on the canal. We entered the ground along a trail no wider than her body and as devious and complex as her reasons for showing me her land. Da-duh strode briskly ahead, her slight form filled out this morning by the layers of sacking petticoats she wore under her working dress to protect her against the damp. A fresh white cloth, elaborately arranged around her head, added to her height, and lent her a vain, almost roguish air.

Her pace slowed once we reached the orchard, and glancing back at me occasionally over her shoulder, she pointed out the various trees.

"This here is a breadfruit," she said. "That one yonder is a papaw. Here's a guava. This is a mango. I know you don't have anything like these in New York. Here's a sugar apple [the fruit looked more like artichokes than apples to me]. This one bears limes. . . ." She went on for some time, intoning the names of the trees as though they were those of her gods. Finally, turning to me, she said, "I know you don't have anything this nice where you come from." Then, as I hesitated: "I said I know you don't have anything this nice where you come from. . . ."

"No," I said and my world did seem suddenly lacking.

Da-dau nodded and passed on. The orchard ended and we were on the narrow cart road that led through the canepiece, the canes clashing like swords above my cowering head. Again she turned and her thin muscular arms spread wide, her dim gaze embracing the small field of canes, she said—and her voice almost broke under the weight of her pride, "Tell me, have you got anything like these in that place where you were born?"

"No."

"I din' think so. I bet you don't even know that these canes here and the sugar you eat is one and the same thing. That they does throw the canes into some damn machine at the factory and squeeze out all the little life in them to make sugar for you all so in New York to eat. I bet you don't know that."

"I've got two cavities and I'm not allowed to eat a lot of sugar."

But Da-duh didn't hear me. She had turned with an inexplicably angry motion and was making her way rapidly out of the canes and down the slope at the edge of the field which led to the gully below. Following her apprehensively down the incline amid a stand of banana plants whose leaves flapped like elephants ears in the wind, I found myself in the middle of a small tropical wood—a place dense and damp and gloomy and tremulous with the fitful play of light and shadow as the leaves high above moved against the sun that was almost hidden from view. It was a violent place, the tangled foliage fighting each other for a chance at the sunlight, the branches of the trees locked in what seemed an immemorial struggle, one both necessary and inevitable. But despite the violence, it was pleasant, almost peaceful in the gully, and beneath the thick undergrowth the earth smelled like spring.

This time Da-duh didn't even bother to ask her usual question, but simply turned and waited for me to speak.

"No," I said, my head bowed. "We don't have anything like this in New York."

"Ah," she cried, her triumph complete. "I din' think so. Why, I've heard that's a place where you can walk till you near drop and never see a tree."

"We've got a chestnut tree in front of our house," I said.

"Does it bear?" She waited. "I ask you, does it bear?"

"Not anymore," I muttered. "It used to, but not anymore."

She gave the nod that was like a nervous twitch. "You see," she said. "Nothing can bear there." Then, secure behind her scorn, she added, "But tell me, what's this snow like that you hear so much about?"

Looking up, I studied her closely, sensing my chance, and then I told her, describing at length and with as much drama as I could summon not only what snow in the city was like, but what it would be like here, in her perennial summer kingdom.

". . . And you see all these trees you got here," I said. "Well, they'd be bare. No leaves, no fruit, nothing. They'd be covered in snow. You see your canes. They'd be buried under tons of snow. The snow would be higher than your head, higher than your house, and you wouldn't be able to come down into this here gully because it would be snowed under. . . ."

She searched my face for the lie, still scornful but intrigued. "What a thing, huh?" she said finally, whispering it softly to herself.

"And when it snows you couldn't dress like you are now," I said. "Oh no, you'd freeze to death. You'd have to wear a hat and gloves and galoshes and ear muffs so your ears wouldn't freeze and drop off, and a heavy coat. I've got a Shirley Temple coat with fur on the collar. I can dance. You wanna see?"

Before she could answer I began, with a dance called the Truck which was popular back then in the 1930's. My right forefinger waving, I trucked around the nearby trees and around Da-duh's awed and rigid form. After the Truck I did the Suzy-Q, my lean hips swishing, my sneakers sidling zigzag over the ground. "I can sing," I said and did so, starting with "I'm Gonna Sit Right Down and Write Myself a Letter," then without pausing, "Tea For Two," and ending with "I Found a Million Dollar Baby in a Five and Ten Cent Store."

For long moments afterwards Da-duh stared at me as if I were a creature from Mars, an emissary from some world she did not know but which intrigued her and whose power she both felt and feared. Yet something about my performance must have pleased her, because bending down she slowly lifted her long skirt and then, one by one, the layers of petticoats until she came to a drawstring purse dangling at the end of a long strip of cloth tied round her waist. Opening the purse she handed me a penny. "Here," she said half-smiling against her will. "Take this to buy yourself a sweet at the shop up the road. There's nothing to be done with you, soul."

From then on, whenever I wasn't taken to visit relatives, I accompanied Da-duh out into the ground, and alone with her amid the canes or down in the gully I told her about New York. It always began with some slighting remark on her part: "I know they don't have anything this nice where you come from," or "Tell me, I hear those foolish people in New York does do such and such. . . ." But as I answered, recreating my towering world of steel and concrete and machines for her, building the city out of words, I would feel her give way. I came to know the signs of her surrender: the total stillness that would come over her little hard dry form, the probing gaze that like a surgeon's knife sought to cut through my skull to get at the images there, to see if I were lying; above all, her fear, a fear nameless and profound, the same one I had felt beating in the palm of her hand that day in the lorry.

Over the weeks I told her about refrigerators, radios, gas

stoves, elevators, trolley cars, wringer washing machines, movies, airplanes, the cyclone at Coney Island, subways, toasters, electric lights: "At night, see, all you have to do is flip this little switch on the wall and all the lights in the house go on. Just like that. Like magic. It's like turning on the sun at night."

"But tell me," she said to me once with a faint mocking smile, "do the white people have all these things too or it's only the people looking like us?"

I laughed. "What d'ya mean," I said. "The white people have even better." Then: "I beat up a white girl in my class last term."

"Beating up white people!" Her tone was incredulous.

"How you mean!" I said, using an expression of hers. "She called me a name."

For some reason Da-duh could not quite get over this and repeated in the same hushed, shocked voice, "Beating up white people now! Oh, the lord, the world's changing up so I can scarce recognize it anymore."

One morning toward the end of our stay, Da-duh led me into a part of the gully that we had never visited before, an area darker and more thickly overgrown than the rest, almost impenetrable. There in a small clearing amid the dense bush, she stopped before an incredibly tall royal palm which rose cleanly out of the ground, and drawing the eye up with it, soared high above the trees around it into the sky. It appeared to be touching the blue dome of sky, to be flaunting its dark crown of fronds right in the blinding white face of the late morning sun.

Da-duh watched me a long time before she spoke, and then she said very quietly, "All right, now, tell me if you've got anything this tall in that place you're from."

I almost wished, seeing her face, that I could have said no. "Yes," I said. "We've got buildings hundreds of times this tall in New York. There's one called the Empire State building that's the tallest in the world. My class visited it last year and I went all the way to the top. It's got over a hundred floors. I can't describe how tall it is. Wait a minute. What's the name of that hill I went to visit the other day, where they have the police station?"

"You mean Bissex?"

"Yes, Bissex. Well, the Empire State Building is way taller than that."

"You're lying now!" she shouted, trembling with rage. Her hand lifted to strike me.

"No, I'm not," I said. "It really is, If you don't believe me

I'll send you a picture postcard of it soon as I get back home so you can see for yourself. But it's way taller than Bissex."

All the fight went out of her at that. The hand poised to strike me fell limp to her side, and as she stared at me, seeing not me but the building that was taller than the highest hill she knew, the small stubborn light in her eyes (it was the same amber as the flame in the kerosene lamp she lit at dusk) began to fail. Finally, with a vague gesture that even in the midst of her defeat still tried to dismiss me and my world, she turned and started back through the gully, walking slowly, her steps groping and uncertain, as if she was suddenly no longer sure of the way, while I followed triumphant yet strangely saddened behind.

The next morning I found her dressed for our morning walk but stretched out on the Berbice chair in the tiny drawing room where she sometimes napped during the afternoon heat, her face turned to the window beside her. She appeared thinner and suddenly indescribably old.

"My Da-duh," I said.

"Yes, nuh," she said. Her voice was listless and the face she slowly turned my way was, now that I think back on it, like a Benin mask, the features drawn and almost distorted by an ancient abstract sorrow.

"Don't you feel well?" I asked.

"Girl, I don't know."

"My Da-duh, I goin' boil you some bush tea," my aunt, Da-duh's youngest child, who lived with her, called from the shed roof kitchen.

"Who tell you I need bush tea?" she cried, her voice assuming for a moment its old authority. "You can't even rest nowadays without some malicious person looking for you to be dead. Come girl," she motioned me to a place beside her on the old-fashioned lounge chair, "give us a tune."

I sang for her until breakfast at eleven, all my brash irreverent Tin Pan Alley songs, and then just before noon we went out into the ground. But it was a short, dispirited walk. Da-duh didn't even notice that the mangoes were beginning to ripen and would have to be picked before the village boys got to them. And when she paused occasionally and looked out across the canes or up at her trees it wasn't as if she were seeing them but something else. Some huge, monolithic shape had imposed itself, it seemed, between her and the land, obstructing her vision. Returning to the house she slept the entire afternoon on the Berbice chair.

She remained like this until we left, languishing away the mornings on the chair at the window gazing out at the land as if it were already doomed; then, at noon, taking the brief stroll with me through the ground during which she seldom spoke, and afterwards returning home to sleep till almost dusk sometimes.

On the day of our departure she put on the austere, ankle length white dress, the black shoes and brown felt hat (her town clothes she called them), but she did not go with us to town. She saw us off on the road outside her house and in the midst of my mother's tearful protracted farewell, she leaned down and whispered in my ear, "Girl, you're not to forget now to send me the picture of that building, you hear."

By the time I mailed her the large colored picture postcard of the Empire State building she was dead. She died during the famous '37 strike which began shortly after we left. On the day of her death England sent planes flying low over the island in a show of force—so low, according to my aunt's letter, that the downdraft from them shook the ripened mangoes from the trees in Da-duh's orchard. Frightened, everyone in the village fled into the canes. Except Da-duh. She remained in the house at the window so my aunt said, watching as the planes came swooping and screaming like monstrous birds down over the village, over her house, rattling her trees and flattening the young canes in her field. It must have seemed to her lying there that they did not intend pulling out of their dive, but like the hardback beetles which hurled themselves with suicidal force against the walls of the house at night, those menacing silver shapes would hurl themselves in an ecstasy of self-immolation onto the land, destroying it utterly.

When the planes finally left and the villagers reurned they found her dead on the Berbice chair at the window.

She died and I lived, but always, to this day even, within the shadow of her death. For a brief period after I was grown I went to live alone, like one doing penance, in a loft above a noisy factory in downtown New York and there painted seas of sugarcane and huge swirling Van Gogh suns and palm trees striding like brightly-plumed Watussi across a tropical landscape, while the thunderous tread of the machines downstairs jarred the floor beneath my easel, mocking my efforts.

DIANE OLIVER (1943–1966)

Death in an automobile accident at the age of twenty-three brought a tragic end to the promising literary talent of Diane Alene Oliver, a student at the famous Writer's Workshop of the University of Iowa. She was born in Charlotte, North Carolina, and graduated from the University of North Carolina at Greensboro in 1964. She served as feature editor and later as managing editor of the student newspaper The Carolinian. *In 1964 she was selected as a guest editor of* Mademoiselle *magazine, and during the summer of that year spent eight weeks in Switzerland with the Experiment in International Living. She published short stories in* Red Clay Reader, Negro Digest, The Sewanee Review, *and* New Writing of the Sixties. *The University of Iowa conferred the Master of Fine Arts degree on Miss Oliver posthumously. Her story "Neighbors," which follows, was published in* The Sewanee Review *(Spring, 1966) and was selected for inclusion in* Prize Stories 1967: The O. Henry Awards.

Neighbors

The bus turning the corner of Patterson and Talford Avenue was dull this time of evening. Of the four passengers standing in the rear, she did not recognize any of her friends. Most of the people tucked neatly in the double seats were women, maids and cooks on their way from work or secretaries who had worked late and were riding from the office building at the mill. The cotton mill was out from town, near the house where she worked. She noticed that a few men were riding too. They were obviously just working men, except for one gentleman dressed very neatly in a dark grey suit and carrying what she imagined was a push-button umbrella.

He looked to her as though he usually drove a car to work.

She immediately decided that the car probably wouldn't start this morning so he had to catch the bus to and from work. She was standing in the rear of the bus, peering at the passengers, her arms barely reaching the over-head railing, trying not to wobble with every lurch. But every corner the bus turned pushed her head toward a window. And her hair was coming down too, wisps of black curls swung between her eyes. She looked at the people around her. Some of them were white, but most of them were her color. Looking at the passengers at least kept her from thinking of tomorrow. But really she would be glad when it came, then everything would be over.

She took a firmer grip on the green leather seat and wished she had on her glasses. The man with the umbrella was two people ahead of her on the other side of the bus, so she could see him between other people very clearly. She watched as he unfolded the evening newspaper, craning her neck to see what was on the front page. She stood, impatiently trying to read the headlines, when she realized he was staring up at her rather curiously. Biting her lips she turned her head and stared out of the window until the downtown section was in sight.

She would have to wait until she was home to see if they were in the newspaper again. Sometimes she felt that if another person snapped a picture of them she would burst out screaming. Last Monday reporters were already inside the pre-school clinic when she took Tommy for his last polio shot. She didn't understand how anyone could be so heartless to a child. The flashbulb went off right when the needle went in and all the picture showed was Tommy's open mouth.

The bus pulling up to the curb jerked to a stop, startling her and confusing her thoughts. Clutching in her hand the paper bag that contained her uniform, she pushed her way toward the door. By standing in the back of the bus, she was one of the first people to step to the ground. Outside the bus, the evening air felt humid and uncomfortable and her dress kept sticking to her. She looked up and remembered that the weatherman had forecast rain. Just their luck—why, she wondered, would it have to rain on top of everything else?

As she walked along, the main street seemed unnaturally quiet but she decided her imagination was merely playing tricks. Besides, most of the stores had been closed since five o'clock.

She stopped to look at a reversible raincoat in Ivey's window, but although she had a full time job now, she couldn't keep her mind on clothes. She was about to continue walking when she heard a horn blowing. Looking around, half-scared but also curious, she saw a man beckoning to her in a grey car. He was nobody she knew but since a nicely dressed woman was with him in the front seat, she walked to the car.

"You're Jim Mitchell's girl, aren't you?" he questioned. "You Ellie or the other one?"

She nodded yes, wondering who he was and how much he had been drinking.

"Now honey," he said leaning over the woman, "you don't know me but your father does and you tell him that if anything happens to that boy of his tomorrow we're ready to set things straight." He looked her straight in the eye and she promised to take home the message.

Just as the man was about to step on the gas, the woman reached out and touched her arm. "You hurry up home, honey, it's about dark out here."

Before she could find out their names, the Chevrolet had disappeared around a corner. Ellie wished someone would magically appear and tell her everything that had happened since August. Then maybe she could figure out what was real and what she had been imagining for the past couple of days.

She walked past the main shopping district up to Tanner's where Saraline was standing in the window peeling oranges. Everything in the shop was painted orange and green and Ellie couldn't help thinking that poor Saraline looked out of place. She stopped to wave to her friend who pointed the knife to her watch and then to her boyfriend standing in the rear of the shop. Ellie nodded that she understood. She knew Sara wanted her to tell her grandfather that she had to work late again. Neither one of them could figure out why he didn't like Charlie. Saraline had finished high school three years ahead of her and it was time for her to be getting married. Ellie watched as her friend stopped peeling the orange long enough to cross her fingers. She nodded again but she was afraid all the crossed fingers in the world wouldn't stop the trouble tomorrow.

She stopped at the traffic light and spoke to a shrivelled woman hunched against the side of a building. Scuffing the bottom of her sneakers on the curb she waited for the woman to open her mouth and grin as she usually did. The kids used to bait her to talk, and since she didn't have but one tooth in her whole head they called her Doughnut Puncher. But the woman was still, the way everything else had been all week.

From where Ellie stood, across the street from the Sears and Roebuck parking lot, she could see their house, all of the houses on the single street white people called Welfare Row. Those newspaper men always made her angry. All of their articles showed how rough the people were on their street. And the reporters never said her family wasn't on welfare, the papers always said the family lived on that street. She paused to look across the street at a group of kids pouncing on one rubber ball. There were always white kids around their neighborhood mixed up in the games, but playing with them was almost an unwritten rule. When everybody started going to school nobody played together any more.

She crossed at the corner ignoring the cars at the stop light and the closer she got to her street the more she realized that the newspaper was right. The houses were ugly, there were not even any trees, just patches of scraggly bushes and grasses. As she cut across the sticky asphalt pavement covered with cars she was conscious of the parking lot floodlights casting a strange glow on her street. She stared from habit at the house on the end of the block and except for the way the paint was peeling they all looked alike to her. Now at twilight the flaking grey paint had a luminous glow and as she walked down the dirt sidewalk she noticed Mr. Paul's pipe smoke added to the hazy atmosphere. Mr. Paul would be sitting in that same spot waiting until Saraline came home. Ellie slowed her pace to speak to the elderly man sitting on the porch.

"Evening, Mr. Paul," she said. Her voice sounded clear and out of place on the vacant street.

"Eh, who's that?" Mr. Paul leaned over the rail. "What you say, girl?"

"How are you?" she hollered louder. "Sara said she'd be late tonight, she has to work." She waited for the words to sink in.

His head had dropped and his eyes were facing his lap. She could see that he was disappointed. "Couldn't help it," he said finally. "Reckon they needed her again." Then as if he suddenly remembered he turned toward her.

"You people be ready down there? Still gonna let him go tomorrow?"

She looked at Mr. Paul between the missing rails on his porch, seeing how his rolled up trousers seemed to fit exactly in the vacant banister space.

"Last I heard this morning we're still letting him go," she said.

Mr. Paul had shifted his weight back to the chair. "Don't reckon they'll hurt him," he mumbled, scratching the side of his face. "Hope he don't mind being spit on though. Spitting ain't like cutting. They can spit on him and nobody'll ever know who did it," he said, ending his words with a quiet chuckle.

Ellie stood on the sidewalk grinding her heel in the dirt waiting for the old man to finish talking. She was glad somebody found something funny to laugh at. Finally he shut up.

"Goodbye, Mr. Paul," she waved. Her voice sounded loud to her own ears. But she knew the way her head ached intensified noises. She walked home faster, hoping they had some aspirin in the house and that those men would leave earlier tonight.

From the front of her house she could tell that the men were still there. The living room light shone behind the yellow shades, coming through brighter in the patched places. She thought about moving the geranium pot from the porch to catch the rain but changed her mind. She kicked a beer can under a car parked in the street and stopped to look at her reflection on the car door. The tiny flowers of her printed dress made her look as if she had a strange tropical disease. She spotted another can and kicked it out of the way of the car, thinking that one of these days some kid was going to fall and hurt himself. What she wanted to do she knew was kick the car out of the way. Both the station wagon and the Ford had been parked in front of her house all week, waiting. Everybody was just sitting around waiting.

Suddenly she laughed aloud. Reverend Davis' car was big and black and shiny just like, but no, the smile disappeared from her face, her mother didn't like for them to say things about other people's color. She looked around to see who else came, and saw Mr. Moore's old beat up blue car. Somebody had torn away half of his NAACP sign. Sometimes she really felt sorry for the man. No matter how hard he glued on his stickers somebody always yanked them off again.

Ellie didn't recognize the third car but it had an Alabama license plate. She turned around and looked up and down the street, hating to go inside. There were no lights on their street, but in the distance she could see the bright lights of the parking lot. Slowly she did an about face and climbed the steps.

She wondered when her mama was going to remember to get a yellow bulb for the porch. Although the lights hadn't been turned on, usually June bugs and mosquitoes swarmed all around the porch. By the time she was inside the house she always felt like they were crawling in her hair. She pulled on the screen and saw that Mama finally had made Hezekiah patch up the holes. The globs of white adhesive tape scattered over the screen door looked just like misshapen butterflies.

She listened to her father's voice and could tell by the tone that the men were discussing something important again. She rattled the door once more but nobody came.

"Will somebody please let me in?" Her voice carried through the screen to the knot of men sitting in the corner.

"The door's open," her father yelled. "Come on in."

"The door is not open," she said evenly. "You know we stopped leaving it open." She was feeling tired again and her voice had fallen an octave lower.

"Yeah, I forgot, I forgot," he mumbled walking to the door.

She watched her father almost stumble across a chair to let her in. He was shorter than the light bulb and the light seemed to beam down on him, emphasizing the wrinkles around his eyes. She could tell from the way he pushed open the screen that he hadn't had much sleep either. She'd overheard him telling Mama that the people down at the shop seemed to be piling on the work harder just because of this thing. And he couldn't do anything or say anything to his boss because they probably wanted to fire him.

"Where's Mama?" she whispered. He nodded toward the back.

"Good evening, everybody," she said looking at the three men who had not looked up since she entered the room. One of the men half stood, but his attention was geared back to something another man was saying. They were sitting on the sofa in their shirt sleeves and there was a pitcher of ice water on the window sill.

"Your mother probably needs some help," her father said. She looked past him trying to figure out who the white man was sitting on the end. His face looked familiar and she tried to remember where she had seen him before. The men were paying no attention to her. She bent to see what they were studying and saw a large sheet of white drawing paper. She could see blocks and lines and the man sitting in the middle was marking a trail with the eraser edge of the pencil.

The quiet stillness of the room was making her head ache more. She pushed her way through the red embroidred curtains that led to the kitchen.

"I'm home, Mama," she said, standing in front of the back door facing the big yellow sun Hezekiah and Tommy had painted on the wall above the iron stove. Immediately she felt a warmth permeating her skin. "Where is everybody?" she asked, sitting at the table where her mother was peeling potatoes.

"Mrs. McAllister is keeping Helen and Teenie," her

mother said. "Your brother is staying over with Harry to-night." With each name she uttered, a slice of potato peeling tumbled to the newspaper on the table. "Tommy's in the bed-room reading that Uncle Wiggily book."

Ellie looked up at her mother but her eyes were straight ahead. She knew that Tommy only read the Uncle Wiggily book by himself when he was unhappy. She got up and walked to the kitchen cabinet.

"The other knives dirty?" she asked.

·"No," her mother said, "look in the next drawer."

Ellie pulled open the drawer, flicking scraps of white paint with her fingernail. She reached for the knife and at the same time a pile of envelopes caught her eye.

"Any more come today?" she asked, pulling out the knife and slipping the envelopes under the dish towels.

"Yes, seven more came today," her mother accentuated each word carefully. "Your father has them with him in the other room."

"Same thing?" she asked picking up a potato and wishing she could think of some way to change the subject.

The white people had been threatening them for the past three weeks. Some of the letters were aimed at the family, but most of them were directed to Tommy himself. About once a week in the same handwriting somebody wrote that he'd better not eat lunch at school because they were going to poison him.

They had been getting those letters ever since the school board made Tommy's name public. She sliced the potato and dropped the pieces in the pan of cold water. Out of all those people he had been the only one the board had accepted for transfer to the elementary school. The other children, the members said, didn't live in the district. As she cut the eyes out of another potato she thought about the first letter they had received and how her father just set fire to it in the ash-tray. But then Mr. Belk said they'd better save the rest, in case anything happened, they might need the evidence for court.

She peeped up again at her mother, "Who's that white man in there with Daddy?"

"One of Lawyer Belk's friends," she answered. "He's pas-tor of the church that's always on television Sunday morning. Mr. Belk seems to think that having him around will do some good." Ellie saw that her voice was shaking just like her hand as she reached for the last potato. Both of them could hear Tommy in the next room mumbling to himself. She was afraid to look at her mother.

Suddenly Ellie was aware that her mother's hands were

trembling violently. "He's so little," she whispered and suddenly the knife slipped out of her hands and she was crying and breathing at the same time.

Ellie didn't know what to do but after a few seconds she cleared away the peelings and put the knives in the sink. "Why don't you lie down?" she suggested. "I'll clean up and get Tommy in bed." Without saying anything her mother rose and walked to her bedroom.

Ellie wiped off the table and draped the dishcloth over the sink. She stood back and looked at the rusting pipes powdered with a whitish film. One of these days they would have to paint the place. She tiptoed past her mother who looked as if she had fallen asleep from exhaustion.

"Tommy," she called softly, "come in and get ready for bed."

Tommy sitting in the middle of the floor did not answer. He was sitting the way she imagined he would be, crosslegged, pulling his ear lobe as he turned the ragged pages of *Uncle Wiggily at the Zoo.*

"What you doing, Tommy?" she said squatting on the floor beside him. He smiled and pointed at the picture of the ducks.

"School starts tomorrow," she said, turning a page with him. "Don't you think it's time to go to bed?"

"Oh Ellie, do I have to go now?" She looked down at the serious brown eyes and the closely cropped hair. For a minute she wondered if he questioned having to go to bed now or to school tomorrow.

"Well," she said, "aren't you about through with the book?" He shook his head. "Come on," she pulled him up, "you're a sleepy head." Still he shook his head.

"When Helen and Teenie coming home?"

"Tomorrow after you come home from school they'll be here."

She lifted him from the floor thinking how small he looked to be facing all those people tomorrow.

"Look," he said breaking away from her hand and pointing to a blue shirt and pair of cotton twill pants, "Mama got them for me to wear tomorrow."

While she ran water in the tub, she heard him crawl on top of the bed. He was quiet and she knew he was untying his sneakers.

"Put your shoes out," she called through the door, "and maybe Daddy will polish them."

"Is Daddy still in there with those men? Mama made me be quiet so I wouldn't bother them."

He padded into the bathroom with bare feet and crawled into the water. As she scrubbed him they played Ask Me A Question, their own version of Twenty Questions. She had just dried him and was about to have him step into his pajamas when he asked: "Are they gonna get me tomorrow?"

"Who's going to get you?" She looked into his eyes and began rubbing him furiously with the towel.

"I don't know," he answered. "Somebody I guess."

"Nobody's going to get you," she said, "who wants a little boy who gets bubblegum in his hair anyway—but us?" He grinned but as she hugged him she thought how much he looked like his father. They walked to the bed to say his prayers and while they were kneeling she heard the first drops of rain. By the time she covered him up and tucked the spread off the floor the rain had changed to a steady downpour.

When Tommy had gone to bed her mother got up again and began ironing clothes in the kitchen. Something, she said, to keep her thoughts busy. While her mother folded and sorted the clothes Ellie drew up a chair from the kitchen table. They sat in the kitchen for a while listening to the voices of the men in the next room. Her mother's quiet speech broke the stillness in the room.

"I'd rather," she said making sweeping motions with the iron, "that you stayed home from work tomorrow and went with your father to take Tommy. I don't think I'll be up to those people."

Ellie nodded. "I don't mind," she said, tracing circles on the oil cloth covered table.

"Your father's going," her mother continued. "Belk and Reverend Davis are too. I think that white man in there will probably go."

"They may not need me," Ellie answered.

"Tommy will," her mother said, folding the last dish towel and storing it in the cabinet.

"Mama, I think he's scared," the girl turned toward the woman. "He was so quiet while I was washing him."

"I know," she answered sitting down heavily. "He's been that way all day." Her brown wavy hair glowed in the dim lighting of the kitchen. "I told him he wasn't going to school with Jakie and Bob any more but I said he was going to meet some other children just as nice."

Ellie saw that her mother was twisting her wedding band around and around on her finger.

"I've already told Mrs. Ingraham that I wouldn't be able to come out tomorrow." Ellie paused. "She didn't say very much. She didn't even say anything about his pictures in the newspaper. Mr. Ingraham said we were getting right crazy but even he didn't say anything else."

She stopped to look at the clock sitting near the sink. "It's almost time for the cruise cars to begin," she said. Her mother followed Ellie's eyes to the sink. The policemen circling their block every twenty minutes was supposed to make them feel safe, but hearing the cars come so regularly and that light flashing through the shade above her bed only made her nervous.

She stopped talking to push a wrinkle out of the shiny red cloth, dragging her finger along the table edges. "How long before those men going to leave?" she asked her mother. Just as she spoke she heard one of the men say something about getting some sleep. "I didn't mean to run them away," she said smiling. Her mother half-smiled too. They listened for the sound of motors and tires and waited for her father to shut the front door.

In a few seconds her father's head pushed through the curtain. "Want me to turn down your bed now, Ellie?" She felt uncomfortable staring up at him, the whole family looked drained of all energy.

"That's all right," she answered. "I'll sleep in Helen and Teenie's bed tonight."

"How's Tommy?" he asked looking toward the bedroom. He came in and sat down at the table with them.

They were silent before he spoke. "I keep wondering if we should send him." He lit a match and watched the flame disappear into the ashtray, then he looked into his wife's eyes. "There's no telling what these fool white folks will do."

Her mother reached over and patted his hand. "We're doing what we have to do, I guess," she said. "Sometimes though I wish the others weren't so much older than him."

"But it seems so unfair," Ellie broke in, "sending him there all by himself like that. Everybody keeps asking me why the MacAdams didn't apply for their children."

"Eloise." Her father's voice sounded curt. "We aren't answering for the MacAdams, we're trying to do what's right for your brother. He's not old enough to have his own say so. You and the others could decide for yourselves, but we're the ones that have to do for him."

She didn't say anything but watched him pull a handful of envelopes out of his pocket and tuck them in the cabinet drawer. She knew that if anyone had told him in August that Tommy would be the only one going to Jefferson Davis they would not have let him go.

"Those the new ones?" she asked. "What they say?"

"Let's not talk about the letters," her father said. "Let's go to bed."

Outside they heard the rain become heavier. Since early evening she had become accustomed to the sound. Now it blended in with the rest of the noises that had accumulated in the back of her mind since the whole thing began.

As her mother folded the ironing board they heard the quiet wheels of the police car. Ellie noticed that the clock said twelve-ten and she wondered why they were early. Her mother pulled the iron cord from the switch and they stood silently waiting for the police car to turn around and pass the house again, as if the car's passing were a final blessing for the night.

Suddenly she was aware of a noise that sounded as if everything had broken loose in her head at once, a loudness that almost shook the foundation of the house. At the same time the lights went out and instinctively her father knocked them to the floor. They could hear the tinkling of glass near the front of the house and Tommy began screaming.

"Tommy, get down," her father yelled.

She hoped he would remember to roll under the bed the way they had practiced. She was aware of objects falling and breaking as she lay perfectly still. Her breath was coming in jerks and then there was a second noise, a smaller explosion but still drowning out Tommy's cries.

"Stay still," her father commanded. "I'm going to check on Tommy. They may throw another one."

She watched him crawl across the floor, pushing a broken flower vase and an iron skillet out of his way. All of the sounds, Tommy's crying, the breaking glass, everything was echoing in her ears. She felt as if they had been crouching on the floor for hours but when she heard the police car door slam, the luminous hands of the clock said only twelve-fifteen.

She heard other cars drive up and pairs of heavy feet trample on the porch. "You folks all right in there?"

She could visualize the hands pulling open the door, because she knew the voice. Sergeant Kearns had been responsible for patrolling the house during the past three weeks. She heard him click the light switch in the living room but the darkness remained intense.

Her father deposited Tommy in his wife's lap and went to what was left of the door. In the next fifteen minutes policemen were everywhere. While she rummaged around underneath the cabinet for a candle, her mother tried to hush up

Tommy. His cheek was cut where he had scratched himself on the springs of the bed. Her mother motioned for her to dampen a cloth and put some petroleum jelly on it to keep him quiet. She tried to put him to bed again but he would not go, even when she promised to stay with him for the rest of the night. And so she sat in the kitchen rocking the little boy back and forth on her lap.

Ellie wandered around the kitchen but the light from the single candle put an eerie glow on the walls making her nervous. She began picking up pans, stepping over pieces of broken crockery and glassware. She did not want to go into the living room yet, but if she listened closely, snatches of the policemen's conversation came through the curtain.

She heard one man say that the bomb landed near the edge of the yard, that was why it had only gotten the front porch. She knew from their talk that the living room window was shattered completely. Suddenly Ellie sat down. The picture of the living room window kept flashing in her mind and a wave of feeling invaded her body making her shake as if she had lost all muscular control. She slept on the couch, right under that window.

She looked at her mother to see if she too had realized, but her mother was looking down at Tommy and trying to get him to close his eyes. Ellie stood up and crept toward the living room trying to prepare herself for what she would see. Even that minute of determination could not make her control the horror that she felt. There were jagged holes all along the front of the house and the sofa was covered with glass and paint. She started to pick up the picture that had toppled from the book shelf, then she just stepped over the broken frame.

Outside her father was talking and, curious to see who else was with him, she walked across the splinters to the yard. She could see pieces of the geranium pot and the red blossoms turned face down. There were no lights in the other houses on the street. Across from their house she could see forms standing in the door and shadows being pushed back and forth. "I guess the MacAdams are glad they just didn't get involved." No one heard her speak, and no one came over to see if they could help; she knew why and did not really blame them. They were afraid their house could be next.

Most of the policemen had gone now and only one car was left to flash the revolving red light in the rain. She heard the tall skinny man tell her father they would be parked outside for the rest of the night. As she watched the reflection of the police cars returning to the station, feeling sick on her stomach, she wondered now why they bothered.

Ellie went back inside the house and closed the curtain behind her. There was nothing anyone could do now, not even to the house. Everything was scattered all over the floor and poor Tommy still would not go to sleep. She wondered what would happen when the news spread through their section of town, and at once remembered the man in the grey Chevrolet. It would serve them right if her father's friends got one of them.

Ellie pulled up an overturned chair and sat down across from her mother who was crooning to Tommy. What Mr. Paul said was right, white people just couldn't be trusted. Her family had expected anything but even though they had practiced ducking, they didn't really expect anybody to try tearing down the house. But the funny thing was the house belonged to one of them. Maybe it was a good thing her family were just renters.

Exhausted, Ellie put her head down on the table. She didn't know what they were going to do about tomorrow, in the day time they didn't need electricity. She was too tired to think any more about Tommy, yet she could not go to sleep. So, she sat at the table trying to sit still, but every few minutes she would involuntarily twitch. She tried to steady her hands, all the time listening to her mother's sing-songy voice and waiting for her father to come back inside the house.

She didn't know how long she lay hunched against the kitchen table, but when she looked up, her wrists bore the imprints of her hair. She unfolded her arms gingerly, feeling the blood rush to her fingertips. Her father sat in the chair opposite her, staring at the vacant space between them. She heard her mother creep away from the table, taking Tommy to his room.

Ellie looked out the window. The darkness was turning to grey and the hurt feeling was disappearing. As she sat there she could begin to look at the kitchen matter-of-factly. Although the hands of the clock were just a little past five-thirty, she knew somebody was going to have to start clearing up and cook breakfast.

She stood and tipped across the kitchen to her parents' bedroom. "Mama," she whispered, standing near the door of Tommy's room. At the sound of her voice, Tommy made a funny throaty noise in his sleep. Her mother motioned for her to go out and be quiet. Ellie knew then that Tommy had just fallen asleep. She crept back to the kitchen and began picking up the dishes that could be salvaged, being careful not to go into the living room.

She walked around her father, leaving the broken glass underneath the kitchen table. "You want some coffee?" she asked.

He nodded silently, in strange contrast she thought to the water faucet that turned with a loud gurgling noise. While she let the water run to get hot she measured out the instant coffee in one of the plastic cups. Next door she could hear people moving around in the Williams' kitchen, but they too seemed much quieter than usual.

"You reckon everybody knows by now?" she asked, stirring the coffee and putting the saucer in front of him.

"Everybody will know by the time the city paper comes out," he said. "Somebody was here last night from the *Observer*. Guess it'll make front page."

She leaned against the cabinet for support watching him trace endless circles in the brown liquid with the spoon. "Sergeant Kearns says they'll have almost the whole force out there tomorrow," he said.

"Today," she whispered.

Her father looked at the clock and then turned his head.

"When's your mother coming back in here?" he asked, finally picking up the cup and drinking the coffee.

"Tommy's just off to sleep," she answered. "I guess she'll be in here when he's asleep for good."

She looked out the window of the back door at the row of tall hedges that had separated their neighborhood from the white people for as long as she remembered. While she stood there she heard her mother walk into the room. To her ears the steps seemed much slower than usual. She heard her mother stop in front of her father's chair.

"Jim," she said, sounding very timid, "what we going to do?" Yet as Ellie turned toward her she noticed her mother's face was strangely calm as she looked down on her husband.

Ellie continued standing by the door listening to them talk. Nobody asked the question to which they all wanted an answer.

"I keep thinking," her father said finally, "that the policemen will be with him all day. They couldn't hurt him inside the school building without getting some of their own kind."

"But he'll be in there all by himself," her mother said softly. "A hundred policemen can't be a little boy's only friends."

She watched her father wrap his calloused hands, still

splotched with machine oil, around the salt shaker on the table.

"I keep trying," he said to her, "to tell myself that somebody's got to be the first one and then I just think how quiet he's been all week."

Ellie listened to the quiet voices that seemed to be a room apart from her. In the back of her mind she could hear phrases of a hymn her grandmother used to sing, something about trouble, her being born for trouble.

"Jim, I cannot let my baby go." Her mother's words, although quiet, were carefully pronounced.

"Maybe," her father answered, "it's not in our hands. Reverend Davis and I were talking day before yesterday how God tested the Israelites, maybe he's just trying us."

"God expects you to take care of your own," his wife interrupted. Ellie sensed a trace of bitterness in her mother's voice.

"Tommy's not going to understand why he can't go to school," her father replied. "He's going to wonder why, and how are we going to tell him we're afraid of them?" Her father's hand clutched the coffee cup. "He's going to be fighting them the rest of his life. He's got to start sometime."

"But he's not on their level. Tommy's too little to go around hating people. One of the others, they're bigger, they understand about things."

Ellie still leaning against the door saw that the sun covered part of the sky behind the hedges and the light slipping through the kitchen window seemed to reflect the shiny red of the table cloth.

"He's our child," she heard her mother say. "Whatever we do, we're going to be the cause." Her father had pushed the cup away from him and sat with his hands covering part of his face. Outside Ellie could hear a horn blowing.

"God knows we tried but I guess there's just no use." Her father's voice forced her attention back to the two people sitting in front of her. "Maybe when things come back to normal, we'll try again."

He covered his wife's chunky fingers with the palm of his hand and her mother seemed to be enveloped in silence. The three of them remained quiet, each involved in his own thoughts, but related, Ellie knew, to the same thing. She was the first to break the silence.

"Mama," she called after a long pause, "do you want me to start setting the table for breakfast?"

Her mother nodded.

Ellie turned the clock so she could see it from the sink

while she washed the dishes that had been scattered over the floor.

"You going to wake up Tommy or you want me to?"

"No," her mother said, still holding her father's hand, "let him sleep. When you wash your face, you go up the street and call Hezekiah. Tell him to keep up with the children after school, I want to do something to this house before they come home."

She stopped talking and looked around the kitchen, finally turning to her husband. "He's probably kicked the spread off by now," she said. Ellie watched her father, who without saying anything walked toward the bedroom.

She watched her mother lift herself from the chair and automatically push in the stuffing underneath the cracked plastic cover. Her face looked set, as it always did when she was trying hard to keep her composure.

"He'll need something hot when he wakes up. Hand me the oatmeal," she commanded, reaching on top of the icebox for matches to light the kitchen stove.

2.

Autobiography

FREDERICK DOUGLASS (1817?–1895)

Born a slave in Talbot County, Maryland, Frederick Douglass escaped from bondage in 1838 to become the leading Negro in the antislavery movement and, after the Civil War, in the fight for Negro rights. He wrote three autobiographies at different stages of his life, classics of the rich, extensive, and still not fully mined body of writing known as "slave narratives." The first, Narrative of the Life of Frederick Douglass, An American Slave, *was published in 1845 at the Anti-Slavery Office in Boston. It was written when his memories of the realities of his life as a slave were sharpest and most vivid. Ten years later his enlarged autobiography,* My Bondage and My Freedom, *was published in New York. His third autobiography,* Life and Times of Frederick Douglass, *was first published in 1881 and was then revised, expanded, and published in its final form in 1892. He was famous as an antislavery*

*orator and, during the Civil War, helped recruit Negro soldiers
for the 54th and 55th Massachusetts Regiments. A consistent
proponent of the emancipation of the slaves, after the war he
remained active in the fight to secure and protect the rights of
Negro freemen. In his later life he held various official offices,
including Secretary of the Santo Domingo Commission, Mar-
shal and Recorder of the Deeds of the District of Columbia,
and Minister of the United States of Haiti. The selections that
follow are from his 1845 autobiography.*

Narrative of the Life of Frederick Douglass,
An American Slave

Chapter I

I was born in Tuckahoe, near Hillsborough, and about twelve miles
from Easton, in Talbot county, Maryland. I have no accurate
knowledge of my age, never having seen any authentic record
containing it. By far the larger part of the slaves know as little of
their ages as horses know of theirs, and it is the wish of most
masters within my knowledge to keep their slaves thus ignorant. I
do not remember to have ever met a slave who could tell of his
birthday. They seldom come nearer to it than planting-time,
harvest-time, cherry-time, spring-time, or fall-time. A want of information concerning my own was a source of unhappiness to me
even during childhood. The white children could tell their ages. I
could not tell why I ought to be deprived of the same privilege.
I was not allowed to make any inquiries of my master concerning
it. He deemed all such inquiries on the part of a slave improper
and impertinent, and evidence of a restless spirit. The nearest
estimate I can give makes me now between twenty-seven and
twenty-eight years of age. I come to this, from hearing my master
say, some time during 1835, I was about seventeen years old.

My mother was named Harriet Bailey. She was the daughter of
Isaac and Betsey Bailey, both colored, and quite dark. My mother
was of a darker complexion than either my grandmother or
grandfather.

My father was a white man. He was admitted to be such
by all I ever heard speak of my parentage. The opinion was
also whispered that my master was my father; but of the cor-
rectness of this opinion, I know nothing; the means of know-

ing was withheld from me. My mother and I were separated when I was but an infant—before I knew her as my mother. It is a common custom, in the part of Maryland from which I ran away, to part children from their mothers at a very early age. Frequently, before the child has reached its twelfth month, its mother is taken from it, and hired out on some farm a considerable distance off, and the child is placed under the care of an old woman, too old for field labor. For what this separation is done, I do not know, unless it be to hinder the development of the child's affection toward its mother, and to blunt and destroy the natural affection of the mother for the child. This is the inevitable result.

I never saw my mother, to know her as such, more than four or five times in my life; and each of these times was very short in duration, and at night. She was hired by a Mr. Stewart, who lived about twelve miles from my home. She made her journeys to see me in the night, travelling the whole distance on foot, after the performance of her day's work. She was a field hand, and a whipping is the penalty of not being in the field at sunrise, unless a slave has special permission from his or her master to the contrary—a permission which they seldom get, and one that gives to him that gives it the proud name of being a kind master. I do not recollect of ever seeing my mother by the light of day. She was with me in the night. She would lie down with me, and get me to sleep, but long before I waked she was gone. Very little communication ever took place between us. Death soon ended what little we could have while she lived, and with it her hardships and suffering. She died when I was about seven years old, on one of my master's farms near Lee's Mill. I was not allowed to be present during her illness, at her death, or burial. She was gone long before I knew any thing about it. Never having enjoyed, to any considerable extent, her soothing presence, her tender and watchful care, I received the tidings of her death with much the same emotions I should have probably felt at the death of a stranger.

Called thus suddenly away, she left me without the slightest intimation of who my father was. The whisper that my master was my father, may or may not be true; and, true or false, it is of but little consequence to my purpose whilst the fact remains, in all its glaring odiousness, that slaveholders have ordained, and by law established, that the children of slave women shall in all cases follow the condition of their mothers; and this is done too obviously to administer to their own lusts, and make a gratification of their wicked desires profitable as well as pleasurable; for by this cunning arrangement, the slaveholder, in cases not a few, sustains to his slaves the double relation of master and father.

I know of such cases; and it is worthy of remark that such slaves invariably suffer greater hardships, and have more to contend with, than others. They are, in the first place, a constant offence to their mistress. She is ever disposed to find fault with them; they can seldom do any thing to please her; she is never better pleased than when she sees them under the lash, especially when she suspects her husband of showing to his mulatto children favors which he withholds from his black slaves. The master is frequently compelled to sell this class of his slaves, out of deference to the feelings of his white wife; and, cruel as the deed may strike any one to be, for a man to sell his own children to human flesh-mongers, it is often the dictate of humanity for him to do so; for, unless he does this, he must not only whip them himself, but must stand by and see one white son tie up his brother, of but few shades darker complexion than himself, and ply the gory lash to his naked back; and if he lisp one word of disapproval, it is set down to his parental partiality, and only makes a bad matter worse, both for himself and the slave whom he would protect and defend.

Every year brings with it multitudes of this class of slaves. It was doubtless in consequence of a knowledge of this fact, that one great statesman of the south predicted the downfall of slavery by the inevitable laws of population. Whether this prophecy is ever fulfilled or not, it is nevertheless plain that a very different-looking class of people are springing up at the south, and are now held in slavery, from those originally brought to this country from Africa; and if their increase will do no other good, it will do away the force of the argument, that God cursed Ham, and therefore American slavery is right. If the lineal descendants of Ham are alone to be scripturally enslaved, it is certain that slavery at the south must soon become unscriptural; for thousands are ushered into the world, annually, who, like myself, owe their existence to white fathers, and those fathers most frequently their own masters.

I have had two masters. My first master's name was Anthony. I do not remember his first name. He was generally called Captain Anthony—a title which, I presume, he acquired by sailing a craft on the Chesapeake Bay. He was not considered a rich slaveholder. He owned two or three farms, and about thirty slaves. His farms and slaves were under the care of an overseer. The overseer's name was Plummer. Mr. Plummer was a miserable drunkard, a profane swearer, and a savage monster. He always went armed with a cowskin and a heavy cudgel. I have known him to cut and slash the women's heads so horribly, that even master would be enraged at his cruelty, and would threaten to whip him if he did not mind himself. Master, however, was not a humane slaveholder. It required extraordinary barbarity on the part of an overseer to affect him. He was a cruel man, hardened by a long life of slaveholding. He would at times seem to take great pleasure in whipping a slave. I have often been awakened at the dawn of day by the most heart-rending shrieks of an own aunt of mine, whom he used to tie up to a joist, and whip upon her naked back till she was literally covered with blood. No words, no tears, no prayers, from his gory victim, seemed to move his iron heart from its bloody purpose. The louder she screamed, the harder he whipped; and where the blood ran fastest, there he whipped longest. He would whip her to make her scream, and whip her to make her hush; and not until overcome by fatigue, would he cease to swing the blood-clotted cowskin. I remember the first time I ever witnessed this horrible exhibition. I was quite a child, but I well remember it. I never shall forget it whilst I remember any thing. It was the first of a long series of such outrages, of which I was doomed to be a witness and a participant. It struck me with awful force. It was the blood-stained gate, the entrance to the hell of slavery, through which I was about to pass. It was a most terrible spectacle. I wish I could commit to paper the feelings with which I beheld it.

This occurrence took place very soon after I went to live with my old master, and under the following circumstances. Aunt Hester went out one night,—where or for what I do not know,—and happened to be absent when my master desired her presence. He had ordered her not to go out evenings, and warned her that she must never let him catch her in company with a young man, who was paying attention to her belonging to Colonel Lloyd. The young man's name was Ned Roberts, generally called Lloyd's Ned. Why master was so careful of her, may be safely left to conjecture. She was a woman of noble form, and of graceful proportions, having very few equals, and fewer superiors, in personal appearance, among the colored or white women of our neighborhood.

Aunt Hester had not only disobeyed his orders in going out, but had been found in company with Lloyd's Ned; which circumstance, I found, from what he said while whipping her, was the chief offence. Had he been a man of pure morals himself, he might have been thought interested in protecting the innocence of my aunt; but those who knew him will not suspect him of any such virtue. Before he commenced whipping Aunt Hester, he took her into the kitchen, and stripped her from neck to waist, leaving her neck, shoulders, and back, entirely naked. He then told her to cross her hands, calling her at the same time a d——d b——h. After crossing her hands, he tied them with a strong rope, and led her to a stool under a large hook in the joist, put in for the purpose. He made her get upon the stool, and tied her hands to the hook. She now stood fair for his infernal purpose. Her arms were stretched up at their full length, so that she stood upon the ends of her toes. He then said to her, "Now, you d——d b——h, I'll learn you how to disobey my orders!" and after rolling up his sleeves, he commenced to lay on the heavy cowskin, and soon the warm, red blood (amid heart-rending shrieks from her, and horrid oaths from him) came dripping to the floor. I was so terrified and horror-stricken at the sight, that I hid myself in a closet, and dared not venture out till long after the bloody transaction was over. I expected it would be my turn next. It was all new to me. I have never seen any thing like it before. I had always lived with my grandmother on the outskirts of the plantation, where she was put to raise the children of the younger women. I had therefore been, until now, out of the way of the bloody scenes that often occurred on the plantation.

Chapter VI

My new mistress proved to be all she appeared when I first met her at the door,—a woman of the kindest heart and finest feelings. She had never had a slave under her control previously to myself, and prior to her marriage she had been dependent upon her own industry for a living. She was by trade a weaver; and by constant application to her business, she had been in a good degree preserved from the blighting and dehumanizing effects of slavery. I was utterly astonished at her goodness. I scarcely knew how to behave towards her. She was entirely unlike any other white woman I had ever seen. I could not approach her as I was accustomed to approach other white ladies. My early instruction was all out of place. The crouching servility, usually so acceptable a quality in a slave, did not answer when manifested toward her. Her favor was not gained by it; she seemed to be disturbed by it. She did not deem it impudent or unmannerly for a slave to look her in the face. The meanest slave was put fully at east in her presence, and none left without feeling better for having seen her. Her face was made of heavenly smiles, and her voice of tranquil music.

But, alas! this kind heart had but a short time to remain such. The fatal poison of irresponsible power was already in her hands, and soon commenced its infernal work. That cheerful eye, under the influence of slavery, soon became red with rage; that voice, made all of sweet accord, changed to one of harsh and horrid discord; and that angelic face gave place to that of a demon.

Very soon after I went to live with Mr. and Mrs. Auld, she very kindly commenced to teach me the A, B, C. After I had learned this, she assisted me in learning to spell words of three or four letters. Just at this point of my progress, Mr. Auld found out what was going on, and at once forbade Mrs. Auld to instruct me further, telling her, among other things, that it was unlawful, as well as unsafe, to teach a slave to read. To use his own words, further, he said, "If you give a nigger an inch, he will take an ell. A nigger should know nothing but to obey his master—to do as he is told to do. Learning would *spoil* the best nigger in the world. Now," said he, "if you teach that nigger (speaking of myself) how to read, there would be no keeping him. It would forever unfit him to be a slave. He would at once become unmanageable, and of no value to his master. As to himself, it could do him no good, but a great deal of harm. It would make him discontented and unhappy." These words sank deep into my heart, stirred up sentiments within that lay slumbering, and called into existence an entirely new train of thought. It was a new and special revelation, explaining dark and mysterious things, with which my youthful understanding had struggled, but struggled in vain. I now understood what had been to me a most perplexing difficulty—to wit, the white man's power to enslave the black man. It was a grand achievement, and I prized it highly. From that moment, I understood the pathway from slavery to freedom. It was just what I wanted, and I got it at a time when I 'the least expected it. Whilst I was saddened by the thought of losing the aid of my kind mistress, I was gladdened by the invaluable instruction which, by the merest accident, I had gained from my master. Though conscious of the difficulty of learning without a teacher, I set out with high hope, and a fixed purpose, at whatever cost of trouble, to learn how to read. The very decided manner with which he spoke, and strove to impress his wife with the evil consequences of giving me instruction, served to convince me that he was deeply sensible of the truths he was uttering. It gave me the best assurance that I might rely with the utmost

confidence on the results which, he said, would flow from
teaching me to read. What he most dreaded, that I most desired. What he most loved, that I most hated. That which to
him was a great evil, to be carefully shunned, was to me a
great good, to be diligently sought; and the argument which
he so warmly urged, against my learning to read, only served
to inspire me with a desire and determination to learn. In
learning to read, I owe almost as much to the bitter opposition of my master, as to the kindly aid of my mistress. I acknowledge the benefit of both.

I had resided but a short time in Baltimore before I observed a marked difference, in the treatment of slaves, from
that which I had witnessed in the country. A city slave is almost a freeman, compared with a slave on the plantation. He
is much better fed and clothed, and enjoys privileges altogether unknown to the slave on the plantation. There is a ves-
tige of decency, a sense of shame, that does much to curb
and check those outbreaks of atrocious cruelty so commonly
enacted upon the plantation. He is a desperate slaveholder,
who will shock the humanity of his non-slaveholding neighbors with the cries of his lacerated slave. Few are willing to
incur the odium attaching to the reputation of being a cruel
master; and above all things, they would not be known as not
giving a slave enough to eat. Every city slaveholder is anxious
to have it known of him, that he feeds his slaves well; and it
is due to them to say, that most of them do give their slaves
enough to eat. There are, however, some painful exceptions
to this rule. Directly opposite to us, on Philpot Street, lived
Mr. Thomas Hamilton. He owned two slaves. Their names
were Henrietta and Mary. Henrietta was about twenty-two
years of age, Mary was about fourteen; and of all the mangled and emaciated creatures I ever looked upon, these two
were the most so. His heart must be harder than stone, that
could look upon these unmoved. The head, neck, and shoulders of Mary were literally cut to pieces. I have frequently
felt her head, and found it nearly covered with festering
sores, caused by the lash of her cruel mistress. I do not know
that her master ever whipped her, but I have been an eye-wit-
ness to the cruelty of Mrs. Hamilton. I used to be in Mr.
Hamilton's house nearly every day. Mrs. Hamilton used to sit
in a large chair in the middle of the room, with a heavy
cowskin always by her side, and scarce an hour passed during
the day but was marked by the blood of one of these slaves.
The girls seldom passed her without her saying, "Move faster,
you *black gip!*" at the same time giving them a blow with the
cowskin over the head or shoulders, often drawing the blood.

She would then say, "Take that, you *black gip!*"—continuing, "If you don't move faster, I'll move you!" Added to the cruel lashings to which these slaves were subjected, they were kept nearly half-starved. They seldom knew what it was to eat a full meal. I have seen Mary contending with the pigs for the offal thrown into the street. So much was Mary kicked and cut to pieces, that she was oftener called *"pecked"* than by her name.

Chapter VII

I lived in Master Hugh's family about seven years. During this time, I succeeded in learning to read and write. In accomplishing this, I was compelled to resort to various stratagems. I had no regular teacher. My mistress, who had kindly commenced to instruct me, had, in compliance with the advice and direction of her husband, not only ceased to instruct, but had set her face against my being instructed by any one else. It is due, however, to my mistress to say of her, that she did not adopt this course of treatment immediately. She at first lacked the depravity indispensable to shutting me up in mental darkness. It was at least necessary for her to have some training in the exercise of irresponsible power, to make her equal to the task of treating me as though I were a brute.

My mistress was, as I have said, a kind and tender-hearted woman; and in the simplicity of her soul she commenced, when I first went to live with her, to treat me as she supposed one human being ought to treat another. In entering upon the duties of a slaveholder, she did not seem to perceive that I sustained to her the relation of a mere chattel, and that for her to treat me as a human being was not only wrong, but dangerously so. Slavery proved as injurious to her as it did to me. When I went there, she was a pious, warm, and tender-hearted woman. There was no sorrow or suffering for which she had not a tear. She had bread for the hungry, clothes for the naked, and comfort for every mourner that came within her reach. Slavery soon proved its ability to divest her of these heavenly qualities. Under its influence, the tender heart became stone, and the lamblike disposition gave way to one of tiger-like fierceness. The first step in her downward course was in her ceasing to instruct me. She now commenced to practise her husband's precepts. She finally became even more violent in her opposition than her husband himself. She was not satisfied with simply doing as well as he had commanded; she seemed anxious to do better. Nothing seemed to make her more angry than to see me with a newspaper. She seemed to think that here lay the danger. I have had her rush at me with a face made all up of fury, and snatch from me a newspaper, in a manner that fully revealed her apprehension. She was an apt woman; and a little experience soon demonstrated, to her satisfaction, that education and slavery were incompatible with each other.

From this time I was most narrowly watched. If I was in a separate room any considerable length of time, I was sure to be suspected of having a book, and was at once called to give an account of myself. All this, however, was too late. The first step had been taken. Mistress, in teaching me the alphabet, had given me the *inch*, and no precaution could prevent me from taking the *ell*.

The plan which I adopted, and the one by which I was most successful, was that of making friends of all the little white boys whom I met in the street. As many of these as I could, I converted into teachers. With their kindly aid, obtained at different times and in different places, I finally succeeded in learning to read. When I was sent on errands, I always took my book with me, and by going one part of my errand quickly, I found time to get a lesson before my return. I used also to carry bread with me, enough of which was always in the house, and to which I was always welcome; for I was much better off in this regard than many of the poor white children in our neighborhood. This bread I used to bestow upon the hungry little urchins, who, in return, would give me that more valuable bread of knowledge. I am strongly tempted to give the names of two or three of those little boys, as a testimonial of the gratitude and affection I bear them; but prudence forbids;—not that it would injure me, but it might embarrass them; for it is almost an unpardonable offence to teach slaves to read in this Christian country. It is enough to say of the dear little fellows, that they lived on Philpot Street, very near Durgin and Bailey's shipyard. I used to talk this matter of slavery over with them. I would sometimes say to them, I wished I could be as free as they would be when they got to be men. "You will be free as soon as you are twenty-one, *but I am a slave for life!* Have not I as good a right to be free as you have?" These words used to trouble them; they would express for me the liveliest sympathy, and console me with the hope that something would occur by which I might be free.

I was now about twelve years old, and the thought of being *a slave for life* began to bear heavily upon my heart. Just about this time, I got hold of a book entitled "The Colum-

bian Orator." Every opportunity I got, I used to read this
book. Among much of other interesting matter, I found in it
a dialogue between a master and his slave. The slave was represented as having run away from his master three times. The
dialogue represented the conversation which took place between them, when the slave was retaken the third time. In
this dialogue, the whole argument in behalf of slavery was
brought forward by the master, all of which was disposed of
by the slave. The slave was made to say some very smart as
well as impressive things in reply to his master—things
which had the desired though unexpected effect; for the conversation resulted in the voluntary emancipation of the slave
on the part of the master.

In the same book, I met with one of Sheridan's mighty
speeches on and in behalf of Catholic emancipation. These
were choice documents to me. I read them over and over
again with unabated interest. They gave tongue to interesting
thoughts of my own soul, which had frequently flashed
through my mind, and died away for want of utterance. The
moral which I gained from the dialogue was the power of
truth over the conscience of even a slaveholder. What I got
from Sheridan was a bold denunciation of slavery, and a
powerful vindication of human rights. The reading of these
documents enabled me to utter my thoughts, and to meet the
arguments brought forward to sustain slavery; but while they
relieved me of one difficulty, they brought on another even
more painful than the one of which I was relieved. The more
I read, the more I was led to abhor and detest my enslavers. I
could regard them in no other light than a band of successful
robbers, who had left their homes, and gone to Africa, and
stolen us from our homes, and in a strange land reduced us
to slavery. I loathed them as being the meanest as well as the
most wicked of men. As I read and contemplated the subject,
behold! that very discontentment which Master Hugh had
predicted would follow my learning to read had already
come, to torment and sting my soul to unutterable anguish.
As I writhed under it, I would at times feel that learning to
read had been a curse rather than a blessing. It had given me
a view of my wretched condition, without the remedy. It
opened my eyes to the horrible pit, but to no ladder upon
which to get out. In moments of agony, I envied my fellow-
slaves for their stupidity. I have often wished myself a beast.
I preferred the condition of the meanest reptile to my own.
Any thing, no matter what, to get rid of thinking! It was this
everlasting thinking of my condition that tormented me.
There was no getting rid of it. It was pressed upon me by

every object within sight or hearing, animate or inanimate.
The silver trump of freedom had roused my soul to eternal
wakefulness. Freedom now appeared, to disappear no more
forever. It was heard in every sound, and seen in every thing.
It was ever present to torment me with a sense of my
wretched condition. I saw nothing without seeing it, I heard
nothing without hearing it, and felt nothing without feeling it.
It looked from every star, it smiled in every calm, breathed in
every wind, and moved in every storm.

I often found myself regretting my own existence, and
wishing myself dead; and but for the hope of being free, I
have no doubt but that I should have killed myself, or done
something for which I should have been killed. While in this
state of mind, I was eager to hear any one speak of slavery. I
was a ready listener. Every little while, I could hear something about the abolitionists. It was some time before I found
what the word meant. It was always used in such connec-
tions as to make it an interesting word to me. If a slave ran
away and succeeded in getting clear, or if a slave killed his
master, set fire to a barn, or did any thing very wrong in the
mind of a slaveholder, it was spoken of as the fruit of *abolition*. Hearing the word in this connection very often, I set
about learning what it meant. The dictionary afforded me little or no help. I found it was "the act of abolishing"; but
then I did not know what was to be abolished. Here I was
perplexed. I did not dare to ask any one about its meaning,
for I was satisfied that it was something they wanted me to
know very little about. After a patient waiting, I got one of
our city papers, containing an account of the number of peti-
tions from the north, praying for the abolition of slavery in
the District of Columbia, and of the slave trade between the
States. From this time I understood the words *abolition* and
abolitionist, and always drew near when that word was spoken, expecting to hear something of importance to myself
and fellow-slaves. The light broke in upon me by degrees. I
went one day down on the wharf of Mr. Waters; and seeing
two Irishmen unloading a scow of stone, I went, unasked,
and helped them. When we had finished, one of them came
to me and asked, "Are ye a slave for life?" I told him that I
was. The good Irishman seemed to be deeply affected by the
statement. He said to the other that it was a pity so fine a
little fellow as myself should be a slave for life. He said it
was a shame to hold me. They both advised me to run away
to the north; that I should find friends there, and that I
should be free. I pretended not to be interested in what they
said, and treated them as if I did not understand them; for I

feared they might be treacherous. White men have been known to encourage slaves to escape, and then, to get the reward, catch them and return them to their masters. I was afraid that these seemingly good men might use me so; but I nevertheless remembered their advice, and from that time I resolved to run away. I looked forward to a time at which it would be safe for me to escape. I was too young to think of doing so immediately; besides, I wished to learn how to write, as I might have occasion to write my own pass. I consoled myself with the hope that I should one day find a good chance. Meanwhile, I would learn to write.

The idea as to how I might learn to write was suggested to me by being in Durgin and Bailey's ship-yard, and frequently seeing the ship carpenters, after hewing, and getting a piece of timber ready for use, write on the timber the name of that part of the ship for which it was intended. When a piece of timber was intended for the larboard side, it would be marked thus—"L." When a piece was for the starboard side, it would be marked thus—"S." A piece for the larboard side forward, would be marked thus—"L. F." When a piece was for starboard side forward, it would be marked thus—"S. F." For larboard aft, it would be marked thus—"L. A." For starboard aft, it would be marked thus—"S. A." I soon learned the names of these letters, and for what they were intended when placed upon a piece of timber in the ship-yard. I immediately commenced copying them, and in a short time was able to make the four letters named. After that, when I met with any boy who I knew could write, I would tell him I could write as well as he. The next word would be, "I don't believe you. Let me see you try it." I would then make the letters which I had been so fortunate as to learn, and ask him to beat that. In this way I got a good many lessons in writing, which it is quite possible I should never have gotten in any other way. During this time, my copy-book was the board fence, brick wall, and pavement; my pen and ink was a lump of chalk. With these, I learned mainly how to write. I then commenced and continued copying the Italics in Webster's Spelling Book, until I could make them all without looking on the book. By this time, my little Master Thomas had gone to school, and learned how to write, and had written over a number of copy-books. These had been brought home, and shown to some of our near neighbors, and then laid aside. My mistress used to go to class meeting at the Wilk Street meetinghouse every Monday afternoon, and leave me to take care of the house. When left thus, I used to spend this time writing in the spaces left in

Master Thomas's copy-book, copying what he had written. I continued to do this until I could write a hand very similar to that of Master Thomas. Thus, after a long, tedious effort for years, I finally succeeded in learning how to write.

Chapter X

I left Master Thomas's house, and went to live with Mr. Covey, on the 1st of January, 1833. I was now, for the first time in my life, a field hand. In my new employment, I found myself even more awkward than a country boy appeared to be in a large city. I had been at my new home but one week before Mr. Covey gave me a severe whipping, cutting my back, causing the blood to run, and raising ridges on my flesh as large as my little finger. The details of this affair are as follows: Mr. Covey sent me, very early in the morning of one of our coldest days in the month of January, to the woods, to get a load of wood. He gave me a team of unbroken oxen. He told me which was the in-hand ox, and which the off-hand one. He then tied the end of a large rope around the horns of the in-hand ox, and gave me the other end of it, and told me, if the oxen started to run, that I must hold on upon the rope. I had never driven oxen before, and of course I was very awkward. I, however, succeeded in getting to the edge of the woods with little difficulty; but I had got a very few rods into the woods, when the oxen took fright, and started full tilt, carrying the cart against trees, and over stumps, in the most frightful manner. I expected every moment that my brains would be dashed out against the trees. After running thus for a considerable distance, they finally upset the cart, dashing it with great force against a tree, and threw themselves into a dense thicket. How I escaped death, I do not know. There I was, entirely alone, in a thick wood, in a place new to me. My cart was upset and shattered, my oxen were entangled among the young trees, and there was none to help me. After a long spell of effort, I succeeded in getting my cart righted, my oxen disentangled, and again yoked to the cart. I now proceeded with my team to the place where I had, the day before, been chopping wood, and loaded my cart pretty heavily, thinking in this way to tame my oxen. I then proceeded on my way home. I had now consumed one half of the day. I got out of the woods safely, and now felt out of danger. I stopped my oxen to open the woods gate; and just as I did so, before I could get hold of my ox-rope, the oxen again started, rushed through the gate, catching it between the wheel and the body of the cart, tearing it to pieces, and coming within a few inches of crushing me against the gate-post. Thus twice, in one short day, I escaped death by the merest chance. On my return, I told Mr. Covey what had happened, and how it happened. He ordered me to return to the woods again immediately. I did so, and he followed on after me. Just as I got into the woods, he came up and told me to stop my cart, and that he would teach me how to trifle away my time, and break gates. He then went to a large gum-tree, and with his axe cut three large switches, and, after trimming them up neatly with his pocket-knife, he ordered me to take off my clothes. I made him no answer, but stood with my clothes on. He repeated his order. I still made him no answer, nor did I move to strip myself. Upon this he rushed at me with the fierceness of a tiger, tore off my clothes, and lashed me till he had worn out his switches, cutting me so savagely as to leave the marks visible for a long time after. This whipping was the first of a number just like it, and for similar offenses.

I lived with Mr. Covey one year. During the first six months, of that year, scarce a week passed without his whipping me. I was seldom free from a sore back. My awkwardness was almost always his excuse for whipping me. We were worked fully up to the point of endurance. Long before day we were up, our horses fed, and by the first approach of day we were off to the field with our hoes and ploughing teams. Mr. Covey gave us enough to eat, but scarce time to eat it. We were often less than five minutes taking our meals. We were often in the field from the first approach of day till its last lingering ray had left us; and at saving-fodder time, midnight often caught us in the field binding blades.

Covey would be out with us. The way he used to stand it, was this. He would spend the most of his afternoons in bed. He would then come out fresh in the evening, ready to urge us on with his words, example, and frequently with the whip. Mr. Covey was one of the few slaveholders who could and did work with his hands. He was a hard-working man. He knew by himself just what a man or a boy could do. There was no deceiving him. His work went on in his absence almost as well as in his presence; and he had the faculty of making us feel that he was ever present with use. This he did by surprising us. He seldom approached the spot where we were at work openly, if he could do it secretly. He always aimed at taking us by surprise. Such was his cunning, that we used to call him, among ourselves, "the snake." When we were at work in the cornfield, he would sometimes crawl on his hands and knees to avoid detection, and all at once he

would rise nearly in our midst, and scream out, "Ha, ha!
Come, come! Dash on, dash on!" This being his mode of at-
tack, it was never safe to stop a single minute. His comings
were like a thief in the night. He appeared to us as being ever
at hand. He was under every tree, behind every stump, in
every bush, and at every window, on the plantation. He
would sometimes mount his horse, as if bound to St. Michael's, a distance of seven miles, and in half an hour afterwards you would see him coiled up in the corner of the
wood-fence, watching every motion of the slaves. He would,
for this purpose, leave his horse tied up in the woods. Again,
he would sometimes walk up to us, and give us orders as
though he was upon the point of starting on a long journey,
turn his back upon us, and make as though he was going to
the house to get ready; and, before he would get half way
thither, he would turn short and crawl into a fence-corner, or
behind some tree, and there watch us till the going down of
the sun.

Mr. Covey's *forte* consisted in his power to deceive. His
life was devoted to planning and perpetrating the grossest de-
ceptions. Every thing he possessed in the shape of learning or
religion, he made conform to his disposition to deceive. He
seemed to think himself equal to deceiving the Almighty. He
would make a short prayer in the morning, and a long prayer
at night; and, strange as it may seem, few men would at
times appear more devotional than he. The exercises of his
family devotions were always commenced with singing; and,
as he was a very poor singer himself, the duty of raising the
hymn generally came upon me. He would read his hymn, and
nod at me to commence. I would at times do so; at others, I
would not. My non-compliance would almost always produce
much confusion. To show himself independent of me, he
would start and stagger through with his hymn in the most
discordant manner. In this state of mind, he prayed with
more than ordinary spirit. Poor man! such was his disposition, and success at deceiving, I do verily believe that he
sometimes deceived himself into the solemn belief, that he
was a sincere worshipper of the most high God; and this, too,
at a time when he may be said to have been guilty of compelling his woman slave to commit the sin of adultery. The facts
in the case are these: Mr. Covey was a poor man; he was just
commencing in life; he was only able to buy one slave; and,
shocking as is the fact, he bought her, as he said, for *a
breeder*. This woman was named Caroline. Mr. Covey bought
her from Mr. Thomas Lowe, about six miles from St. Michael's. She was a large, able-bodied woman, about twenty

years old. She had already given birth to one child, which proved her to be just what he wanted. After buying her, he hired a married man of Mr. Samuel Harrison, to live with him one year; and him he used to fasten up with her every night! The result was, that, at the end of the year, the miserable woman gave birth to twins. At this result Mr. Covey seemed to be highly pleased, both with the man and the wretched woman. Such was his joy, and that of his wife, that nothing they could do for Caroline during her confinement was too good, or too hard, to be done. The children were regarded as being quite an addition to his wealth.

If at any one time of my life more than another, I was made to drink the bitterest dregs of slavery, that time was during the first six months of my stay with Mr. Covey. We were worked in all weathers. It was never too hot or too cold; it could never rain, blow, hail, or snow, too hard for us to work in the field. Work, work, work, was scarcely more the order of the day than of the night. The longest days were too short for him, and the shortest nights too long for him. I was somewhat unmanageable when I first went there, but a few months of this discipline tamed me. Mr. Covey succeeded in breaking me. I was broken in body, soul, and spirit. My natural elasticity was crushed, my intellect languished, the disposition to read departed, the cheerful spark that lingered about my eye died; the dark night of slavery closed in upon me; and behold a man transformed into a brute!

Sunday was my only leisure time. I spent this in a sort of beast-like stupor, between sleep and wake, under some large tree. At times I would rise up, a flash of energetic freedom would dart through my soul, accompanied with a faint beam of hope, that flickered for a moment, and then vanished. I sank down again, mourning over my wretched condition. I was sometimes prompted to take my life, and that of Covey, but was prevented by a combination of hope and fear. My sufferings on this plantation seem now like a dream rather than a stern reality.

Our house stood within a few rods of the Chesapeake Bay, whose broad bosom was ever white with sails from every quarter of the habitable globe. Those beautiful vessels, robed in the purest white, so delightful to the eye of freemen, were to me so many shrouded ghosts, to terrify and torment me with thoughts of my wretched condition. I have often, in the deep stillness of summer's Sabbath, stood all alone upon the lofty banks of that noble bay, and traced, with saddened heart and tearful eye, the countless number of sails moving off to the mighty ocean. The sight of these always affected me powerfully. My thoughts would compel utterance; and there, with no audience but the Almighty, I would pour out my soul's complaint, in my rude way, with an apostrophe to the moving multitude of ships:—

"You are loosed from your moorings, and are free; I am fast in my chains, and am a slave! You move merrily before the gentle gale, and I sadly before the bloody whip! You are freedom's swift-winged angels, that fly round the world; I am confined in bands of iron! O that I were free! O, that I were on one of your gallant decks, and under your protecting wing! Alas! betwixt me and you, the turbid waters roll. Go on, go on. O that I could also go! Could I but swim! If I could fly! O, why was I born a man, of whom to make a brute! The glad ship is gone; she hides in the dim distance. I am left in the hottest hell of unending slavery. O God, save me! God, deliver me! Let me be free! Is there any God? Why am I a slave? I will run away. I will not stand it. Get caught, or get clear, I'll try it. I had as well die with ague as the fever. I have only one life to lose. I had as well be killed running as die standing. Only think of it; one hundred miles straight north, and I am free! Try it? Yes! God helping me, I will. It cannot be that I shall live and die a slave. I will take to the water. This very bay shall yet bear me to freedom. The steamboats steered in a north-east course from North Point. I will do the same; and when I get to the head of the bay, I will turn my canoe adrift, and walk straight through Delaware into Pennsylvania. When I get there, I shall not be required to have a pass; I can travel without being disturbed. Let but the first opportunity offer, and, come what will, I am off. Meanwhile, I will try to bear up under the yoke. I am not the only slave in the world. Why should I fret? I can bear as much as any of them. Besides, I am but a boy, and all boys are bound to some one. It may be that my misery in slavery will only increase my happiness when I get free. There is a better day coming."

Thus I used to think, and thus I used to speak to myself; goaded almost to madness at one moment, and at the next reconciling myself to my wretched lot.

I have already intimated that my condition was much worse, during the first six months of my stay at Mr. Covey's, than in the last six. The circumstances leading to the change in Mr. Covey's course toward me form an epoch in my humble history. You have seen how a man was made a slave; you shall see how a slave was made a man. On one of the hottest days of the month of August 1833, Bill Smith, William Hughes, a slave named Eli, and myself, were engaged in fanning wheat. Hughes was clearing the fanned wheat from before the fan. Eli was turning. Smith was feeding, and I was carrying wheat to the fan. The work was simple, requiring strength rather than intellect; yet, to one entirely unused to such work, it came very hard. About three o'clock of that day, I broke down; my strength failed me; I was seized with a violent aching of the head, attended with extreme dizziness; I trembled in every limb. Finding what was coming, I nerved myself up, feeling it would never do to stop work. I stood as long as I could stagger to the hopper with grain. When I could stand no longer, I fell, and felt as if held down by an immense weight. The fan of course stopped; every one had his own work to do; and no one could do the work of the other, and have his own go on at the same time.

Mr. Covey was at the house, about one hundred yards from the treading-yard where we were fanning. On hearing the fan stop, he left immediately, and came to the spot where we were. He hastily inquired what the matter was. Bill answered that I was sick, and there was no one to bring wheat to the fan. I had by this time crawled away under the side of the post and rail-fence by which the yard was enclosed, hoping to find relief by getting out of the sun. He then asked where I was. He was told by one of the hands. He came to the spot, and, after looking at me awhile, asked me what was the matter. I told him as well as I could, for I scarce had strength to speak. He then gave me a savage kick in the side, and told me to get up. I tried to do so, but fell back in the attempt. He gave me another kick, and again told me to rise. I again tried, and succeeded in gaining my feet; but, stooping to get the tub with which I was feeding the fan, I again staggered and fell. While down in this situation, Mr. Covey took up the hickory slat with which Hughes had been striking off the half-bushel measure, and with it gave me a heavy blow upon the head, making a large wound, and the blood ran freely; and with this again told me to get up. I made no effort to comply, having now made up my mind to let him do his worst. In a short time after receiving this blow, my head grew better. Mr. Covey had now left me to my fate. At this moment I resolved, for the first time, to go to my master, enter a complaint, and ask his protection. In order to do this, I must that afternoon walk seven miles; and this, under the circumstances, was truly a severe undertaking. I was exceedingly feeble; made so as much by the kicks and blows which I received, as by the severe fit of sickness to which I had been subjected. I, however, watched my chance, while Covey was looking in an opposite direction, and started for St. Michael's. I succeeded in getting a considerable distance on my way to the woods, when Covey discovered me and called after me to come back, threatening what he would do if I did not come. I disregarded both his calls and his threats, and made my way to the woods as fast as my feeble state would allow; and thinking I might be overhauled by him if I kept the road, I walked through the woods, keeping far enough from the road to avoid detection, and near enough to prevent losing my way. I had not gone far before my little strength again failed me. I could go no farther. I fell down, and lay for a considerable time. The blood was yet oozing from the wound on my head. For a time I thought I should bleed to death; and think now that I should have done so, but that the blood so matted my hair as to stop the wound. After lying there about three quarters of an hour, I nerved myself up again, and started on my way, through bogs and briers, barefooted and bareheaded, tearing my feet sometimes at nearly every step; and after a journey of about seven miles, occupying some five hours to perform it, I arrived at master's store. I then presented an appearance enough to affect any but a heart of iron. From the crown of my head to my feet, I was covered with blood; my shirt was stiff with blood. My legs and feet were torn in sundry places with briers and thorns, and were also covered with blood. I suppose I looked like a man who had escaped a den of wild beasts, and barely escaped them. In this state I appeared before my master, humbly entreating him to interpose his authority for my protection. I told him all the circumstances as well as I could, and it seemed, as I spoke, at times to affect him. He would then walk the floor, and seek to justify Covey by saying he expected I deserved it. He asked me what I wanted. I told him, to let me get a new home; that as sure as I lived with Mr. Covey again, I should live with but to die with him; that Covey would surely kill me; he was in a fair way for it. Master Thomas ridiculed the idea that there was any danger of Mr. Covey's killing me, and said that he knew Mr. Covey; that he was a good man, and that he could not think of taking me from him; that, should he do so, he would lose the whole year's wages; that I belonged to Mr. Covey for one year, and that I must go back to him, come what might; and that I must not trouble him with any more stories, or that he would himself *get hold of me*. After threatening me thus, he gave me a very large dose of salts, telling me that I might remain in St. Michael's that night, (it being quite late,) but that I must be off back to Mr. Covey's early in the morning; and that if I did not, he would *get hold of me*, which meant that he would whip me. I remained all night, and, according to his orders, I started off to Covey's in the morning, (Saturday morning,) wearied in body and broken in spirit. I got no supper that night, or breakfast that morning. I reached Covey's about nine o'clock; and just as I was getting over the fence that divided Mrs. Kemp's fields from ours, out ran Covey with his cowskin, to give me another whipping. Before he could reach me, I succeeded in getting to the cornfield and as the corn was very high, it afforded me the means of hiding. He seemed very angry, and searched for me a long time. My behavior was altogether unaccountable. He finally gave up the chase, thinking, I suppose, that I must come home for something to eat; he would give himself no further trouble in looking for me. I spent that day mostly in the woods, having the alternative before me,—to go home and be whipped to death, or stay in the woods and be starved to death. That night, I fell in with Sandy Jenkins, a slave with whom I was somewhat acquainted. Sandy had a free wife who lived about four miles from Mr. Covey's; and it being Saturday, he was on his way to see her. I told him my circumstances, and he very kindly invited me to go home with him. I went home with him, and talked this whole matter over, and got his advice as to what course it was best for me to pursue. I found Sandy an old adviser. He told me, with great solemnity, I must go back to Covey; but that before I went, I must go with him into another part of the woods, where there was a certain *root,* which, if I would take some of it with me, carrying it *always on my right side,* would render it impossible for Mr. Covey, or any other white man, to whip me. He said he had carried it for years; and since he had done so, he had never received a blow, and never expected to while he carried it. I at first rejected the idea, that the simple carrying of a root in my pocket would have any such effect as he had said, and was not disposed to take it; but Sandy impressed the necessity with much earnestness, telling me it could do no harm, if it did no good. To please him, I at length took the root, and, according to his direction, carried it upon my right side. This was Sunday morning. I immediately started for home; and upon entering the yard gate, out came Mr. Covey on his way to meeting. He spoke to me very kindly, bade me drive the pigs from a lot near by, and passed on towards the church. Now, this singular conduct of Mr. Covey really made me begin to think that there was something in the *root* which Sandy had given me; and had it been on any other day than Sunday, I could have attributed the conduct to no other cause than the influence of that root; and as it was, I was half inclined to think the root to be something more than I at first had taken it to be. All went well till Monday morning. On this morning, the virtue of the *root* was fully tested. Long before daylight, I was called to go and rub, curry, and feed, the horses. I obeyed, and was glad to obey. But whilst thus engaged, whilst in the act of throwing down some blades from the loft, Mr. Covey entered the stable with a long rope; and just as I was half out of the loft, he caught hold of my legs, and was about tying me. As soon as I found what he was up to, I gave a sudden spring, and as I did so, he holding to my legs, I was brought sprawling on the stable floor. Mr. Covey seemed now to think he had me, and could do what he pleased; but at this moment —from whence came the spirit I don't know—I resolved to fight; and, suiting my action to the resolution, I seized Covey hard by the throat; and as I did so, I rose. He held on to me, and I to him. My resistance was so entirely unexpected, that Covey seemed taken all aback. He trembled like a leaf. This gave me assurance, and I held him uneasy, causing the blood to run where I touched him with the ends of my fingers. Mr. Covey soon called out to Hughes for help. Hughes came, and, while Covey held me, attempted to tie my right hand. While he was in the act of doing so, I watched my chance, and gave him a heavy kick close under the ribs. This kick fairly sickened Hughes, so that he left me in the hands of Mr. Covey. This kick had the effect of not only weakening Hughes, but Covey also. When he saw Hughes bending over with pain, his courage quailed. He asked me if I meant to persist in my resistance. I told him I did, come what might; that he had used me like a brute for six months, and that I was determined to be used so no longer. With that, he strove to drag me to a stick that was lying just out of the stable door. He meant to knock me down. But just as he was leaning over to get the stick, I seized him with both hands by his collar, and brought him by a sudden snatch to the ground. By this time, Bill came. Covey called upon him for assistance. Bill wanted to know what he could do. Covey said, "Take hold of him, take hold of him!" Bill said his master hired him out to work, and not to help to whip me; so he left Covey and myself to fight our own battle out. We were at it for nearly two hours. Covey at length let me go, puffing and blowing at a great rate, saying that if I had not resisted, he would not have whipped me half so much. The truth was, that he had not whipped me at all. I considered him as getting entirely the worst end of the bargain; for he had drawn no blood from me, but I had from him. The whole six months afterwards, that I spent with Mr. Covey, he never laid the weight of his finger upon me in anger. He would occasionally say, he didn't want to get hold of me again. "No," thought I, "you need not; for you will come off worse than you did before."

This battle with Mr. Covey was the turning-point in my career as a slave. It rekindled the few expiring embers of freedom, and revived within me a sense of my own manhood. It recalled the departed self-confidence, and inspired me again with a determination to be free. The gratification afforded by the triumph was a full compensation for whatever else might follow, even death itself. He only can understand the deep satisfaction which I experienced, who has himself repelled by force the bloody arm of slavery. I felt as I never felt before. It was a glorious resurrection, from the tomb of slavery, to the heaven of freedom. My long-crushed spirit rose, cowardice departed, bold defiance took its place; and I now resolved that, however long I might remain a slave in form, the day had passed forever when I could be a slave in fact. I did not hesitate to let it be known of me, that the white man who expected to succeed in whipping, must also succeed in killing me.

From this time I was never again what might be called fairly whipped, though I remained a slave four years afterwards. I had several fights, but was never whipped.

It was for a long time a matter of surprise to me why Mr. Covey did not immediately have me taken by the constable to the whipping-post, and there regularly whipped for the crime of raising my hand against a white man in defence of myself. And the only explanation I can now think of does not entirely satisfy me; but such as it is, I will give it. Mr. Covey enjoyed the most unbounded reputation for being a first-rate overseer and negro-breaker. It was of considerable importance to him. That reputation was at stake; and had he sent me—a boy about sixteen years old—to the public whipping-post, his reputation would have been lost; so, to save his reputation, he suffered me to go unpunished.

My term of actual service to Mr. Edward Covey ended on Christmas day, 1833. The days between Christmas and New Year's day are allowed as holidays; and, accordingly, we were not required to perform any labor, more than to feed and take care of the stock. This time we regarded as our own, by the grace of our masters; and we therefore used or abused it nearly as we pleased. Those of us who had families at a distance, were generally allowed to spend the whole six days in their society. This time, however, was spent in various ways. The staid, sober, thinking and industrious ones of our number would employ themselves in making corn-brooms, mats, horse-collars, and baskets; and another class of us would spend the time in hunting opossums, hares, and coons. But by far the larger part engaged in such sports and merriments as playing ball, wrestling, running foot-races, fiddling, dancing, and drinking whisky; and this latter mode of spending the time was by far the most agreeable to the feelings of our masters. A slave who would work during the holidays was considered by our masters as scarcely deserving them. He was regarded as one who rejected the favor of his master. It was deemed a disgrace not to get drunk at Christmas; and he was regarded as lazy indeed, who had not provided himself with the necessary means, during the year, to get whisky enough to last him through Christmas.

From what I know of the effect of these holidays upon the slave, I believe them to be among the most effective means in the hands of the slaveholder in keeping down the spirit of insurrection. Were the slaveholders at once to abandon this practice, I have not the slightest doubt it would lead to an immediate insurrection among the slaves. These holidays serve as conductors, or safety-valves, to carry off the rebellious spirit of enslaved humanity. But for these, the slave would be forced up to the wildest desperation; and woe betide the slaveholder, the day he ventures to remove or hinder the operation of those conductors! I warn him that, in such an event, a spirit will go forth in their midst, more to be dreaded than the most appalling earthquake.

The holidays are part and parcel of the gross fraud, wrong, and inhumanity of slavery. They are professedly a custom established by the benevolence of the slaveholders; but I undertake to say, it is the result of selfishness, and one of the grossest frauds committed upon the down-trodden slave. They do not give the slaves this time because they would not like to have their work during its continuance, but because they know it would be unsafe to deprive them of it. This will be seen by the fact, that the slaveholders like to have their slaves spend those days just in such a manner as to make them as glad of their ending as of their beginning. Their object seems to be, to disgust their slaves with freedom, by plunging them into the lowest depths of dissipation. For instance, the slaveholders not only like to see the slave drink of his own accord, but will adopt various plans to make him drunk. One plan is, to make bets on their slaves, as to who can drink the most whisky without getting drunk; and in this way they succeed in getting whole multitudes to drink to excess. Thus, when the slave asks for virtuous freedom, the cunning slaveholder, knowing his ignorance, cheats him with a dose of vicious dissipation, artfully labelled with the name of liberty. The most of us used to drink it down, and the result was just what might be supposed: many of us were led to think that there was little to choose between liberty and slavery. We felt, and very properly too, that we had almost as well be slaves to man as to rum. So, when the holidays ended, we staggered up from the filth of our wallowing, took a long breath, and marched to the field,—feeling, upon the whole, rather glad to go, from what our master had deceived us into a belief was freedom, back to the arms of slavery.

I have said that this mode of treatment is a part of the whole system of fraud and inhumanity of slavery. It is so. The mode here adopted to disgust the slave with freedom, by allowing him to see only the abuse of it, is carried out in other things. For instance, a slave loves molasses; he steals some. His master, in many cases, goes off to town, and buys a large quantity; he returns, takes his whip, and commands the slave to eat the molasses, until the poor fellow is made sick at the very mention of it. The same mode is sometimes adopted to make the slaves refrain from asking for more food than their regular allowance. A slave runs through his allowance and applies for more. His master is enraged at him; but, not willing to send him off without food, gives him more than is necessary, and compels him to eat it within a given time. Then, if he complains that he cannot eat it, he is said to be satisfied neither full nor fasting, and is whipped for being hard to please! I have an abundance of such illustrations of the same principle, drawn from my own observation, but think the cases I have cited sufficient. The practice is a very common one.

On the first of January, 1834, I left Mr. Covey, and went to live with Mr. William Freeland, who lived about three miles from St. Michael's. I soon found Mr. Freeland a very different man from Mr. Covey. Thought not rich, he was what would be called an educated southern gentleman. Mr. Covey, as I have shown, was a well-trained negro-breaker and slave-driver. The former (slaveholder though he was) seemed to possess some regard for honor, some reverence for justice, and some respect for humanity. The latter seemed totally insensible to all such sentiments. Mr. Freeland had many of the faults peculiar to slaveholders, such as being very passionate and fretful; but I must do him the justice to say, that he was exceedinly free from those degrading vices to which Mr. Covey was constantly addicted. The one was open and frank, and we always knew where to find him. The other was a most artful deceiver, and could be understood only by such as were skilful enough to detect his cunningly-devised frauds. Another advantage I gained in my new master was, he made no pretensions to, or profession of, religion; and this, in my opinion, was truly a great advantage. I assert most unhesitatingly, that the religion of the south is a mere covering for the most horrid crimes,—a justifier of the most appalling barbarity,—a sanctifer of the most hateful frauds,—and a dark shelter under which the darkest, foulest, grossest, and most infernal deeds of slaveholders find the strongest protection. Were I to be again reduced to the chains of slavery, next to that enslavement, I should regard being the slave of a religious master the greatest calamity that could befall me. For of all slaveholders with whom I have ever met, religious slaveholders are the worst. I have ever found them the meanest and basest, the most cruel and cowardly, of all others. It was my unhappy lot not only to belong to a religious slaveholder, but to live in a community of such religionists. Very near Mr. Freeland lived the Rev. Daniel Weeden, and in the same neighborhood lived the Rev. Rigby Hopkins. These were members and ministers in the Reformed Methodist Church. Mr. Weeden owned, among others, a woman slave, whose name I have forgotten. This woman's back, for weeks, was kept literally raw, made so by the lash of this merciless, *religious* wretch. He used to hire hands. His maxim was, Behave well or behave ill, it is the duty of a master occasionally to whip a slave, to remind him of his master's authority. Such was his theory, and such his practice.

Mr. Hopkins was even worse than Mr. Weeden. His chief boast was his ability to manage slaves. The peculiar feature of his government was that of whipping slaves in advance of deserving it. He always managed to have one or more of his slaves to whip every Monday morning. He did this to alarm their fears, and strike terror into those who escaped. His plan was to whip for the smallest offences, to prevent the commission of large ones. Mr. Hopkins could always find some excuse for whipping a slave. It would astonish one, unaccustomed to a slaveholding life, to see with what wonderful ease a slaveholder can find things, of which to make occasion to whip a slave. A mere look, word, or motion,—a mistake, accident, or want of power,—are all matters for which a slave may be whipped at any time. Does a slave look dissatisfied? It is said, he has the devil in him, and it must be whipped out. Does he speak loudly when spoken to by his master?

Then he is getting high-minded, and should be taken down a button-hole lower. Does he forget to pull off his hat at the approach of a white person? Then he is wanting in reverence, and should be whipped for it. Does he ever venture to vindicate his conduct, when censured for it? Then he is guilty of impudence,—one of the greatest crimes of which a slave can be guilty. Does he ever venture to suggest a different mode of doing things from that pointed out by his master? He is indeed presumptuous, and getting above himself; and nothing less than a flogging will do for him. Does he, while ploughing, break a plough,—or, while hoeing, break a hoe? It is owing to his carelessness, and for it a slave must always be whipped. Mr. Hopkins could always find something of this sort to justify the use of the lash, and he seldom failed to embrace such opportunities. There was not a man in the whole county, with whom the slaves who had the getting their own home, would not prefer to live, rather than with this Rev. Mr. Hopkins. And yet there was not a man any where round, who made higher professions of religion, or was more active in revivals,—more attentive to the class, love-feast, prayer and preaching meetings, or more devotional in his family,— that prayed earlier, later, louder, and longer,—than this same reverend slave-driver, Rigby Hopkins.

But to return to Mr. Freeland, and to my experience while in his employment. He, like Mr. Covey, gave us enough to eat; but, unlike Mr. Covey, he also gave us sufficient time to take our meals. He worked us hard, but always between sunrise and sunset. He required a good deal of work to be done, but gave us good tools with which to work. His farm was large, but he employed hands enough to work it, and with ease, compared with many of his neighbors. My treatment, while in his employment, was heavenly, compared with what I experienced at the hands of Mr. Edward Covey.

Mr. Freeland was himself the owner of but two slaves. Their names were Henry Harris and John Harris. The rest of his hands he hired. These consisted of myself, Sandy Jenkins,* and Handy Caldwell. Henry and John were quite intelligent, and in a very little while after I went there, I succeeded in creating in them a strong desire to learn how to read. This desire soon sprang up in the others also. They very

---

*This is the same man who gave me the roots to prevent my being whipped by Mr. Covey. He was "a clever soul." We used frequently to talk about the fight with Covey, and as often as we did so, he would claim my success as the result of the roots which he gave me. This superstition is very common among the more ignorant slaves. A slave seldom dies but that his death is attributed to trickery.

soon mustered up some old spelling-books, and nothing
would do but that I must keep a Sabbath school. I agreed to
do so, and accordingly devoted my Sundays to teaching these
my loved fellow-slaves how to read. Neither of them knew
his letters when I went there. Some of the slaves of the neigh-
boring farms found what was going on, and also availed
themselves of the little opportunity to learn to read. It was
understood, among all who came, that there must be as little
display about it as possible. It was necessary to keep our religious masters at St. Michael's unacquainted with the fact,
that, instead of spending the Sabbath in wrestling, boxing,
and drinking whisky, we were trying to learn how to read the
will of God; for they had much rather see us engaged in
those degrading sports, than to see us behaving like intellectual, moral, and accountable beings. My blood boils as I
think of the bloody manner in which Messrs. Wright Fair-
banks and Garrison West, both class-leaders, in connection
with many others, rushed in upon us with sticks and stones,
and broke up our virtuous little Sabbath school, at St. Michael's—all calling themselves Christians! humble followers
of the Lord Jesus Christ! But I am again digressing.

I held my Sabbath school at the house of a free colored
man, whose name I deem it imprudent to mention; for should
it be known, it might embarrass him greatly, though the
crime of holding the school was committed ten years ago. I
had at one time over forty scholars, and those of the right
sort, ardently desiring to learn. They were of all ages, though
mostly men and women. I look back to those Sundays with an
amount of pleasure not to be expressed. They were great days
to my soul. The work of instructing my dear fellow-slaves
was the sweetest engagement with which I was ever blessed.
We loved each other, and to leave them at the close of the
Sabbath was a severe cross indeed. When I think that these
precious souls are to-day shut up in the prison-house of slavery, my feelings overcome me, and I am almost ready to ask,
"Does a righteous God govern the universe? and for what
does he hold the thunders in his right hand, if not to smite
the oppressor, and deliver the spoiled out of the hand of the
spoiler?" These dear souls came not to Sabbath school because it was reputable to be thus engaged. Every moment
they spent in that school, they were liable to be taken up, and
given thirty-nine lashes. They came because they wished to
learn. Their minds had been starved by their cruel masters.
They had been shut up in mental darkness. I taught them, because it was the delight of my soul to be doing something
that looked like bettering the condition of my race. I kept up

my school nearly the whole year I lived with Mr. Freeland; and, beside my Sabbath school, I devoted three evenings in the week, during the winter, to teaching the slaves at home. And I have the happiness to know, that several of those who came to Sabbath school learned how to read; and that one, at least, is now free through my agency.

The year passed off smoothly. It seemed only about half as long as the year which preceded it. I went through it without receiving a single blow. I will give Mr. Freeland the credit of being the best master I ever had, *till I became my own master.* For the ease with which I passed the year, I was, however, somewhat indebted to the society of my fellow-slaves. They were noble souls; they not only possessed loving hearts, but brave ones. We were linked and interlinked with each other. I loved them with a love stronger than any thing I have experienced since. It is sometimes said that we slaves do not love and confide in each other. In answer to this assertion, I can say, I never loved any or confided in any people more than my fellow-slaves, and especially those with whom I lived at Mr. Freeland's. I believe we would have died for each other. We never undertook to do any thing, of any importance, without a mutual consultation. We never moved separately. We were one; and as much so by our tempers and dispositions, as by the mutual hardships to which we were necessarily subjected by our condition as slaves.

At the close of the year 1834, Mr. Freeland again hired me of my master, for the year 1835. But, by this time, I began to want to live *upon free land* as well as *with Freeland;* and I was no longer content, therefore, to live with him or any other slave-holder. I began, with the commencement of the year, to prepare myself for a final struggle, which should decide my fate one way or the other. My tendency was upward. I was fast approaching manhood, and year after year had passed, and I was still a slave. These thoughts roused me—I must do something. I therefore resolved that 1835 should not pass without witnessing an attempt, on my part, to secure my liberty. But I was not willing to cherish this determination alone. My fellow-slaves were dear to me. I was anxious to have them participate with me in this, my life-giving determination. I therefore, though with great prudence, commenced early to ascertain their views and feelings in regard to their condition, and to imbue their minds with thoughts of freedom. I bent myself to devising ways and means for our escape, and meanwhile strove, on all fitting occasions, to impress them with the gross fraud and inhumanity of slavery. I went first to Henry, next to John, then to the others. I found, in them all, warm hearts and noble spirits. They were ready to hear, and ready to act when a feasible plan should be proposed. This was what I wanted. I talked to them of our want of manhood, if we submitted to our enslavement without at least one noble effort to be free. We met often, and consulted frequently, and told our hopes and fears, recounted the difficulties, real and imagined, which we should be called on to meet. At times we were almost disposed to give up, and try to content ourselves with our wretched lot; at others, we were firm and unbending in our determination to go. Whenever we suggested any plan, there was shrinking —the odds were fearful. Our path was beset with the greatest obstacles; and if we succeeded in gaining the end of it, our right to be free was yet questionable—we were yet liable to be returned to bondage. We could see no spot, this side of the ocean, where we could be free. We knew nothing about Canada. Our knowledge of the north did not extend farther than New York; and to go there, and be forever harassed with the frightful liability of being returned to slavery—with the certainty of being treated tenfold worse than before—the thought was truly a horrible one, and one which it was not easy to overcome. The case sometimes stood thus: At every gate through which we were to pass, we saw a watchman—at every ferry a guard—on every bridge a sentinel—and in every wood a patrol. We were hemmed in upon every side. Here were the difficulties, real or imagined—the good to be sought, and the evil to be shunned. On the one hand, there stood slavery, a stern reality, glaring frightfully upon us—its robes already crimsoned with the blood of millions, and even now feasting itself greedily upon our own flesh. On the other hand, away back in the dim distance, under the flickering light of the north star, behind some craggy hill or snow-covered mountain, stood a doubtful freedom—half frozen— beckoning us to come and share its hospitality. This in itself was sometimes enough to stagger us; but when we permitted ourselves to survey the road, we were frequently appalled. Upon either side we saw grim death, assuming the most horrid shapes. Now it was starvation, causing us to eat our own flesh;—now we were contending with the waves, and were drowned;—now we were overtaken, and torn to pieces by the fangs of the terrible bloodhound. We were stung by scorpions, chased by wild beasts, bitten by snakes, and finally, after having nearly reached the desired spot,—after swimming rivers, encountering wild beasts, sleeping in the woods, suffering hunger and nakedness,—we were overtaken by our pursuers, and, in our resistance, we were shot dead upon the spot! I say, this picture sometimes appalled us, and made us

"rather bear those ills we had,
Than fly to others, that we knew not of."

In coming to a fixed determination to run away, we did more than Patrick Henry, when he resolved upon liberty or death. With us it was a doubtful liberty at most, and almost certain death if we failed. For my part, I should prefer death to hopeless bondage.

Sandy, one of our number, gave up the notion, but still encouraged us. Our company then consisted of Henry Harris, John Harris, Henry Bailey, Charles Roberts, and myself. Henry Bailey was my uncle, and belonged to my master. Charles married my aunt: he belonged to my master's father-in-law, Mr. William Hamilton.

The plan we finally concluded upon was, to get a large canoe belonging to Mr. Hamilton, and upon the Saturday night previous to Easter holidays, paddle directly up the Chesapeake Bay. On our arrival at the head of the bay, a distance of seventy or eighty miles from where we lived, it was our purpose to turn our canoe adrift, and follow the guidance of the north star till we got beyond the limits of Maryland. Our reason for taking the water route was, that we were less liable to be suspected as runaways; we hoped to be regarded as fishermen; whereas, if we should take the land route, we should be subjected to interruptions of almost every kind. Any one having a white face, and being so disposed, could stop us, and subject us to examination.

The week before our intended start, I wrote several protections, one for each of us. As well as I can remember, they were in the following words, to wit:—

"This is to certify that I, the undersigned, have given the bearer, my servant, full liberty to go to Baltimore, and spend the Easter holidays. Written with mine own hand, &c., 1835.
"WILLIAM HAMILTON,
"Near St. Michael's, in Talbot county, Maryland."

We were not going to Baltimore; but, in going up the bay, we went toward Baltimore, and these protections were only intended to protect us while on the bay.

As the time drew near for our departure, our anxiety became more and more intense. It was truly a matter of life and death with us. The strength of our determination was about to be fully tested. At this time, I was very active in explaining every difficulty, removing every doubt, dispelling every fear, and inspiring all with the firmness indispensable to success in our undertaking; assuring them that half was gained the instant we made the move; we had talked long enough; we were now ready to move; if not now, we never should be; and if we did not intend to move now, we had as well fold our arms, sit down, and acknowledge ourselves fit only to be slaves. This none of us were prepared to acknowledge. Every man stood firm; and at our last meeting, we pledged ourselves afresh, in the most solemn manner, that, at the time appointed, we would certainly start in pursuit of freedom. This was in the middle of the week, at the end of which we were to be off. We went, as usual, to our several fields of labor, but with bosoms highly agitated with thoughts of our truly hazardous undertaking. We tried to conceal our feelings as much as possible; and I think we succeeded very well.

After a painful waiting, the Saturday morning, whose night was to witness our departure, came. I hailed it with joy, bring what of sadness it might. Friday night was a sleepless one for me. I probably felt more anxious than the rest, because I was, by common consent, at the head of the whole affair. The responsibility of success or failure lay heavily upon me. The glory of the one, and the confusion of the other, were alike mine. The first two hours of that morning were such as I never experienced before, and hope never to again. Early in the morning, we went, as usual, to the field. We were spreading manure; and all at once, while thus engaged, I was overwhelmed with an indescribable feeling, in the fulness of which I turned to Sandy, who was near by, and said, "We are betrayed!" "Well," said he, "that thought has this moment struck me." We said no more. I was never more certain of any thing.

The horn was blown as usual, and we went up from the field to the house for breakfast. I went for the form more than for want of any thing to eat that morning. Just as I got to the house, in looking out at the lane gate, I saw four white men, with two colored men. The white men were on horseback, and the colored ones were walking behind, as if tied. I watched them a few moments till they got up to our lane gate. Here they halted, and tied the colored men to the gatepost. I was not yet certain as to what the matter was. In a few moments, in rode Mr. Hamilton, with a speed betokening great excitement. He came to the door, and inquired if Master William was in. He was told he was at the barn. Mr. Hamilton, without dismounting, rode up to the barn with extraordinary speed. In a few moments, he and Mr. Freeland returned to the house. By this time, the three constables rode up, and in great haste dismounted, tied their horses, and met Master William and Mr. Hamilton returning from the barn; and after talking awhile, they all walked up to the kitchen door. There was no one in the kitchen but myself and John. Henry and Sandy were up at the barn. Mr. Freeland put his head in at the door, and called me by name, saying, there were some gentlemen at the door who wished to see me. I stepped to the door, and inquired what they wanted. They at once seized me, and, without giving me any satisfaction, tied me—lashing my hands closely together. I insisted upon knowing what the matter was. They at length said, that they had learned I had been in a "scrape," and that I was to be examined before my master; and if their information proved false, I should not be hurt.

In a few moments, they succeeded in tying John. They then turned to Henry, who had by this time returned, and commanded him to cross his hands. "I won't!" said Henry, in a firm tone indicating his readiness to meet the consequences of his refusal. "Won't you?" said Tom Graham, the constable. "No, I won't!" said Henry, in a still stronger tone. With this, two of the constables pulled out their shining pistols, and swore, by their Creator, that they would make him cross his hands or kill him. Each cocked his pistol, and, with fingers on the trigger, walked up to Henry, saying, at the same time, if he did not cross his hands, they would blow his damned heart out. "Shoot me, shoot me!" said Henry; "you can't kill me but once. Shoot, shoot,—and be damned! *I won't be tied!*" This he said in a tone of loud defiance; and at the same time, with a motion as quick as lightning, he with one single stroke dashed the pistols from the hand of each constable. As he did this, all hands fell upon him, and after beating him some time, they finally overpowered him, and got him tied.

During the scuffle, I managed, I know not how, to get my pass out, and, without being discovered, put it into the fire. We were all now tied; and just as we were to leave for Easton jail, Betsy Freeland, mother of William Freeland, came to the door with her hands full of biscuits, and divided them between Henry and John. She then delivered herself of a speech, to the following effect:—addressing herself to me, she said, *"You devil! You yellow devil!* it was you that put it into the heads of Henry and John to run away. But for you, you long-legged mulatto devil! Henry nor John would never have thought of such a thing." I made no reply, and was immediately hurried off towards St. Michael's. Just a moment previous to the scuffle with Henry, Mr. Hamilton suggested

the propriety of making a search for the protections which he
had understood Frederick had written for himself and the
rest. But, just at the moment he was about carrying his proposal into effect, his aid was needed in helping to tie Henry;
and the excitement attending the scuffle caused them either to
forget, or to deem it unsafe, under the circumstances, to
search. So we were not yet convicted of the intention to run
away.

When we got about half way to St. Michael's, while the
constables having us in charge were looking ahead, Henry inquired of me what he should do with his pass. I told him to
eat it with his biscuit, and own nothing; and we passed the
word around, *"Own nothing"*; and *"Own nothing!"* said we
all. Our confidence in each other was unshaken. We were resolved to succeed or fail together, after the calamity had be-
fallen us as much as before. We were now prepared for any
thing. We were to be dragged that morning fifteen miles behind horses, and then to be placed in the Easton jail. When
we reached St. Michael's, we underwent a sort of examination. We all denied that we ever intended to run away. We
did this more to bring out the evidence against us, than from
any hope of getting clear of being sold; for, as I have said,
we were ready for that. The fact was, we cared but little
where we went, so we went together. Our greatest concern
was about separation. We dreaded that more than any thing
this side of death. We found the evidence against us to be the
testimony of one person; our master would not tell who it
was; but we came to a unanimous decision among ourselves
as to who their informant was. We were sent off to the jail at
Easton. When we got there, we were delivered up to the
sheriff, Mr. Joseph Graham, and by him placed in jail.
Henry, John, and myself, were placed in one room together
—Charles, and Henry Bailey, in another. Their object in sep-
arating us was to hinder concert.

We had been in jail scarcely twenty minutes, when a
swarm of slave traders, and agents for slave traders, flocked
into jail to look at us, and to ascertain if we were for sale.
Such a set of beings I never saw before! I felt myself surrounded by so many fiends from perdition. A band of pirates
never looked more like their father, the devil. They laughed
and grinned over us, saying, "Ah, my boys! we have got you,
haven't we?" And after taunting us in various ways, they one
by one went into an examination of us, with intent to ascertain our value. They would impudently ask us if we would
not like to have them for our masters. We would make them
no answer, and leave them to find out as best they could.

Then they would curse and swear at us, telling us that they could take the devil out of us in a very little while, if we were only in their hands.

While in jail, we found ourselves in much more comfortable quarters than we expected when we went there. We did not get much to eat, nor that which was very good; but we had a good clean room, from the windows of which we could see what was going on in the street, which was very much better than though we had been placed in one of the dark, damp cells. Upon the whole, we got along very well, so far as the jail and its keeper were concerned. Immediately after the holidays were over, contrary to all our expectations, Mr. Hamilton and Mr. Freeland came up to Easton, and took Charles, the two Henrys, and John, out of jail, and carried them home, leaving me alone. I regarded this separation as a final one. It caused me more pain than any thing else in the whole transaction. I was ready for any thing rather than separation. I supposed that they had consulted together, and had decided that, as I was the whole cause of the intention of the others to run away, it was hard to make the innocent suffer with the guilty; and that they had, therefore, concluded to take the others home, and sell me, as a warning to the others that remained. It is due to the noble Henry to say, he seemed almost as reluctant at leaving the prison as at leaving home to come to the prison. But we knew we should, in all probability, be separated, if we were sold; and since he was in their hands, he concluded to go peaceably home.

I was now left to my fate. I was all alone, and within the walls of a stone prison. But a few days before, and I was full of hope. I expected to have been safe in a land of freedom; but now I was covered with gloom, sunk down to the utmost despair. I thought the possibility of freedom was gone. I was kept in this way about one week, at the end of which, Captain Auld, my master, to my surprise and utter astonishment, came up, and took me out, with the intention of sending me, with a gentleman of his acquaintance, into Alabama. But, from some cause or other, he did not send me to Alabama, but concluded to send me back to Baltimore, to live again with his brother Hugh, and to learn a trade.

Thus, after an absence of three years and one month, I was once more permitted to return to my old home at Baltimore. My master sent me away, because there existed against me a very great prejudice in the community, and he feared I might be killed.

In a few weeks after I went to Baltimore, Master Hugh hired me to Mr. William Gardner, an extensive ship-builder,

on Fell's Point. I was put there to learn how to calk. It, however, proved a very unfavorable place for the accomplishment
of this object. Mr. Gardner was engaged that spring in building two large man-of-war brigs, professedly for the Mexican
government. The vessels were to be launched in the July of
that year, and in failure thereof, Mr. Gardner was to lose a
considerable sum; so that when I entered, all was hurry.
There was no time to learn any thing. Every man had to do
that which he knew how to do. In entering the shipyard, my
orders from Mr. Gardner were, to do whatever the carpenters
commanded me to do. This was placing me at the beck and
call of about seventy-five men. I was to regard all these as
master. Their word was to be my law. My situation was a
most trying one. At times I needed a dozen pair of hands. I
was called a dozen ways in the space of a single minute.
Three or four voices would strike my ear at the same moment. It was—"Fred., come help me to cant this timber
here."—Fred., come carry this timber yonder."—Fred., bring
that roller here."—"Fred., go get a fresh can of water."—
Fred., come help saw off the end of this timber."—"Fred., go
quick, and get the crowbar."—"Fred., hold on the end of this
fall."—"Fred., go to the blacksmith's shop, and get a new
punch."—"Hurra, Fred.! run and bring me a cold chisel."—
"I say, Fred., bear a hand, and get up a fire as quick as
lightning under that steam-box."—"Halloo, nigger! come, turn
this grindstone."—"Come, come! move, move! and bowse this
timber forward."—"I say, darky, blast your eyes, why don't
you heat up some pitch?"—"Halloo! halloo! halloo!" (Three
voices at the same time.) "Come here!—Go there!—Hold on
where you are! Damn you, if you move, I'll knock your brains
out!"

This was my school for eight months; and I might have remained there longer, but for a most horrid fight I had with
four of the white apprentices, in which my left eye was
nearly knocked out, and I was horribly mangled in other respects. The facts in the case were these: Until a very little
while after I went there, white and black ship-carpenters
worked side by side, and no one seemed to see any impro-
priety in it. All hands seemed to be very well satisfied. Many
of the black carpenters were freemen. Things seemed to be
going on very well. All at once, the white carpenters knocked
off, and said they would not work with free colored workmen. Their reason for this, as alleged, was, that if free colored carpenters were encouraged, they would soon take the
trade into their own hands, and poor white men would be
thrown out of employment. They therefore felt called upon

at once to put a stop to it. And, taking advantage of Mr. Gardner's necessities, they broke off, swearing they would work no longer, unless he would discharge his black carpenters. Now, though this did not extend to me in form, it did reach me in fact. My fellow-apprentices very soon began to feel it degrading to them to work with me. They began to put on airs, and talk about the "niggers" taking the country, saying we all ought to be killed; and, being encouraged by the journeymen, they commenced making my condition as hard as they could, by hectoring me around, and sometimes striking me. I, of course, kept the vow I made after the fight with Mr. Covey, and struck back again, regardless of consequences; and while I kept them from combining, I succeeded very well; for I could whip the whole of them, taking them separately. They, however, at length combined, and came upon me, armed with sticks, stones, and heavy handspikes. One came in front with a half brick. There was one at each side of me, and one behind me. While I was attending to those in front, and on either side, the one behind ran up with the handspike, and struck me a heavy blow upon the head. It stunned me. I fell, and with this they all ran upon me, and fell to beating me with their fists. I let them lay on for a while, gathering strength. In an instant, I gave a sudden surge, and rose to my hands and knees. Just as I did that, one of their number gave me, with his heavy boot, a powerful kick in the left eye. My eyeball seemed to have burst. When they saw my eye closed, and badly swollen, they left me. With this I seized the handspike, and for a time pursued them. But here the carpenters interfered, and I thought I might as well give it up. It was impossible to stand my hand against so many. All this took place in sight of not less than fifty white ship-carpenters, and not one interposed a friendly word; but some cried, "Kill the damned nigger! Kill him! kill him! He struck a white person." I found my only chance for life was in flight. I succeeded in getting away without an additional blow, and barely so; for to strike a white man is death by Lynch law,—and that was the law in Mr. Gardner's shipyard nor is there much of any other out of Mr. Gardner's ship-yard.

I went directly home, and told the story of my wrongs to Master Hugh; and I am happy to say of him, irreligious as he was, his conduct was heavenly, compared with that of his brother Thomas under similar circumstances. He listened attentively to my narration of the circumstances leading to the savage outrage, and gave many proofs of his strong indignation at it. The heart of my once overkind mistress was again melted into pity. My puffed-out eye and blood-covered face moved her to tears. She took a chair by me, washed the blood from my face, and, with a mother's tenderness, bound up my head, covering the wounded eye with a lean piece of fresh beef. It was almost compensation for my suffering to witness, once more, a manifestation of kindness from this, my once affectionate old mistress. Master Hugh was very much enraged. He gave expression to his feelings by pouring out curses upon the heads of those who did the deed. As soon as I got a little the better of my bruises, he took me with him to Esquire Watson's, on Bond Street, to see what could be done about the matter. Mr. Watson inquired who saw the assault committed. Master Hugh told him it was done in Mr. Gardner's ship-yard, at midday, where there were a large company of men at work. "As to that," he said, "the deed was done, and there was no question as to who did it." His answer was, he could do nothing in the case, unless some white man would come forward and testify. He could issue no warrant on my word. If I had been killed in the presence of a thousand colored people, their testimony combined would have been insufficient to have arrested one of the murderers. Master Hugh, for once, was compelled to say this state of things was too bad. Of course, it was impossible to get any white man to volunteer his testimony in my behalf, and against the white young men. Even those who may have sympathized with me were not prepared to do this. It required a degree of courage unknown to them to do so; for just at that time, the slightest manifestation of humanity toward a colored person was denounced as abolitionism, and that name subjected its bearer to frightful liabilities. The watchwords of the bloody-minded in that region, and in those days were, "Damn the abolitionists!" and "Damn the niggers!" There was nothing done, and probably nothing would have been done if I had been killed. Such was, and such remains, the state of things in the Christian city of Baltimore.

Master Hugh, finding he could get no redress, refused to let me go back again to Mr. Gardner. He kept me himself, and his wife dressed my wound till I was again restored to health. He then took me into the ship-yard of which he was foreman, in the employment of Mr. Walter Price. There I was immediately set to calking, and very soon learned the art of using my mallet and irons. In the course of one year from the time I left Mr. Gardner's, I was able to command the highest wages given to the most experienced calkers. I was now of some importance to my master. I was bringing him from six to seven dollars per week. I sometimes brought him nine dollars per week: my wages were a dollar and a half a day. After learning how to calk, I sought my own employment, made my own contracts, and collected the money which I earned. My pathway became much more smooth than before; my condition was now much more comfortable. When I could get no calking to do, I did nothing. During these leisure times, those old notions about freedom would steal over me again. When in Mr. Gardner's employment, I was kept in such a perpetual whirl of excitement, I could think of nothing, scarcely, but my life; and in thinking of my life, I almost forgot my liberty. I have observed this in my experience of slavery,—that whenever my condition was improved, instead of its increasing my contentment, it only increased my desire to be free, and set me to thinking of plans to gain my freedom. I have found that, to make a contented slave, it is necessary to make a thoughtless one. It is necessary to darken his moral and mental vision, and, as far as possible, to annihilate the power of reason. He must be able to detect no inconsistencies in slavery; he must be made to feel that slavery is right; and he can be brought to that only when he ceases to be a man.

I was now getting, as I have said, one dollar and fifty cents per day. I contracted for it; I earned it; it was paid to me; it was rightfully my own; yet, upon each returning Saturday night, I was compelled to deliver every cent of that money to Master Hugh. And why? Not because he earned it,—not because he had any hand in earning it,—not because I owed it to him,—nor because he possessed the slightest shadow of a right to it; but solely because he had the power to compel me to give it up. The right of the grim-visaged pirate upon the high seas is exactly the same.

JAMES WELDON JOHNSON (1871–1938)

A major figure in the creation and development of Negro American literature and culture, James Weldon Johnson contributed in many ways: as a poet and songwriter, novelist, es-

*sayist and critic, collector of spirituals, pioneer anthologist
and interpreter of Negro poetry, pioneer student of the history of the Negro in the drama, educator, and active participant in the early development of the civil rights movement.
He was born in Jacksonville, Florida, went to Atlanta University, and returned to Jacksonville as a teacher and public-
school principal. He was the first Negro to pass the Florida
bar examination but did not devote his energies to the practice of law. He wrote songs which his composer brother, Rosamond, set to music. They both went to New York in 1901
and achieved success in musical comedy. Johnson also pursued the study of literature and drama at Columbia University. From 1906 to 1913 he was in the U.S. diplomatic service as a consul, first in Venezuela and later in Nicaragua,
and, while in the consular service, he wrote his landmark
novel* The Autobiography of an Ex-Colored Man *(1912). On
returning to the United States, he became associated with the
National Association for the Advancement of Colored People.
He served as Field Secretary of the N.A.A.C.P. from 1916 to
1920, and as General Secretary from 1920 to 1930. During
these years he became a recognized poet, collected and published* The Book of American Negro Poetry *and, with his
brother, edited* The Books of American Negro Spirituals. *In
1930 he was appointed Professor of Creative Literature at
Fisk University, in Nashville, Tennessee, and also served as a
visiting professor at New York University. His autobiography,*
Along This Way, *from which we present selected episodes,
was published in 1933.*

Along This Way (Selected Episodes)

I was born June 17, 1871, in the old house on the corner; but
I have no recollection of having lived in it. Before I could be
aware of such a thing my father had built a new house near
the middle of his lot. In this new house was formed my first
consciousness of home. My childish idea of it was that it was
a great mansion. I saw nothing in the neighborhood that sur-
passed it in splendor. Of course, it was only a neat cottage.
The house had three bedrooms, a parlor, and a kitchen. The
four main rooms were situated, two on each side of a hall
that ran through the center of the house. The kitchen, used
also as a room in which the family ate, was at the rear of the
house and opened on a porch that was an extension of the
hall. On the front a broad piazza ran the width of the house.

Under the roof was an attic to which a narrow set of steps in one of the back rooms gave access.

But the house was painted, and there were glass windows and green blinds. Before long there were some flowers and trees. One of the first things my father did was to plant two maple trees at the front gate and a dozen or more orange trees in the yard. The maples managed to live; the orange trees, naturally, flourished. The hallway of the house was covered with a strip of oilcloth and the floors of the rooms with matting. There were curtains at the windows and some pictures on the walls. In the parlor there were two or three dozen books and a cottage organ. When I was seven or eight years old, the organ gave way to a square piano. It was a tinkling old instrument, but a source of rapturous pleasure. It is one of the indelible impressions on my mind. I can still remember just how the name "Bacon" looked, stamped in gold letters above the keyboard. There was a center marble-top table on which rested a big, illustrated Bible and a couple of photograph albums. In a corner stood a what-not filled with bric-a-brac and knickknacks. On a small stand was a glass-domed receptacle in which was a stuffed canary perched on a diminutive tree; on this stand there was also kept a stereoscope and an assortment of views photographed in various parts of the world. For my brother and me, in our childhood (my brother, John Rosamond, was born in the new house August 11, 1873), this room was an Aladdin's cave. We used to stand before the what-not and stake out our claims to the objects on its shelves with a "that's mine" and a "that's mine." We never tired of looking at the stereoscopic scenes, examining the photographs in the album, or putting the big Bible and other books on the floor and exploring for pictures. Two large conch shells decorated the ends of the hearth. We greatly admired their pink, polished inner surface; and loved to put them to our ears to hear the "roar of the sea" from their cavernous depths. But the undiminishing thrill was derived from our experiments on the piano.

When I was born, my mother was very ill, too ill to nurse me. Then she found a friend and neighbor in an unexpected quarter. Mrs. McCleary, her white neighbor who lived a block away, had a short while before given birth to a girl baby. When this baby was christened she was named Angel. The mother of Angel, hearing of my mother's plight, took me and nursed me at her breast until my mother had recovered sufficiently to give me her own milk. So it appears that in the land of black mammies I had a white one. Between her and

me there existed an affectionate relation through all my childhood; and even in after years when I had grown up and
moved away I never, up to the time of her death, went back
to my old home without paying her a visit and taking her
some small gift.

I do not intend to boast about a white mammy, for I have
perceived bad taste in those Southern white people who
are continually boasting about their black mammies. I know
the temptation for them to do so is very strong, because the
honor point on the escutcheon of Southern aristocracy, the
sine qua non of a background of family, of good breeding
and social prestige, in the South is the Black Mammy. Of
course, many of the white people who boast of having had
black mammies are romancing. Naturally, Negroes had black
mammies, but black mammies for white people were expensive luxuries, and comparatively few white people had them.

When I was about a year old, my father made a trip to
New York, taking my mother and me with him. It was during this visit that I developed from a creeping infant into a
walking child. Without doubt, my mother welcomed this trip.
She was, naturally, glad to see again the city and friends of
her girlhood; and it is probable that she brought some pressure on my father to make another move—back to New
York. If she did, it was without effect. I say she probably
made some such effort because I know what a long time it
took her to become reconciled to life in the South; in fact,
she never did entirely. The New York of her childhood and
youth was all the United States she knew. Latterly she had
lived in a British colony under conditions that rendered the
weight of race comparatively light. During the earlier days of
her life in Jacksonville she had no adequate conception of
her "place."

And so it was that one Sunday morning she went to worship at St. John's Episcopal Church. As one who had been a
member of the choir of Christ Church Cathedral she went
quite innocently. She went, in fact, not knowing any better.
In the chanting of the service her soprano voice rang out
clear and beautiful, and necks were craned to discover the
singer. On leaving the church she was politely but definitely
informed that the St. John's congregation would prefer to
have her worship the Lord elsewhere. Certainly she never
went back to St. John's nor to any other Episcopal church;
she followed her mother and joined Ebenezer, the colored
Methodist Episcopal Church in Jacksonville, and became the
choir leader.

Racially she continued to be a nonconformist and a rebel.

A decade or so after the St. John's Church incident Lemuel W. Livingston, a student at Cookman Institute, the Negro school in Jacksonville founded and maintained by the Methodist Church (North), was appointed as a cadet to West Point. Livingston passed his written examinations, and the colored people were exultant. The members of Ebenezer Church gave a benefit that netted for him a purse of several hundred dollars. There was good reason for a show of pride; Livingston was a handsome, bronze-colored boy with a high reputation as a student, and appeared to be ideal material for a soldier and officer. But at the Academy he was turned down. The examining officials there stated that his eyesight was in some manner defective. The news that Livingston had been denied admission to West Point was given out at a Sunday service at Ebenezer Church. When at the same service the minister announced "America" as a hymn, my mother refused to sing it.

My mother was artistic and more or less impractical and in my father's opinion had absolutely no sense about money. She was a splendid singer and she had a talent for drawing. One day when I was about fifteen years old, she revealed to me that she had written verse, and showed me a thin sheaf of poems copied out in her almost perfect handwriting. She was intelligent and possessed a quick though limited sense of humor. But the limitation of her sense of humor was quite the normal one: she had no relish for a joke whose butt was herself or her children; my father had the rarer capacity for laughing even at himself. . . .

My father was a quiet, unpretentious man. He was naturally conservative and cautious, and generally displayed common sense in what he said and did. He never went to school; such education as he had was self-acquired. Later in life, I appreciated the fact that his self-development was little less than remarkable. He had a knowledge of general affairs and was familiar with many of the chief events and characters in the history of the world. I have the old sheepskin bound volume of *Plutarch's Lives* which he owned before I was born. He had gained by study a working knowledge of the Spanish language; this he had done to increase his value as a hotel employee. When he was a young man in New York, he attended the theater a good deal, and, before I was aware of where the lines came from or of what they meant, I used to go around the house parroting after him certain snatches from the Shakespearean plays. I particularly recall: "To be or not to be; that is the question" and "A horse! a horse! my kingdom for a horse!"

The quality in my father that impressed me most was his high and rigid sense of honesty. I simply could not conceive of him as a party to any monetary transaction that was questionable in the least. I think he got his greatest satisfaction in life out of the reputation he had built up as a man of probity, and took his greatest pride in the consequent credit standing that he enjoyed. This element in his character was a source of gratification to my pride and also, more than once, to my needs. One instance of double gratification was when I was at home in Jacksonville in 1910, just a few weeks before I was to be married. My father and mother discussed an appropriate gift to me and, finally, to my undisguised joy, decided upon a check for a thousand dollars. My father, excusably, did not have a thousand dollars in cash; but he said to me, "My boy, we'll go down town tomorrow and see if we can get the money." We went the next morning to one of the principal banks and my father spoke with John C. L'Engle, the president. The transaction was put through without any delay; he got the money on his note, without collateral security, without even an endorser. I was as proud to see him able to do such a thing as I was glad to have the money. . . .

Atlanta disappointed me. It was a larger city than Jacksonville, but did not seem to me to be nearly so attractive. Many of the thoroughfares were still red clay roads. It was a long time before I grew accustomed to the bloody aspect of Atlanta's highways. Trees were rare and there was no city park or square within walking distance. The city was neither picturesque nor smart; it was merely drab. Atlanta University was a pleasant relief. The Confederate ramparts on the hill where the school was built had been leveled, the ground terraced, and grass and avenues of trees planted. The three main buildings were ivy-covered. Here was a spot fresh and beautiful, a rest for the eyes from what surrounded it, a green island in a dull, red sea. The University, as I was soon to learn, was a little world in itself, with ideas of social conduct and of the approach to life distinct from those of the city within which it was situated. When students or teachers stepped off the campus into West Mitchell Street, they underwent as great a transition as would have resulted from being instantaneously shot from a Boston drawing room into the wilds of Borneo. They had to make an immediate readjustment of many of their fundamental notions about life. When I was at the University, there were twenty-odd teachers, of whom all, except four, were white. These white teachers by eating at table with the students rendered themselves "unclean," not fit to sit at table with any Atlanta white family. The president was Horace Bumstead, a cultured gentleman, educated at Yale and in Germany, yet there was only one white door in all Atlanta thrown open to him socially, the door of a German family. No observance of caste in India was more cruelly rigid. The year before I entered, the state of Georgia had cut off its annual appropriation of $8000 because the school stood by its principles and refused to exclude the children of the white teachers from the regular classes.

I was at the University only a short time before I began to get an insight into the ramifications of race prejudice and an understanding of the American race problem. Indeed, it was in this early period that I received my initiation into the arcana of "race." I perceived that education for me meant, fundamentally: preparation to meet the tasks and exigencies of life as a Negro, a realization of the peculiar responsibilities due to my own racial group, and a comprehension of the application of American democracy to Negro citizens. Of course, I had not been entirely ignorant of these conditions and requirements, but now they rose before me in such sudden magnitude as to seem absolutely new knowledge. This knowledge was no part of classroom instruction—the college course at Atlanta University was practically the old academic course at Yale; the founder of the school was Edmund Asa Ware, a Yale man, and the two following presidents were graduates of Yale—it was simply in the spirit of the institution; the atmosphere of the place was charged with it. Students talked "race." It was the subject of essays, orations, and debates. Nearly all that was acquired, mental and moral, was destined to be fitted into a particular system of which "race" was the center. . . .

I now began to get my bearings with regard to the world and particularly with regard to my own country. I began to get the full understanding of my relationship to America, and to take on my share of the peculiar responsibilities and burdens additional to those of the common lot, which every Negro in the United States is compelled to carry. I began my mental and spiritual training to meet and cope not only with the hardships that are common, but with planned wrong, concerted injustice, and applied prejudice. Here was a deepening, but narrowing experience; an experience so narrowing that the inner problem of a Negro in America becomes that of not allowing it to choke and suffocate him. I am glad that this fuller impact of the situation came to me as late as it did, when my apprehension of it could be more or less objective.

As an American Negro, I consider the most fortunate thing in my whole life to be the fact that through childhood I was reared free from undue fear of or esteem for white people as a race; otherwise, the deeper implications of American race prejudice might have become a part of my subconscious as well as of my conscious self.

I began also in this period to find myself, to think of life not only as it touched me from without but also as it moved me from within. I went in for reading, and spent many of the winter afternoons that settle down so drearily on the bleak hills of North Georgia absorbed in a book. The university library was then the Graves Memorial Library. It contained ten thousand or so volumes, an array of books that seemed infinite to me. Many of the titles snared me, but I was often disappointed to find that the books were written from the point of view of divine revelation and Christian dogma or with a bald moral purpose. Among all the books in the Graves Library it was from books of fiction that I gained the greatest satisfaction. I read more Dickens; I read George Eliot; I read *Vanity Fair*, and that jewel among novels, *Lorna Doone*. It was during this period that I also read with burning interest Alphonse Daudet's *Sapho*, a book which was not in the library but was owned by one of the boys and circulated until it was all but worn out. The episode in which Sapho is carried up the flight of stairs left a disquieting impression on my mind that lingered long.

Before I left Stanton I had begun to scribble. I had written a story about my first plug (derby) hat. Mr. Artrell thought it was fine, and it made a hit when I read it before the school. Now an impulse set me at writing poetry, and I filled several notebooks with verses. I looked over these juvenilia recently and noted that the first of my poems opened with these three lines:

Miserable, miserable, weary of life,
Worn with its turmoil, its din and its strife,
And with its burden of grief.

I did not follow this vein. Perhaps even then I sensed that there was already an over-supply of poetry by people who mistake a torpid liver for a broken heart, and frustrated sex desires for yearnings of the soul. I wrote a lot of verses lampooning certain students and teachers and conditions on the campus. However, the greater part of my output consisted of rather ardent love poems. A number of these latter circulated with success in North Hall, and brought me considerable prestige as a gallant. It has struck me that the potency possessed by a few, fairly well written lines of passionate poetry is truly astounding, and altogether disproportionate to what really goes into the process of producing them. It is probable that the innate hostility of the average man toward the poet has its basis in this fact. . . .

In the fall Rosamond * and I went back to our teaching in Jacksonville and to do more writing. Before we left New York we met Bob Cole. Bob was one of the most talented and versatile Negroes ever connected with the stage. He could write a play, stage it, and play a part. Although he was not a trained musician, he was the originator of a long list of catchy songs. We also met Williams and Walker and Ernest Hogan, the comedians; Will Marion Cook, the Negro composer; Harry T. Burleigh, the musician and singer; and a number of others, doing pioneer work in Negro theatricals. I attended rehearsals of two Negro companies that were preparing for the coming season, and I took in something of night life in Negro Bohemia, then flourishing in the old Tenderloin District. Into one of the rehearsals I was attending walked Paul Laurence Dunbar, the Negro poet. The year before he had written in collaboration with Cook an operetta called, *Clorindy—The Origin of the Cakewalk*, which had been produced with an all-Negro cast and Ernest Hogan as star by George Lederer at the Casino Theater Roof Garden, and had run with great success the entire summer. Mr. Lederer was the principal and most skillful musical play producer of the period. His production, *The Belle of New York*, with Dan Daly and Edna May, was one of the greatest successes the American stage had seen. But he learned some new things from *Clorindy*. He judged correctly that the practice of the Negro chorus, to dance strenuously and sing at the same time, if adapted by the white stage would be a profitable novelty; so he departed considerably from the model of the easy, leisurely movements of the English light opera chorus. He also judged that some injection of Negro syncopated music would produce a like result. Mr. Lederer was, at least, the grandfather of the modern American musical play. Ironi-

---

*James Weldon Johnson's brother, a composer and musician. They collaborated on many occasions as a songwriting team, producing popular tunes and songs for Broadway musicals. They worked together as co-editors of *The Book of American Negro Spirituals* (1925) and *The Second Book of Negro Spirituals* (1926), which included the words and music (voice and piano arrangement) for 124 spirituals—*Ed.*

cally, these adaptations from the Negro stage, first made
years ago, give many present-day critics reason for condemning Negro musical comedy on the ground that it is too slavish
an imitation of the white product. I had met Dunbar five
years before, when he was almost unknown; now he was at
the height of his fame. When he walked into the hall, those
who knew him rushed to welcome him; among those who did
not know him personally there were awed whispers. But it
did not appear that celebrity had puffed him up; he did not
meet the homage that was being shown him with anything
but friendly and hearty response. There was no hint of vain-
glory in his bearing. He sat quiet and unassuming while the
rehearsal proceeded. He was then twenty-seven years old, of
medium height and slight of figure. His black, intelligent face
was grave, almost sad, except when he smiled or laughed. But
notwithstanding this lack of ostentation, there was on him the
hallmark of distinction. He had an innate courtliness of manner, his speech was unaffectedly polished and brilliant, and he
carried himself with that dignity of humility which never fails
to produce a sense of the presence of greatness. Paul and I
were together a great deal during those last few weeks. I was
drawn to him and he to me; and a friendship was begun that
grew closer and lasted until his death. A day or two before I
left he took me into Dutton's on 23rd Street, where he
bought a copy of his *Lyrics of Lowly Life* and inscribed it
for me. It is one of my most treasured books.

These glimpses of life that I caught during our last two or
three weeks in New York were not wholly unfamiliar to Rosamond, but they showed me a new world—an alluring
world, a tempting world, a world of greatly lessened re-
straints, a world of fascinating perils; but, above all, a world
of tremendous artistic potentialities. Up to this time, outside
of polemical essays on the race question, I had not written a
single line that had any relation to the Negro. I now began to
grope toward a realization of the importance of the American Negro's cultural background and his creative folk-art,
and to speculate on the superstructure of conscious art that
might be reared upon them. My first step in this general direction was taken in a song that Bob Cole, my brother, and I
wrote in conjunction during the last days in New York. It
was an attempt to bring a higher degree of artistry to Negro
songs, especially with regard to the text. The Negro songs
then the rage were known as "coon songs" and were concerned with jamborees of various sorts and the play of razors,
with the gastronomical delights of chicken, pork chops and
watermelon, and with the experiences of red-hot "mammas"

and their never too faithful "papas." These songs were for the most part crude, raucous, bawdy, often obscene. Such elements frequently are excellencies in folk-songs, but rarely so in conscious imitations. The song we did was a little love song called *Louisiana Lize* and was forerunner of a style that displaced the old "coon songs." We sold the singing rights to May Irwin for fifty dollars—our first money earned. With the check the three of us proceeded joyfully to the Garfield National Bank, then at Sixth Avenue and 23rd Street, where Bob was slightly known. The paying teller looked at the check and suggested we take it over on the next corner to the Fifth Avenue Bank, on which it was drawn and have it O.K.'d It is always disconcerting to have a bank teller shove a check back to you, whatever his reasons may be, so we went over to the other bank not without some misgivings. The teller there looked at it and said, "Tell them over at the Garfield Bank that the check would be good if it was for fifty thousand dollars." Bob delivered the message. Next, we took the manuscript to Jos. W. Stern and Co., who published the song.

When I got back to Jacksonville I found that my artistic ideas and plans were undergoing a revolution. Frankly, I was floundering badly: the things I had been trying to do seemed vapid and nonessential, and the thing I felt a yearning to do was so nebulous that I couldn't take hold of it or even quite make it out. In this state, satisfactory expression first came through writing a short dialect poem. One night, just after I had finished the poem, I was at Mr. McBeath's house talking about school matters; then about books and literature. He read me a long poem he had written on Lincoln—a Lincoln poem, the expression of a Southern white man. I thought it was good and told him so. I also thought but did not say that there was yet to be written a great poem on Lincoln, the expression of a Negro. Aloud, I repeated for him my dialect poem, *Sence You Went Away*. He thought it was good enough for me to try it on one of the important magazines. I sent it to *Century,* and it was promptly accepted and printed. Outside of what had appeared in Atlanta University periodicals and in the local newspapers, this was my first published poem. Some years later my brother set this little poem to music. It has proved to be one of the most worthwhile and lasting songs he has written. It was first sung by Amato, the Metropolitan Opera baritone; it was afterwards recorded for the phonograph by John McCormack, with a violin obbligato played by Kreisler; and was again recorded by Louis Graveure and still again by Paul Robeson. It continues to find a place on concert programs.

During the winter I wrote more dialect poems, some of them very trite, written with an eye on Broadway. Rosamond made some pretty songs out of these trivialities and put them aside for our next migration to New York. In the same winter Rosamond planned a concert such as had not before been given by or for colored people in Jacksonville. He brought Sidney Woodward down from Boston. The affair was successful, artistically and financially, beyond our expectations. The concert sent the level of musical entertainment among the colored people many degrees higher. Nor were its effects limited to the colored people; it was a treat for the hundred or so local white music lovers who were present, for, indeed, not all of them had before heard a tenor with Woodward's voice and technical finish.

A group of young men decided to hold on February 12 a celebration of Lincoln's birthday. I was put down for an address, which I began preparing; but I wanted to do something else also. My thoughts began buzzing round a central idea of writing a poem on Lincoln, but I couldn't net them. So I gave up the project as beyond me; at any rate, beyond me to carry out in so short a time; and my poem on Lincoln is still to be written. My central idea, however, took on another form. I talked over with my brother the thought I had in mind, and we planned to write a song to be sung as a part of the exercises. We planned, better still, to have it sung by schoolchildren—a chorus of five hundred voices.

I got my first line:—Lift ev'ry voice and sing. Not a startling line; but I worked along grinding out the next five. When, near the end of the first stanza, there came to me the lines:

Sing a song full of the faith that the dark past has taught us
Sing a song full of the hope that the present has brought us.

the spirit of the poem had taken hold of me. I finished the stanza and turned it over to Rosamond.

In composing the two other stanzas I did not use pen and paper. While my brother worked at his musical setting I paced back and forth on the front porch, repeating the lines over and over to myself, going through all of the agony and ecstasy of creating. As I worked through the opening and middle lines of the last stanza:

God of our weary years,
God of our silent tears,
Thou who hast brought us thus far on our way,

Thou who hast by Thy might
Let us into the light,
Keep us forever in the path, we pray;
Lest our feet stray from the places, our God, where we met Thee,
Lest, our hearts drunk with the wine of the world, we forget
  Thee . . . .

I could not keep back the tears, and made no effort to do so.
I was experiencing the transports of the poet's ecstasy. Fever-
ish ecstasy was followed by that contentment—that sense
of serene joy—which makes artistic creation the most complete of all human experiences.

When I had put the last stanza down on paper I at once
recognized the Kiplingesque touch in the two longer lines
quoted above; but I knew that in the stanza the American
Negro was, historically and spiritually, immanent; and I decided to let it stand as it was written.

As soon as Rosamond had finished his noble setting of the
poem he sent a copy of the manuscript to our publishers in
New York, requesting them to have a sufficient number of
mimeographed copies made for the use of the chorus. The
song was taught to the children and sung very effectively at
the celebration; and my brother and I went on with other
work. After we had permanently moved away from Jacksonville, both the song and the occasion passed out of our minds.
But the schoolchildren of Jacksonville kept singing the song;
some of them went off to other schools and kept singing it;
some of them became schoolteachers and taught it to their
pupils. Within twenty years the song was being sung in
schools and churches and on special occasions throughout the
South and in some other parts of the country. Within that
time the publishers had recopyrighted it and issued it in several arrangements. Later it was adopted by the National Association for the Advancement of Colored People, and is now
quite generally used throughout the country as the "Negro
National Hymn." The publishers consider it a valuable piece
of property; however, in traveling round I have commonly
found printed or typewritten copies of the words pasted in
the backs of hymnals and the songbooks used in Sunday
schools, Y.M.C.A.'s, and similar institutions; and I think that
is the method by which it gets its widest circulation. Recently
I spoke for the summer labor school at Bryn Mawr College
and was surprised to hear it fervently sung by the white students there and to see it in their mimeographed folio of
songs.

Nothing that I have done has paid me back so fully in satisfaction as being the part creator of this song. I am always

thrilled deeply when I hear it sung by Negro children. I am lifted up on their voices, and I am also carried back and enabled to live through again the exquisite emotions I felt at the birth of the song. My brother and I, in talking, have often marveled at the results that have followed what we considered an incidental effort, an effort made under stress and with no intention other than to meet the needs of a particular moment. The only comment we can make is that we wrote better than we knew. . . .

I went down to Atlanta University on the tenth anniversary of my graduation to receive an honorary degree. There it was that I first met W. E. B. Du Bois, who was now one of the professors. The year before, he had issued *The Souls of Black Folk* (a work which, I think, has had a greater effect upon and within the Negro race in America than any other single book published in this country since *Uncle Tom's Cabin*) and was already a national figure. I had been deeply moved and influenced by the book, and was anxious to meet the author. I met a quite handsome and unpedantic young man—Dr. Du Bois was then thirty-six. Indeed, it was, at first, slightly difficult to reconcile the brooding but intransigent spirit of *The Souls of Black Folk* with this apparently so light-hearted man, this man so abundantly endowed with the gift of laughter. I noted then what, through many years of close association, I have since learned well, and what the world knows not at all: that Du Bois in battle is a stern, bitter, relentless fighter, who, when he has put aside his sword, is among his paricular friends the most jovial and fun-loving of men. This quality has been a saving grace for him, but his lack of the ability to unbend in his relations with people outside the small circle has gained him the reputation of being cold, stiff, supercilious, and has been a cause of criticism amongst even his adherents. This disposition, due perhaps to an inhibition of spontaneous impulse, has limited his scope of leadership to less than what it might have been, in that it has hindered his attracting and binding to himself a body of zealous liegemen —one of the essentials to the headship of a popular or an unpopular cause. The great influence Du Bois has exercised has been due to the concentrated force of his ideas, with next to no reinforcement from that wide appeal of personal magnetism which is generally a valuable asset of leaders of men. . . .

I began earnest work on *The Autobiography of an Ex-Colored Man*, of which I had already made a first draft of the opening. The story developed in my mind more rapidly than I had expected that it would; at times, outrunning my speed in getting it down. The use of prose as a creative medium was new to me; and its latitude, its flexibility, its comprehensiveness, the variety of approaches it afforded for surmounting technical difficulties gave me a feeling of exhilaration, exhilaration similar to that which goes with freedom of motion. I turned over in my mind again and again my original idea of making the book anonymous. I also debated with myself the aptness of *The Autobiography of an Ex-Colored Man* as a title. Brander Matthews had expressed a liking for the title, but my brother had thought it was clumsy and too long; he had suggested *The Chameleon*. In the end, I stuck to the original idea of issuing the book without the author's name, and kept the title that had appealed to me first. But I have never been able to settle definitely for myself whether I was sagacious or not in these two decisions. When I chose the title, it was without the slightest doubt that its meaning would be perfectly clear to anyone; there were people, however, to whom it proved confusing. When the book was published (1912) most of the reviewers, though there were some doubters, accepted it as a human document. This was a tribute to the writing, for I had done the book with the intention of its being so taken. But, perhaps, it would have been more far-sighted had I originally affixed my name to it as a frank piece of fiction. But I did get a certain pleasure out of anonymity, that no acknowledged book could have given me. The authorship of the book excited the curiosity of literate colored people, and there was speculation among them as to who the writer might be—to every such group some colored man who had married white, and so coincided with the main point on which the story turned, is known. I had the experience of listening to some of these discussions. I had a rarer experience, that of being introduced to and talking with one man who tacitly admitted to those present that he was the author of the book. Only two or three people knew that I was the writer of the story—the publishers themselves never knew me personally; yet the fact gradually leaked out and spread. The first printed statement was made by George A. Towns, my classmate at Atlanta University, who wrote a piece in which he gave his reasons for thinking I was the man. When the book was republished,* I affixed my name to it, and Carl

* Alfred A. Knopf, New York, 1925.

Van Vechten was good enough to write an Introduction, and
in it to inform the reader that the story was not the story of
my life. Nevertheless, I continue to receive letters from persons who have read the book inquiring about this or that
phase of my life as told in it. That is, probably, one of the
reasons why I am writing the present book. . . .

Nineteen-seventeen was a busy year for me. Yet I made the
time to collect my published and unpublished poems and
issue them in a little volume entitled *Fifty Years and Other
Poems*. Brander Matthews wrote a word of introduction for
the book. In the middle of the summer, I attended a three-
day conference of the Intercollegiate Socialist Society that was
held at Belleport, Long Island. I was on the program, but I
did not make a talk on economic or social conditions; instead, I read a paper on the contribution of the Negro to
American culture.

Some of the contributions that the Negro has made to
America are quite obvious—for example, his contribution of
labor—and their importance, more or less, has long been recognized. But the idea of his being a generous contributor to
the common cultural store and a vital force in the formation
of American civilization was a new approach to the race
question.

The common-denominator opinion in the United States
about American Negroes is, I think, something like this:
these people are here; they are here to be shaped and
molded and made into something different and, of course,
better; they are here to be helped; here to be given something; in a word, they are beggars under the nation's table
waiting to be thrown the crumbs of civilization. However
true this may be, it is also true that the Negro has helped to
shape and mold and make America; that he has been a creator as well as a creature; that he has been a giver as well as a
receiver. It is, no doubt, startling to contemplate that America would not and could not be precisely the America it is,
except for the influence, often silent, but nevertheless potent,
that the Negro has exercised in its making. That influence has
been both active and passive. Any contemplation of the Negro's passive influence ought to make America uneasy. Estimate, if you can, the effect upon the making of the character
of the American people caused by the opportunity which the
Negro has involuntarily given the dominant majority to practice injustice, wrong, and brutality for three hundred years
with impunity upon a practically defenseless minority. There

can be no estimate of the moral damage done to every American community that has indulged in the bestial orgy of torturing and mutilating a human being and burning him alive. The active influences of the Negro have come out of his strength; his passive influences out of his weaknesses. And it would be well for the nation to remember that for the good of one's own soul, what he needs most to guard against, most to fear, in dealing with another, is that one's weakness, not his strength.

My paper, despite the fact that it was removed from the main topic of the conference, was received well, and gave rise to some interesting discussion. A young man, Herbert J. Seligmann, who was reporting the conference for the *New York Evening Post* was enthusiastic about it. He asked for my manuscript and made a summary of it for his newspaper. Paragraphs of his summary actually went round the world; they were copied in American and European periodicals, and I got clippings from as far away as South Africa and Australia. The statement that evoked the greatest interest—and some controversy—was that the only things artistic in America that have sprung from American soil, permeated American life, and been universally acknowledged as distinctively American, had been the creations of the American Negro.

I was, of course, speaking of the principal folk-art creations of the Negro—his folklore, collected by Joel Chandler Harris under the title of *Uncle Remus,* his dances, and his music, sacred and secular. Some years later, I modified that statement by excepting American skyscraper architecture. In making the original statement I certainly had no inention of disparaging the accomplishments of the other groups, the aboriginal Indians and the white groups. The Indians have wrought finely, and what they have done sprang from the soil of America; but it must be admitted that their art-creations have in no appreciable degree permeated American life. In all that the white groups have wrought, there is no artistic creation—with the exception noted above—born of the physical and spiritual forces at work peculiarly in America, none that has made a universal appeal as something distinctively American.

One other statement in Mr. Seligmann's summary of my paper which was widely copied was that the finest artistic contribution that this country could offer as its own to the world was the American Negro spirituals.

It is, however, in his lighter music that the Negro has given America its best-known distinctive form of art. I would make no extravagant claims for this music, but I say "form of art," without apology. This lighter music has been fused and then developed, chiefly by Jewish musicians, until it has become our national medium for expressing ourselves musically in popular form, and it bids fair to become a basic element in the future great American music. The part it plays in American life and its acceptance by the world at large cannot be ignored. It is to this music that America in general gives itself over in its leisure hours, when it is not engaged in the struggles imposed upon it by the exigencies of present-day American life. At these times, the Negro drags his captors captive. On occasions, I have been amazed and amused watching white people dancing to a Negro band in a Harlem cabaret; attempting to throw off the crusts and layers of inhibitions laid on by sophisticated civilization; striving to yield to the feel and experience of abandon; seeking to recapture a taste of primitive joy in life and living; trying to work their way back into that jungle which was the original Garden of Eden; in a word, doing their best to pass for colored. . . .

Often I am asked if I think the Negro will remain a racial entity or merge; and if I am in favor of amalgamation. I answer that, if I could have my wish, the Negro would retain his racial identity, with unhampered freedom to develop his own qualities—the best of those qualities American civilization is much in need of as a complement to its other qualities —and finally stand upon a plane with other American citizens. To convince America and the world that he was capable of doing this would be the greatest triumph he could wish and work for. But what *I* may wish and what others may not wish can have no effect on the elemental forces at work; and it appears to me that the result of those forces will, in time, be the blending of the Negro into the American Race of the future. It seems probable that, instead of developing them independently to the utmost, the Negro will fuse his qualities with those of the other groups in the making of the ultimate American people; and that he will add a tint to America's complexion and put a perceptible permanent wave in America's hair. It may be that nature plans to work out on the North American continent a geographical color scheme similar to that of Europe, with the Gulf of Mexico as our Mediterranean. My hope is that in the process the Negro will be not merely sucked up but, through his own advancement and development, will go in on a basis of equal partnership.

If I am wrong in these opinions and conclusions, if the Negro is always to be given a heavy handicap back of the common scratch, or if the antagonistic forces are destined to dominate and bar all forward movement, there will be only one way of salvation for the race that I can see, and that will be through the making of its isolation into a religion and the cultivation of a hard, keen, relentless hatred for everything white. Such a hatred would burn up all that is best in the Negro, but it would also offer the sole means that could enable him to maintain a saving degree of self-respect in the midst of his abasement.

But the damage of such a course would not be limited to the Negro. If the Negro is made to fail, America fails with him. If America wishes to make democratic institutions secure, she must deal with this question right and righteously. For it is in the nature of a truism to say that this country can actually have no more democracy than it accords and guarantees to the humblest and weakest citizen.

It is both a necessity and to the advantage of America that she deal with this question right and righteously; for the well-being of the nation as well as that of the Negro depends upon taking that course. And she must bear in mind that it is a question which can be neither avoided nor postponed; it is not distant in position or time; it is immediately at hand and imminent; it must be squarely met and answered. And it cannot be so met and answered by the mere mouthings of the worn platitudes of humanitarianism, of formal religion, or of abstract democracy. For the Negroes directly concerned are not in far-off Africa; they are in and within our midst.

RICHARD WRIGHT (1908–1960)

A biographical note on Richard Wright appears in the Fiction section (see pp. 113–114). His autobiographical essay, which follows, was first published in 1937 in American Stuff, *a collection of writing by members of the Federal Writers' Project.*

The Ethics of Living Jim Crow: An Autobiographical Sketch

My first lesson in how to live as a Negro came when I was quite small. We were living in Arkansas. Our house stood behind the railroad tracks. Its skimpy yard was paved with black cinders. Nothing green ever grew in that yard. The only touch of green we could see was far away, beyond the tracks, over where the white folks lived. But cinders were good enough for me and I never missed the green growing things. And anyhow cinders were fine weapons. You could always have a nice hot war with huge black cinders. All you had to do was crouch behind the brick pillars of a house with your hands full of gritty ammunition. And the first woolly black head you saw pop out from behind another row of pillars was your target. You tried your very best to knock it off. It was great fun.

I never fully realized the appalling disadvantages of a cinder environment till one day the gang to which I belonged found itself engaged in a war with the white boys who lived beyond the tracks. As usual we laid down our cinder barrage, thinking that this would wipe the white boys out. But they replied with a steady bombardment of broken bottles. We doubled our cinder barrage, but they hid behind trees, hedges, and the sloping embankments of their lawns. Having no such fortifications, we retreated to the brick pillars of our homes. During the retreat a broken milk bottle caught me behind the ear, opening a deep gash which bled profusely. The sight of blood pouring over my face completely demoralized our ranks. My fellow-combatants left me standing paralyzed in the center of the yard, and scurried for their homes. A kind neighbor saw me and rushed me to a doctor, who took three stitches in my neck.

I sat brooding on my front steps, nursing my wound and waiting for my mother to come from work. I felt that a grave injustice had been done me. It was all right to throw cinders. The greatest harm a cinder could do was leave a bruise. But broken bottles were dangerous; they left you cut, bleeding, and helpless.

When night fell, my mother came from the white folks' kitchen. I raced down the street to meet her. I could just feel in my bones that she would understand. I knew she would tell me exactly what to do next time. I grabbed her hand and babbled out the whole story. She examined my wound, then slapped me.

"How come yuh didn't hide?" she asked me. "How come yuh awways fightin'?"

I was outraged, and bawled. Between sobs I told her that I didn't have any trees or hedges to hide behind. There wasn't a thing I could have used as a trench. And you couldn't throw very far when you were hiding behind the brick pillars of a house. She grabbed a barrel stave, dragged me home, stripped me naked, and beat me till I had a fever of one hundred and two. She would smack my rump with the stave, and while the skin was still smarting, impart to me gems of Jim Crow wisdom. I was never to throw cinders any more. I was never to fight any more wars. I was never, never, under any conditions, to fight *white* folks again. And they were absolutely right in clouting me with the broken milk bottle. Didn't I know she was working hard every day in the hot kitchens of the white folks to make money to take care of me? When was I ever going to learn to be a good boy? She couldn't be bothered with my fights. She finished by telling me that I ought to be thankful to God as long as I lived that they didn't kill me.

All that night I was delirious and could not sleep. Each time I closed my eyes I saw monstrous white faces suspended from the ceiling, leering at me.

From that time on, the charm of my cinder yard was gone. The green trees, the trimmed hedges, the cropped lawns grew very meaningful, became a symbol. Even today when I think of white folks, the hard, sharp outlines of white houses surrounded by trees, lawns, and hedges are present somewhere in the background of my mind. Through the years they grew into an overreaching symbol of fear.

It was a long time before I came in close contact with white folks again. We moved from Arkansas to Mississippi. Here we had the good fortune not to live behind the railroad tracks, or close to white neighborhoods. We lived in the very heart of the local Black Belt. There were black churches and black preachers; there were black schools and black teachers; black groceries and black clerks. In fact, everything was so solidly black that for a long time I did not even think of white folks, save in remote and vague terms. But this could not last forever. As one grows older one eats more. One's clothing costs more. When I finished grammar school I had to go to work. My mother could no longer feed and clothe me on her cooking job.

There is but one place where a black boy who knows no trade can get a job, and that's where the houses and faces are white, where the trees, lawns, and hedges are green. My first job was with an optical company in Jackson, Mississippi. The morning I applied I stood straight and neat before the boss, answering all his questions with sharp yessirs and nosirs. I was very careful to pronounce my *sirs* distinctly, in order that he might know that I was polite, that I knew where I was, and that I knew he was a *white* man. I wanted that job badly.

He looked me over as though he were examining a prize poodle. He questioned me closely about my schooling, being particularly insistent about how much mathematics I had had. He seemed very pleased when I told him I had had two years of algebra.

"Boy, how would you like to learn something around here?" he asked me.

"I'd like it fine, sir," I said, happy. I had visions of "working my way up." Even Negroes have those visions.

"All right," he said. "Come on."

I followed him to the small factory.

"Pease," he said to a white man of about thirty-five, "this is Richard. He's going to work for us."

Pease looked at me and nodded.

I was then taken to a white boy of about seventeen.

"Morrie, this is Richard, who's going to work for us."

"Whut yuy sayin' there, boy!" Morrie boomed at me.

"Fine!" I answered.

The boss instructed these two to help me, teach me, give me jobs to do, and let me learn what I could in my spare time.

My wages were five dollars a week.

I worked hard, trying to please. For the first month I got along O.K. Both Pease and Morrie seemed to like me. But one thing was missing. And I kept thinking about it. I was not learning anything and nobody was volunteering to help me. Thinking they had forgotten that I was to learn something about the mechanics of grinding lenses, I asked Morrie one day to tell me about the work. He grew red.

"Whut yuh tryin' t' do, nigger, get smart?" he asked.

"Naw; I ain' tryin' t' git smart," I said.

"Well, don't, if yuh know whut's good for yuh!"

I was puzzled. Maybe he just doesn't want to help me, I thought. I went to Pease.

"Say, are yuh crazy, you black bastard?" Pease asked me, his gray eyes growing hard.

I spoke out, reminding him that the boss had said I was to be given a chance to learn something.

"Nigger, you think you're *white*, don't you?"

"Naw, sir!"

"Well, you're acting mighty like it!"

"But, Mr. Pease, the boss said . . ."

Pease shook his fist in my face.

"This is a *white* man's work around here, and you better watch yourself!"

From then on they changed toward me. They said good-morning no more. When I was a bit slow performing some duty, I was called a lazy black son-of-a-bitch.

Once I thought of reporting all this to the boss. But the mere idea of what would happen to me if Pease and Morrie should learn that I had "snitched" stopped me. And after all the boss was a white man, too. What was the use?

The climax came at noon one summer day. Pease called me to his work-bench. To get to him I had to go between two narrow benches and stand with my back against a wall.

"Yes, sir," I said.

"Richard, I want to ask you something," Pease began pleasantly, not looking up from his work.

"Yes, sir," I said again.

Morrie came over, blocking the narrow passage between the benches. He folded his arms, staring at me solemnly.

I looked from one to the other, sensing that something was coming.

"Yes, sir," I said for the third time.

Pease looked up and spoke very slowly.

"Richard, *Mr.* Morrie here tells me you called me *Pease*."

I stiffened. A void seemed to open up in me. I knew this was the show-down.

He meant that I had failed to call him Mr. Pease. I looked at Morrie. He was gripping a steel bar in his hands. I opened my mouth to speak, to protest, to assure Pease that I had never called him simply *Pease*, and that I had never had any intentions of doing so, when Morrie grabbed me by the collar, ramming my head against the wall.

"Now, be careful, nigger!" snarled Morrie, baring his teeth. "*I* heard yuh call 'im *Pease!* 'N' if you say yuh didn't, yuh're callin' me a *lie*, see?" He waved the steel bar threateningly.

If I had said: No, sir, Mr. Pease, I never called you *Pease*, I would have been automatically calling Morrie a liar. And if I had said: Yes, sir, Mr. Pease, I called you *Pease*, I would have been pleading guilty to having uttered the worst insult that a Negro can utter to a southern white man. I stood hesitating, trying to frame a neutral reply.

"Richard, I asked you a question!" said Pease. Anger was creeping into his voice.

"I don't remember calling you *Pease*, Mr. Pease," I said cautiously. "And if I did, I sure didn't mean . . ."

"You black son-of-a-bitch! You called me *Pease*, then!" he spat, slapping me till I bent sideways over a bench. Morrie was on top of me, demanding:

"Didn't yuh call 'im *Pease?* If yuh say yuh didn't I'll rip yo' gut string loose with this bar, yuh black granny dodger! Yuh can't call a white man a lie 'n' git erway with it, you black son-of-a-bitch!"

I wilted. I begged them not to bother me. I knew what they wanted. They wanted me to leave.

"I'll leave," I promised. "I'll leave right *now*."

They gave me a minute to get out of the factory. I was warned not to show up again, or tell the boss.

I went.

When I told the folks at home what had happened, they called me a fool. They told me that I must never again attempt to exceed my boundaries. When you are working for white folks, they said, you got to "stay in your place" if you want to keep working.

2

My Jim Crow education continued on my next job, which was portering in a clothing store. One morning, while polishing brass out front, the boss and his twenty-year-old son got out of their car and half dragged and half kicked a Negro

woman into the store. A policeman standing at the corner
looked on, twirling his night-stick. I watched out of the corner of my eye, never slackening the strokes of my chamois
upon the brass. After a few minutes, I heard shrill screams
coming from the rear of the store. Later the woman stumbled
out, bleeding, crying, and holding her stomach. When she
reached the end of the block, the policeman grabbed her and
accused her of being drunk. Silently, I watched him throw
her into a patrol wagon.

When I went to the rear of the store, the boss and his son
were washing their hands in the sink. They were chuckling.
The floor was bloody and strewn with wisps of hair and
clothing. No doubt I must have appeared pretty shocked, for
the boss slapped me reassuringly on the back.

"Boy, that's what we do to niggers when they don't want to
pay their bills," he said, laughing.

His son looked at me and grinned.

"Here, hava cigarette," he said.

Not knowing what to do, I took it. He lit his and held the
match for me. This was a gesture of kindness, indicating that
even if they had beaten the poor old woman, they would not
beat me if I knew enough to keep my mouth shut.

"Yes, sir," I said, and asked no questions.

After they had gone, I sat on the edge of a packing box
and stared at the bloody floor till the cigarette went out.

That day at noon, while eating in a hamburger joint, I told
my fellow Negro porters what had happened. No one seemed
surprised. One fellow, after swallowing a huge bite, turned to
me and asked:

"Huh! Is tha' all they did t' her?"

"Yeah. Wasn't tha' enough?' I asked.

"Shucks! Man, she's a lucky bitch!" he said, burying his
lips deep into a juicy hamburger. "Hell, it's a wonder they
didn't lay her when they got through."

3

I was learning fast, but not quite fast enough. One day, while
I was delivering packages in the suburbs, my bicycle tire was
punctured. I walked along the hot, dusty road, sweating and
leading my bicycle by the handle-bars.

A car slowed at my side.

"What's the matter, boy?" a white man called.

I told him my bicycle was broken and I was walking back
to town.

"That's too bad," he said. "Hop on the running board."

He stopped the car. I clutched hard at my bicycle with one hand and clung to the side of the car with the other.

"All set?"

"Yes, sir," I answered. The car started.

It was full of young white men. They were drinking. I watched the flask pass from mouth to mouth.

"Wanna drink, boy?" one asked.

I laughed as the wind whipped my face. Instinctively obeying the freshly planted precepts of my mother, I said:

"Oh, no!"

The words were hardly out of my mouth before I felt something hard and cold smash me between the eyes. It was an empty whisky bottle. I saw stars, and fell backwards from the speeding car into the dust of the road, my feet becoming entangled in the steel spokes of my bicycle. The white men piled out and stood over me.

"Nigger, ain' yuh learned no better sense'n tha' yet?" asked the man who hit me. "Ain' yuh learned t' say *sir* t' a white man yet?"

Dazed, I pulled to my feet. My elbows and legs were bleeding. Fists doubled, the white man advanced, kicking my bicycle out of the way.

"Aw, leave the bastard alone. He's got enough," said one.

They stood looking at me. I rubbed my shins, trying to stop the flow of blood. No doubt they felt a sort of contemptuous pity, for one asked:

"Yuh wanna ride t' town now, nigger? Yuh reckon yuh know enough t' ride now?"

"I wanna walk," I said, simply.

Maybe it sounded funny. They laughed.

"Well, walk, yuh black son-of-a-bitch!"

When they left they comforted me with:

"Nigger, yuh sho better be damn glad it wuz us yuh talked t' tha' way. Yuh're a lucky bastard, 'cause if yuh'd said tha' t' somebody else, yuh might've been a dead nigger now."

4

Negroes who have lived South know the dread of being caught alone upon the streets in white neighborhoods after the sun has set. In such a simple situation as this the plight of the Negro in America is graphically symbolized. While white strangers may be in these neighborhoods trying to get home, they can pass unmolested. But the color of a Negro's skin makes him easily recognizable, makes him suspect, converts him into a defenseless target.

Late one Saturday night I made some deliveries in a white neighborhood. I was pedaling my bicycle back to the store as fast as I could, when a police car, swerving toward me, jammed me into the curbing.

"Get down and put up your hands!" the policemen ordered.

I did. They climbed out of the car, guns drawn, faces set, and advanced slowly.

"Keep still!" they ordered.

I reached my hands higher. They searched my pockets and packages. They seemed dissatisfied when they could find nothing incriminating. Finally, one of them said:

"Boy, tell your boss not to send you out in white neighborhoods after sundown."

As usual, I said:

"Yes, sir."

5

My next job was a hall-boy in a hotel. Here my Jim Crow education broadened and deepened. When the bell-boys were busy, I was often called to assist them. As many of the rooms in the hotel were occupied by prostitutes, I was constantly called to carry them liquor and cigarettes. These women were nude most of the time. They did not bother about clothing, even for bell-boys. When you went into their rooms, you were supposed to take their nakedness for granted, as though it startled you no more than a blue vase or a red rug. Your presence awoke in them no sense of shame, for you were not regarded as human. If they were alone, you could steal sidelong glimpses at them. But if they were receiving men, not a flicker of your eyelids could show. I remember one incident vividly. A new woman, a huge, snowy-skinned blonde, took a room on my floor. I was sent to wait upon her. She was in bed with a thick-set man; both were nude and uncovered. She said she wanted some liquor and slid out of bed and waddled across the floor to get her money from a dresser drawer. I watched her.

"Nigger, what in hell are you looking at?" the white man asked me, raising himself upon his elbows.

"Nothing," I answered, looking miles deep into the blank wall of the room.

"Keep your eyes where they belong, if you want to be healthy!" he said.

"Yes, sir."

6

One of the bell-boys I knew in this hotel was keeping steady
company with one of the Negro maids. Out of a clear sky the
police descended upon his home and arrested him, accusing
him of bastardy. The poor boy swore he had had no intimate
relations with the girl. Nevertheless, they forced him to
marry her. When the child arrived, it was found to be much
lighter in complexion than either of the two supposedly legal
parents. The white men around the hotel made a great joke
of it. They spread the rumor that some white cow must have
scared the poor girl while she was carrying the baby. If you
were in their presence when this explanation was offered, you
were supposed to laugh.

7

One of the bell-boys was caught in bed with a white prosti-
tute. He was castrated and run out of town. Immediately
after this all the bell-boys and hall-boys were called together
and warned. We were given to understand that the boy who
had been castrated was a "mighty, mighty lucky bastard." We
were impressed with the fact that next time the management
of the hotel would not be responsible for the lives of "trou-
ble-makin' niggers." We were silent.

8

One night just as I was about to go home, I met one of the
Negro maids. She lived in my direction, and we fell in to
walk part of the way home together. As we passed the white
night-watchman, he slapped the maid on her buttock. I
turned around, amazed. The watchman looked at me with a
long, hard, fixed-under stare. Suddenly he pulled his gun and
asked:

"Nigger, don't yuh like it?"

I hesitated.

"I asked yuh don't yuh like it?" he asked again, stepping
forward.

"Yes, sir," I mumbled.

"Talk like it, then!"

"Oh, yes, sir!" I said with as much heartiness as I could
muster.

Outside, I walked ahead of the girl, ashamed to face her.
She caught up with me and said:

"Don't be a fool! Yuh couldn't help it!"

This watchman boasted of having killed two Negroes in self-defense.

Yet, in spite of all this, the life of the hotel ran with an amazing smoothness. It would have been impossible for a stranger to detect anything. The maids, the hall-boys, and the bell-boys were all smiles. They had to be.

9

I had learned my Jim Crow lessons so thoroughly that I kept the hotel job till I left Jackson for Memphis. It so happened that while in Memphis I applied for a job at a branch of the optical company. I was hired. And for some reason, as long as I worked there, they never brought my past against me.

Here my Jim Crow education assumed quite a different form. It was no longer brutally cruel, but subtly cruel. Here I learned to lie, steal, to dissemble. I learned to play that dual role which every Negro must play if he wants to eat and live.

For example, it was almost impossible to get a book to read. It was assumed that after a Negro had imbibed what scanty schooling the state furnished he had no further need for books. I was always borrowing books from men on the job. One day I mustered enough courage to ask one of the men to let me get books from the library in his name. Surprisingly, he consented. I cannot help but think that he consented because he was a Roman Catholic and felt a vague sympathy for Negroes, being himself an object of hatred. Armed with a library card, I obtained books in the following manner: I would write a note to the librarian, saying: "Please let this nigger boy have the following books." I would then sign it with the white man's name.

When I went to the library, I would stand at the desk, hat in hand, looking as unbookish as possible. When I received the books desired I would take them home. If the books listed in the note happened to be out, I would sneak into the lobby and forge a new one. I never took any chances guessing with the white librarian about what the fictitious white man would want to read. No doubt if any of the white patrons had suspected that some of the volumes they enjoyed had been in the home of a Negro, they would not have tolerated it for an instant.

The factory force of the optical company in Memphis was much larger than that in Jackson, and more urbanized. At least they liked to talk, and would engage the Negro help in conversation whenever possible. By this means I found that many subjects were taboo from the white man's point of

view. Among the topics they did not like to discuss with
Negroes were the following: American white women; the Ku
Klux Klan; France, and how Negro soldiers fared while
there; French women; Jack Johnson; the entire northern part
of the United States; the Civil War; Abraham Lincoln; U. S.
Grant; General Sherman; Catholics; the Pope; Jews; the Re-
publican Party; slavery; social equality; Communism; Social-
ism; the 13th and 14th Amendments to the Constitution; or
any topic calling for positive knowledge or manly self-asser-
tion on the part of the Negro. The most accepted topics were
sex and religion.

There were many times when I had to exercise a great deal
of ingenuity to keep out of trouble. It is a southern custom
that all men must take off their hats when they enter an elevator. And especially did this apply to us blacks with rigid
force. One day I stepped into an elevator with my arms full
of packages. I was forced to ride with my hat on. Two white
men stared at me coldly. Then one of them very kindly lifted
my hat and placed it upon my armful of packages. Now the
most accepted response for a Negro to make under such circumstances is to look at the white man out of the corner of
his eye and grin. To have said: "Thank you!" would have
made the white man *think* that you *thought* you were receiving from him a personal service. For such an act I have seen
Negroes take a blow in the mouth. Finding the first alternative distasteful, and the second dangerous, I hit upon an acceptable course of action which fell safely between these two
poles. I immediately—no sooner than my hat was lifted—
pretended that my packages were about to spill, and appeared
deeply distressed with keeping them in my arms. In this fashion I evaded having to acknowledge his service, and, in spite
of adverse circumstances, salvaged a slender shred of personal pride.

How do Negroes feel about the way they have to live?
How do they discuss it when alone among themselves? I
think this question can be answered in a single sentence. A
friend of mine who ran an elevator once told me:

"Lawd, man! Ef it wuzn't fer them polices 'n' them ol'
lynch-mobs, there wouldn't be nothin' but uproar down
here!"

J. SAUNDERS REDDING (1906–1988)

When Redding's autobiographical book No Day of Triumph *was published in 1942, it included a brief Introduction by Richard Wright, which opened with the following paragraph:*

It has long been my conviction that the next quarter of a century will disclose a tremendous struggle *among* the Negro people for self-expression, self-possession, self-consciousness, individuality, new values, new loyalties, and, above all, for a new leadership. My reading of Redding's *No Day of Triumph* has confirmed and strengthened this conviction, for his book contains honesty, integrity, courage, grownup thinking and feeling, all rendered in terms of vivid prose. *No Day of Triumph* is another hallmark in the coming-of-age of the modern Negro; it is yet another signal in the turn of the tide from sloppy faith and cheap cynicism to fruitful seeking and passionate questioning.

J. Saunders Redding was born in Delaware, received a B.A. from Lincoln University and a Ph.D. in English from Brown University. He established a national reputation with his essays, literary criticism, fiction, and educational activities as Professor of English at Hampton Institute. He left this post when he was named Director of the Division of Research and Publication of the National Foundation on the Arts and the Humanities in Washington, D.C., in 1966, filling that post until 1970 when he was named conservator. In 1968, he moved to Cornell University as the Ernest I. White Professor of American Studies. He retired as professor emeritus in 1975. He has received Rockefeller and Guggenheim awards, won the Mayflower Award from the North Carolina Historical Society, and was honorary conservator of American Culture, Library of Congress, from 1973 to 1977. We present here three chapters from Part I (subtitled "Troubled in Mind:") of No Day of Triumph. *An address by Professor Redding at the First Conference of Negro Writers (March, 1959) appears in the Literary Criticism section.*

No Day of Triumph

Chapter One—Troubled in Mind

1

Consciousness of my environment began with the sound of talk. It was not hysterical talk, not bravado, though it might well have been, for my father had bought in a neighborhood formerly forbidden, and we lived, I realize now, under an armistice. But in the early years, when we were a young family, there was always talk at our house; a great deal of it mere talk, a kind of boundless and robustious overflow of family feeling. Our shouts roared through the house with the exuberant gush of flood waters through an open sluice, for talk, generated by any trifle, was the power that turned the wheels of our inner family life. It was the strength and that very quality of our living that made impregnable, it seemed, even to time itself, the walls of our home. But it was in the beginning of the second decade of the century, when the family was an institution still as inviolate as the swing of the earth.

There was talk of school, of food, of religion, of people. There were the shouted recitations of poems and Biblical passages and orations from Bryan, Phillips, and John Brown. My mother liked rolling apostrophes. We children were all trained at home in the declining art of oratory and were regular contestants for prizes at school. My father could quote with appropriate gestures bits from Beveridge, whom he had never heard, and from Teddy Roosevelt and Fred Douglass, whom he had. There was talk of the "race problem," reasonable and unembittered unless Grandma Redding was there, and then it became a kind of spiritual poison, its virulence destructive of its own immediate effects, almost its own catharsis. Some of the poison we absorbed.

I remember Grandma Redding coming on one of her visits and finding us playing in the back yard. My brother and sister were there and we were playing with Myrtle Lott and Elwood Carter, white children who were neighbors. Grandma came in the back way through the alley, as she always did, and when we heard the gate scrape against the bricks we stopped. She stepped into the yard and looked fixedly at us. Holding her ancient, sagging canvas bag under one arm, she slowly untied the ribbons of her black bonnet. The gate fell shut behind her. Her eyes were like lashes on our faces. Reaching out her long arm, she held open the gate. Then she said, "Git. You white trash, git!" Our companions, pale with fright, ducked and scampered past her. When they had gone, Grandma nodded curtly to us. "Chillen," she said, and went into the house.

Grandma Redding's visits were always unannounced. She came the fifty-odd miles up from Still Pond, Maryland, as casually as if she had come from around the nearest corner. A sudden cold silence would fall, and there would be Grandma. I do not know how she managed to give the impression of shining with a kind of deadly hard glare, for she was always clothed entirely in black and her black, even features were as hard and lightless as stone. I never saw a change of expression on her features. She never smiled. In anger her face turned slowly, dully gray, but her thin nostrils never flared, her long mouth never tightened. She was tall and fibrous and one of her ankles had been broken when she was a girl and never properly set, so that she walked with a defiant limp.

She hated white people. In 1858, as a girl of ten, she had escaped from slavery on the eastern shore of Maryland with a young woman of eighteen. They made their way to Camden, New Jersey, but there was no work and little refuge there. Across the river, bustling Philadelphia swarmed with slave hunters. By subterfuge or by violence even free people were sometimes kidnaped and sent south. Near Bridgeton, New Jersey, the runaways heard, there was a free Negro settlement, but one night they were stopped on the docks by a constable who asked them for papers. They had none. Within two weeks after their escape they were slaves again. When my grandmother tried to run away from the flogging that was her punishment, Caleb Wrightson, her master, flung a chunk of wood at her and broke her ankle.

It was not until we were quite large children that Grandma Redding told us this story. She did not tell it for our pleasure, as one tells harrowing tales to children. It was without the dramatic effects that Grandma Conway delighted in. What *she* would have done with such a tale! No. Grandma Redding's telling was as bare and imageless as a lesson recited from the head and as coldly furious as the whine of a shot.

"An' ol' man Calub flane a hick'ry chunk an' brist my anklebone."

I can see her now as she sits stooped in the wooden rocker by the kitchen stove, her sharp elbows on her sharp knees and her long black fingers with their immense purple nails clawing upward at the air. Her undimmed eyes whipped at ours, and especially at mine, it seemed to me; her thin lips scarcely parted. She had just come in or was going out, for she wore her bonnet and it sat on the very top of her harsh, dull hair. Hatred shook her as a strong wind shakes a boughless tree.

"An' ol' man Calub stank lik'a pes'-house from the rottin' of his stomick 'fore he died an' went t' hell, an' his boys died in the wo' an' went to hell."

But her implacable hatred needed no historical recall, and so far as I remember, she never told the tale to us again.

But generally Grandma Redding's taciturnity was a hidden rock in the sea of our talk. The more swift the tide, the more the rock showed, bleak and unavoidable. At other times the talk flowed smoothly around her: the bursts of oratory and poetry, the chatter of people and events, the talk of schooling and sometimes of money and often of God. Even the talk of God did not arouse her. I think she was not especially religious; and in this, too, she was unlike Grandma Conway.

My grandmothers met at our house but once. They did not like each other. . . .

5

My mother was tall, with a smooth, rutilant skin and a handsome figure. Her hair began to whiten in her late twenties and whitened very rapidly. I especially liked to be on the street with her, for I enjoyed the compliment of staring which was paid to her. I think she was not aware of these stares. There was pride in her, a kind of glowing consciousness that showed in her carriage in exactly the same way that good blood shows in a horse. But she had no vanity. Her pride gave to everything she did a certain ritualistic élan.

It is surprising to me now how little I learned about my mother in the sixteen years she lived after my birth. It was not that I lacked opportunity, but insight. She was never withdrawn or restrained, purposefully shading out her personality from us. And her speech and actions seemed to have the simple directness and the sharp impact of thrown stones. But she was a woman of many humors, as if, knowing her time to be short, she would live many lives in one. Gaiety and soberness, anger and benignity, joy and woe possessed her with equal force. In all her moods there was an intensity as in a spinning top.

I vividly recall the day when in rage and tears she stormed because another Negro family moved into our neighborhood. When her rage had passed and she had dropped into that stilly tautness that sometimes kept her strained for days, she said to my father:

"That's all it takes, Fellow. Today our house is worth one-third of what it was last night. When those people . . ." She shrugged her wide shoulders and stared at my father.

"Oh, Girl! Girl!" my father said gently. "You mustn't be so hard on them. They may be respectable people."

"Hard! Hard! And respectable people!" She laughed brittlely. "What has respectability got to do with it?"

Then she tried to find the words for what she thought, for we children were present and she did not wish to appear unreasonable before us. The subject of race was for her a narrow bridge over a chasmal sea, and the walking of it was not a part of her daily living. Only when she felt she must save herself from the abyss did she venture to walk. At other times she ignored it, not only in word, but I think in thought as well. She knew the speeches of John Brown and Wendell Phillips, the poetry of Whittier and Whitman, but not as my father knew them; not as battering stones hurled against the strong walls of a prison. She was not imprisoned. Stones, perhaps, but dropped into a dark sea whose tides licked only at the farthest shores of her life. She took this for reasonableness.

I remember she laughed a brittle laugh and said, "The first thing they moved in was one of those pianola things. Oh, we shall have music," she said bitterly, "morning, noon, and midnight. And they're not buying. They're renting. Why can't they stay where they belong!"

"Belong?" my father said.

"Yes. Over the bridge."

"They are our people, Girl," my father said.

My mother looked at him, tears of vexation dewing her eyes. She blinked back the tears and looked fixedly at my father's dark face shining dully under the chandelier, his bald head jutting back from his forehead like a brown rock. As if the words were a bad taste to be rid of, she said:

"Yours maybe. But not mine."

"Oh, Girl. Girl!"

But Mother had already swept from the dining room.

It is strange how little my deep affection for my mother (and hers for all of us) taught me about her while she lived. I have learned much more about her since her death. It is as if the significance of remembered speech and action unfolded to me gradually a long time after. My mother was the most complex personality I have ever known.

But no will of my mother's could abate the heave of the social tide just then beginning to swell. Our new neighbors were the first that we saw of that leaderless mass of blacks that poured up from the South during and after the war years. It was a trickle first, and then a dark flood that soon inundated the east side and burbled restively at our street. Within five months of the time my mother had raged, the whites were gone. But rents and prices in our street were too high for the laborers in morocco and jute mills, shipyards and foundries, the ditch-diggers, coal-heavers, and the parasites. They crowded sometimes as many as eight to a room in the houses below us, and I knew of at least one house of six small rooms in which fifty-one people lived.

Our street and the diagonal street above it were a more exclusive preserve. A few middle-class Jews, a clannish community of Germans clustered about their Turn Hall, and some Catholic Irish lived there. But they were nudged out. The Germans first, for they became the victims of mass hatred during the war, and the last German home was stoned just before the day of the Armistice. Landlords and realtors inflated prices to profit by Negro buyers who clamored for houses as if for heaven. Into our street moved the prosperous class of mulattoes, a physician and a dentist, a minister, an insurance agent, a customs clerk, a well-paid domestic, and several school teachers. Nearly all of these were buying at prices three times normal.

The atmosphere of our street became purely defensive. No neighborhood in the city was so conscious of its position and none, trapped in a raw materialistic struggle between the well-being of the west side and the grinding poverty of the east, fought harder to maintain itself. This struggle was the satanic bond, the blood-pact that held our street together.

But there was also the spiritual side to this struggle. It remained for me for a long time undefined but real. It was not clear and cold in the brain as religion was and taxes and food to eat and paint to buy. It was in the throat like a warm clot of phlegm or blood that no expectorant could dislodge. It was in the bowels and bone. It was memory and history, the pound of the heart, the pump of the lungs. It was Weeping Joe making bursting flares of words on the Court House wall and murmuring like a priest in funeral mass on our back steps of summer evenings. It was east side, west side, the white and the black, the word nigger, the cry of exultation, of shame, of fear when black Lemuel Price shot and killed a white policeman. It was Paul Dunbar, whose great brooding eyes spirit-flowed from his drawn face in a photograph over our mantel. It was sleeping and waking. It was Wilson and Hughes in 1917, Harding and Cox in 1921. It was a science teacher saying sarcastically, "Yes. I know. They won't hire you because you're colored," and, "Moreover, the dog licked Lazarus' wounds," and getting very drunk occasionally and reeling about, his yellow face gone purple, blubbering, "A good chemist, God damn it. A Goddamn good chemist! And here I am teaching a school full of niggers. Oh, damn my unwhite skin! And God damn it!" It was the music of pianolas played from dusk to dawn. And it was books read and recited and hated and loved: fairy tales, *Up From Slavery*, *Leaves of Grass*, *Scaramouche*, *Othello*, *The Yoke*, *Uncle Tom's Cabin*, *The Heroic Story of the Negro in the Spanish-American War*, *The Leopard's Spots*, *Door of the Night*, *Sentimental Tommy*, *The Negro, Man or Beast?*, and the rolling apostrophes of the *World's Best Orations*.

And on this plane allegiances were confused, divided. There was absolute cleavage between those spiritual values represented by Grandma Conway, who thought and lived according to ideas and ideals inherited from a long line of free ancestors and intimates (her father had been white, her mother part Irish, Indian, Negro. Her first husband was a mulatto carriage maker with a tradition of freedom three generations old) and those ill-defined, uncertain values represented by Grandma Redding and which, somehow, seemed to be close to whatever values our neighbors on the east held. What these were I never knew, nor, I suspect, did Grandma Redding. Certainly she would have cast equal scorn on the east side's black Lizzie Gunnar, who ran a whore house and who two days before every Christmas gathered up all the Negro children she could find and led them to the Court House for the city's party to the poor, because, "Niggahs is jus' about de poores' folks dere is," and white and foreign-born Weeping Joe, who spoke of linking the spirits of men together in the solvent bond of Christ. Her closeness to them was more a sympathetic prepossession than an alliance. They were her people, whether their values were the same as hers or not. Blood was stronger than ideal, and the thing that was between them sprang from emotion rather than mind. It was unreasoning, and as ineluctable as the flight of time. Grandma Redding was the outright inheritor of a historical situation.

But not so Grandma Conway. She had assumed—not to say usurped—both the privileges and the penalties of a tradition that was hers only disingenuously, and therefore all the more fiercely held. The privileges gave her power; the penalties strength. She was certain of her values and she held them to be inviolate. She believed in a personal God and that He was in His heaven and all was right with the world. She believed in a rigid code of morality, but in a double standard, because she believed that there was something in the male animal that made him naturally incontinent, and that some women, always of a class she scornfully pitied, had no other purpose in life than to save good women from men's incontinence. In her notion, such women were not loose any more than rutting bitches were loose. A loose woman was a woman of her own class who had wilfully assumed the privileges and shunned the penalties of her birth. Such women she hated with face-purpling hatred. She believed in banks and schools and prisons. She believed that the world was so ordered that in the end his just desserts came to every man. This latter belief was very comprehensive, for she thought in terms of reciprocal responsibility of man and his class—that man did not live for himself alone and that he could not escape the general defections (she called it "sin") of the group into which he was born.

These beliefs must have been conspicuous to Grandma Conway's most casual acquaintance, but to me—and I have no doubt, to the rest of us long familiar with them—they were past both realizing and remarking, like the skin of one's body.

But realization of her most occult belief must have come quite early. Perhaps it came to me in 1917, when, on one of her visits, she first found the lower boundary of our neighborhood roiling with strange black folk and brazen with conspicuous life. It may have come to me imperceptibly, along with the consciousness of the stigma attaching to blackness of skin. But this stigma was a blemish, not a taint. A black skin was uncomely, but not inferior. My father was less beautiful than my mother, but he was not inferior to her. There were soot-black boys whom I knew in school who could outrun, outplay, and outthink me, but they were less personable than I. And certainly we did not think in any conscious way that Grandma Redding was a lesser person than Grandma Conway. The very core of awareness was this distinction.

But gradually, subtly, depressingly and without shock there entered into my consciousness the knowledge that Grandma Conway believed that a black skin was more than a blemish. In her notion it was a taint of flesh and bone and blood, varying in degree with the color of the skin, overcome sometimes by certain material distinctions and the grace of God, but otherwise fixed in the blood.

To Grandma Conway, as to my mother, our new neighbors on the east were a threat.

In our house a compromise was struck. No one ever talked about it. In the careless flow of our talk, it was the one subject avoided with meticulous concern. My parents were stern disciplinarians, and this subject was so fraught with punishable possibilities and yet so conscious a part of our living that by the time the three older ones of us were in grammar and high school our care for the avoidance of it took on at times an almost hysterical intensity. Many a time, as we heard schoolmates do and as we often did ourselves outside, one or the other of us wished to hurl the epithet "black" or "nigger," or a combination, and dared only sputter, "You, you . . . monkey!" For being called a monkey was not considered half so grave an insult as being called the other; and it was at least as grave a sin to avoid as using the Lord's name in vain. My parents, of course, never used either black or nigger, and avoided mentioning color in describing a person. One was either dark or light, never black or yellow—and between these two was that indeterminate group of browns of which our family was largely composed. We grew up in the very center of a complex.

I think my older brother and sister escaped most of the adolescent emotional conflict and vague melancholy (it came later to them, and especially to my brother, and in decidedly greater force) which were the winds of my course through teenhood. For me it was a matter of choices, secret choices really. For them there was no choice. And yet I had less freedom than they. They went off to a New England college in 1919. Up to then their associates had been first the white and then the mulatto children on our street. Even the children whom they met in high school were largely of the mulatto group, for the dark tide of migration had not then swept the schools. Going to school was distinctly an upper-class pursuit, and the public school was almost as exclusive as the summer playground which Miss Grinnage conducted along stubbornly select lines for "children of the best blood" (it was her favorite phrase), almost as exclusive as the Ethical Culture lectures we attended once each month, or the basement chapel of St. Andrews Episcopal church, where Father Tatnall held segregated services for us twice a month. For my older brother and sister, the road through childhood was straight, without sideroads or crossings.

But by the time I reached high school in the fall of 1919, life was undergoing a tumultuous change. It was as if a placid river had suddenly broken its banks and in blind and senseless rage was destroying old landmarks, leveling the face of the country farther and farther beyond the shore line.

The migrants not only discovered our neighborhood, they discovered the church where we went to Sunday school and where my father was superintendent. They discovered the vast, beautiful reaches of the Brandywine where we used to walk on fair Sundays. They discovered the school. I remember the sickening thrill with which I heard a long-headed black boy arraign the mulatto teachers for always giving the choice parts in plays, the choice chores, the cleanest books to mulatto children. He called the teachers "color-struck," a phrase that was new to me, and "sons-of-bitches," a phrase that was not. He was put out of school. Many black children were put out of school, or not encouraged to continue. Two incidents stand out in my mind.

In my first oratorical competiton, I knew—as everyone else knew—that the contestant to beat was a gangling dark fellow named Tom Cephus. He had a fervor that I did not have and for which I was taught to substitute craft. His voice, already changed, boomed with a vibrant quality that was impressive to hear. Moreover, he was controlled, self-possessed, and I was not. For days before the competition I was unable to rest, and when I did finally face the audience, I uttered a sentence or two and from sheer fright and nervous exhaustion burst into uncontrollable tears. Somehow, bawling like a baby, I got through. I was certain that I had lost.

Cephus in his turn was superb. The greater part of the audience was with him. Beyond the first rows of benches, which were friendly to me, stretched row after increasingly dark row of black faces and beaming eyes. It was more than an oratorical contest to them. It was a class and caste struggle as intense as any they would ever know, for it was immediate and possible of compromise and assuagement, if not of victory. Mouths open, strained forward, they vibrated against that booming voice, transfixed in ecstasy. The applause was deafening and vindicative. In the back of the crowded hall someone led three cheers for Cephus (a wholly unheard-of thing) and while the teacher-judges were conferring, cheer after cheer swelled from the audience like the approaching, humming, booming bursting of ocean waves.

A pulsing hush fell on them when the judges returned.

They watched the announcer as leashed and hungry dogs watch the approach of food. But the judge was shrewd. She wanted that excitement to simmer down. Flicking a smile at the first rows, she calmly announced the singing of a lullaby and waited, a set smile on her face, until three verses had been sung. Then icily, in sprung-steel Bostonian accents, she announced to an audience whose soft-skinned faces gradually froze in spastic bewilderment, "Third place, Edith Miller. Second place, Thomas Cephus. First place . . ." My name was lost in a void of silence. "Assembly dismissed!"

Stunned beyond expression and feeling, the back rows filed out. The front rows cheered. Cephus's lips worked and he looked at me. I could not look at him. I wanted to fall on my knees.

I was truant from school for a week. When my parents discovered it, I took my punishment without a word. A little later that year, Cephus dropped out of school.

But I was stubborn in my resistance to these lessons. My stubbornness was not a rational thing arrived at through intellection. It was not as simple and as hard as that. I was not a conscious rebel. I liked people, and, for all the straitening effects of environment, I was only lightly color-struck. A dark skin was perhaps not as comely as a brown or yellow, but it was sometimes attractive. In matters of class morality and custom and thought I was perhaps too young to make distinctions. I liked people. When I was sixteen and a senior in high school, I liked a doe-soft black girl named Viny. After school hours, Viny was a servant girl to kindly, dumpy, near-white Miss Kruse, the school principal, who lived across the street from us. I saw a good bit of Viny, for I ran Miss Kruse's confidential errands and did innumerable small things for her. There was nothing clandestine about my relations with her servant girl. We talked and joked in the kitchen. We sometimes walked together from school. We were frequently alone in the house.

But one day Miss Kruse called me to the front porch, where in fine, warm weather she ensconced herself in a rocker especially braced to support her flabby weight. She sat with her back turned squarely to the street. She was very fair, and because she ate heavily of rich, heavy foods, at forty-five she was heavy-jowled, with a broad, pleasant, doughy face. A sack of flesh swelled beneath her chin and seemed to hold her mouth open in a tiny O. She was reading.

"Sit down," she said.

I sat in the chair next to hers, but facing the street, so that we could look directly at each other. Both sides of the street were still lined with trees at that time, and it was June. Hedges were green. Miss Kruse read for a while longer, then she crumpled the paper against herself and folded her fingers over it.

"You like Viny, don't you?" she asked, looking at me with a heavy frown.

"Yes, ma'am," I said.

"Well, you be careful. She'll get you in trouble," she said.

"Trouble?"

"How would you like to marry her?"

I did not answer, for I did not know what to say.

"How?"

"I don't know'm."

This provoked her. She threw the newspaper on the floor. The network of fine pink veins on the lobes of her nose turned purple.

"Well, let her alone! Or she'll trap you to marry her. And what would you look like married to a girl like that?" she said bitingly. "No friends, no future. You might as well be dead! How would you like to spend the rest of your life delivering ice or cleaning outdoor privies? Don't you know girls like her haven't any shame, haven't any decency? She'll get you in trouble."

I stared stupidly at her. I do not know what my reaction was. I remember being confused and hotly embarrassed, and after that a kind of soggy lethargy settled in my stomach, like indigestible food. I distinctly remember that I felt no resentment and no shock, and that my confusion was due less to this first frank indictment of blackness than to the blunt reference to sex. Boys talked about sex in giggly whispers among themselves, but between male and female talk of sex was taboo. In the midst of my embarrassment, I heard Miss Kruse's voice again, calm and gentle now, persuasive, admonitory.

"You're going to college. You're going to get a fine education. You're going to be somebody. You'll be ashamed you ever knew Viny. There'll be fine girls for you to know, to marry."

She sighed, making a round sound of it through her O-shaped mouth, and rubbing her hands hard together as if they were cold.

"Viny. Well, Viny won't ever be anything but what she is already."

And what is she? And what and where are the others? One, who wore the flashy clothes and made loud laughter in the halls, is now a man of God, a solemn, earnest pulpiteer.

Cephus, the boy who won and lost, is dead. And Pogie Walker's dead. It is remarkable how many of those I came to know in 1919 are dead. Birdie, Sweetie Pie, and Oliver. Viny? After she quit and moved away, she used to write me once a year on cheap, lined paper. "I'm doing alrite." (She never learned to spell). "I'm living alrite. I gess I'm geting along alrite. How do these few lines fine you?" And Brunson, the smartest of that migrant lot, who outran, outfought, outthought all of us. He was expelled for writing a letter and passing it among the students. Most of the things he said were true—the exclusion of the very black from the first yearbook, the way one teacher had of referring to the black-skinned kids as "You, Cloudy, there," and never remembering their names. Well, Brunson is a week-end drunk. At other times he's very bitter. Not long ago I saw him. I spoke to him. "You don't remember me," I said. "Yeah. I remember you all right. So what?" He lives down on the east side, way down, where in the spring the river comes. . . .

7

In my senior year I met Lebman. For several lonely months I had been the only Negro in the college, and the sense of competitive enmity, which began to develop slowly in me in my second year, was now at its height. It was more than a sense of competition. It was a perverted feeling of fighting alone against the whole white world. I raged with secret hatred and fear. I hated and feared the whites. I hated and feared and was ashamed of Negroes. (The memory of it even now is painful to me.) I shunned contacts with the general run of the latter, confining myself to the tight little college group centered around Boston. But even this group was no longer as satisfying as once it had been, and I gradually withdrew from it, though the bond of frustration was strong. But my own desperation was stronger. I wished to be alone. My room in University Hall had almost no visitors, but it was peopled by a thousand nameless fears.

Furtively trying to burn out the dark, knotted core of emotion, I wrote acidulous verse and sent bitter essays and stories to various Negro magazines. One editor wrote, "You must be crazy!" Perhaps I was. I was obsessed by nihilistic doctrine. Democracy? It was a failure. Religion? A springe to catch woodcocks. Truth? There was no objective ground of truth, nothing outside myself that made morality a principle. Destroy and destroy, and perhaps, I remember writing cynically, "from the ashes of nothingness will spring a phoenix not altogether devoid of beauty." All my thoughts and feelings were but symptomatic of a withering, grave sickness of doubt.

And then I met Lebman.

He was a Jew. He had lived across the hall from me since the fall, and I had seen him once or twice in only the most casual way. Then late one night he knocked at my door. When I opened it, he was standing there pale and smiling, a lock of damp, dark hair falling across his wide, knotty forehead.

"I saw your light. Do you mind if I ask you something?"

"Come in," I said automatically; but all my defenses immediately went up.

Still smiling shyly, he came into the room and stood in the center of the floor. He carried a book in his hand, his longer fingers marking the place. He was wearing pajamas and a robe. I remember I did not close the door nor sit down at first, but stood awkwardly waiting, trying to exorcise my suspicion and fear. He looked around the room with quiet, friendly curiosity.

"I've been reading your stuff in the *Quarterly*," he said. "It's good."

"Thanks," I said. And I remember thinking, 'Don't try to flatter me, damn you. I don't fall for that stuff.' Then I tried to get ahold of myself, groping at my tangled feelings with clumsy fingers of thought in an action almost physical. "Thanks."

"I think you're after something," he said. It was a cliché, and I did not like talking about my writing. It was always like undressing before strangers. But Lebman was sincere, and now unembarrassed.

"You do?" I said, trying to say it in a tone that would end it.

"Yes."

"Why?"

"Oh, it's plain in your writing. You know, I correct papers in philosophy too. Your paper on Unamuno, it was plain there. That paper was all right too."

"I wish I knew what I was after, or that I was after something," I said defensively, cynically. I closed the door. Then in the still, sharp silence that followed, I moved to the desk and turned the chair to face the other chair in the corner. Lebman sat down.

"What I came in to see you about was this," he said, holding the book up. And in another moment, without really asking me anything, he had plunged into a brilliant, brooding discussion of Rudolph Fisher's *Walls of Jericho*, the book he

held in his hand, and of men and books. I listened captiously
at first. He did not speak in the rhapsodic way of one who
merely loves books and life. He spoke as one who understands
and both loves and hates. He sat in the chair in the corner,
where the light from the reading lamp fell upon his pale face,
his narrow, angular shoulders. Through the window at his
elbow we could see the mist-shrouded lights outlining the
walks of the middle campus. Lebman talked and talked. I listened.

I do not remember all he said between that midnight and
dawn, but one thing I do remember.

"I'm a Jew. I tried denying it, but it was no use. I suppose
everyone at some time or other tries to deny some part or all
of himself. Suicides, some crazy people go all the way. But
spiritual schizophrenes aren't so lucky as suicides and the
hopelessly insane. I used to think that only certain Jews
suffered from this—the Jews who turn Christian and marry
Christian and change their names from Lowenstein to Lowe
and Goldberg to Goldsborough and still aren't happy. But
they're not the only ones. Fisher makes a point of that. I
thought so until I read him. You ought to read him, if you
haven't."

"I've read him," I said, trying to remember the point.

"Schizophrenia in the mind, that's the curse of God; but in
the spirit, it's man's curse upon himself. It took me a long
time—all through college, through three years of reading
manuscripts for a publisher, through another two years of
graduate school—it took me years to realize what a thing it
is. I'm a thirty-six-year-old bird, and I've only just found my
roost.

"That's what you want, a roost, a home. And not just a
place to hang your hat, but someplace where your spirit's
free, where you belong. That's what everybody wants. Not a
place in space, you understand. Not a marked place, geographically bounded. Not a place at all in fact. It's hard to
tell others," he said. "But it's a million things and people, a
kind of life and thought that your spirit touches, absorbed
and absorbing, understood and understanding, and feels completely free and whole and one."

That midnight conversation—though it was scarcely that
—recurred to me many times in the years immediately following.

When I came up for graduation in 1928, it still had not
occurred to me to think of finding work to do that would
turn my education to some account. My brother had been
graduated from Harvard Law, and I thought randomly of

earning money to follow him there. My credits were transferred. But I earnèd very little and I could discover in myself no absorbing interest, no recognition of a purpose. The summer blazed along to August. Then, out of the blue, John Hope offered me a job at Morehouse College in Atlanta. I took it. I was twenty-one in October of that fall, a lonely, random-brooding youth, uncertain, purposeless, lost, and yet so tightly wound that every day I lived big-eyed as death in sharp expectancy of a mortal blow or a vitalizing fulfillment of the unnamable aching emptiness within me.

But Morehouse College and the southern environment disappointed me. The college tottered with spiritual decay. Its students were unimaginative, predatory, pretentious. Theirs was a naked, metal-hard world, stripped of all but its material values, and these glittered like artificial gems in the sun of their ambition. An unwholesome proportion of the faculty was effete, innocuous, and pretentious also, with a flabby softness of intellectual and spiritual fiber and even a lack of personal force. They clustered together like sheared sheep in a storm. They were a sort of mass-man, conscious of no spiritual status even as men, much less as a people. They were a futile, hamstrung group, who took a liberal education (they despised mechanical and technical learning) to be a process of devitalization and to be significant in extrinsics only. They awarded a lot of medallions and watch charms. Try as I might, I could feel no kinship with them. Obviously my home was not among them.

I thought often of Lebman in the pre-dawn quiet of my room, saying, "Not a place in geography, but a million things and people your spirit touches, absorbed and absorbing." I did not want sanctuary, a soft nest protected from the hard, strengthening winds that blew hot and cold through the world's teeming, turbulent valley. I wanted to face the wind. I wanted the strength to face it to come from some inexpressibly deep well of feeling of oneness with the wind, of belonging to something, some soul-force outside myself, bigger than myself, but yet a part of me. Not family merely, or institution, or race; but a people and all their topless strivings; a nation and its million destinies. I did not think in concrete terms at first. Indeed, I had but the shadow of this thought and feeling. But slowly the shadow grew, taking form and outline, until at last I felt and knew that my estrangement from my fellows and theirs from me was but a failure to realize that we were all estranged from something fundamentally ours. We were all withdrawn from the heady, brawling, lusty stream of culture which had nourished us and which was the stream by whose turbid waters all of America fed. We were spiritually homeless, dying and alone, each on his separate hammock of memory and experience.

This was emotional awareness. Intellectual comprehension came slowly, painfully, as an abscess comes. I laid no blame beyond immediate experience. Through hurt and pride and fear, they of this class (and of what others I did not know) had deliberately cut themselves off not only from their historical past but also from their historical future. Life had become a matter of asylum in some extra time-sphere whose hard limits were the rising and setting sun. Each day was another and a different unrelated epoch in which they had to learn again the forgetting of ancestral memory, to learn again to bar the senses from the sights and sounds and tastes of a way of life that they denied, to close the mind to the incessant close roar of a world to which they felt unrelated. This vitiated them, wilted them, dwarfed their spirits, and they slunk about their gray astringent world like ghosts from the shores of Lethe.

I tried fumblingly to tell them something of this, for my desire for spiritual wholeness was great. I yearned for some closer association with these men and women, some bond that was not knit of frustration and despair. In impersonal terms I tried to tell them something of this. They snubbed me. They looked upon me as a pariah who would destroy their societal bond, their asylum. They called me fool—and perhaps I was. Certainly I was presumptuous. Their whispers and their sterile laughter mocked me. They were at pains to ridicule me before the students. They called me radical, and it was an expletive the way they used it, said in the same way that one calls another a snake. For three years I held on, and then I was fired.

But my seeking grew in intensity and the need to find became an ache almost physical. For seven, eight years after that I sought with the same frantic insatiability with which one lives through a brutal, lustful dream. It was planless seeking, for I felt then that I would not know the thing I sought until I found it. It was both something within and something without myself. Within, it was like the buried memory of a name that will not come to the tongue for utterance. Without, it was the muffled roll of drums receding through a darkling wood. And so, restricted in ways I had no comprehension of, I sought, and everywhere—because I sought among the things and folk I knew—I went unfinding.

JAMES BALDWIN (1924–1987)

Notes of a Native Son, Nobody Knows My Name, *and* The Fire Next Time *established the reputation of James Baldwin as an undisputed master of the contemporary American essay. With his novels, a collection of short stories, essays, and plays, Baldwin joined Ralph Ellison in the mainstream of contemporary American letters and in the limelight of critical attention as one of two Negro writers who shared in the expression of the American literary zeitgeist of the 1950's and 1960's. He was born and brought up in New York City and lived in Europe for a number of years. The following autobiographical sketch opened his first collection of essays in book form,* Notes of a Native Son *(1955). Baldwin's views on many questions, literary and social, appear in "James Baldwin . . . in Conversation" in the Literary Criticism section.*

Autobiographical Notes

I was born in Harlem thirty-one years ago. I began plotting novels at about the time I learned to read. The story of my childhood is the usual bleak fantasy, and we can dismiss it with the unrestrained observation that I certainly would not consider living it again. In those days my mother was given to the exasperating and mysterious habit of having babies. As they were born, I took them over with one hand and held a book with the other. The children probably suffered, though they have since been kind enough to deny it, and in this way I read *Uncle Tom's Cabin* and *A Tale of Two Cities* over and over and over again; in this way, in fact, I read just about everything I could get my hands on—except the Bible, probably because it was the only book I was encouraged to read. I must also confess that I wrote—a great deal—and my first professional triumph, in any case, the first effort of mine to be seen in print, occurred at the age of twelve or thereabouts, when a short story I had written about the Spanish revolution won some sort of prize in an extremely short-lived church newspaper. I remember the story was censored by the lady editor, though I don't remember why, and I was outraged.

Also wrote plays, and songs, for one of which I received a letter of congratulations from Mayor La Guardia, and poetry, about which the less said, the better. My mother was delighted by all these goings-on, but my father wasn't; he wanted me to be a preacher. When I was fourteen I became a preacher, and when I was seventeen I stopped. Very shortly thereafter I left home. For God knows how long I struggled with the world of commerce and industry—I guess they would say they struggled with *me*—and when I was about twenty-one I had enough done of a novel to get a Saxton Fellowship. When I was twenty-two the fellowship was over, the novel turned out to be unsalable, and I started waiting on tables in a Village restaurant and writing book reviews—mostly, as it turned out, about the Negro problem, concerning which the color of my skin made me automatically an expert. Did another book, in company with photographer Theodore Pelatowski, about the store-front churches in Harlem. This book met exactly the same fate as my first—fellowship, but no sale. (It was a Rosenwald Fellowship.) By the time I was twenty-four I had decided to stop reviewing books about the Negro problem—which, by this time, was only slightly less horrible in print than it was in life—and I packed my bags and went to France, where I finished, God knows how, *Go Tell It on the Mountain*.

Any writer, I suppose, feels that the world into which he was born is nothing less than a conspiracy against the cultivation of his talent—which attitude certainly has a great deal to support it. On the other hand, it is only because the world looks on his talent with such a frightening indifference that the artist is compelled to make his talent important. So that any writer, looking back over even so short a span of time as I am here forced to assess, finds that the things which hurt him and the things which helped him cannot be divorced from each other; he could be helped in a certain way only because he was hurt in a certain way; and his help is simply to be enabled to move from one conundrum to the next—one is tempted to say that he moves from one disaster to the next. When one begins looking for influences one finds them by the score. I haven't thought much about my own, not enough anyway; I hazard that the King James Bible, the rhetoric of the store-front church, something ironic and violent and perpetually understated in Negro speech—and something of Dickens' love for bravura—have something to do with me today; but I wouldn't stake my life on it. Likewise, innumerable people have helped me in many ways; but finally, I suppose, the most difficult (and most rewarding) thing in my life has been the fact that I was born a Negro and was forced, therefore, to effect some kind of truce with this reality. (Truce, by the way, is the best one can hope for.)

One of the difficulties about being a Negro writer (and this is not special pleading, since I don't mean to suggest that he has it worse than anybody else) is that the Negro problem is written about so widely. The bookshelves groan under the weight of information, and everyone therefore considers himself informed. And this information, furthermore, operates usually (generally, popularly) to reinforce traditional attitudes. Of traditional attitudes there are only two—For or Against—and I, personally, find it difficult to say which attitude has caused me the most pain. I am perfectly aware that the change from ill-will to good-will, however motivated, however imperfect, however expressed, is better than no change at all.

But it is part of the business of the writer—as I see it—to examine attitudes, to go beneath the surface, to tape the source. From this point of view the Negro problem is nearly inaccessible. It is not only written about so widely; it is written about so badly. It is quite possible to say that the price a Negro pays for becoming articulate is to find himself, at length, with nothing to be articulate about. ("You taught me the language," says Caliban to Prospero, "and my profit on't is I know how to curse.") Consider: the tremendous social activity that this problem generates imposes on whites and Negroes alike the necessity of looking forward, of working to bring about a better day. This is fine, it keeps the waters troubled; it is all, indeed, that has made possible the Negro's progress. Nevertheless, social affairs are not generally speaking the writer's prime concern, whether they ought to be or not; it is absolutely necessary that he establish between himself and these affairs a distance that will allow, at least, for clarity, so that before he can look forward in any meaningful sense, he must first be allowed to take a long look back. In the context of the Negro problem neither whites nor blacks, for excellent reasons of their own, have the faintest desire to look back; but I think that the past is all that makes the present coherent, and further, that the past will remain horrible for exactly as long as we refuse to assess it honestly.

I know, in any case, that the most crucial time in my own development came when I was forced to recognize that I was a kind of bastard of the West; when I followed the line of my past I did not find myself in Europe but in Africa. And this meant that in some subtle way, in a really profound way, I brought to Shakespeare, Bach, Rembrandt, to the stones of Paris, to the cathedral at Chartres, and to the Empire State Building, a special attitude. These were not really my creations, they did not contain my history; I might search in them in vain forever for any reflection of myself. I was an interloper; this was not my heritage. At the same time I had no other heritage which I could possibly hope to use—I had certainly been unfitted for the jungle or the tribe. I would have to appropriate these white centuries, I would have to make them mine—I would have to accept my special attitude, my special place in this scheme—otherwise I would have no place in *any* scheme. What was the most difficult was the fact that I was forced to admit something I had always hidden from myself, which the American Negro has had to hide from himself as the price of his public progress; that I hated and feared white people. This did not mean that I loved black people; on the contrary, I despised them, possibly because they failed to produce Rembrandt. In effect, I hated and feared the world. And this meant, not only that I thus gave the world an altogether murderous power over me, but also that in such a self-destroying limbo I could never hope to write.

One writes out of one thing only—one's own experience. Everything depends on how relentlessly one forces from this experience the last drop, sweet or bitter, it can possibly give. This is the only real concern of the artist, to recreate out of the disorder of life that order which is art. The difficulty then, for me, of being a Negro writer was the fact that I was, in effect, prohibited from examining my own experience too closely by the tremendous demands and the very real dangers of my social situation.

I don't think the dilemma outlined above is uncommon. I do think, since writers work in the disastrously explicit medium of language, that it goes a little way towards explaining why, out of the enormous resources of Negro speech and life, and despite the example of Negro music, prose written by Negroes has been generally speaking so pallid and so harsh. I have not written about being a Negro at such length because I expect that to be my only subject, but only because it was the gate I had to unlock before I could hope to write about anything else. I don't think that the Negro problem in Amer-

ica can be even discussed coherently without bearing in mind
its context; its context being the history, traditions, customs,
the moral assumptions and preoccupations of the country; in
short, the general social fabric. Appearances to the contrary,
no one in America escapes its effects and everyone in America bears some responsibility for it. I believe this the more
firmly because it is the overwhelming tendency to speak of
this problem as though it were a thing apart. But in the work
of Faulkner, in the general attitude and certain specific passages in Robert Penn Warren, and, most significantly, in the
advent of Ralph Ellison, one sees the beginnings—at least—
of a more genuinely penetrating search. Mr. Ellison, by the
way, is the first Negro novelist I have ever read to utilize in
language, and brilliantly, some of the ambiguity and irony of
Negro life.

About my interests: I don't know if I have any, unless the
morbid desire to own a sixteen-millimeter camera and make
experimental movies can be so classified. Otherwise, I love to
eat and drink—it's my melancholy conviction that I've
scarcely ever had enough to eat (this is because it's *impossible* to eat enough if you're worried about the next meal)—
and I love to argue with people who do not disagree with me
too profoundly, and I love to laugh. I do *not* like bohemia, or
bohemians, I do not like people whose principal aim is pleasure, and I do not like people who are *earnest* about anything. I don't like people who like me because I'm a Negro;
neither do I like people who find in the same accident
grounds for contempt. I love America more than any other
country in the world, and, exactly for this reason, I insist on
the right to criticize her perpetually. I think all theories are
suspect, that the finest principles may have to be modified, or
may even be pulverized by the demands of life, and that one
must find, therefore, one's own moral center and move
through the world hoping that this center will guide one
aright. I consider that I have many responsibilities, but none
greater than this: to last, as Hemingway says, and get my
work done.

I want to be an honest man and a good writer.

ARNA BONTEMPS (1902–1973)

A biographical note on Arna Bontemps appears in the Fiction section (see p. 87). The autobiographical essay which follows first appeared in "The South Today . . . 100 Years After Appomattox," a Special Supplement to Harper's *magazine, April, 1965.*

Why I Returned

At our request Arna Bontemps, whose books include American Negro Poetry, Story of the Negro, *and* 100 Years of Negro Freedom, *explains why he finally came South to live. These reminiscences of his father, his Uncle Buddy, the Scottsboro trials, and the early assaults on Jim Crow provide a fresh perspective on the present struggle for Negro rights.*

The last time I visited Louisiana, the house in which I was born was freshly painted. To my surprise, it seemed almost attractive. The present occupants, I learned, were a Negro minister and his family. Why I expected the place to be run down and the neighborhood decayed is not clear, but somewhere in my subconscious the notion that rapid deterioration was inevitable where Negroes live had been planted and allowed to grow. Moreover, familiar as I am with the gloomier aspects of living Jim Crow, this assumption did not appall me. I could reject the snide inferences. Seeking my birthplace again, however, after many years, I felt apologetic on other grounds.

Mine had not been a varmint-infested childhood so often the hallmark of Negro American autobiography. My parents and grandparents had been well-fed, well-clothed, and well-housed, although in my earliest recollections of the corner at Ninth and Winn in Alexandria both streets were rutted and sloppy. On Winn there was an abominable ditch where water settled for weeks at a time. I can remember Crazy George, the town idiot, following a flock of geese with the bough of a tree in his hand, standing in slush while the geese paddled about or probed into the muck. So fascinated was I, in fact, I did not hear my grandmother calling from the kitchen door. It was after I felt her hand on my shoulder shaking me out of my daydream that I said something that made her laugh. "You called me Arna," I protested, when she insisted on knowing why I had not answered. "My name is George." But I became Arna for the rest of her years.

I had already become aware of nicknames among the people we regarded as members of the family. Teel, Mousie, Buddy, Pinkie, Ya-ya, Mat, and Pig all had other names which one heard occasionally. I got the impression that to be loved intensely one needed a nickname. I was glad my grandmother, whose love mattered so much, had found one she liked for me.

As I recall, my hand was in my grandmother's a good part of the time. If we were not standing outside the picket gate waiting for my young uncles to come home from school, we were under the tree in the front yard picking up pecans after one of the boys had climbed up and shaken the branches. If we were not decorating a backyard bush with eggshells, we were driving in our buggy across the bridge to Pineville on the other side of the Red River.

This idyll came to a sudden, senseless end at a time when everything about it seemed flawless. One afternoon my mother and her several sisters had come out of their sewing room with thimbles still on their fingers, needles and thread stuck to their tiny aprons, to fill their pockets with pecans. Next, it seemed, we were at the railroad station catching a train to California, my mother, sister, and I, with a young woman named Susy.

The story behind it, I learned, concerned my father. When he was not away working at brick or stone construction, other things occupied his time. He had come from a family of builders. His oldest brother had married into the Metoyer family on Cane River, descendants of the free Negroes who were the original builders of the famous Melrose plantation mansion. Another brother older than my father went down to New Orleans, where his daughter married one of the prominent jazzmen. My father was a bandman himself and, when he was not working too far away, the chances were he would be blowing his horn under the direction of Claiborne Williams, whose passion for band music awakened the impulse that worked its way up the river and helped to quicken American popular music.

My father was one of those dark Negroes with "good" hair, meaning almost straight. This did not bother anybody in Avoyelles Parish, where the type was common and "broken French" accents expected, but later in California people who had traveled in the Far East wondered if he were not a Ceylonese or something equally exotic. In Alexandria his looks, good clothes, and hauteur were something of a disadvantage in the first decade of this century.

He was walking on Lee Street one night when two white men wavered out of a saloon and blocked his path. One of them muttered, "Let's walk over the big nigger." My father was capable of fury, and he might have reasoned differently at another time, but that night he calmly stepped aside, allowing the pair to have the walk to themselves. The decision he made as he walked on home changed everything for all of us.

My first clear memory of my father as a person is of him waiting for us outside the Southern Pacific Depot in Los Angeles. He was shy about showing emotion, and he greeted us quickly on our arrival and let us know this was the place he had chosen for us to end our journey. We had tickets to San Francisco and were prepared to continue beyond if necessary.

We moved into a house in a neighborhood where we were the only colored family. The people next door and up and down the block were friendly and talkative, the weather was perfect, there wasn't a mud puddle anywhere, and my mother seemed to float about on the clean air. When my grandmother and a host of others followed us to this refreshing new country, I began to pick up comment about the place we had left, comment which had been withheld from me while we were still in Louisiana.

They talked mainly about my grandmother's younger brother, nicknamed Buddy. I could not remember seeing him in Louisiana, and I now learned he had been at the Keeley Institute in New Orleans taking a cure for alcoholism. A framed portrait of Uncle Buddy was placed in my grandmother's living room in California, a young mulatto dandy in elegant cravat and jeweled stickpin. All the talk about him gave me an impression of style, grace, éclat.

That impression vanished a few years later, however, when we gathered to wait for him in my grandmother's house; he entered wearing a detachable collar without a tie. His clothes did not fit. They had been slept in for nearly a week on the train. His shoes had come unlaced. His face was pock-marked. Nothing resembling the picture in the living room.

Two things redeemed the occasion, however. He opened his makeshift luggage and brought out jars of syrup, bags of candy my grandmother had said in her letters that she missed, pecans, and filé for making gumbo. He had stuffed his suitcase with these instead of clothes; he had not brought an overcoat or a change of underwear. As we ate the sweets, he began to talk. He was not trying to impress or even enter-tain us. He was just telling how things were down home, how he had not taken a drink or been locked up since he came back from Keeley the last time, how the family of his em-ployer and benefactor had been scattered or died, how the schoolteacher friend of the family was getting along, how high the Red River had risen along the levee, and such things.

Someone mentioned his white employer's daughter. A rumor persisted that Buddy had once had a dangerous crush on her. This, I took it, had to be back in the days when the picture in the living room was made, but the dim suggestion of interracial romance had an air of unreality. It was all mostly gossip, he commented, with only a shadow of a smile. Never had been much to it, and it was too long ago to talk about now. He did acknowledge, significantly, I thought, that his boss's daughter had been responsible for his enjoyment of poetry and fiction and had taught him perhaps a thousand songs, but neither of these circumstances had undermined his life-long employment in her father's bakery, where his spe-cialty was fancy cakes. Buddy had never married. Neither had the girl.

When my mother became ill, a year or so after Buddy's arrival, we went to live with my grandmother in the country for a time. Buddy was there. He had acquired a rusticity wholly foreign to his upbringing. He had never before worked out of doors. Smoking a corncob pipe and wearing oversized clothes provided by my uncles, he resembled a scare-crow in the garden, but the dry air and the smell of green vegetables seemed to be good for him. I promptly became his companion and confidant in the corn rows.

At mealtime we were occasionally joined by my father, home from his bricklaying. The two men eyed each other with suspicion, but they did not quarrel immediately. Mostly they reminisced about Louisiana. My father would say, "Sometimes I miss all that. If I was just thinking about myself, I might want to go back and try it again. But I've got the children to think about—their education."

"Folks talk a lot about California," Buddy would reply thoughtfully, "but I'd a heap rather be down home than here, if it wasn't for the *conditions*."

Obviously their remarks made sense to each other, but they left me with a deepening question. Why was this exchange repeated after so many of their conversations? What was it that made the South—excusing what Buddy called the *conditions* —so appealing for them?

There was less accord between them in the attitudes they revealed when each of the men talked to me privately. My father respected Buddy's ability to quote the whole of Thomas Hood's "The Vision of Eugene Aram," praised his reading and spelling ability, but he was concerned, almost troubled, about the possibility of my adopting the old derelict as an example. He was horrified by Buddy's casual and frequent use of the word *nigger*. Buddy even forgot and used it in the presence of white people once or twice that year, and was soundly criticized for it. Buddy's new friends, moreover, were sometimes below the level of polite respect. They were not bad people. They were what my father described as don't-care folk. To top it all, Buddy was still crazy about the minstrel shows and minstrel talk that had been the joy of his young manhood. He loved dialect stories, preacher stories, ghost stories, slave and master stories. He half-believed in signs and charms and mumbo-jumbo, and he believed wholeheartedly in ghosts.

I took it that my father was still endeavoring to counter Buddy's baneful influence when he sent me away to a white boarding school during my high school years, after my mother had died. "Now don't go up there acting colored," he cautioned. I believe I carried out his wish. He sometimes threatened to pull me out of school and let me scuffle for myself the minute I fell short in any one of several ways he indicated. Before I finished college, I had begun to feel that in some large and important areas I was being miseducated, and that perhaps I should have rebelled.

How dare anyone, parent, schoolteacher, or merely literary critic, tell me not to act *colored*? White people have been enjoying the privilege of acting like Negroes for more than a hundred years. The minstrel show, their most popular form of entertainment in America for a whole generation, simply epitomized, while it exaggerated, this privilege. Today nearly everyone who goes on a dance floor starts acting colored immediately, and this had been going on since the cakewalk was picked up from Negroes and became the rage. Why should I be ashamed of such influences? In popular music, as in the music of religious fervor, there is a style that is unmistakable, and its origin is certainly no mystery. On the playing field a Willie Mays could be detected by the way he catches a ball, even if his face were hidden. Should the way some Negroes walk be changed or emulated? Sometimes it is possible to tell whether or not a cook is a Negro without going into the kitchen. How about this?

In their opposing attitudes toward roots my father and my great uncle made me aware of a conflict in which every educated American Negro, and some who are not educated, must somehow take sides. By implication at least, one group advocates embracing the riches of the folk heritage; their opposites demand a clean break with the past and all it represents. Had I not gone home summers and hobnobbed with Negroes, I would have finished college without knowing that any Negro other than Paul Laurence Dunbar ever wrote a poem. I would have come out imagining that the story of the Negro could be told in two short paragraphs: a statement about jungle people in Africa and an equally brief account of the slavery issue in American history.

So what did one do after concluding that for him a break with the past and the shedding of his Negro-ness were not only impossible but unthinkable? First, perhaps, like myself, he went to New York in the 'twenties, met young Negro writers and intellectuals who were similarly searching, learned poems like Claude McKay's "Harlem Dancer" and Jean Toomer's "Song of the Son," and started writing and publishing things in this vein himself.

My first book was published just after the Depression struck. Buddy was in it, conspicuously, and I sent him a copy, which I imagine he read. In any case, he took the occasion to celebrate. Returning from an evening with his don't-care friends, he wavered along the highway and was hit and killed by an automobile. He was sixty-seven, I believe.

Alfred Harcourt, Sr. was my publisher. When he invited me to the office, I found that he was also to be my editor. He explained with a smile that he was back on the job doing editorial work because of the hard times. I soon found out what he meant. Book business appeared to be as bad as every other kind, and the lively and talented young people I had met in Harlem were scurrying to whatever brier patches they could find. I found one in Alabama.

It was the best of times and the worst of times to run to that state for refuge. Best, because the summer air was so laden with honeysuckle and spiraea it almost drugged the senses at night. I have occasionally returned since then but never at a time when the green of trees, of countryside, or even of swamps seemed so wanton. While paying jobs were harder to find here than in New York, indeed scarcely existed, one did not see evidences of hunger. Negro girls worked in kitchens not for wages but for the toting privilege —permission to take home leftovers.

The men and boys rediscovered woods and swamps and streams with which their ancestors had been intimate a century earlier, and about which their grandparents still talked wistfully. The living critters still abounded. They were as wild and numerous as anybody had ever dreamed, some small, some edible, some monstrous. I made friends with these people and went with them on possum hunts, and I was astonished to learn how much game they could bring home without gunpowder, which they did not have. When the possum was treed by the dogs, a small boy went up and shook him off the limb, and the bigger fellows finished him with sticks. Nets and traps would do for birds and fish. Cottontail rabbits driven into a clearing were actually run down and caught by barefoot boys.

Such carryings-on amused them while it delighted their palates. It also took their minds off the hard times, and they were ready for church when Sunday came. I followed them there, too, and soon began to understand why they enjoyed it so much. The preaching called to mind James Weldon Johnson's "The Creation" and "Go Down Death." The long-meter singing was from another world. The shouting was ecstasy itself. At a primitive Baptist foot washing I saw bench-walking for the first time, and it left me breathless. The young woman who rose from her seat and skimmed from the front of the church to the back, her wet feet lightly touching the tops of the pews, her eyes upward, could have astounded me no more had she walked on water. The members fluttered and wailed, rocked the church with their singing, accepted the miracle for what it was.

It was also the worst times to be in northern Alabama. That was the year, 1931, of the nine Scottsboro boys and their trials in nearby Decatur. Instead of chasing possums at night and swimming in creeks in the daytime, this group of kids without jobs and nothing else to do had taken to riding empty boxcars. When they found themselves in a boxcar with two white girls wearing overalls and traveling the same way, they knew they were in bad trouble. The charge against them was rape, and the usual finding in Alabama, when a Negro man was so much as remotely suspected, was guilty; the usual penalty, death.

To relieve the tension, as we hoped, we drove to Athens one night and listened to a program of music by young people from Negro high schools and colleges in the area. A visitor arrived from Decatur during the intermission and reported shocking developments at the trial that day. One of the girls involved had given testimony about herself which reasonably should have taken the onus from the boys. It had only succeeded in infuriating the crowd around the courthouse. The rumor that reached Athens was that crowds were spilling along the highway, lurking in unseemly places, threatening to vent their anger. After the music was over, someone suggested nervously that those of us from around Huntsville leave at the same time, keep our cars close together as we drove home, be prepared to stand by, possibly help, if anyone met with mischief.

We readily agreed. Though the drive home was actually uneventful, the tension remained, and I began to take stock with a seriousness comparable to my father's when he stepped aside for the Saturday night bullies on Lee Street in Alexandria. I was younger than he had been when he made his move, but my family was already larger by one. Moreover, I had weathered a Northern as well as a Southern exposure. My education was different, and what I was reading in newspapers differed greatly from anything he could have found in the Alexandria *Town Talk* in the first decade of this century.

With Ghandi making world news in India while the Scottsboro case inflamed passions in Alabama and awakened consciences elsewhere, I thought I could sense something beginning to shape up, possibly something on a wide scale. As a matter of fact, I had already written a stanza foreshadowing the application of a nonviolent strategy to the Negro's efforts in the South:

We are not come to wage a strife
  With swords upon this hill;
It is not wise to waste the life
  Against a stubborn will.
Yet would we die as some have done:
Beating a way for the rising sun.

Even so, deliverance did not yet seem imminent, and it was becoming plain that an able-bodied young Negro with a healthy family could not continue to keep friends in that community if he sat around trifling with a typewriter on the shady side of his house when he should have been working or at least trying to raise something for the table. So we moved on to Chicago.

Crime seemed to be the principal occupation of the South Side at the time of our arrival. The openness of it so startled us we could scarcely believe what we saw. Twice our small apartment was burglarized. Nearly every week we witnessed a stickup, purse-snatching, or something equally dismaying in the street. Once I saw two men get out of a car, enter one of those blinded shops around the corner from us, return dragging a resisting victim, slam him into the back seat of the car, and speed away. We had fled from the jungle of Alabama's Scottsboro era to the jungle of Chicago's crime-ridden South Side, and one was as terrifying as the other.

Despite literary encouragement, and the heartiness of a writing clan that adopted me and bolstered my courage, I never felt that I could settle permanently with my family in Chicago. I could not accept the ghetto, and ironclad residential restrictions against Negroes situated as we were made escape impossible, confining us to neighborhoods where we had to fly home each evening before darkness fell and honest people abandoned the streets to predators. Garbage was dumped in alleys around us. Police protection was regarded as a farce. Corruption was everywhere.

When I inquired about transfers for two of our children to integrated schools which were actually more accessible to our address, I was referred to a person not connected with the school system or the city government. He assured me he could arrange the transfers—at an outrageous price. This represented ways in which Negro leadership was operating in the community at that time and by which it had been reduced to impotence.

I did not consider exchanging this way of life for the institutionalized assault on Negro personality one encountered in the Alabama of the Scottsboro trials, but suddenly the campus of a Negro college I had twice visited in Tennessee began to seem attractive. A measure of isolation, a degree of security seemed possible there. If a refuge for the harassed Negro could be found anywhere in the 1930s, it had to be in such a setting.

Fisk University, since its beginnings in surplus barracks, provided by a general of the occupying army six months after the close of the Civil War, had always striven to exemplify racial concord. Integration started immediately with children of white teachers and continued till state laws forced segregation after the turn of the century. Even then, a mixed faculty was retained, together with a liberal environment, and these eventually won a truce from an outside community that gradually changed from hostility to indifference to acceptance and perhaps a certain pride. Its founders helped fight the battle for public schools in Nashville, and donated part of the college's property for this purpose. Its students first introduced Negro spirituals to the musical world. The college provided a setting for a continuing dialogue between scholars across barriers and brought to the city before 1943 a pioneering Institute of Race Relations and a Program of African Studies, both firsts in the region. When a nationally known scholar told me in Chicago that he found the atmosphere *yeasty*, I thought I understood what he meant.

We had made the move, and I had become the Librarian at Fisk when a series of train trips during World War II gave me an opportunity for reflections of another kind. I started making notes for an essay to be called "Thoughts in a Jim Crow Car." Before I could finish it, Supreme Court action removed the curtains in the railway diners, and the essay lost its point. While I had been examining my own feelings and trying to understand the need men have for customs like this, the pattern had altered. Compliance followed with what struck me, surprisingly, as an attitude of relief by all concerned. White passengers, some of whom I recognized by their positions in the public life of Nashville, who had been in a habit of maintaining a frozen silence until the train crossed the Ohio River, now nodded and began chatting with Negroes before the train left the Nashville station. I wanted to stand up and cheer. When the Army began to desegregate its units, I was sure I detected a fatal weakness in our enemy. Segregation, the monster that had terrorized my parents and driven them out of the green Eden in which they had been born, was itself vulnerable and could be attacked, possibly destroyed. I felt as if I had witnessed the first act of a spectacular drama. I wanted to stay around for the second.

Without the miseries of segregation, the South as a home-place for a Negro of my temperament had clear advantages. In deciding to wait and see how things worked out, I was also betting that progress toward this objective in the Southern region would be more rapid, the results more satisfying, than could be expected in the metropolitan centers of the North, where whites were leaving the crumbling central areas to Negroes while they themselves moved into restricted suburbs and began setting up another kind of closed society.

The second act of the spectacular on which I had focused began with the 1954 decision of the Supreme Court. While this was a landmark, it provoked no wild optimism. I had no doubt that the tide would now turn, but it was not until the freedom movement began to express itself that I felt reassured. We were in the middle of it in Nashville. Our little world commenced to sway and rock with the fury of a resurrection. I tried to discover just how the energy was generated. I think I found it. The singing that broke out in the ranks of protest marchers, in the jails where sit-in demonstrators were held, in the mass meetings and boycott rallies, was gloriously appropriate. The only American songs suitable for a resurrection—or a revolution, for that matter—are Negro spirituals. The surge these awakened was so mighty it threatened to change the name of our era from the "space age" to the "age of freedom."

The Southern Negro's link with his past seems to me worth preserving. His greater pride in being himself, I would say, is all to the good, and I think I detect a growing nostalgia for these virtues in the speech of relatives in the North. They talk a great deal about "Soulville" nowadays, when they mean "South." "Soulbrothers" are simply the homefolks. "Soulfood" includes black-eyed peas, chitterlings, grits, and gravy. Aretha Franklin, originally from Memphis, sings, "Soulfood—it'll make you limber; it'll make you quick." Vacations in Soulville by these expatriates in the North tend to become more frequent and to last longer since times began to get better.

Colleagues of mine at Fisk who like me have pondered the question of staying or going have told me their reasons. The effective young Dean of the Chapel, for example, who since has been wooed away by Union Theological Seminary, felt constrained mainly by the opportunities he had here to guide a large number of students and by the privilege of identifying with them. John W. Work, the musicologist and composer, finds the cultural environment more stimulating than any he could discover in the North. Aaron Douglas, an art professor, came down thirty-four years ago to get a "real, concrete experience of the touch and feel of the South." Looking back, he reflects, "If one could discount the sadness, the misery, the near-volcanic intensity of Negro life in most of the South, and concentrate on the mild, almost tropical climate and the beauty of the landscape, one is often tempted to forget the senseless cruelty and inhumanity the strong too often inflict on the weak."

For my own part, I am staying on in the South to write something about the changes I have seen in my lifetime, and about the Negro's awakening and regeneration. That is my theme, and this is where the main action is. There is also the spectacular I am watching. Was a climax reached with the passage of the Civil Rights Act last year? Or was it with Martin Luther King's addressing Lyndon B. Johnson as "my fellow Southerner"? Having stayed this long, it would be absurd not to wait for the third act—and possibly the most dramatic.

MALCOLM X (1925–1965)

The legend, aura, and mystique surrounding Malcolm X, an epitome of the new black nationalism, was clearly reflected in 1967 with the publication of For Malcolm, *an anthology of poems on the life and death of Malcolm X, edited by Dudley Randall and Margaret G. Burroughs. Malcolm X was born in Omaha, Nebraska, the seventh child of Reverend Earl Little, a Baptist minister from the West Indies and an organizer for Marcus Garvey's Universal Negro Improvement Association. The family was continually on the move, and the young Malcolm's early years were spent in Omaha, Milwaukee, Lansing, Michigan, and Roxbury, a suburb of Boston. He became a Black Muslim, was an assistant minister in Detroit and a founder of Muslim temples throughout the United States. He rose to prominence in the hierarchy of the black Islamic movement, second only to the prophet, Elijah Muhammed. Malcolm visited Mecca and made two trips to Africa. In 1964 he broke with Elijah Muhammed, formed his own organization—the Organization of Afro-American Unity—to con-*

centrate on political rights for black Americans and also organized his own Islamic religious center, the Muslim Mosque, Inc. On February 21, 1965, during a meeting of his political organization in the Audubon Ballroom in Harlem, he was shot and killed. The Autobiography of Malcolm X, published in 1965, has become a classic of contemporary black nationalist thinking. Following is the first chapter of the book.

The Autobiography of Malcolm X

Chapter One—Nightmare

When my mother was pregnant with me, she told me later, a party of hooded Ku Klux Klan riders galloped up to our home in Omaha, Nebraska, one night. Surrounding the house, brandishing their shotguns and rifles, they shouted for my father to come out. My mother went to the front door and opened it. Standing where they could see her pregnant condition, she told them that she was alone with her three small children, and that my father was away, preaching, in Milwaukee. The Klansmen shouted threats and warnings at her that we had better get out of town because "the good Christian white people" were not going to stand for my father's "spreading trouble" among the "good" Negroes of Omaha with the "back to Africa" preachings of Marcus Garvey.

My father, the Reverend Earl Little, was a Baptist minister, a dedicated organizer for Marcus Aurelius Garvey's U.N.I.A. (Universal Negro Improvement Association). With the help of such disciples as my father, Garvey, from his headquarters in New York City's Harlem, was raising the banner of black-race purity and exhorting the Negro masses to return to their ancestral African homeland—a cause which had made Garvey the most controversial black man on earth.

Still shouting threats, the Klansmen finally spurred their horses and galloped around the house, shattering every window pane with their gun butts. Then they rode off into the night, their torches flaring, as suddenly as they had come.

My father was enraged when he returned. He decided to wait until I was born—which would be soon—and then the family would move. I am not sure why he made this decision, for he was not a frightened Negro, as most then were, and many still are today. My father was a big, six-foot-four, very black man. He had only one eye. How he had lost the other one I have never known. He was from Reynolds, Georgia, where he had left school after the third or maybe fourth grade. He believed, as did Marcus Garvey, that freedom, independence and self-respect could never be achieved by the Negro in America, and that therefore the Negro should leave America to the white man and return to his African land of origin. Among the reasons my father had decided to risk and dedicate his life to help disseminate this philosophy among his people was that he had seen four of his six brothers die by violence, three of them killed by white men, including one by lynching. What my father could not know then was that of the remaining three, including himself, only one, my Uncle Jim, would die in bed, of natural causes. Northern white police were later to shoot my Uncle Oscar. And my father was finally himself to die by the white man's hands.

It has always been my belief that I, too, will die by violence. I have done all that I can to be prepared. . . .

One afternoon in 1931 when Wilfred, Hilda, Philbert, and I came home, my mother and father were having one of their arguments. There had lately been a lot of tension around the house because of Black Legion threats. Anyway, my father had taken one of the rabbits which we were raising, and ordered my mother to cook it. We raised rabbits, but sold them to whites. My father had taken a rabbit from the rabbit pen. He had pulled off the rabbit's head. He was so strong, he needed no knife to behead chickens or rabbits. With one twist of his big black hands he simply twisted off the head and threw the bleeding-necked thing back at my mother's feet.

My mother was crying. She started to skin the rabbit, preparatory to cooking it. But my father was so angry he slammed on out of the front door and started walking up the road toward town.

It was then that my mother had this vision. She had always been a strange woman in this sense, and had always had a strong intuition of things about to happen. And most of her children are the same way, I think. When something is about to happen, I can feel something, sense something. I never have known something to happen that has caught me completely off guard—except once. And that was when, years later, I discovered facts I couldn't believe about a man who, up until that discovery, I would gladly have given my life for.

My father was well up the road when my mother ran screaming out onto the porch. *"Early! Early!"* She screamed his name. She clutched up her apron in one hand, and ran down across the yard and into the road. My father turned around. He saw her. For some reason, considering how angry he had been when he left, he waved at her. But he kept on going.

She told me later, my mother did, that she had a vision of my father's end. All the rest of the afternoon, she was not herself, crying and nervous and upset. She finished cooking the rabbit and put the whole thing in the warmer part of the black stove. When my father was not back home by our bedtime, my mother hugged and clutched us, and we felt strange, not knowing what to do, because she had never acted like that.

I remember waking up to the sound of my mother's screaming again. When I scrambled out, I saw the police in the living room; they were trying to calm her down. She had snatched on her clothes to go with them. And all of us children who were staring knew without anyone having to say it that something terrible had happened to our father.

My mother was taken by the police to the hospital, and to a room where a sheet was over my father in a bed, and she wouldn't look, she was afraid to look. Probably it was wise that she didn't. My father's skull, on one side, was crushed in, I was told later. Negroes in Lansing have always whispered that he was attacked, and then laid across some tracks for a streetcar to run over him. His body was cut almost in half.

He lived two and a half hours in that condition. Negroes then were stronger than they are now, especially Georgia Negroes. Negroes born in Georgia had to be strong simply to survive.

It was morning when we children at home got the word that he was dead. I was six. I can remember a vague commotion, the house filled up with people crying, saying bitterly that the white Black Legion had finally gotten him. My mother was hysterical. In the bedroom, women were holding smelling salts under her nose. She was still hysterical at the funeral.

I don't have a very clear memory of the funeral, either. Oddly, the main thing I remember is that it wasn't in a church, and that surprised me, since my father was a preacher, and I had been where he preached people's funerals in churches. But his was in a funeral home.

And I remember that during the service a big black fly came down and landed on my father's face, and Wilfred sprang up from his chair and he shooed the fly away, and he came groping back to his chair—there were folding chairs for us to sit on—and the tears were streaming down his face. When we went by the casket, I remember that I thought that it looked as if my father's strong black face had been dusted with flour, and I wished they hadn't put on such a lot of it.

Back in the big four-room house, there were many visitors for another week or so. They were good friends of the family, such as the Lyons from Mason, twelve miles away, and the Walkers, McGuires, Liscoes, the Greens, Randolphs, and the Turners, and others from Lansing, and a lot of people from other towns, whom I had seen at the Garvey meetings.

We children adjusted more easily than our mother did. We couldn't see, as clearly as she did, the trials that lay ahead. As the visitors tapered off, she became very concerned about collecting the two insurance policies that my father had always been proud he carried. He had always said that families should be protected in case of death. One policy apparently paid off without any problem—the smaller one. I don't know the amount of it. I would imagine it was not more than a thousand dollars, and maybe half of that.

But after that money came, and my mother had paid out a lot of it for the funeral and expenses, she began going into town and returning very upset. The company that had issued the bigger policy was balking at paying off. They were claiming that my father had committed suicide. Visitors came again, and there was bitter talk about white people: how could my father bash himself in the head, then get down across the streetcar tracks to be run over?

So there we were. My mother was thirty-four years old now, with no husband, no provider or protector to take care of her eight children. But some kind of a family routine got going again. And for as long as the first insurance money lasted, we did all right.

Wilfred, who was a pretty stable fellow, began to act older than his age. I think he had the sense to see, when the rest of us didn't, what was in the wind for us. He quietly quit school and went to town in search of work. He took any kind of job he could find and he would come home, dog-tired, in the evenings, and give whatever he had made to my mother.

Hilda, who always had been quiet, too, attended to the babies. Philbert and I didn't contribute anything. We just fought all the time—each other at home, and then at school we would team up and fight white kids. Sometimes the fights would be racial in nature, but they might be about anything.

Reginald came under my wing. Since he had grown out of the toddling stage, he and I had become very close. I suppose I enjoyed the fact that he was the little one, under me, who looked up to me.

My mother began to buy on credit. My father had always been very strongly against credit. "Credit is the first step into debt and back into slavery," he had always said. And then she went to work herself. She would go into Lansing and find different jobs—in housework, or sewing—for white people. They didn't realize, usually, that she was a Negro. A lot of white people around there didn't want Negroes in their houses.

She would do fine until in some way or other it got to people who she was, whose widow she was. And then she would be let go. I remember how she used to come home crying, but trying to hide it, because she had lost a job that she needed so much.

Once when one of us—I cannot remember which—had to go for something to where she was working, and the people saw us, and realized she was actually a Negro, she was fired on the spot, and she came home crying, this time not hiding it.

When the state Welfare people began coming to our house, we would come from school sometimes and find them talking with our mother, asking a thousand questions. They acted and looked at her, and at us, and around in our house, in a way that had about it the feeling—at least for me—that we were not people. In their eyesight we were just *things*, that was all.

My mother began to receive two checks—a Welfare check and, I believe, a widow's pension. The checks helped. But they weren't enough, as many of us as there were. When they came, about the first of the month, one always was already owed in full, if not more, to the man at the grocery store. And, after that, the other one didn't last long.

We began to go swiftly downhill. The physical downhill wasn't as quick as the psychological. My mother was, above everything else, a proud woman, and it took its toll on her that she was accepting charity. And her feelings were communicated to us.

She would speak sharply to the man at the grocery store for padding the bill, telling him that she wasn't ignorant, and he didn't like that. She would talk back sharply to the state

Welfare people, telling them that she was a grown woman, able to raise her children, that it wasn't necessary for them to keep coming around so much, meddling in our lives. And they didn't like that.

But the monthly Welfare check was their pass. They acted as if they owned us, as if we were their private property. As much as my mother would have liked to, she couldn't keep them out. She would get particularly incensed when they began insisting upon drawing us older children aside, one at a time, out on the porch or somewhere, and asking us questions, or telling us things—against our mother and against each other.

We couldn't understand why, if the state was willing to give us packages of meat, sacks of potatoes and fruit, and cans of all kinds of things, our mother obviously hated to accept. We really couldn't understand. What I later understood was that my mother was making a desperate effort to preserve her pride—and ours.

Pride was just about all we had to preserve, for by 1934, we really began to suffer. This was about the worst depression year, and no one we knew had enough to eat or live on. Some old family friends visited us now and then. At first they brought food. Though it was charity, my mother took it.

Wilfred was working to help. My mother was working, when she could find any kind of job. In Lansing, there was a bakery where, for a nickel, a couple of us children would buy a tall flour sack of day-old bread and cookies, and then walk the two miles back out into the country to our house. Our mother knew, I guess, dozens of ways to cook things with bread and out of bread. Stewed tomatoes with bread, maybe that would be a meal. Something like French toast, if we had any eggs. Bread pudding, sometimes with raisins in it. If we got hold of some hamburger, it came to the table more bread than meat. The cookies that were always in the sack with the bread, we just gobbled down straight.

But there were times when there wasn't even a nickel and we would be so hungry we were dizzy. My mother would boil a big pot of dandelion greens, and we would eat that. I remember that some small-minded neighbor put it out, and children would tease us, that we ate "fried grass." Sometimes, if we were lucky, we would have oatmeal or cornmeal mush three times a day. Or mush in the morning and cornbread at night.

Philbert and I were grown up enough to quit fighting long enough to take the .22 caliber rifle that had been our father's, and shoot rabbits that some white neighbors up or down the road would buy. I know now that they just did it to help us, because they, like everyone, shot their own rabbits. Sometimes, I remember, Philbert and I would take little Reginald along with us. He wasn't very strong, but he was always so proud to be along. We would trap muskrats out in the little creek in back of our house. And we would lie quiet until unsuspecting bullfrogs appeared, and we could spear them, cut off their legs, and sell them for a nickel a pair to people who lived up and down the road. The whites seemed less restricted in their dietary tastes.

Then, about in late 1934, I would guess, something began to happen. Some kind of psychological deterioration hit our family circle and began to eat away our pride. Perhaps it was the constant tangible evidence that we were destitute. We had known other families who had gone on relief. We had known without anyone in our home ever expressing it that we had felt prouder not to be at the depot where the free food was passed out. And, now, we were among them. At school, the "on relief" finger suddenly was pointed at us, too, and sometimes it was said aloud.

It seemed that everything to eat in our house was stamped Not To Be Sold. All Welfare food bore this stamp to keep the recipients from selling it. It's a wonder we didn't come to think of Not To Be Sold as a brand name.

Sometimes, instead of going home from school, I walked the two miles up the road into Lansing. I began drifting from store to store, hanging around outside where things like apples were displayed in boxes and barrels and baskets, and I would watch my chance and steal me a treat. You know what a treat was to me? Anything!

Or I began to drop in about dinnertime at the home of some family that we knew. I knew that they knew exactly why I was there, but they never embarrassed me by letting on. They would invite me to stay for supper, and I would stuff myself.

Especially, I liked to drop in and visit at the Gohannas' home. They were nice, older people, and great churchgoers. I had watched them lead the jumping and shouting when my father preached. They had, living with them—they were raising him—a nephew whom everyone called "Big Boy," and he and I got along fine. Also living with the Gohannas was old Mrs. Adcock, who went with them to church. She was always trying to help anybody she could, visiting anyone she heard was sick, carrying them something. She was the one who, years later, would tell me something that I remembered a long time: "Malcolm, there's one thing I like about you.

You're no good, but you don't try to hide it. You are not a hypocrite."

The more I began to stay away from home and visit people and steal from the stores, the more aggressive I became in my inclinations. I never wanted to wait for anything.

I was growing up fast, physically more so than mentally. As I began to be recognized more around the town, I started to become aware of the peculiar attitude of white people toward me. I sensed that it had to do with my father. It was an adult version of what several white children had said at school, in hints, or sometimes in the open, which really expressed what their parents had said—that the Black Legion or the Klan had killed my father, and the insurance company had pulled a fast one in refusing to pay my mother the policy money.

When I began to get caught stealing now and then, the state Welfare people began to focus on me when they came to our house. I can't remember how I first became aware that they were talking of taking me away. What I first remember along that line was my mother raising a storm about being able to bring up her own children. She would whip me for stealing, and I would try to alarm the neighborhood with my yelling. One thing I have always been proud of is that I never raised my hand against my mother.

In the summertime, at night, in addition to all the other things we did, some of us boys would slip out down the road, or across the pastures, and go "cooning" watermelons. White people always associated watermelons with Negroes, and they sometimes called Negroes "coons" among all the other names, and so stealing watermelons became "cooning" them. If white boys were doing it, it implied that they were only acting like Negroes. Whites have always hidden or justified all of the guilts they could by ridiculing or blaming Negroes.

One Halloween night, I remember that a bunch of us were out tipping over those old country outhouses, and one old farmer—I guess he had tipped over enough in his day—had set a trap for us. Always, you sneak up from behind the outhouse, then you gang together and push it, to tip it over. This farmer had taken his outhouse off the hole, and set it just in *front* of the hole. Well, we came sneaking up in single file, in the darkness, and the two white boys in the lead fell down into the outhouse hole neck deep. They smelled so bad it was all we could stand to get them out, and that finished us all for that Halloween. I had just missed falling in myself. The whites were so used to taking the lead, this time it had really gotten them in the hole.

Thus, in various ways, I learned various things. I picked strawberries, and though I can't recall what I got per crate for picking, I remember that after working hard all one day, I wound up with about a dollar, which was a whole lot of money in those times. I was so hungry, I didn't know what to do. I was walking away toward town with visions of buying something good to eat, and this older white boy I knew, Richard Dixon, came up and asked me if I wanted to match nickels. He had plenty of change for my dollar. In about a half hour, he had all the change back, including my dollar, and instead of going to town to buy something, I went home with nothing, and I was bitter. But that was nothing compared to what I felt when I found out later that he had cheated. There is a way that you can catch and hold the nickel and make it come up the way you want. This was my first lesson about gambling: if you see somebody winning all the time, he isn't gambling, he's cheating. Later on in life, if I were continuously losing in any gambling situation, I would watch very closely. It's like the Negro in America seeing the white man win all the time. He's a professional gambler; he has all the cards and the odds stacked on his side, and he has always dealt to our people from the bottom of the deck.

About this time, my mother began to be visited by some Seventh Day Adventists who had moved into a house not too far down the road from us. They would talk to her for hours at a time, and leave booklets and leaflets and magazines for her to read. She read them, and Wilfred, who had started back to school after we had begun to get the relief food supplies, also read a lot. His head was forever in some book.

Before long, my mother spent much time with the Adventists. It's my belief that what influenced her was that they had even more diet restrictions than she always had taught and practiced with us. Like us, they were against eating rabbit and pork; they followed the Mosaic dietary laws. They ate nothing of the flesh without a split hoof, or that didn't chew a cud. We began to go with my mother to the Adventist meetings that were held further out in the country. For us children, I know that the major attraction was the good food they served. But we listened, too. There were a handful of Negroes, from small towns in the area, but I would say that it was ninety-nine percent white people. The Adventists felt that we were living at the end of time, that the world soon was coming to an end. But they were the friendliest white people I had ever seen. In some ways, though, we children noticed, and, when we were back at home, discussed, that they were different from us—such as the lack of enough seasoning in their food, and the different way that white people smelled.

Meanwhile, the state Welfare people kept after my mother. By now, she didn't make it any secret that she hated them, and didn't want them in her house. But they exerted their right to come, and I have many, many times reflected upon how, talking to us children, they began to plant the seeds of division in our minds. They would ask such things as who was smarter than the other. And they would ask me why I was "so different."

I think they felt that getting children into foster homes was a legitimate part of their function, and the result would be less troublesome, however they went about it.

And when my mother fought them, they went after her—first, through me. I was the first target. I stole; that implied that I wasn't being taken care of by my mother.

All of us were mischievous at some time or another, I more so than any of the rest. Philbert and I kept a battle going. And this was just one of a dozen things that kept building up the pressure on my mother.

I'm not sure just how or when the idea was first dropped by the Welfare workers that our mother was losing her mind.

But I can distinctly remember hearing "crazy" applied to her by them when they learned that the Negro farmer who was in the next house down the road from us had offered to give us some butchered pork—a whole pig, maybe even two of them—and she had refused. We all heard them call my mother "crazy" to her face for refusing good meat. It meant nothing to them even when she explained that we had never eaten pork, that it was against her religion as a Seventh Day Adventist.

They were as vicious as vultures. They had no feelings, understanding, compassion, or respect for my mother. They told us, "She's crazy for refusing food." Right then was when our home, our unity, began to disintegrate. We were having a hard time, and I wasn't helping. But we could have made it, we could have stayed together. As bad as I was, as much trouble and worry as I caused my mother, I loved her.

The state people, we found out, had interviewed the Gohannas family, and the Gohannas' had said that they would take me into their home. My mother threw a fit, though, when she heard that—and the home wreckers took cover for a while.

It was about this time that the large, dark man from Lansing began visiting. I don't remember how or where he and my mother met. It may have been through some mutual friends. I don't remember what the man's profession was. In 1935, in Lansing, Negroes didn't have anything you could call a profession. But the man, big and black, looked something like my father. I can remember his name, but there's no need to mention it. He was a single man, and my mother was a widow only thirty-six years old. The man was independent; naturally she admired that. She was having a hard time disciplining us, and a big man's presence alone would help. And if she had a man to provide, it would send the state people away forever.

We all understood without ever saying much about it. Or at least we had no objection. We took it in stride, even with some amusement among us, that when the man came, our mother would be all dressed up in the best that she had—she still was a good-looking woman—and she would act differently, lighthearted and laughing, as we hadn't seen her act in years.

It went on for about a year, I guess. And then, about 1936, or 1937, the man from Lansing jilted my mother suddenly. He just stopped coming to see her. From what I later understood, he finally backed away from taking on the responsibility of those eight mouths to feed. He was afraid of so many of us. To this day, I can see the trap that Mother was in, saddled with all of us. And I can also understand why he would shun taking on such a tremendous responsibility.

But it was a terrible shock to her. It was the beginning of the end of reality for my mother. When she began to sit around and walk around talking to herself—almost as though she was unaware that we were there—it became increasingly terrifying.

The state people saw her weakening. That was when they began the definite steps to take me away from home. They began to tell me how nice it was going to be at the Gohannas' home, where the Gohannas' and Big Boy and Mrs. Adcock had all said how much they liked me, and would like to have me live with them.

I liked all of them, too. But I didn't want to leave Wilfred. I looked up to and admired my big brother. I didn't want to leave Hilda, who was like my second mother. Or Philbert; even in our fighting, there was a feeling of brotherly union. Or Reginald, especially, who was weak with his hernia condition, and who looked up to me as his big brother who looked out for him, as I looked up to Wilfred. And I had nothing, either, against the babies, Yvonne, Wesley, and Robert.

As my mother talked to herself more and more, she gradually became less responsive to us. And less responsible. The house became less tidy. We began to be more unkempt. And usually, now, Hilda cooked.

We children watched our anchor giving way. It was something terrible that you couldn't get your hands on, yet you couldn't get away from. It was a sensing that something bad was going to happen. We younger ones leaned more and more heavily on the relative strength of Wilfred and Hilda, who were the oldest.

When finally I was sent to the Gohannas' home, at least in a surface way I was glad. I remember that when I left home with the state man, my mother said one thing: "Don't let them feed him any pig."

It was better, in a lot of ways, at the Gohannas'. Big Boy and I shared his room together, and we hit it off nicely. He just wasn't the same as my blood brothers. The Gohannas' were very religious people. Big Boy and I attended church with them. They were sanctified Holy Rollers now. The preachers and congregations jumped even higher and shouted even louder than the Baptists I had known. They sang at the top of their lungs, and swayed back and forth and cried and moaned and beat on tambourines and chanted. It was spooky, with ghosts and spirituals and "ha'nts" seeming to be in the very atmosphere when finally we all came out of the church, going back home.

The Gohannas' and Mrs. Adcock loved to go fishing, and some Saturdays Big Boy and I would go along. I had changed schools now, to Lansing's West Junior High School. It was right in the heart of the Negro community, and a few white kids were there, but Big Boy didn't mix much with any of our schoolmates, and I didn't either. And when we went fishing, neither he nor I liked the idea of just sitting and waiting for the fish to jerk the cork under the water—or make the tight line quiver, when we fished that way. I figured there should be some smarter way to get the fish—though we never discovered what it might be.

Mr. Gohannas was close cronies with some other men who, some Saturdays, would take me and Big Boy with them hunting rabbits. I had my father's .22 caliber rifle; my mother had said it was all right for me to take it with me. The old men had a set rabbit-hunting strategy that they had always used. Usually when a dog jumps a rabbit, and the rabbit gets away, that rabbit will always somehow instinctively run in a circle and return sooner or later past the very spot where he originally was jumped. Well, the old men would just sit and wait in hiding somewhere for the rabbit to come back, then get their shots at him. I got to thinking about it, and finally I thought of a plan. I would separate from them and Big Boy and I would go to a point where I figured that the rabbit, returning, would have to pass me first.

It worked like magic. I began to get three and four rabbits before they got one. The astonishing thing was that none of the old men ever figured out why. They outdid themselves exclaiming what a sure shot I was. I was about twelve, then. All I had done was to improve on their strategy, and it was the beginning of a very important lesson in life—that anytime you find someone more successful than you are, especially when you're both engaged in the same business—you know they're doing something that you aren't.

I would return home to visit fairly often. Sometimes Big Boy and one or another, or both, of the Gohannas' would go with me—sometimes not. I would be glad when some of them did go, because it made the ordeal easier.

Soon the state people were making plans to take over all of my mother's children. She talked to herself nearly all of the time now, and there was a crowd of new white people entering the picture—always asking questions. They would even visit me at the Gohannas'. They would ask me questions out on the porch, or sitting out in their cars.

Eventually my mother suffered a complete breakdown, and the court orders were finally signed. They took her to the State Mental Hospital at Kalamazoo.

It was seventy-some miles from Lansing, about an hour and a half on the bus. A Judge McClellan in Lansing had authority over me and all of my brothers and sisters. We were "state children," court wards; he had the full say-so over us. A white man in charge of a black man's children! Nothing but legal, modern slavery—however kindly intentioned.

My mother remained in the same hospital at Kalamazoo for about twenty-six years. Later, when I was still growing up in Michigan, I would go to visit her every so often. Nothing that I can imagine could have moved me as deeply as seeing her pitiful state. In 1963, we got my mother out of the hospital, and she now lives there in Lansing with Philbert and his family.

It was so much worse than if it had been a physical sickness, for which a cause might be known, medicine given, a cure effected. Every time I visited her, when finally they led her—a case, a number—back inside from where we had been sitting together, I felt worse.

My last visit, when I knew I would never come to see her again—there—was in 1952. I was twenty-seven. My brother Philbert had told me that on his last visit, she had recognized him somewhat. "In spots," he said.

But she didn't recognize me at all.

She stared at me. She didn't know who I was.

Her mind, when I tried to talk, to reach her, was somewhere else. I asked, "Mama, do you know what day it is?"

She said, staring, "All the people have gone."

I can't describe how I felt. The woman who had brought me into the world, and nursed me, and advised me, and chastised me, and loved me, didn't know me. It was as if I was trying to walk up the side of a hill of feathers. I looked at her. I listened to her "talk." But there was nothing I could do.

I truly believe that if ever a state social agency destroyed a family, it destroyed ours. We wanted and tried to stay together. Our home didn't have to be destroyed. But the Welfare, the courts, and their doctor, gave us the one-two-three punch. And ours was not the only case of this kind.

I knew I wouldn't be back to see my mother again because it could make me a very vicious and dangerous person—knowing how they had looked at us as numbers and as a case in their book, not as human beings. And knowing that my mother in there was a statistic that didn't have to be, that existed because of a society's failure, hypocrisy, greed, and lack of mercy and compassion. Hence I have no mercy or compassion in me for a society that will crush people, and then penalize them for not being able to stand up under the weight.

I have rarely talked to anyone about my mother, for I believe that I am capable of killing a person, without hesitation, who happened to make the wrong kind of remark about my mother. So I purposely don't make any opening for some fool to step into.

Back then when our family was destroyed, in 1937, Wilfred and Hilda were old enough so that the state let them stay on their own in the big four-room house that my father had built. Philbert was placed with another family in Lansing, a Mrs. Hackett, while Reginald and Wesley went to live with a family called Williams, who were friends of my mother's. And Yvonne and Robert went to live with a West Indian family named McGuire.

Separated though we were, all of us maintained fairly close touch around Lansing—in school and out—whenever we could get together. Despite the artificially created separation and distance between us, we still remained very close in our feelings toward each other.

STANLEY SANDERS (1942–   )

Born and educated in the Watts district of Los Angeles, Stanley Sanders became president of the student body at Whittier College, went to Oxford University as a Rhodes Scholar in 1965, and studied at Yale Law School. Active in community affairs, Sanders is a cofounder of the Watts Summer Festival, and he is currently on the board of trustees of Whittier College Alumni Fund and the NCAA Foundation. He practices law with the firm of Barnes, McGhee & Pryce. He has published articles in The Nation *and in numerous educational journals. The following autobiographical article is reprinted from the special issue of* Ebony *magazine (August, 1967) devoted to "Negro Youth in America."*

"I'll Never Escape the Ghetto"

I was born, raised and graduated from high school in Watts. My permanent Los Angeles home address is in Watts. My father, a brother and sister still live in Watts. By ordinary standards these are credentials enough to qualify one as coming from Watts.

But there is more to it than that. I left Watts. After I was graduated from the local high school I went away to college. A college venture in Watts terms is a fateful act. There are no retractions or future deliverances. Watts, like other black ghettos across the country, is, for ambitious youths, a transient status. Once they have left, there is no returning. In this sense, my credentials are unsatisfactory. To some people, I am not from Watts. I can never be.

The Watts-as-a-way-station mentality has a firm hold on
both those who remain and those who leave. Such as it is, the
ghetto is regarded as no place to make a career for those who
have a future. Without exception, the prime American values
underscore the notion. Negroes, inside it or out, and whites
too, behave toward the ghetto like travelers.

Accordingly, I was considered one of the lucky ones. My
scholarship to college was a ticket. People did not expect me
to return. Understanding this, I can understand the puzzle-
ment in the minds of those in Watts when I was home last
summer, working in the local poverty program. Rumors
spread quickly that I was an FBI agent. I was suspect because I was not supposed to return. Some people said I was
either a federal agent or a fool, for no reasonable man, they
said, returns to Watts by choice. Outside of Watts, reports
stated that I had "given up" a summer vacation to work in
Watts. For my part, I had come home to work in my community, but to some people I could not come home to Watts.
To them I was no longer from Watts.

My own state of mind, when I left Watts eight years ago to
take up the freshman year at Whittier College, was different.
It was to me less of a departure; it was the stepping-off point
of an Odyssey that was to take me through Whittier College
and Oxford University, to Yale Law School, and back to
Watts. I had intended then, as now, to make Watts my home.

A career in Watts had been a personal ambition for many
years. In many ways the career I envisioned was antithetical
to ghetto life. In the ghetto, a career was something on the
outside. In Los Angeles, this meant a pursuit founded in a
world beyond Alameda street, at a minimum in the largely
Negro middle-class Westside of Los Angeles. The talk among
the ambitious and future-minded youth in Watts was on getting out so that careers could begin. And they did just that.
The talented young people left Watts in droves. The one skill
they had in common was the ability to escape the ghetto.

I was especially intrigued by a career in Watts because it
was supposed to be impossible. I wanted to demonstrate that
it could be done more than anything else. I recall a moment
during a city-wide high school oratorical contest when one of
the judges asked whether anything good could come out of
Watts. Our high school won the contest. We showed that
judge. I saw that achievement as a possible pattern for the
entire ghetto. I was pleased.

I had not realized in leaving for Whittier College that,
however worthy my intention of returning was, I was nevertheless participating in the customary exodus from Watts. It

was not long after leaving that my early ambitions began to wear thin. The stigma of Watts was too heavy to bear. I could easily do without the questioning looks of my college classmates. I did not want my being from Watts to arouse curiosity.

I followed the instructions of those who fled Watts. I adopted the language of escape. I resorted to all the devices of those who wished to escape. I was from South Los Angeles, thereafter, not Watts. "South Los Angeles," geographically identical to Watts, carried none of the latter's stigma. South Los Angeles was a cleaner—safer—designation. It meant having a home with possibilities.

It never occurred to me at the time what I was doing. I thought of it only as being practical. It was important to me to do well in college. Community identity was secondary, if a consideration at all. Somehow, the Watts things interfered with my new college life. Moreover, Negro college youth during those undergraduate years had none of its present mood. Its theme was campus involvement. Good grades, athletics, popularity—these were the things that mattered. The word "ghetto" had not even entered the lexicon of race relations. Students were not conscious of the ghetto as a separate phenomenon. Civil rights, in the Southern sense, was academically fashionable. But the ghetto of the North was not. The concern for the ghetto was still in the future.

It was to occur to me later, at the time of the Watts riots, two years after I graduated from college, if my classmates at Whittier realized that the epochal conflagration taking place was in the home of one of their very own student body presidents. They had no reason to think it was. I had never told them that I was from Watts.

A lot of things changed during the two years at Oxford. My attitude toward home was one of them. It was there, ironically enough, that the Odyssey turned homeward. Those years were bound to be meaningful as a Yankee foreign student or Rhodes Scholar. I knew that much. But I would never have imagined when receiving the award that Oxford would be significant as a Negro experience. After all, it was part of the faith gained during four years at Whittier that everything concerning me and Watts would remain conveniently buried.

It emerged in an odd context. England then, for the most part, was free of the fine distinctions between blacks and whites traditionally made in America. Except for some exclusive clubs in London, there were few occasions where racial lines were drawn. The color-blindness of England was especially true in the student life at Oxford. (This relatively mild racial climate in England during the last three years has, with the large influx of blacks from the West Indies and Southern Asia, adopted some very American-like features. It was in such a relaxed racial atmosphere that all my defenses, about race and home, came down. At Oxford, I could reflect on the American black man.

My ghetto roots became crucially important in this examination. Englishmen were not concerned about the distinctions I was making in my own mind, between Watts and "South Los Angeles," between Watts and Whittier. They were not imagined distinctions. I was discovering that I could not escape the ghetto after all. A fundamental change was taking place in the ghettos, the Wattses, across the country. These changes were making the distinction. I realized I was a part of them, too.

By far the most traumatic of the new changes was ghetto rioting. I was studying at the University of Vienna, between semesters at Oxford, during the summer of 1964. News of Harlem rioting jolted the multi-national student community there. The typical European response was unlike anything I had seen before. They had no homes or businesses to worry about protecting. They wanted to know why Negroes did not riot more often. As the only Negro in the summer session I felt awkward for a time. I was being asked questions about the black man in America that no one had ever asked me before. I was embarrassed because I did not have any answers.

My own lack of shame in the rioting then taking place in America surprised me. In one sense, I was the archetype of the ghetto child who through hard work and initiative, was pulling himself toward a better life. I was the example, the exception. It was my life that was held up to Watts youth to emulate.

In another sense, however, my feelings toward the rioting were predictable. I had always been bothered by the passivity of the ghetto. The majority of black men in the North had remained outside the struggle. Nothing was happening in the ghettos. No one was making it happen. Ghetto rioting then was the first representation I perceived of movement and activity among the mass of Negroes in the North. It marked a break with the passive tradition of dependency and indifference. The ghetto was at least no longer content with its status as bastard child of urban America. The currents set in motion had a hopeful, irreversible quality about them. The ghetto wanted legitimation. That was a beginning.

The parallel between a single individual's success and the

boot-strap effort of the mass of ghetto youth is and remains too tenuous to comport with reality. This was made clear to me during the discussions of the Harlem riots on those hot summer days in Vienna. It shattered the notion that my individual progress could be hailed as an advance for all Negroes. Regrettably, it was an advance only for me. Earlier I had thought the success I had won satisfied an obligation I had to all Negroes. It is part of the lip service every successful Negro is obliged to pay to the notion of race progress whenever he achieves. In the face of mass rioting, the old shibboleths were reduced to embarrassing emptiness. I was enjoying the privileges of studying at the world's finest universities; Negroes at home were revolting against their miserable condition. To them, my experience and example were as remost as if I had never lived or been there. At best, only the top students could identify with my example—but they were few. And besides, the top students were not the problem.

When I returned to Oxford in the fall, following a spate of summer rioting in Eastern cities, I was convinced that some momentous changes had been wrought for all Negroes, not just those in the ghetto. It certainly meant a new militancy and a militancy of action, not the passive fulminations of the demi-militants. This was for Watts.

I returned home in August, 1965, from two years at Oxford just in time for the beginning of the Watts riots. As I walked the streets I was struck by the sameness of the community. There were few changes. Everything seemed to be in the same place where I had last seen it. It was unsettling for me to recall so easily the names of familiar faces I saw on the street. It was that feeling one gets when he feels he has done this one same thing before.

Streets remained unswept; sidewalks, in places, still unpaved. During this same time the growth rate in the rest of Southern California had been phenomenal, one of the highest in the country. L. A. suburbs had flourished. Watts, however, remained an unacknowledged child in an otherwise proud and respectable family of new towns.

The intellectual journey back to Watts after the Vienna summer and during the last year at Oxford had partly prepared me for what was soon to erupt into revolutionary scale violence. My first reaction after the riot began was to have it stopped. But I was not from Watts for the past six years. I, nor anyone outside of Watts, was in no moral position to condemn this vicious expression of the ghetto.

I enrolled in Yale Law School in the fall after the riots. This time I did not leave Watts. Nor did I wish to leave

Watts. Watts followed me to Yale. In fact, Watts was at Yale before I was. The discussions about riots and ghettos were more lively and compelling than the classroom discussions on the law. There were no word games or contrived problems. The questions raised were urgent ones.

Not surprisingly, Watts, too, was in the throes of painful discussion about the riots. It was beginning to look as though the deepest impact of the riots was on the people of Watts themselves. Old attitudes about the community were in upheaval. There were no explanations that seemed complete. No one knew for sure how it all began. There was no agreement on how it was continued as long as it was—and why. We only knew it happened. What I had often mistaken for pointless spoutings was in reality a manifestation of this desperate search for a truth about the riots.

The new intellectual climate in Watts was hard-wrought. It was rich enough to support even a communist bookstore. Writers, poets, artists flourished. I was handed full manuscripts of unpublished books by indigenous writers and asked to criticize them. I have not seen during eight years of college life as many personal journals kept and sketches written than in Watts since the 1965 riots. A new, rough wisdom of the street corner was emerging.

I suspected at the time and now realize that the riots were perhaps the most significant massive action taken by Northern Negroes. It was a watershed in the ghetto's history. Before the riots, the reach of the Negro movement in America seemed within the province of a small civil rights leadership. Now Watts, and places like Watts, were redefining the role of black men in their city's life.

I have affectionate ties to Watts. I bear the same mark as a son of Watts now that I did during that oratorical contest in high school. I may be personally less vulnerable to it today, but I am nevertheless influenced by it. While a group in Whittier, Calif. may regard it as unfortunate that its college's first Rhodes Scholar comes from Watts, I, for my part, could not feel more pride about that than I do now. I feel no embarrassment for those who think ill of Watts. I had once felt it. Now I only feel the regret for once having been embarrassed. "South Los Angeles" is a sour memory. Watts is my home.

Then I have my logical ties to Watts, too. My interest in the law stems from a concern for the future of Watts. The problem of the poor and of the city in America, simplified, is the problem of the ghetto Negro. I regard it as *the* problem of the last third of this century. Plainly, Watts is where the action is. The talents and leadership which I saw leave Watts as a child are the very things it needs most today. Many of the ghetto's wandering children are choosing a city to work in. My choice was made for me—long ago.

There is a difference between my schooling and the wisdom of the street corner. I know the life of a black man in Watts is larger than a federal poverty program. If there is no future for the black ghetto, the future of all Negroes is diminished. What affects it, affects me, for I am a child of the ghetto. When they do it to Watts, they do it to me, too. I'll never escape from the ghetto. I have staked my all on its future. Watts is my home.

3.

Poetry

PAUL LAURENCE DUNBAR (1872–1906)

*Although the first Negro poet of record in America is Lucy
Terry, a woman who wrote poems in the 1740's, and the
names of Jupiter Hammon and Phillis Wheatley stand out in
the history of Negro poetry in the eighteenth century, Paul
Laurence Dunbar was the first Negro poet to win national recognition and full acceptance in America. Born and educated
in Dayton, Ohio, the son of former slaves, he began writing
verse as a youth. His first book of poems,* Oak and Ivy *(1893)
was distributed and sold by the poet, but his second volume,*
Majors and Minors *(1895), also very much a private venture, was very favorably reviewed by William Dean Howells.
This led to the publication of his third volume,* Lyrics of
Lowly Life *(1896), by Dodd, Mead and Company, with an introduction by Howells, which was an instant success and
made him a celebrity. James Weldon Johnson, in the revised
edition of* The Book of American Negro Poetry *(1931),
noted:*

There have been many changes in the estimates of Negro poetry since Dunbar died [February 9, 1906], but he still holds his place as the first American Negro poet of real literary distinction. There are some who will differ with this statement, feeling that it should be made about Phillis Wheatley. It is true that Phillis Wheatley did measure up to the best of her contemporaries; but it must be remembered that not one of her contemporaries was a poet of real literary distinction. Dunbar was the first to demonstrate a high degree of poetic talent combined with literary training and technical proficiency. In the field in which he became best known, Negro dialect poetry, his work has not been excelled. . . . Much of the poetry on which Dunbar's fame rests has passed; just as much of the poetry of his even more popular contemporary, Riley, has passed. Dialect poetry still holds a place in American literature, but the place itself is no longer considered an important one.

His poems and short stories were in demand by the best American magazines, and before his death, at the age of thirty-four, he wrote four novels and numerous stories. We present four of Dunbar's poems, two in the literary English he wanted to be known for, and two of his dialect poems.

We Wear the Mask

We wear the mask that grins and lies,
It hides our cheeks and shades our eyes,—
This debt we pay to human guile;
With torn and bleeding hearts we smile,
And mouth with myriad subtleties.

Why should the world be overwise,
In counting all our tears and sighs?
Nay, let them only see us, while
   We wear the mask.

We smile, but, O great Christ, our cries
To Thee from tortured souls arise.
We sing, but oh, the clay is vile
Beneath our feet, and long the mile;
But let the world dream otherwise,
   We wear the mask.

A Death Song

Lay me down beneaf de willers in de grass,
Whah de branch 'll go a-singin' as it pass.
   An' w'en I's a-layin' low,
   I kin hyeah it as it go
Singin', "Sleep, my honey, tek yo' res' at las'."

Lay me nigh to whah hit meks a little pool,
An' de watah stan's so quiet lak an' cool,
   Whah de little birds in spring,
   Ust to come an' drink an' sing,
An' de chillen waded on dey way to school.

Let me settle w'en my shouldahs draps dey load
Nigh enough to hyeah de noises in de road;
   Fu' I t'ink de las' long res'
   Gwine to soothe my sperrit bes'
Ef I's layin' 'mong de t'ings I's allus knowed.

Sympathy

I know what the caged bird feels, alas!
When the sun is bright on the upland slopes;
When the wind stirs soft through the springing grass,
And the river flows like a stream of glass;
When the first bird sings and the first bud opes,
And the faint perfume from its chalice steals—
I know what the caged bird feels!

I know why the caged bird beats his wing
Till its blood is red on the cruel bars;
For he must fly back to his perch and cling
When he fain would be on the bough a-swing;
And a pain still throbs in the old, old scars
And they pulse again with a keener sting—
I know why he beats his wing!

I know why the caged bird sings, ah me,
When his wing is bruised and his bosom sore,—
When he beats his bars and he would be free;

It is not a carol of joy or glee,
But a prayer that he sends from his heart's deep core,
But a plea, that upward to Heaven he flings—
I know why the caged bird sings!

A Negro Love Song

Seen my lady home las' night,
　Jump back, honey, jump back.
Hel' huh han' an' sque'z it tight,
　Jump back, honey, jump back.
Hyeahd huh sigh a little sigh,
Seen a light gleam f'om huh eye,
An' a smile go flittin' by—
　Jump back, honey, jump back.

Hyeahd de win' blow thoo de pine,
　Jump back, honey, jump back.
Mockin'-bird was singin' fine,
　Jump back, honey, jump back.
An' my hea't was beatin' so,
When I reached my lady's do',
Dat I couldn't ba' to go—
　Jump back, honey, jump back.

Put my ahm aroun' huh wais',
　Jump back, honey, jump back.
Raised huh lips an' took a tase,
　Jump back, honey, jump back.
Love me, honey, love me true?
Love me well ez I love you?
An' she answe'd, " 'Cose I do"—
　Jump back, honey, jump back.

WILLIAM EDWARD BURGHART DuBOIS (1868–1963)

It is no exaggeration to say that, in many respects, W. E. B. DuBois is the intellectual father of modern Negro scholarship, modern Negro militancy and self-consciousness, and modern Negro cultural development. His figure looms large as writer, editor, scholar, educator, historian, sociologist, and student of Africa. He was born in Great Barrington, Massachusetts, and graduated from Fisk University in 1888. He completed four years of graduate studies at Harvard, and his Ph.D. dissertation, The Suppression of the African Slave Trade, *was hailed as the "first scientific historical work" written by a Negro. It achieved publication as the first volume of the then new series of Harvard Historical Studies (1896). His* The Philadelphia Negro: A Social Study, *published by the University of Pennsylvania in 1899, is a pioneer work in the sociological study of the American Negro. He was a professor at Atlanta University from 1896 to 1910. In 1905 he founded the Niagara Movement, an early expression of the fight to end racial discrimination and segregation in the United States. In 1908 he was among the founders of the N.A.A.C.P. DuBois was the founder and served as the first editor of* The Crisis. *In an article in this journal in April, 1915, he stated the cultural program which was to be realized in the Negro Renaissance of the following decade: "In art and literature we should try to loose the tremendous emotional wealth of the Negro and the dramatic strength of his problems through writing, the stage, pageantry, and other forms of art. We should resurrect forgotten ancient Negro art and history, and we should set the black man before the world as both a creative artist and a strong subject for artistic treatment." He edited* The Atlanta Studies *(see Bibliography) and founded and edited* Phylon, *the famous scholarly "Atlanta University Review of Race and Culture." DuBois was the founder of the Pan-African Congresses and first director of the Secretariat for* Encyclopaedia Africana. *In addition to his scholarly studies and essays, he wrote fiction (see Bibliography) and poetry. We present two of his poems: "The Song of the Smoke," a poem written in 1899, which appeared anew in the special DuBois Memorial Issue of the quarterly review* Freedomways *(Winter, 1965) and has never before been anthologized, and the widely reprinted "A Litany at Atlanta," written after the Atlanta race riot in 1906. Two chapters from DuBois's classic,* The Souls of Black Folk, *appear in the Literary Criticism section.*

The Song of the Smoke

I am the smoke king,
I am black.
I am swinging in the sky.
I am ringing worlds on high:
I am the thought of the throbbing mills,
I am the soul toil kills,
I am the ripple of trading rills,

Up I'm curling from the sod,
I am whirling home to God.
I am the smoke king,
I am black.

I am the smoke king,
I am black.
I am wreathing broken hearts,
I am sheathing devils' darts;
Dark inspiration of iron times,
Wedding the toil of toiling climes
Shedding the blood of bloodless crimes.

Down I lower in the blue,
Up I tower toward the true,
I am the smoke king,
I am black.

I am the smoke king,
I am black.

I am darkening with song,
I am hearkening to wrong;
I will be black as blackness can,

The blacker the mantle the mightier the man,
My purpl'ing midnights no day dawn may ban.

I am carving God in night,
I am painting hell in white.
I am the smoke king,
I am black.

I am the smoke king,
I am black.

I am cursing ruddy morn,
I am nursing hearts unborn;
Souls unto me are as mists in the night,
I whiten my blackmen, I beckon my white,
What's the hue of a hide to a man in his might!

Sweet Christ, pity toiling lands!
Hail to the smoke king,
Hail to the black!

A Litany at Atlanta

Done at Atlanta, in the Day of Death, 1906.
O Silent God, Thou whose voice afar in mist and mystery
hath left our ears an-hungered in these fearful days—
Hear us, good Lord!

Listen to us, Thy children: our faces dark with doubt are
made a mockery in Thy sanctuary. With uplifted hands we
front Thy heaven, O God, crying:
We beseech Thee to hear us, good Lord!

We are not better than our fellows, Lord, we are but weak
and human men. When our devils do deviltry, curse Thou the
doer and the deed: curse them as we curse them, do to them
all and more than ever they have done to innocence and
weakness, to womanhood and home.
Have mercy upon us, miserable sinners!

And yet whose is the deeper guilt? Who made these devils?
Who nursed them in crime and fed them on injustice? Who
ravished and debauched their mothers and their grandmoth-

ers? Who bought and sold their crime, and waxed fat and rich on public iniquity?
Thou knowest, good God!

Is this Thy justice, O Father, that guile be easier than innocence, and the innocent crucified for the guilt of the untouched guilty?
Justice, O judge of men!

Wherefore do we pray? Is not the God of the fathers dead? Have not seers seen in Heaven's halls Thine hearsed and lifeless forms stark amidst the black and rolling smoke of sin, where all along bow bitter forms of endless dead?
Awake, Thou that sleepest!

Thou art not dead, but flown afar, up hills of endless light through blazing corridors of suns, where worlds do swing of good and gentle men, of women strong and free—far from the cozenage, black hypocrisy, and chaste prostitution of this shameful speck of dust!
Turn again, O Lord, leave us not to perish in our sin!

From lust of body and lust of blood,
  Great God, deliver us!

From lust of power and lust of gold,
  Great God, deliver us!

From the leagued lying of despot and of brute,
  Great God, deliver us!

A city lay in travail, God our Lord, and from her loins sprang twin Murder and Black Hate. Red was the midnight; clang, crack and cry of death and fury filled the air and trembled underneath the stars when church spires pointed silently to Thee. And all this was to sate the greed of greedy men who hide behind the veil of vengeance!
Bend us Thine ear, O Lord!

In the pale, still morning we looked upon the deed. We stopped our ears and held our leaping hands, but they—did they not wag their heads and leer and cry with bloody jaws: *Cease from Crime!* The word was mockery, for thus they train a hundred crimes while we do cure one.
Turn again our captivity, O Lord!

Behold this maimed and broken thing; dear God, it was an humble black man who toiled and sweat to save a bit from the pittance paid him. They told him: *Work and Rise.* He worked. Did this man sin? Nay, but some one told how some one said another did—one whom he had never seen nor known. Yet for that man's crime this man lieth maimed and murdered, his wife naked to shame, his children, to poverty and evil.

Hear us, O heavenly Father!

Doth not this justice of hell stink in Thy nostrils, O God? How long shall the mounting flood of innocent blood roar in Thine ears and pound in our hearts for vengeance? Pile the pale frenzy of blood-crazed brutes who do such deeds high on Thine altar, Jehovah Jireh, and burn it in hell forever and forever.

Forgive us, good Lord; we know not what we say!

Bewildered we are, and passion-tost, mad with the madness of a mobbed and mocked and murdered people; straining at the armposts of Thy Throne, we raise our shackled hands and charge Thee, God, by the bones of our stolen fathers, by the tears of our dead mothers, by the very blood of Thy crucified Christ: *What meaneth this?* Tell us the Plan; give us the Sign!

Keep not Thou silence, O God!

Sit no longer blind, Lord God, deaf to our prayer and dumb to our dumb suffering. Surely Thou too art not white, O Lord, a pale, bloodless, heartless thing?

Ah! Christ of all the Pities!

Forgive the thought! Forgive these wild, blasphemous words. Thou art still the God of our black fathers, and in Thy soul's soul sit some soft darkenings of the evening, some shadowings of the velvet night.

But whisper—speak—call, great God, for Thy silence is white terror to our hearts! The way, O God, show us the way and point us the path.

Whither? North is greed and South is blood; within, the coward, and without the liar. Whither? To Death?

Amen! Welcome dark sleep!

Whither? To life? But not this life, dear God, not this. Let the cup pass from us, tempt us not beyond our strength, for there is that clamoring and clawing within, to whose voice we

would not listen, yet shudder lest we must,—and it is red,
Ah! God! It is a red and awful shape.
Selah!

In yonder East trembles a star.
*Vengeance is mine; I will repay, saith the
Lord!*

Thy will, O Lord, be done!
Kyrie Eleison!

Lord, we have done these pleading, wavering
words
We beseech Thee to hear us, good Lord!

We bow our heads and hearken soft to the sobbing of women and little children.
We beseech Thee to hear us, good Lord!

Our voices sink in silence and in night.
Hear us, good Lord!

In night, O God of a godless land!
Amen!

In silence, O silent God.
Selah!

JAMES WELDON JOHNSON (1871–1938)

*A biographical note on James Weldon Johnson appears in the
Autobiography section (see pp. 269–270). Johnson's poem,
"The Creation," is reprinted from* God's Trombones *(1927).*

The Creation

A Negro Sermon

And God stepped òut on space,
And He looked around and said,
"I'm lonely—
I'll make me a world."

And far as the eye of God could see
Darkness covered everything,
Blacker than a hundred midnights
Down in a cypress swamp.

Then God smiled,
And the light broke,
And the darkness rolled up on one side,
And the light stood shining on the other,
And God said, *"That's good!"*

Then God reached out and took the light in His hands,
And God rolled the light around in His hands,
Until He made the sun;
And He set that sun a-blazing in the heavens.
And the light that was left from making the sun
God gathered up in a shining ball
And flung against the darkness,
Spangling the night with the moon and stars.

Then down between
The darkness and the light
He hurled the world;
And God said, *"That's good!"*

Then God himself stepped down—
And the sun was on His right hand,
And the moon was on His left;
The stars were clustered about His head,
And the earth was under His feet.
And God walked, and where He trod
His footsteps hollowed the valleys out
And bulged the mountains up.

Then He stopped and looked and saw
That the earth was hot and barren.
So God stepped over to the edge of the world
And He spat out the seven seas;
He batted His eyes, and the lightnings flashed;
He clapped His hands, and the thunders rolled;
And the waters above the earth came down,
The cooling waters came down.

Then the green grass sprouted,
And the little red flowers blossomed,
The pine-tree pointed his finger to the sky,
And the oak spread out his arms;
The lakes cuddled down in the hollows of the ground,
And the rivers ran down to the sea;
And God smiled again,
And the rainbow appeared,
And curled itself around His shoulder.

Then God raised His arm and He waved His hand
Over the sea and over the land,
And He said, *"Bring forth! Bring forth!"*
And quicker than God could drop His hand,
Fishes and fowls
And beast and birds
Swam the rivers and the seas,
Roamed the forests and the woods,
And split the air with their wings,
And God said, *"That's good!"*

Then God walked around
And God looked around

On all that He had made.
He looked at His sun,
And He looked at His moon,
And He looked at His little stars;
He looked on His world
With all its living things,
And God said, *"I'm lonely still."*

Then God sat down
On the side of a hill where He could think;
By a deep, wide river He sat down;
With His head in His hands,
God thought and thought,
Till He thought, *"I'll make me a man!"*

Up from the bed of the river
God scooped the clay;
And by the bank of the river
He kneeled Him down;
And there the great God Almighty,
Who lit the sun and fixed it in the sky,
Who flung the stars to the most far corner of the night,
Who rounded the earth in the middle of His hand—
This Great God,
Like a mammy bending over her baby,
Kneeled down in the dust
Toiling over a lump of clay
Till He shaped it in His own image;

Then into it He blew the breath of life,
And man became a living soul.
Amen. Amen.

FENTON JOHNSON (1888–1958)

*From beginnings with verse in conventional forms and often
trite in content, Fenton Johnson became one of the very first
Negro poets to turn to the revolutionary "new poetry" move-*

ment in America. In 1918 and 1919 he published poems in Poetry *magazine and Alfred Kreymborg's* Others, *where he appeared along with William Carlos Williams, Wallace Stevens, and Marianne Moore. He never became a major figure, but he cultivated his own distinctive voice and a fatalistic, nihilistic vision of life which was very rare in Negro American literature. He was born and raised in Chicago, attended the University of Chicago, and was active in the Chicago literary circles. In an autobiographical note that he prepared for* Caroling Dusk, An Anthology of Verse by Negro Poets *(1927), edited by Countee Cullen, Johnson wrote:*

> Taught school one year and repented. Having scribbled since the age of nine, had some plays produced on the stage of the old Pekin Theatre, Chicago, at the time I was nineteen. When I was twenty-four my first volume *A Little Dreaming* was published. Since then *Visions of the Dusk* (1915) and *Songs of the Soil* (1916) represent my own collections of my work. Also published a volume of short stories *Tales of Darkest America* and a group of essays on American politics *For the Highest Good* . . . Edited two or three magazines and published one or two of them myself.

The Negro Collection of the Fisk University Library has an unpublished collection of Fenton Johnson poems in manuscript. The eight poems that follow are from Johnson's published works.

The Daily Grind

If Nature says to you,
"I intend you for something fine,
For something to sing the song
That only my whirling stars can sing,
For something to burn in the firmament
With all the fervor of my golden sun,
For something to moisten the parched souls
As only my rivulets can moisten the parched,"

What can you do?

If the System says to you,
"I intend you to grind and grind
Grains of corn beneath millstones;
I intend you to shovel and sweat

Before a furnace of Babylon;
I intend you for grist and meat
To fatten my pompous gods
As they wallow in an alcoholic nectar,"

What can you do?

Naught can you do
But watch that eternal battle
Between Nature and the System.
You cannot blame God,
You cannot blame man;
For God did not make the System,
Neither did man fashion Nature.
You can only die each morning,
And live again in the dreams of the night.
If Nature forgets you,
If the System forgets you,
God has blest you.

The World Is a Mighty Ogre

I could love her with a love so warm
You could not break it with a fairy charm;
I could love her with a love so bold
It would not die, e'en tho' the world grew cold.

I cannot cross the bridge, nor climb the tower,—
I cannot break the spell of magic power;
The rules of man forbid me raise my sword—
Have mercy on a humble bard, O Lord!

A Negro Peddler's Song

*(The pattern of this song was sung by a Negro peddler in a
Chicago alley.)*

Good Lady,
I have corn and beets,
Onions, too, and leeks,
And also sweet potat-y.

Good Lady,
Buy for May and John;
And when work is done
Give a bite to Sadie.

Good Lady,
I have corn and beets,
Onions, too, and leeks,
And also sweet potat-y.

The Old Repair Man

God is the Old Repair Man.
When we are junk in Nature's storehouse he takes us apart.
What is good he lays aside; he might use it some day.
What has decayed he buries in six feet of sod to nurture the
    weeds.
Those we leave behind moisten the sod with their tears;
But their eyes are blind as to where he has placed
    the good.
Some day the Old Repair Man
Will take the good from its secret place
And with his gentle, strong hands will mold
A more enduring work—a work that will defy Nature—
And we will laugh at the old days, the troubled days,
When we were but a crude piece of craftsmanship,
When we were but an experiment in Nature's labora-
    tory. . . .
It is good we have the Old Repair Man.

Rulers

It is said that many a king in troubled Europe would sell his
    crown for a day of happiness.
I have seen a monarch who held tightly the jewel of happi-
    ness.
Oh Lombard Street in Philadelphia, as evening dropped to
    earth, I gazed upon a laborer duskier than a sky devoid
    of moon. He was seated on a throne of flour bags, waving
    his hand imperiously as two small boys played on their
    guitars the ragtime tunes of the day.

God's blessing on the monarch who rules on Lombard Street
in Philadelphia.

The Scarlet Woman

Once I was good like the Virgin Mary and the Minister's
wife.
My father worked for Mr. Pullman and white people's tips;
but he died two days after his insurance expired.
I had nothing, so I had to go to work.
All the stock I had was a white girl's education and a face
that enchanted the men of both races.
Starvation danced with me.
So when Big Lizzie, who kept a house for white men, came
to me with tales of fortune that I could reap from the
sale of my virtue I bowed my head to Vice.
Now I can drink more gin than any man for miles around.
Gin is better than all the water in Lethe.

Tired

I am tired of work; I am tired of building up somebody else's
civilization.
Let us take a rest, M'Lissy Jane.
I will go down to the Last Chance Saloon, drink a gallon or
two of gin, shoot a game or two of dice and sleep the rest
of the night on one of Mike's barrels.
You will let the old shanty go to rot, the white people's
clothes turn to dust, and the Calvary Baptist Church sink
to the bottomless pit.
You will spend your days forgetting you married me and
your nights hunting the warm gin Mike serves the ladies
in the rear of the Last Chance Saloon.
Throw the children into the river; civilization has given us
too many. It is better to die than to grow up and find that
you are colored.
Pluck the stars out of the heavens. The stars mark our destiny. The stars marked my destiny.
I am tired of civilization.